...But was he her true enemy, or her destined lifemate?

Praise for Christine Feehan's Dark Carpathian novels . . .

"AN UTTERLY COMPELLING SERIES."*

DARK SECRET

"A refreshing Carpathian tale." —*Midwest Book Review*

"May be the most horrific of Feehan's Dark series. The erotic heat . . . turns scorching." —*Booklist*

"Without a doubt, Feehan is a high priestess in the world of vampire fiction." —**Romantic Times*

"A fabulous tale." —*Romance Reviews Today*

DARK GUARDIAN

"Feehan's newest is a skillful blend of supernatural thrills and romance that is sure to entice readers."
—*Publishers Weekly*

DARK LEGEND

"Vampire romance at its best!" —*Romantic Times*

DARK FIRE

"If you are looking for something that is fun and different, pick up a copy of this book." —*All About Romance*

continued . . .

Titles by Christine Feehan

DARK SECRET

DARK DESTINY

DARK MELODY

DARK SYMPHONY

DARK GUARDIAN

DARK LEGEND

DARK FIRE

DARK CHALLENGE

DARK MAGIC

DARK GOLD

DARK DESIRE

DARK PRINCE

NIGHT GAME

MIND GAME

SHADOW GAME

OCEANS OF FIRE

WILD RAIN

DARK DEMON

CHRISTINE FEEHAN

JOVE BOOKS, NEW YORK

THE BERKLEY PUBLISHING GROUP
Published by the Penguin Group
Penguin Group (USA) Inc.
375 Hudson Street, New York, New York 10014, USA
Penguin Group (Canada), 90 Eglinton Avenue East, Suite 700, Toronto, Ontario M4P 2Y3, Canada
(a division of Pearson Penguin Canada Inc.)
Penguin Books Ltd., 80 Strand, London WC2R 0RL, England
Penguin Group Ireland, 25 St. Stephen's Green, Dublin 2, Ireland (a division of Penguin Books Ltd.)
Penguin Group (Australia), 250 Camberwell Road, Camberwell, Victoria 3124, Australia
(a division of Pearson Australia Group Pty. Ltd.)
Penguin Books India Pvt. Ltd., 11 Community Centre, Panchsheel Park, New Delhi—110 017, India
Penguin Group (NZ), Cnr. Airborne and Rosedale Roads, Albany, Auckland 1310, New Zealand
(a division of Pearson New Zealand Ltd.)
Penguin Books (South Africa) (Pty.) Ltd., 24 Sturdee Avenue, Rosebank, Johannesburg 2196,
South Africa

Penguin Books Ltd., Registered Offices: 80 Strand, London WC2R 0RL, England

DARK DEMON

A Jove Book / published by arrangement with the author.

PRINTING HISTORY
Jove premium edition / April 2006

Copyright © 2006 by Christine Feehan.
Excerpt from *Dangerous Tides* copyright © 2006 by Christine Feehan.
Cover design by George Long.
Cover illustration by Franco Accernero.
Handlettering by Ron Zinn.

ISBN: 0-515-14088-0

JOVE®
Jove Books are published by The Berkley Publishing Group,
a division of Penguin Group (USA) Inc.,
375 Hudson Street, New York, New York 10014.
JOVE is a registered trademark of Penguin Group (USA) Inc.
The "J" design is a trademark belonging to Penguin Group (USA) Inc.

PRINTED IN THE UNITED STATES OF AMERICA

10 9 8 7 6 5 4 3 2 1

*To Dr. Christopher Tong and Mary Waltrich with much love
And for Kelley Granzow and her lifemate Rick*

Be sure to go to
http://www.christinefeehan.com/members/
to sign up for her PRIVATE book announcement
list and get a FREE EXCLUSIVE Christine Feehan
animated screen saver. Please feel free to e-mail
her at christine@christinefeehan.com.
She would love to hear from you.

Acknowledgments

Special thanks to Dr. Christopher Tong who is a continual source of information. It was his brainchild to use the Carpathian language as the proto-language of the Hungarian and Finnish languages. Dr. Chris Tong (www.christong.com) is fluent in several languages, did undergraduate studies in linguistics at Columbia University and graduate studies in computational linguistics at Stanford University. He has also studied the world's great spiritual, mythic and healing traditions for the past thirty years (and personally participated in several of them). He is also the founder of The Practical Spirituality Press, and the author of several books on "practical spirituality." Thank you, Mary for speaking Hungarian and giving us a place to start!

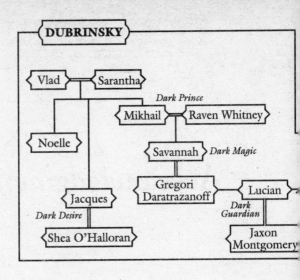

DUBRINSKY

Vlad = Sarantha

Dark Prince
Mikhail = Raven Whitney

Noelle

Savannah = *Dark Magic*

Jacques
Dark Desire

Gregori
Daratrazanoff = Lucian
Dark Guardian

Shea O'Halloran

Jaxon
Montgomery

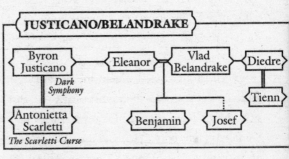

JUSTICANO/BELANDRAKE

Byron
Justicano — Eleanor — Vlad
Belandrake — Diedre
Dark Symphony

Tienn

Antonietta
Scarletti

Benjamin — Josef

The Scarletti Curse

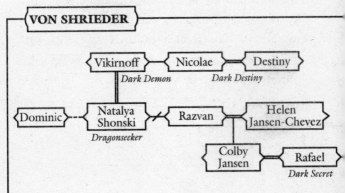

VON SHRIEDER

Vikirnoff = Nicolae = Destiny
Dark Demon *Dark Destiny*

Dominic --- Natalya
Shonski — Razvan = Helen
Jansen-Chevez
Dragonseeker

Colby
Jansen = Rafael
Dark Secret

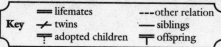

THE CARPATHIANS

Key
- ══ lifemates
- ⫟ twins
- ⋯ adopted children
- --- other relation
- — siblings
- ⊤ offspring

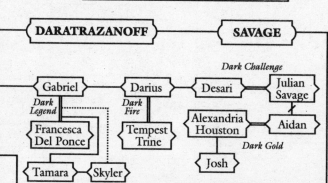

DARATRAZANOFF — **SAVAGE**

Dark Challenge

Gabriel — Darius — Desari — Julian Savage

Dark Legend

Dark Fire

Francesca Del Ponce — Tempest Trine

Alexandria Houston ══ Aidan

Dark Gold

Tamara — Skyler

Josh

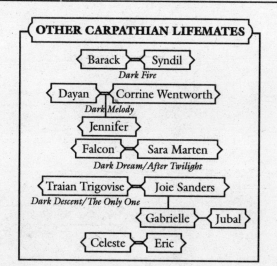

OTHER CARPATHIAN LIFEMATES

Barack ══ Syndil
Dark Fire

Dayan ══ Corrine Wentworth
Dark Melody

Jennifer

Falcon ══ Sara Marten
Dark Dream/After Twilight

Traian Trigovise ══ Joie Sanders
Dark Descent/The Only One

Gabrielle ══ Jubal

Celeste ══ Eric

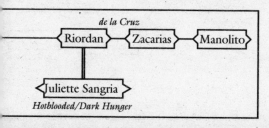

de la Cruz

Riordan — Zacarias — Manolito

Juliette Sangria

Hotblooded/Dark Hunger

1

Natalya Shonski drew the pair of black leather trousers up over her legs and settled them on her hips where they molded to her body. Leather helped prevent injury during battles and she was certain she would be running into trouble tonight. As she pulled on the soft leather camisole, she glanced around the meticulously clean room she'd rented. The inn was small, but colorful with tapestries on the walls and bright patterned covers decorating the bed. Her weapons were laid out with great care over the beautifully woven quilt.

She began to slip various weapons into the specially made compartments and loops in her leather pants. Throwing stars with razor-sharp edges. Several knives. A belt that provided her with room for more weapons and extra clips for the twin guns she fit snugly into the harness under each arm. She put on one of her new peasant blouses and donned the brightly colored fur vest the local women wore for warmth, effectively hiding her arsenal.

The long skirt not only hid the leather pants, but also helped her to blend into the local population. She'd chosen a colorful one, rather than the severe black kind the older women often wore, and tied a scarf over her tawny hair to further disguise herself.

Satisfied she looked as much like a local as possible, she shoved two Arnis sticks into the well-worn loops on her backpack and opened the doors to the balcony. She had deliberately chosen a room on the second floor. Her many enemies would find it difficult to approach unnoticed while she could escape easily to the ground below or go up and over the roof.

Natalya rested her hands on the balcony rail and leaned out to survey the countryside. The small village was nestled at the bottom of one of the tall jagged peaks that formed the formidable Carpathian Mountains. Numerous small farms were scattered across the green, rolling hills. Stacks of hay dotted the meadows and led the way up the mountain to the timberline. Above the heavy forest were rocky peaks, still glistening with snow. She felt as if she'd stepped back in time with the simple homes and the rustic way of life, yet she felt as if she'd come home. And that was truly odd. She had no home.

Natalya sighed and closed her eyes briefly. More than anything in the world, she envied these people their families. Their laughter and children and the love shining in their eyes and on their faces. She longed to belong somewhere. Be needed by someone. To be treasured by one single person. Just to be able to truly be who she was, share a real conversation. . . .

Her fingers found deep grooves in the railing and she found herself rubbing the polished wood, the pads of her fingers stroking along the grooves almost in a caress. Startled, she examined the scores in the hardwood. It looked as if a large bird had dug talons deep into the railing, although the marks were old and the innkeepers kept the intricately carved balcony polished and free of splinters.

She inhaled the night air and stared up toward the top of the mountain. Somewhere up there was her goal. She had no idea what drove her to come to this particular spot, but she trusted her instincts. She needed to climb to the top and find whatever it was that wouldn't let go of her. Thick mist hid the mountaintop, enveloping the peak in an impenetrable cloud. Whether the cloud was natural condensation or a preternatural warning made no difference. She had no choice but to climb the mountain, the compulsion driving her was far too strong to ignore.

Natalya took a last look toward the swirling white mists and headed back into her room. There was no point in putting it off. She'd spent the last week mingling with the people in the village, establishing friendships with a few of the women and getting a feel for the area. She found she needed human companionship although her life was very solitary. She enjoyed the time spent with the local women and had gleaned quite a bit of information from them, but she was always saddened that her friendships could never go beyond the surface. It made for a lonely life and she yearned to belong somewhere, to let someone like the innkeeper, Slavica Ostojic, know who and what she was just so Natalya could have the luxury of being honest with someone she truly liked.

The hallway and stairs were narrow, leading to the sitting room below. The room opened into the dining hall on one end and a bar on the other. Many of the locals drank beer in the evening and visited together after a hard day's work. She waved to two or three people she recognized, her gaze automatically scanning the rooms, noting exits, windows and above all, new faces. Several men sitting at the bar glanced at her. She catalogued the lined faces, the friendly smiles and assessing glances, filed them away just in case she met up with them again.

One pair of eyes flicked over her face, giving her pause. The perusal was quick, but it was thorough. He was reading her in the same way she was reading him. He certainly noticed the backpack with the double Arnis sticks and her ornate walking stick. Natalya turned away with a quick smile for the owner of the inn, grateful she could make her exit gracefully. If there was a sentry watching, she didn't want him to know her plans.

"Slavica." She took the innkeeper's hands in hers. "Thank you so much for the wonderful meal." She spoke in English because Slavica worked hard to perfect her language skills and always practiced. Deliberately she led the woman away from the bar to a more secluded spot in the sitting room where prying ears would not be able to overhear their conversation. "I'm heading up into the mountains and I'm often gone for days at a time while exploring. Don't worry about me. I'll return eventually. Give me a week at least before you panic."

Slavica shook her head. "It is after sunset, Natalya. Here in the mountains and forests there can be . . ." She hesitated searching for the right word—"unrest. It's better if you explore during the day when the sun is bright and there are people around you." She looked up and met her husband's eyes across the room and smiled.

Natalya instantly felt a pang of envy. She loved to watch the innkeeper with her husband, Mirko, and their daughter, Angelina, together. Their love for one another was always so obvious in the small little glances they exchanged and their many touches as they brushed by one another when they worked.

"I've gone out every evening and you've never objected," Natalya reminded her. "And nearly all of those times were after sunset."

Slavica gave her a faint smile. "I feel the difference tonight. I know you will think I'm superstitious, but something is not right this evening and it is better you stay here with us." She patted Natalya's arm. "There is much to do here. Mirko will play chess with you. He is quite good. Or I will teach you more about the local herbs and how to use them to heal." Slavica was a trained nurse and renowned for her healing skills throughout the district and for her knowledge of the local healing herbs and how to use them. The subject fascinated Natalya and she enjoyed spending time in Slavica's company while the woman imparted her knowledge.

Natalya shook her head, regret lingering in her heart. Slavica was the kind of woman that made her ache to be part of a family and community. "Thank you, Slavica, but I have protection." She pulled the cross hanging on the thin silver chain from where it was hidden beneath her shirt. "I appreciate your concern, but I'll be fine."

Slavica started to protest, but stopped herself, pressing her lips together firmly. She simply shook her head.

"I know what I'm doing," Natalya assured her. "I'm going to slip out through the kitchen if you don't mind. I've got food and drink enough for several days and I'll be back in the middle of next week if not sooner."

Slavica walked with her through the dining room. Natalya risked another glance at the man sitting at the bar talking to Mirko. He seemed absorbed in the conversation, but she didn't trust him. He had shown interest in her and it wasn't the interest of a man looking for a woman. She had no idea what it was, but she wasn't going to take any chances. She gave a small nod toward the man. "Who is he? I haven't seen him in here before."

"He travels through this way many times on business." Slavica's expression gave nothing away. "He's very quiet and I don't know what his business is."

"Is he married?"

The innkeeper looked alarmed. "This man is not for

you, Natalya. He is welcome here as all travelers are, but he is not for you."

Natalya didn't dare risk another glance in the man's direction. He was far too observant and she didn't want to draw his attention. She walked through the dining room into the small kitchen. There was the inevitable sheep's cheese and baskets of potatoes. "Don't worry, I'm not looking for a man."

"I have seen the yearning on your face and in your eyes when you look at children. When you see married couples," Slavica said gently. "You wish for a family of your own."

Natalya shrugged carelessly, avoiding the other woman's gaze, not wanting to see the compassion she knew would be there. Was she becoming that obvious? When had it become so difficult for her to hide her feelings beneath her carefully cultivated "flip" personality? "I like traveling. I wouldn't want to be tied down." It was a blatant lie and for the first time in her life, she knew she had given herself away.

"It is natural to want a family and a man for yourself. I waited to find the right one," Slavica counseled. "Even when my parents and neighbors thought I was too old and would never find him, I thought it better to wait than to make a mistake and tie myself to someone I didn't want to spend my life with. I waited for Mirko and it was the right thing to do. We have a beautiful daughter and this place and that is enough. We're happy together. You understand, Natalya? Don't give yourself away to just any man because you think time is running out."

Natalya nodded solemnly. "I understand and agree completely. I'm not feeling desperate to find a man, far from it. I'll see you soon." She pushed open the kitchen door, gave a cheery wave toward the frowning innkeeper and hurried out into the night.

After the warmth of the inn, the air outside was cold, but she was prepared for that. She walked briskly along the narrow road leading toward the mountain trail. An empty horse cart passed her and she called out asking for a ride. The farmer hesitated and then stopped for her. Natalya caught up the hem of her skirt and ran to catch up before he could change his mind. Most of the locals used the horse carts rather than cars. They were simple vehicles, a wagon on tires pulled by one or two horses. They were used for everything from transportation to hauling great sheafs of hay.

"Thank you, sir," she said as she tossed in her walking stick and climbed aboard. She settled herself toward the back of the cart, not wanting to make the farmer more uncomfortable than he already seemed to be hauling a strange woman around.

To her surprise he spoke. Most of the older married men were quite reserved around younger, single women. "What are you doing out this late? The sun has gone down." He glanced nervously around him.

"Yes it has," she agreed, avoiding the question. "You're out late as well."

"It isn't good," he said. "Not this night." He kept his voice very low. The concern in his tone was unmistakable. "Better you should allow my wife and I to put you up for the night. Or I could take you to the inn." He was looking up at the moon, at the clouds swirling over it, partially blocking the light and it was clear he didn't want to turn back. He shook the reins to speed the horse up.

Natalya glanced up at the sky and the boiling clouds that had not been there minutes before. The heavy mist obscuring the top of the mountains spread like bony fingers, reaching up toward the moon and lower for the forest. Lightning edged the mist in golden arcs. Thunder rumbled in the distance, centered mainly over the mountain.

She slid her hand inside her fur vest and touched the handle of her gun. "The weather changed fast this evening." *And it wasn't natural.*

"It happens that way in the mountains," the farmer said, clucking at the horse with urgency. "It's best to take cover until things settle down."

Natalya didn't reply. She had to get to the top of the mountain. Had spies let her enemies know she was close? Were they waiting for her? She turned her attention to the countryside passing by so quickly. Was there movement in the shadows? If so, she had to lead trouble away from the farmer. They had traveled far past the perimeters of the village and well out into the rolling hills where farms dotted the landscape.

She stayed alert, watching for signs of an impending

attack, her senses flaring out into the night, reaching for information. She inhaled, taking the night air deep into her lungs, working to unravel the stories the wind brought her. The wind carried the stench of evil. The whisper of movement in the forest. The scent of wolves, restless beneath the moon. Her chin lifted. So be it. She didn't go looking for fights. She was, in fact, usually the first to walk away, but she was tired of being pursued, of looking over her shoulder every minute of every day. If they wanted to fight, she had come prepared, because this time she wasn't going to turn away.

The farmer pulled the cart onto a narrow lane. The horse slowed to make the sharp turn and Natalya jumped off, waving at the farmer as she hurried away. He called out to her, but she kept going, walking briskly up the hillside toward the timberline.

The moment she was certain she was out of the farmer's sight, she stripped off the brightly colored skirt and blouse, folding them along with the scarf and tucking them into her backpack. The double Arnis sticks went into loops at the back of her belt for easy retrieval. Her entire demeanor changed as she gripped the familiar walking stick. She strode with tremendous confidence, weaving in and out of the hay sheaves until she was clear of the farms. A walking path led up the mountain, a trail for goats, not humans, but she took it because it was the most direct approach.

She crossed through a field of alpine flowers, the blossoms everywhere as she pushed through the high grasses toward the slope of timber. The moon was almost completely hidden by the darkening clouds, and the closer she got to the forest, the louder the thunder boomed. Flowers and grass gave way to bushes and scrub. Large boulders dotted the slope. A few heartier flowers had managed to find their way into the crevices. The trees were small and very scraggly, but as she wound her way through two more switchbacks, the vegetation changed completely, growing fuller and taller.

Natalya had studied the Carpathian Mountains. She knew the range was one of Europe's largest homes for carnivores, rich with brown bear, wolves and lynx. The mountains stretched across seven countries in Central Europe and the heavily wooded forests were one of the last refuges left to Europe's rare and nearly extinct birds and larger predators. Although home to millions of people, the Carpathian Mountains boasted huge tracts of land that remained utterly wild and dangerous.

She paused to examine the pristine forest surrounding her. The area received twice the rainfall of surrounding regions and the amazing forests and green hills gave evidence of the amount of water that fed the river systems below. The vivid colors of green drew her into the coolness of the forest almost as a compulsion would. Why did she know this place? How had she dreamt of it? How did she know that when she took the path on her left, which was no more than a deer path, it would lead her deep into the interior and she would find the faint trail that would take her to the very top of the mountains, right up into the swirling mists where few people ventured to go?

She moved fast along the path, using a light, ground-eating jog that took her through the brush quickly. She had to make it to the top of the mountain and find the entrance to the caves before sunup.

The forest grew more dense, the plants more exotic and lush as she hurried through the seemingly impenetrable trees. Swaying branches interlocked overhead, blocking most of the moonlight. Natalya had no problem seeing where she was going. In addition to excellent night vision, she'd always had a sense of radar that prevented her from running into obstacles.

She moved through the forest swiftly but with instinctive caution, fully alert, aware of the smallest of rustlings, the silence of insects and the faintest of scents that would indicate she wasn't alone.

Her mouth went suddenly dry and her heart rate increased. The hairs on the back of her neck prickled with unease. She was being stalked.

Behind her shadows slipped around the trees in an effort to surround her. Natalya continued jogging at the same steady pace. As she ran she transferred her grip on the walking stick to the familiar grooves at the top of it in preparation for a fight.

The first wolf sprang at her out of the cover of brush as she crossed a small stream. Natalya didn't slow down, but met the charge with a practiced swing of the thick walking stick. The crack was audible; the wolf yelped and leapt back as she swept past. She whirled around, drawing the sword smoothly from the stick and casting the deceptive sheath aside to face the wolf.

"If you wish to fight me, brother, do so. I have places to go and you are delaying my travel." She murmured the words aloud as she glided toward the animal, deliberately stepping into the wind so it could carry her scent to the pack.

The wolf sniffed the air and backed up, suddenly wary. The pack members milled around in confusion. Natalya growled low in her throat, the warning of a wild, dangerous animal. Her vivid green eyes began to swirl with intense blue, going almost opaque as she bared her teeth at the pack. Streaks of midnight black and bright orange—almost red banded through her hair. The wolves broke off, loping away from her. Only the alpha female looked back, snarling and showing her displeasure at the unfamiliar scent. Natalya hissed a warning and the female fled after the pack.

"Yeah, that's what I thought," Natalya called after them, sliding the sword back into the scabbard. She waited to make certain the wolves were gone before continuing up the mountainside, moving steadily toward her goal.

She cleared a downed tree covered with moss and fern and slid to an abrupt halt as a man sauntered out from behind a tree directly in front of her. He was tall with dark hair, very handsome, his shoulders wide and his smile dazzling. Natalya scanned the area with every sense on high alert. He wasn't alone, she was certain of it.

She dropped her pack on the ground and smiled at the man. "I expected you a good hour ago."

He bowed from the waist. "I am sorry to be late then, lady. I arrived here to prepare for your coming." He opened his arms wide to encompass the area around them.

"It wasn't necessary to dress in your Sunday best," Natalya said. "Although the alternative is rather disgusting."

A flicker of anger rippled across the man's face, but he hung onto his smile. His teeth weren't so white and appeared pointy and sharp. "Please put down your stick."

"Do you think I'm going to make it easy on you? I'm not really happy with you, Freddie boy."

This time the anger stayed. Brown stains appeared on his teeth. "I am not Freddie. Who is Freddie? My name is Henrik."

"You don't get out much do you? Haven't you ever watched the late night movies? Freddie's a regular star. A very ugly mass murderer, much like yourself. I really don't care what your name is. I care that you persist in following me and I'm damned tired of it. So take your best shot, Freddie boy, and let's get it over."

Henrik's breath came out in a long hiss of anger. "You will learn respect."

Not bothering with a retort, Natalya launched her attack, freeing her sword as she sprang at him. The sword arced through the air slicing toward his neck.

Henrik dissolved into vapor, streaming away from

her, a shriek of rage echoing through the forest. He faced her several yards away. His thick black hair was gone to be replaced by long white very disheveled strands.

"I should have known you'd be a sissy. Vampires are supposed to be such bad asses, but you're all such babies. You wanted a fight." Natalya continued to goad him. "I've got things to do tonight. I don't have time to play your little games with you."

"You go too far. I don't care what the order is. I'm going to kill you," the vampire snarled.

She smirked at him, giving a small salute. "Nice to know you can think for yourself. I thought your puppet master had you too well trained for free thinking."

The branch above her head cracked and broke off, rocketing toward her head like a missile. Natalya leapt forward, going on the offensive, ramming the sword straight at Henrik's chest. The branch slammed into the ground exactly where she'd been standing.

The vampire parried the sword away with a sweep of his arm. He was enormously strong and the contact sent violent vibrations up and down her arm so that for a moment everything went numb and the sword slid out of her hand. She kept moving, spinning nearly in midair, already reaching for her guns. She drew both, rapidly firing as she raced at him, the bullets slamming into him repeatedly, driving him backwards away from her.

Henrik jerked with each bullet, staggering, but staying upright. As she reached arm's distance, she holstered one gun and drew a knife, holding it low, close to her body as she drove toward him.

He attempted to shift shape, reaching for her with contorting arms and clawed hands. She drove the knife into his chest, deep into his heart and leapt away to keep the blood from touching her skin. She'd learned from experience it burned like acid. She'd also learned vampires could rise again and again.

She whirled around and raced for her sword. The wind rushed over her, a whirling eddy of leaves and twigs. Wings beat strongly above her head and talons materialized out of the sky, dropping at an alarming rate of speed straight toward her eyes. Natalya dove for the ground in a rolling somersault, coming up on one knee, guns in both hands, tracking the huge bird. It had already dissolved into mist. The droplets shimmered and began to take the shape of a human.

She waited. It was impossible to kill a vampire without form. Already Henrik was stirring, tugging at the knife buried in his heart. He called weakly to the new arrival. She heaved a sigh. "Die already! Sheesh, the least you could do is put yourself out of your misery and get it over."

"Good evening, Natalya." The voice was hypnotic, almost mesmerizing.

"Well, if it isn't my good friend Arturo." Natalya faced the vampire with a false smile. "How nice to see you again. It's been a long time." She gestured with her gun toward the writhing vampire. "Your little sissy partner is making so much noise. Would you mind finishing him off so we can talk without the background music? If there's one thing I can't stand, it's a whiney vampire." Deliberately she continued to goad Henrik, knowing the angrier the vampire, the more mistakes they made in battle.

"You haven't changed much."

"I've gotten meaner." She shrugged and grinned at the newcomer. "I'm losing my tolerance for your kind."

Arturo glanced at the bleeding vampire clawing at the ground. "I see that. He is rather loud, isn't he?" He walked over and yanked the knife from his partner's heart and tossed it aside, nudging the vampire with his toe contemptuously. "Get up, Henrik."

Henrik managed to stagger into a standing position. He shrieked and hissed, spittle and blood running down his face. "I'm going to kill you," he snapped, glaring at Natalya.

"Do shut up," Natalya said. "You're becoming so repetitive."

"You will not escape this time," Arturo said. "You cannot best Henrik, me and the wolves. Do you hear them? They are on their way to assist us."

"You take all the fun out of fighting because you never fight fair," Natalya complained. "You have no honor."

Arturo smiled at her with his perfect white teeth. "What is honor after all, Natalya? It is worth nothing."

Vikirnoff Von Shrieder knew the moment he entered the heavy woods that something evil waited there. The warning came in the silence of the forest, the way the earth shuddered and the trees cringed. Not a single living creature moved. It mattered little. He was a hunter and he expected danger to find him. It was his accepted way of life and had been for centuries.

He took a step and stopped abruptly as the grass shivered beneath his feet. He looked down, half expecting to see the stalks shrivel. Was the forest shrinking from direct contact with *him*? Had it sensed the darkness shadowing him with every step, with each breath he took? Nature could very well be naming him monster—vampire, a Carpathian male who had deliberately chosen to give up his soul for the momentary rush of power and emotion a kill while feeding brought.

It was a choice, wasn't it? Had he made a decision and was no longer aware of whether he was good or evil? Was there even such a thing? The thought should have distressed him, but it didn't. He felt nothing at all even as he contemplated the idea that he was no longer fully a Carpathian male; that the predator in him had consumed all but some small spark left in his soul.

He dropped to his knees, his hands digging through layers of leaves and twigs covering the forest floor and plunging deep into the rich, dark soil beneath. He lifted his face to the night sky. "*Susu*," he whispered aloud. "I am home." His native language rolled off his tongue naturally, his accent thicker than usual as if somehow by just being in the Carpathian Mountains he could go back in time.

After so many centuries of exile in service to his people, he had finally returned to his birthplace. He knelt in utter silence waiting for something. Anything. Some flicker of emotion, or remembrance. He expected the soil to bring peace, to bring him serenity, to bring him *something*, but there was the same barren void he woke to every rising.

Nothing. He felt absolutely nothing. He bowed his head and sank back on his heels, looking around him. What he wanted or even needed, he didn't know, but there was no flood of emotion. No elation. No disappointment. Not even despair. The forest looked bleak and gray with twisted, malevolent shadows waiting for him. The endless cycle of his life remained. Kill or be killed.

Hunger was ever present now, a soft seductive whisper in his mind. The call to power, to salvation, and false though he knew it to be, it had gained strength with every rising. He had fought battles, far too many to count, destroying old friends, men he respected and admired, watching the fall of his people and all for what? "Tell me the reason," he whispered to the night. "Let me understand the complete waste of my life."

Had he fed this night? He tried to recall the occasion of his wakening, but it seemed too much trouble. Surely he hadn't taken a life while feeding. Was this how it happened then? Was there no real choice, but a slow indifference pervading one's mind until one kill ran into another? Until one feeding became mixed with a kill and his indifference became the weapon of his own destruction?

He looked toward the south where he knew the prince of his people resided. The wind began to pick up speed and strength, rushing through the forest in a southerly direction. "Honor is a damnable trait and one that may not last eternity." Vikirnoff murmured the words with a small sigh as he rose to his full height and drew back his long hair, securing it at the nape of his neck with a leather tie. Did he still have his honor? After centuries of battling to keep his word, had the crouching beast at last consumed him?

The leaves on the trees closest to him began to tremble and the branches swayed with alarm. He was a Carpathian male, born into an ancient race now on the brink of extinction. They had few women, so all-important to the males and the preservation of life. Two halves of the same whole, darkness ruled the males while light dwelt within the females. Without women to anchor them, the males were falling into the greedy jaws of their own demons.

Vikirnoff coexisted with humans, living among them, trying to maintain honor and discipline in a world where he no longer saw in color or felt even the slightest of emotions. After two hundred years, his feelings had faded and over the long endless centuries the dark predator in him had grown strong and powerful. Only faded memories of laughter and love sustained him, and then only through his link with Nicolae, his brother. Now, that too was gone, with Nicolae an ocean away.

Vikirnoff had lived too long and become far too dangerous. His fighting skills were superb, honed and sharpened in the too numerous encounters with those of his kind who had chosen to give up their souls for the momentary illusion of power, or more likely, more tragically, for a brief moment of feeling. He felt as if he were single-handedly destroying his own race. So many deaths. So many lost friends. "For what?" He asked aloud. "*Möéri*?" He whispered again in his own language.

He deliberately used his own ancient tongue to recall his duty, his promises to his prince. He had volunteered to be sent out into the world. It was his choice. Always his choice. Free will. But he was no longer free. He was so close to being the very thing he hunted, he almost couldn't separate the two.

The ground rolled gently beneath his feet and the night sky rumbled a menacing warning. Somewhere ahead of him was his quarry—a blue-eyed woman who he had pursued across an ocean. Between the woman and Vikirnoff was a vampire—or perhaps more than one.

Vikirnoff pulled the photograph of his quarry from its place close to his heart. He saw only in shades of gray, yet he had known she had eyes as blue as the sea and Nicolae told him her hair appeared midnight black. Blue like the nearly forgotten ice lakes of his homeland. The various shades of blue in the skies overhead. He had thought— hoped—that perhaps knowing instinctively that small detail meant he was pursuing his lifemate. The other half of his soul, light to his darkness, the one woman who could restore the lost colors and most of all, his ability to feel *something*. Anything at all. That hope, too, had faded over time, leaving the world a bleak, ugly place.

The air charged with electricity, crackling and snapping along with the building thunder. Cloud formations built in the sky, great towers churning upward. He drew the pad of his thumb in a small unconscious caress over the picture of the woman as he had done so many times before. He had dreams, of course, of the perfect Carpathian lifemate. A woman with this face, those eyes, a woman who would do as he bid, see to his happiness while he ensured hers. Life would be peaceful and serene and filled with joy and most of all, emotion. He slipped the photograph back inside his shirt, over his heart, where it would be protected. He couldn't even sigh with regret. He didn't feel regret, or despair. Just the endless emptiness.

You have to stop! The words swirled in his mind, a telepathic link of unexpected strength. *Your emotions are so incredibly strong I can't imagine how you don't recognize they exist. You're devastating me, ripping my heart out. I can't afford this right now. Control your emotions or get the hell far away from me!*

The feminine voice swirled in his mind, slid over and into his body, invaded his heart and lungs and rushed through his bloodstream with the raging force of a firestorm. For nearly two thousand years he had existed in the gray shadows feeling nothing at all. He had lived in an endless, starkly barren world without desire or rage or affection. In that one moment everything changed. His mind was instant chaos.

Colors blinded him, running together in vivid, dazzling streaks his eyes and mind could barely accept. His stomach churned and rolled as he fought to maintain alertness when the very ground beneath his feet swelled and buckled. A floodgate opened and where before there had been nothing, now there was *everything,* a wild jumble of every emotion with his tremendous strength and power feeding the chaos.

The trees nearest him split in two, the sound horrendous as trunks hit the ground, shaking the earth. A rift opened in the ground close to him, followed by a second jagged tear and then another. The rocks shifted and buckled and another row of trees split and flattened.

The demon in him lifted its head and roared for release, tearing at him with great claws, fighting for the freedom to abandon honor and go after the one thing that belonged solely to him. His savior. Or maybe she was his damnation. His incisors lengthened and his blood was so hot he feared he might burst into flame.

Oh my God! You're one of them. Terror made her voice tremble.

Just as he had shared his loneliness, pain and sorrow with her, he shared his darkness and the terrible intensity of overwhelming emotions. She felt his edgy need for violence. The rush the kill provided. The primitive, raw, sexual hunger that ruled his body and mixed with the possessive lust to claim her. She shared it all with him, not only the wild elation, but every fierce need and desire pouring into his body. Every questioning of his life, the gradual need to hunt and kill. The madness of his beast rising and fighting to get loose, to be unleashed for the sole purpose of *getting to her*.

Fear hit him, great waves nearly amounting to terror, just as quickly building into resolve. The emotions were so strong his stomach rolled. It took a moment before he realized her feelings were pouring into him with every bit of strength as his own. He touched the stream of feminine passion and found power. She would fight. Surrounded, she had no choice but to fight and win. The fear was banished. The terror gone. She would defeat whatever, whoever came at her because it was the only way left to her to survive.

Vikirnoff closed himself off from her, abruptly halting the sharing of the storm of emotions breaking through him. He searched for a mental path, a trail that would lead him back to the woman. She belonged to him. No other. Not another Carpathian. Not the vampires on her trail. She was *his*. He would have her or many—human and Carpathian alike—would die.

Taking a deep breath to restore his control, Vikirnoff lifted his head slowly and looked around him. The forest seemed to expand and grow and glitter with brilliance, even in the dark of night, as if he had taken a strong hallucinogenic. Above his head the clouds were black with wrath, edged with flickering white-hot lightning. Twisting tendrils of fog snaked through the trees and gathered along the ground.

Vikirnoff remained still, allowing his experience as a

hunter to guide him, rather than following the dictates of his chaotic mind. He waited, sorting through the frenzied sensations, waiting for calm before taking action.

All the while he savored the sound of her voice. The path leading back to her was subtle, almost too subtle to follow. It was puzzling. She was Carpathian, yet not Carpathian. She was human, yet not human. He felt the whisper of power in her voice, the subtle "push" when she tried to force obedience. She had tried to force *his* obedience. He took another deep breath, inhaling to take air deep into his lungs, but most of all to find her scent.

2

Natalya *swiped at* the empathetic tears clouding her vision. Her heart pounded in terror, but she set her teeth grimly. She could kill Henrik and she might even best Arturo. She could even get away from the wolves, but she had just touched a being so powerful she never wanted to tangle with him. At the first touch, she thought him a hunter, one of those who had killed her twin brother and was hunting her. But his emotions had been so sad, so despairing, he'd nearly torn her heart out.

She had never experienced such a strong connection before. She hadn't meant for him to hear her protest. She had no idea how they were on the same mental path to share such intense emotions, but she didn't want to stick around to find out how it had happened. She'd never been bombarded with such an overwhelming explosion of feelings before. His feelings. Lust and possession. Elation and relief. All superceded by the overwhelming need to kill. She needed to escape fast before whatever, *whomever,* she had accidentally touched psychically tracked her down.

"Look who's crying now," Henrik sneered. "I knew you were all talk."

"That's right, Freddie boy, I like to talk," Natalya agreed as she directed three throwing knives in rapid succession at him. Each scored a hit, burying deeply all the way to the hilt, one in the heart, one in the throat and one in the mouth. "But, as I've already said, I hate to listen to whiners."

Henrik dropped to the ground again, howling and writhing, clawing great holes in the soil, his blood withering the vegetation in a broad circle around him.

Arturo sighed. "That wasn't nice, Natalya. He's going to be much more difficult to control. I don't want you dead and he'll insist."

Natalya glanced into the darkened interior of the forest. So far it had just been too easy. Neither vampire was trying to kill her. Her last few encounters with the undead had been strange in that none of them seemed willing to kill her. It gave her a distinct advantage in battle, but it boded ill for her future. She had discovered some years earlier that they were hunting her for a purpose she couldn't fathom and they were very persistent in their pursuit of her.

"I don't think you really need him, Arturo," she said. "He's rather a pathetic fellow, don't you think?"

"But a useful sacrifice," Arturo pointed out.

Natalya was having trouble with her vision. Colors ran together, vivid and brilliant in spite of the darkening clouds spinning around the moon. The leaves glittered silver, dazzling her eyes so that when she launched her attack at Arturo, she was slightly off in her depth perception. She couldn't afford to wait. It was obvious Arturo was using Henrik as a stall tactic, waiting for reinforcements, and she knew the hunter was coming.

Out of necessity she went for the kill, somersaulting through the air, only baring the knife concealed in her hand at the last second, as she plunged it straight for Arturo's chest. He leapt to the side, so that she sliced a long thin cut across his shoulder and arm. As she sprang past him Arturo whipped his other arm around and slammed talons into her side, raking deep.

Pain blossomed, low and deep and bone-jarring. Vikirnoff looked down, shocked to see blood seeping from a gaping wound. He pressed his hand over his side, eyes glowing a hot red, fangs bursting into his mouth. He growled low in his throat, already shifting shape, taking the form of an owl. As his muscles popped, sinews crackled, and then the pain vanished. He glanced down again and there was no blood. None. His clothes, his skin and, as he completed the change, his iridescent feathers, were immaculate.

He had thought the danger she had sensed was within

him, that her resolve had been to fight *him*. Something else, something evil and cunning had led them both into a trap and she had paid a terrible price. If it wasn't his blood, his pain, there was only one other it could belong to. The vampire he had detected earlier wasn't between them, it had already found her. Somewhere ahead of him, his lifemate was fighting for her life.

Deep within the form of the owl, Vikirnoff threw back his head and roared with rage. He raced through the trees, powerful wings flapping hard, skimming the edge of branches, a suicide run through the dense trees. He maneuvered more by instinct than by sight, staying low in the thick canopy. He sensed the disturbance increasing and slowed to a more acceptable speed, moving the way an owl would naturally among the branches of the trees and gaining more height to spot prey.

Below him, he sighted movement, dark shapes slipping silently through the trees, sliding from one shadow to the next. The wild scent of wolf mingled with the sweet aroma of blood. Directly below was a thicket of dense shrubbery surrounded by groves of trees. The branches interlocked, providing a seemingly impenetrable canopy. He dropped lower as he slipped between the branches, making his body smaller, uncaring that the use of power might give away his presence. He could see a vampire writhing on the ground, growling and cursing and swearing vengeance as it attempted to remove several knives from its body.

Vikirnoff knew his lifemate was in that thicket of

trees. Every protective instinct rose up, every possessive Carpathian trait existing in him, his imprinted instincts all told him she was there. He just couldn't see her.

Movement attracted his eye. Vikirnoff settled the owl's body silently onto a thick, twisted branch high above the ground, folding his wings and watching for movement below him. A shadowy form separated itself from a gnarled trunk and slithered along the rich vegetation, ignoring the shriveling leaves and blackened grasses as it glided into a cleared space in the center of the trees.

"You have been wounded. Let me give you aid." The shadow raised his head, taking on a more substantial form as he sniffed the air. "The scent of blood is so intoxicating."

Even the sharp eyes of the owl didn't spot the woman until she moved. She seemed to emerge from the very trees, her body difficult to make out with the bands of light spilling from the moon. Clouds spun overhead shifting the light continually, casting stripes across her. Vikirnoff held his breath as she went from complete stillness to a fluid motion, taking several steps away from the trees toward her shadowy opponent. This then was his lifemate. Natalya Shonski, the woman he had crossed an ocean to find.

She seemed to glow, golden streaks of colors flashing off her hair, black, orange, even platinum. Her eyes, her all important eyes, were no longer blue, but opalescent, a swirling mixture of vibrant colors as turbulent and wild as the raw power emanating from her. Energy crackled around her and the vaporous fog rising from the forest floor churned with renewed vigor, as if by her presence, new life was feeding the grayish mist.

She was dazzling. Vikirnoff stared at her, unable to look away even though the vivid colors hurt his eyes. He had never seen such raw power springing to life. She looked fragile in stillness, yet when she moved, muscles slid suggestively beneath her golden skin. It was how she moved, so fluid, like water over rock, her small form erect, unbending in the face of her enemy. She was exotic and beautiful to him and wholly regal. In spite of the red stain spreading across her side, her gaze remained fixed on the vampire, an unwavering, focused stare, uncannily like that of a wild predator.

Behold. There she stands. Lifemate to Vikirnoff. The awe and splendor of her astonished him. His lungs burned and his throat felt raw. His body flooded with heat and every muscle seized with desire. He couldn't separate lust from rage, or joy from the need to kill those threatening her. He felt almost dizzy with the combination and intensity of his unfamiliar feelings.

Vikirnoff knew he could no longer afford the chaotic emotions. It was that simple. He was a hunter and he had a battle in front of him. He was useless in the state he was in. More than useless—he was dangerous not only to himself but to his lifemate. He called on his years of service, years of experience in battle, and centered himself, reached deep to find the eye in the center of the storm, to find the man he had always been—a man short on speech, but long on action when there was need. A man ruled by logic and duty and honor. He waited until the emotional storm subsided and he was once more balanced and in control before he allowed his gaze to dwell on his lifemate.

Natalya's starkly focused stare shifted, a quick, restless movement sliding around her surroundings in a sweep. She inhaled and her gaze touched briefly on Vikirnoff's owl form before sliding past to observe the gathering shapes slinking through the trees in a loose ring around her.

Arturo inclined his head towards her. "You are bleeding. I do not wish you harm, rather I need you to perform a small task for me and then I will allow you to go free." He swept his arms out from his side in a gesture encompassing the entire forest. "You cannot hope to get away. You are surrounded by those I command and they will cause great damage to you should you try to leave. Come. Be reasonable and come to me." He opened his arms wide to draw her in. His voice was mesmerizing, beautiful, almost singsong. He looked a young, handsome man, nearly as beguiling as Natalya.

Vikirnoff recognized the strong hidden compulsion in the vampire's voice. He studied the face. It was an illusion, of course, as most masks a vampire chose to wear were, but it was a face Vikirnoff recognized. Arturo had once been a hunter of the very thing he had become. Vikirnoff could only hope Arturo had recently turned and did not have centuries of wielding evil behind him.

"How many times must we do this, Arturo?" There was a deliberate contemptuous challenge in Natalya's voice. "I've staked you a couple of times already. Do you really want to dance with me again?"

The vampire growled, his smooth smile disappearing. "You are incapable of staking one of my strength. You are the one bleeding."

"Tell yourself that," she said. "But I think that's blood running down your arm." She remained utterly motionless and once again the light of the moon hit her in bands. Natalya seemed to fade into the background, the stripes lending her a strange camouflage. Only her eyes blazed, a deep ruby red, nearly glowing in the darkness.

The tree branch beneath Vikirnoff's talons trembled as power swelled in the air. He held himself in check when every instinct told him to go to her, to stand between her and the thing of evil. Centuries of battling the undead held him steady. The trap was too neat, too tidy for his liking. He used the owl's hunting instincts to find what was hidden.

"You have always been too confident, Natalya," Arturo said. His voice rose to a thin, ugly screech, his illusion beginning to fade as he grew angrier with her. "You will not escape us this time." His hand went to his chest and rubbed over the area where his blackened, wizened heart lay. "I was unfortunately not in control of my abilities the last time we met, but I have learned much in the years since that time." His humorless smile stretched once more, accenting the flesh taut over bone and revealing the sharp, pointed teeth that filled his mouth.

The vampire crawling on the ground used both hands and jerked the knife from his chest, screaming as he did so. The voice was high and ugly and filled with rage and pain. He turned his head to glare at Natalya with hate-filled eyes, the hilt of a knife still sticking in his mouth and throat.

"Will nothing shut you up?" she snapped, rolling her eyes heavenward.

The rush of wind seemed to come from every direction, crashing together with tremendous force between Arturo and Natalya and bringing a putrid smell of decayed flesh. Twigs and leaves rose up through the whirling mist like a black tornado, weaving together to make a tight net above and around Natalya. For a moment it was impossible to see the empty space between the vampire and injured woman. Voices shrieked and wailed from inside the churning whirlwind.

Vikirnoff had no choice. The wolves pressed closer, ringing the dark net brought by the winds. He could see the ground along the outside of the churning mass lifting ominously as if something evil stalked the woman from beneath the soil. Lightning forked overhead and the sound of thunder boomed loud, shaking the earth. He dropped fast, talons outstretched, plunging from a great height to rip through the shield of churning dirt and leaves. The moment he touched the barrier, he sensed the presence of yet another.

The impression of evil washed over him. It was unlike anything he'd felt before. Vampire? Yes. But, much,

much more. Vampires were evil, treacherous and cunning. Whatever waited to show itself, whatever had constructed this trap for his lifemate, waited beneath the ground and it felt far, far more evil than any vampire he'd ever encountered in all his centuries of hunting.

His heart lurched. *Run. Do not stand and fight. Can you not feel it? Run while you can, before it reveals itself.* He gave the command telepathically, "pushing" as hard as he dared with another creature of unknown power so close.

Virkirnoff shifted at the last possible moment, landing directly in front of the woman, shielding her with his body against the attacking vampire. He was hit simultaneously from the front and back. Natalya clawed his back, rending his flesh from the back of his neck to his waist while the vampire Arturo exploded into action, tearing at his chest with razor-sharp talons, shrieking with rage as he dug to get at Vikirnoff's heart.

Vikirnoff would accept death at the hands of his lifemate, but never a vampire. He slammed his fist through the chest cavity, ignoring the pain searing through him as the vampire's talons dug deeper through flesh and bone and acid blood poured over his arm and hand.

Damn it! You could have let me know you were joining the battle. The attack ended abruptly from behind him and he sensed her fury mixed with guilt.

For a moment there was only the sound of heavy breathing, the outraged scream of the vampire and the terrible pain coursing through his own body. The vampire dissolved, flowing away from him in droplets of mist, a vapor of gray mixed with bright red. Vikirnoff staggered, nearly going to his knees before shoving the pain into some corner of his mind where he could ignore it.

The second vampire, Henrik, dragged yet another knife from his body with a horrific scream and a spray of blood. "Dead," he snarled, the word so slurred it was nearly impossible to understand. "You're dead."

Look out! Natalya called out.

Even as Vikirnoff heard the warning, he was already turning to meet the attack of the first wolf as it leapt at him, trying to knock him off of his feet. The wolf's entire weight hit him in the chest, claws digging deep into the wound left behind by the vampire. The impact was so forceful it drove him backward, but he managed to stay upright. Catching the animal and preventing the teeth from boring into his throat, Vikirnoff hurtled the wolf away from him. His strength was enormous and the snarling creature hit a tree trunk with such force it shook the branches. Vikirnoff whirled to face three other wolves as they advanced on him.

Get out of here. I will take care of this while you make your escape. It was necessary to warn his lifemate, to get her clear of the battle when Henrik clawed his way up a tree trunk in preparation of joining the melee.

You've got to be kidding me! Vikirnoff sensed a distinct impression of feminine disgust. *You couldn't fight your way out of a paper bag right now.* She fired off several rounds at Henrik, closing the distance between them in a single leap and driving a knife for the third time deep into his heart. "Die, damn you!" She jumped back to avoid the raking claws as Henrik once more fell to the ground. She kicked him for good measure. "You are so tiresome, Freddie, and you're making me lose my temper. I'm not nice when I lose my temper."

Vikirnoff's gaze shifted to her face. *You will not address your lifemate with such disrespect. Do as I say at once and leave this place. The battle has only begun and you must remain safe. He will not die if you do not incinerate his heart.*

Natalya shot him a venomous look. *Keep your orders for someone who wants to be hunter's mouse. And these things should come with an instruction manual on killing them.*

I do not want to embarrass you and force your obedience. It was all the warning he was going to give her. The wolves rushed him, one going low for his legs, another leaping for his chest and the third attacking his arm.

Are you out of your tiny little mind? Do your women actually obey when you say jump? She whirled around, back to back with him, facing outward toward the ring of wolves. *And don't think for one moment that you could force my obedience. You don't want to start a war with me.*

Vikirnoff swore under his breath as he kicked at the wolf tearing at his leg with sharp teeth. *The vampire is going for as much blood loss as possible to weaken me. If I try to protect you, which I must do, I will divide my strength.*

Well, try not to let it happen. I've got enough to take care of without worrying about protecting an amateur. I'm a little busy here if you don't mind. Silence would be appreciated.

Vikirnoff slammed a barrier around her, caging her in, away from the wolves as he caught the animal driving at his chest and wrenched at its head with both hands. The neck gave way with a sickening crack. He threw the body aside, but more wolves poured out of the forest, hurtling toward him, slavering, fangs wide open as they dug their back feet into the ground and leapt for his throat.

He waited until the wolves were almost on him, timing his jump, somersaulting over them straight at Arturo who clearly commanded them. The air vibrated with the rift of power as he broke through the flimsy barrier the vampire hastily erected to slow him down. As Vikirnoff landed the ground split open right at his feet, a yawning chasm separating him from the snarling vampire. He teetered precariously on the edge, glancing down at the sharpened rocks beneath him and then up to see the vampire slowly stretch his lips in a parody of a smile.

The ground rolled, throwing Vikirnoff toward the jagged rocks below him. Simultaneously he felt the shove of a howling wind at his back. He couldn't catch himself and began to hastily shift form as he toppled. Half man, half transparent, Vikirnoff hit a strong, invisible wall and bounced back. Turning his head quickly, he saw that Natalya had shred the protective cage he'd placed her in. She had settled the barricade around him, effectively stopping his fall.

Stay put while I take care of this. He isn't even a very powerful vampire. I've killed him twice. Her voice dripped with sarcasm.

Vikirnoff couldn't detect fear, only complete and utter resolve. Natalya seemed to glow as she leaped into the midst of the wolves, her skin a radiant tawny color, her hair blazing with life, colors streaking through wherever bands of light hit her, eyes once more going from a vivid green to brilliant blue to opalscent. She whirled around in the center of the wolves, but they backed away from her, shrinking and trembling, slinking back into deeper forest.

Below you. The vampire is a pawn. Can you not feel where the real power is coming from? Get out of here! Get off the ground. If he destroys you, he destroys us both.

Vikirnoff shredded the barricade she'd erected around him, a simple, easy feat as she'd used what he'd wrought in the first place. There was another trap here, one that had not yet been sprung, but she didn't seem to sense the danger. He felt it everywhere, thrumming in the very air around him. He rushed toward her as the attack came from below her. The ground beneath her fissured and two clawed hands grasped her ankles, the long, razor-sharp talons driving deep into her skin to anchor her to the creature as it jerked her beneath the earth.

Vikirnoff merged minds with her, holding her to him, sending her the image of mist and maintaining the likeness uppermost in her brain. *Merge with me. Merge fully with me.* There was desperation in the command.

Natalya fought to get the creature off her ankles, kicking with all of her strength, but the needle-like talons were buried deep. She could feel the nails digging into her bones.

Vikirnoff dove into the gaping tear in the ground after her, streaking downward, feeling her terror, her pain, as the claws dug deep into her ankles and hung on while her body attempted to make the change without his aid. She feared him. Feared the hold a complete merging with him would have on her.

If you want us to live, you must merge with me. This time he kept any "push" from his voice, using only pure truth.

Vikirnoff felt her brief hesitancy, her fear and resistance of him and what he might want of her. Terror of the creature dragging her underground overcame her fear of the hunter enough for her to reach for him, her arms outstretched, hands open, still fighting to maintain mental barriers against him. He caught her wrists and reversed directions, ruthlessly holding the image of mist in her mind. She screamed as the creature worked the talons deeper into her ankles in an attempt to hold her to him.

Natalya made up her mind and ceased resisting Vikirnoff, embracing the change, allowing the complete merging with him in order to save herself from the unseen monster clawing at her ankles. She shimmered into transparency, dissolved into droplets, streaming upwards like a multicolored comet. The ground shook, and deep in the earth something roared with rage and hatred.

There was an ominous rumble. Vikirnoff veered to the left, leading her straight toward Arturo waiting with his army of wolves. Mud and rock blasted from hole in the ground, a fiery orange, spewing venom after the hunter and his lifemate. Vikirnoff and Natalya streaked past the undead and his puppets, going high toward the heavy canopy where they could conceal themselves in the leaves of the trees.

Behind them, the wolves howled in terror and the vampires shrieked as hot lava spurted and rained down from the ever-widening hole in the ground. The tree shielding Vikirnoff and his lifemate burst into flames. Instantly everything around them went white-hot and the temperature of the droplets soared.

Stay off the ground. Deliberately Vikirnoff gave a hard mental push to emphasize he meant business.

Natalya streaked away from the burning tree, out of range of the boiling mud and spewing fireballs. He received the impression of a snarl, but little else.

Vikirnoff shifted in the air, plummeting down toward Arturo, talons outstretched, driving toward the chest cavity. The vampire was distracted, running for his life from the tantrum the malevolent creature beneath the earth was displaying.

What the hell are you doing? We don't have to stand and fight. Are you completely mad? Natalya's tone was incredulous, as if she couldn't conceive of anyone deliberately fighting a vampire if they had a choice. *And that idiot Henrik is back on his feet. I need a flamethrower in my arsenal. Do you have any idea what they cost?*

I cannot leave vampires loose to prey on the innocent people in this region. He is angry and dangerous in this state and he will retaliate against anyone weaker. Killing a vampire is hardly a game, as you seem to think it is. Attend your wounds and leave Henrik and the others to me, Natalya. She was not acting anything like the woman he had dreamed of. He didn't feel soothed by her, or at peace, instead he wanted to tear out his hair. His cool demeanor was rapidly being challenged, not by vampire, but by his own lifemate.

Vikirnoff's razor-sharp talons ripped through empty air. At the last possible second Arturo sensed the attack from above and dissolved, leaving only blood and vapor in his wake. Vikirnoff shifted form again, taking that of a man, landing lightly on the ground seeking to trace the darker menace below him. He hoped the risk would draw the evil one to him and he would be warned by the reaction of the earth itself.

How did you know my name? Fear and suspicion crept into Natalya's voice. Once Vikirnoff took the image from her mind, she shifted back to her natural form and found herself sitting in a tree. She narrowed her gaze, watching Vikirnoff, trying to look past his handsome face, past the blood he'd shed on her behalf to see who he really was. And what he wanted from her.

Look out! Pay attention to what you are doing.

The knife skimmed her arm and brought her attention to Henrik who faced her with deadly purpose. "Freddie boy, can't you do a girl a favor and just lie down and die?" Natalya sat on the branch and glared down at the blood-smeared vampire. "You're like the little engine that could, except you can't." *Stop distracting me.*

I know your name because you are my lifemate. His beautiful, soothing lifemate who was supposed to hang onto his every word and live to please him. He sent her a small frowning glance of reprimand. She wasn't respectful, or obedient, or anything he had been so certain she would be.

What? Are you freakin' nuts? If you think we're going to be getting it on you're out of your tiny—gorgeous, but tiny—little mind.

Getting it on? Vikirnoff repeated it back, shocked and very certain he couldn't have heard her correctly. He knew next to nothing about women, but she was not what he wanted or envisioned. He wasn't at all certain he approved of her and he certainly couldn't imagine a peaceful life with her around. He whirled around as a shadow detached itself from the trees and Arturo strode out to face him.

I don't want your approval. I can't believe you're so incredibly thick-headed that you'd actually stay here and fight these things. Natalya dodged the volley of knives Henrik threw at her. "That's not nice, Freddie, using my own weapons against me," she scolded aloud.

One blade stuck in the branch she'd been sitting in, but she climbed fast going up the tree, utilizing the close canopy as a shield.

Henrik shifted shape in spite of his wounds, lunging at her as he streaked through the trees in the form of an owl.

Flames burst all around the owl, cutting him off from every direction so that the vampire was forced to aban-

don his efforts to get to Natalya. He traced the power
source back to Vikirnoff and dropped to the ground, facing the hunter with a snarl.

"I've got to hand it to you, Freddie, you just keep on
coming. I like that in a man, but it isn't the best trait in a
vampire." Natalya climbed down the tree to the lower
branches, careful to stay off the ground, but determined
to keep Henrik's wrath and attention squarely on her.
Vikirnoff had lost too much blood thanks to the initial
attack and she was partially responsible for that.

I don't need you to help me. She made the protest as
strongly as she dared. Vikirnoff seemed unwilling to let
her participate in the battle, yet she couldn't make herself
leave, even when she knew it was utter madness to stay
with so many enemies close. *I hope you haven't forgotten
the Troll King just because he's gone surprisingly silent. He's
still there, lurking, ready to do something nasty the moment
you give him an opening.*

You let me worry about what is beneath us.

*Oh, I forgot! I must be the poor ditzy woman incapable of
making my own decisions now that the big strong man is here.*
Natalya snorted in derision. *We should have gotten away
while we had the chance.*

Vikirnoff realized she was angry with herself. She
wanted to leave. Every instinct, every survival sense told
her to leave, but the pull of her lifemate, especially injured as he was, prevented her from doing so. She didn't
understand why he had such power over her and the fact

that she couldn't just leave him made her angry, suspicious and edgy.

The fireballs had ceased abruptly and the forest had grown quiet. Vikirnoff scanned the ground, but whatever lay in hiding had withdrawn to regroup and refused to take the bait, even when Vikirnoff deliberately moved with a heavier tread.

Arturo looked a macabre parody of the handsome man who had faced Natalya earlier. Skin pulled tight over his bones and skull. Wisps of gray-white hair clung to his scalp. When he smiled at them, his pointed teeth were brown with stains. "Vikirnoff. You do not look so well. You cannot even command your woman to your bidding. How sad to see a once-proud hunter fall so low as to have to beg."

"How sad to see a once-great hunter stoop so low as to follow in the shadow of an evil one instead of going his own way," Vikirnoff retaliated. He watched the vampire, but he scanned the ground continually, waiting for the unseen monster to reveal itself.

"The two of you can stop talking about me like I'm not here," Natalya snapped, sick of the entire mess. "I have business elsewhere and you're holding me up." She glanced down at Henrick who had made his way to the base of the tree where she sat.

The lesser vampire's nails dug at the roots of the tree. He was so weak he couldn't gather enough power to use against her, but it didn't stop him from digging at the roots of the tree in an effort to topple her to the forest floor. The tree shuddered each time the vampire touched it, shrinking away from the hideous creature. The blood of the undead dripped on the bark and burned through to the very heart of the tree.

Natalya could hear the tree screaming in pain. The sap ran from the scalding hole and dripped steadily like blood onto the ground. She pressed her hands over her ears and tried not to feel the way her ankles burned and throbbed. Most of all she tried not to notice the vampire licking at the smears of blood left behind from the wounds on her ankles along the trunk of the tree. It sickened her. Why had she stayed? She *despised* hunters nearly as much as she did vampires.

Vikirnoff glanced at her, aware of her distress. He moved, a mere blur so fast it was impossible to see him as he rushed past Arturo and slammed his fist deep into Henrik's chest. The heart was lacerated and wizened, and he threw it a distance away to give himself time to direct the lightning to the blackened organ before it could roll back to its master.

Lightning arced from the heart to the body of the vampire, even before Henrik could fall to the ground, fully incinerating and reducing the undead to a pile of ashes.

"That was not necessary, Vikirnoff. You were always one to take action before talking things out."

"There is no need for talk, Arturo," Vikirnoff answered.

"Do you think I cannot sense the darkness in you?"

Arturo demanded. "*She* senses it. She nearly ripped your back apart earlier and she will again given the chance, when she no longer needs you." The voice turned crafty, wheedling. "The prince is without protection. Now is the time to strike. Join us, Vikirnoff. We can defeat the hunters and come out of the shadows to take our rightful place in the world. We wouldn't rule a mere country or just our people, but all of it. All, Vikirnoff, think of it."

"The prince is not without protection, Arturo. Never think that he is without the full protection of his people." Vikirnoff glided closer without appearing to move, angling toward the vampire, barely skimming the earth with the soles of his feet, yet sending out heavier footsteps a few yards from where he really was, hoping to draw out the creature hiding beneath the ground. "You have been made into a puppet. Whom do you serve, Arturo?" All the while he could feel the gathering of power as Arturo once again summoned the wolf pack to his bidding.

Spittle ran down the mouth of the vampire as he growled and hissed his displeasure at the taunts. "I serve no one, unlike you." He launched his attack, shrieking as he rushed Vikirnoff. Wolves poured from the woods. A forest of sharp, jagged rocks speared through the ground aimed at the hunter.

Vikirnoff took to the air, meeting the vampire's rush with astonishing speed, slamming his fist through the chest wall, reaching for the heart. A wolf sprang at him, clamped around his calf and hung on grimly, clawing and clamping down in an effort to protect his master. Several others leapt at him, snapping and howling to get to the hunter.

Vikirnoff found the heart, even as the vampire repeatedly tore at his face and throat with sharpened talons.

Use fire to get rid of the wolves! Natalya sounded frantic. *I know your kind can do that. Hurry!*

They are innocents, under the command of the undead. It would destroy the entire pack. Go while you can. The other rises from beneath the earth. I feel its triumph.

She screamed in frustration and sheer exasperation, the sound only in his mind. Fire rained from the sky. Hot embers like glowing orange arrows, streaking down to find live targets. *You are the most stubborn, idiotic man I've ever had the misfortune to run across. Finish him now!*

Vikirnoff had the impression of her grinding her teeth together. She was furious as she drove off the wolf pack, with the one exception being the male attached to his calf. Ignoring the excruciating pain, he settled his fingers around the vampire's shriveled heart and wrenched it from the body. Arturo's shriek became high-pitched and vengeful. The wolf began to saw frantically at Vikirnoff's leg and the vampire sprang after the blackened heart as Vikirnoff tossed it to the ground, calling lightning to incinerate it.

The ground opened and the heart dropped through the widening fissure. A furred arm stretched, the bony fingers seizing Arturo to drag him beneath the earth. Before Vikirnoff could follow, the crevice slammed closed. Lightning slammed into the ground in the precise spot where the heart had been, but it was too late.

Vikirnoff caught at a tree branch as he plummeted toward the forest floor. He hung there for a moment, fighting to breathe when his body felt torn apart, weighted down by the wolf still hanging on to his leg. His leg was so slippery with blood, the animal finally fell to the ground and began to leap over and over at him.

Vikirnoff's hand and arm burned from the acid of the vampire blood and his fingers were slippery. He could see blood pooling below his body and it seemed a tremendous amount. Unexpectedly weakness rushed over him and he felt himself falling straight toward the open jaws of the wolf below him.

A rush of flames sent the animal howling and tumbling backward away from him. He landed hard and looked up at the face of a very exasperated woman. Natalya leapt from the tree and landed beside him, crouching down to do a quick examination of his wounds. "You're a mess."

"How did you send fire like that?"

"I followed the instructions in your head," Natalya said. "You have a tremendous amount of information in your brain. I wish I'd known about incinerating the heart. It would have helped. Can you stand up?" He was horribly wounded. She told herself to leave him, but his body had been far too ravaged in her defense.

"Of course." He had lost too much blood and dawn was fast approaching. "You need to get out of here."

"Don't bother giving me orders," Natalya said. "I've always had a problem with authority figures. I'm getting

you somewhere safe and then I never want to see you
again."

"That will be a little difficult." Vikirnoff made an effort to rise. He was far weaker than he imagined. If he
took his lifemate's blood, he would have the necessary
strength to get them both to safety.

Natalya leapt away from him, hand on her sword.
"Don't you even think about taking my blood. If necessary, I'll sit here and wait until you become so leaden you
can't move before I'll touch you. I'm not the blood donor
type." She pinned him with her gaze. "Not now, not *ever*.
If and that's a big if, I ever give it to you, it will be voluntarily. Don't ever think of taking it by force."

Vikirnoff forced his body into a sitting position, his
back against a tree trunk. "You have a grudge against my
people." He sounded distant, faraway, even to his own
ears. The vivid colors around him, faded in and out,
blurring until everything ran together. He knew it was
necessary to shut down his heart and lungs to prevent
further blood loss, but his lifemate wasn't yet safe. "Go,
Natalya, go now." He said the words aloud, or maybe
they were in his mind, but he was already slipping into
unconsciousness.

3

"**D**amn it," Natalya whispered fiercely as she gathered the fallen hunter into her arms and looked around her, feeling desperate. "Don't do this." Over the years Natalya had tried to gather information about the Carpathians, partly because she knew she carried their blood, but mostly because she believed knowledge gave her advantages. She was fully aware they needed rich earth to heal. She used it on her wounds upon occasion. "I can't even pack your wounds with soil. The vampires have ruined the earth around here." She gave Vikirnoff a small shake. "What's left of the wolf pack might come back drawn by the scent of blood, or worse—that creature with the claws beneath the ground. Come on, wake up."

The man weighed a ton. Okay, not a ton, but he may as well have. She was *not* going to wait around for the

Troll King and his vamp buddies to make another try for her. They'd slunk off with their hearts in their hands and tails between their legs, but if they knew what a predicament she was in, they'd be back. "Fine, you big lug, I'll carry you. You just had to be a hero, didn't you? You couldn't leave when I asked you to, could you?"

Natalya tried a firemen's lift, but nothing happened. She was strong. She was stronger than most humans, but he was a dead weight and slippery with blood loss. She tied her pack on him, not wanting to lose her things and made a second attempt to hoist him to her shoulder.

Woman. What are you doing? In spite of his seemingly unconscious state, he managed to sound wholly exasperated.

Natalya nearly jumped out of her skin. "What does it look like? Someone has to save your butt and since no one else is waving their hand to volunteer, you're stuck with me." There was no way she could haul him down the mountain. No way. The dread inside of her was growing as each minute ticked by. "You were supposed to be unconscious, not waiting to see how you can aggravate me."

Leave me.

"If you aren't going to say anything helpful, just shut up. I need to think. If you hadn't insisted on staying and fighting we'd be long gone." Natalya wanted to shake some sense into him. She'd never seen anyone so battered and wounded manage to survive. By all rights he should be dead. And the thought of his death was frightening to her. The more afraid she was, the more she wanted to lash out at his stupidity. It hadn't been necessary to fight. They could have run. He just had to be gallant and save the world.

"I have one shape-shifting ability," she admitted. Natalya had to deceive just about everyone she met, but she never deceived herself. It was a luxury to be able to admit who and what she was, show what she was capable of for the first time in years. She watched his face for his reaction. "Just one on my own. I'll be able to carry you on my back, but you'll have to stay awake enough to hold on. Do you think you can?"

Vikirnoff didn't open his eyes. *Whatever you need.*

His voice was far away. She swallowed hard. She needed to pack his wounds as soon as possible and that meant moving him immediately. "It's going to hurt."

Natalya stripped, folded her clothes and stuffed them into the pack tied to him. She had wandered alone for years, unable to stay in one place too long for fear of giving herself away. She had been alone without friends or family and it had been long since she had experienced the exhilaration of shifting in front of another being. The freedom to be herself was a powerful lure she couldn't resist.

She was not fully human. She was not fully mage. And she was not fully Carpathian but a combination of all three. Her mage father had gifted her with the nature of the tigress in the hopes it would alleviate the needs of her other side for a family and give her some balance as the endless years passed. To some extent, she supposed it had, but the idea of being able to share a real part of her true self with Vikirnoff, that he would know her for what she was, felt wonderful.

She took a deep breath, losing herself in the familiar shape and feel of the tigress. Muscles rippled beneath her luxurious striped fur coat and she stretched, showing the black and orange camouflage bands to their full advantage. Sharp claws raked the ground and she lifted her muzzle to scent the air before arching her back and lowering her body to the ground. She had no idea she was holding her breath, waiting for his reaction, until he spoke, her eyes blazing a vivid blue at him.

His eyes opened and he reached his hand to stroke the deep fur. *You are beautiful. Your eyes are the exact color of the ice lakes.*

She tried not to be pleased. She didn't want to feel a response to him, only do her duty as a human being, but she couldn't help the rush of warmth his words caused. *Can you slip onto my back and put your arms around my neck?*

The tiger was a solitary creature and in its form, Natalya didn't feel yearnings for a family and community. For a brief time she was able to have respite from her natural needs as a woman, but she found, even deep within the form of the tigress, she was acutely aware of Vikirnoff as a man.

He lay out full length on his stomach, his arms sliding around her neck. The long walking stick stuck in the loop of her backpack poked her body and hurt. He felt it and adjusted immediately, a groan slipping out as he did so. *You do not shift in the same way a Carpathian shifts. Is that why you have only one form?*

She knew he was too weak and shouldn't be trying to converse, but her thoughts were tumbling around in her head so fast, frantic to share with someone. *I wondered about that when you held the image of mist in my head and I was able to change. It was both frightening and wonderful.*

The tiger snarled at a lone wolf slinking through the trees. The wolf backed away from the much larger predator despite the lure of fresh blood.

It is humbling that you gave your trust to me. I will not abuse it.

She started to deny that she'd given him her trust, but she refrained from correcting him. She had wanted to save her life and he had been the lesser of two evils when the underground creature had grabbed her with spiked claws. Even in the form of the tiger, her ankles still burned, a constant reminder of the terror of that moment.

The tiger hurried through the forest, carrying the man on its back until it was several miles from the battlefield, and down near the richer rolling hills. She was much more careful, taking her burden through more open ground cautiously as she approached the farms. Many of the farmers were beginning to start their day. Twice a dog barked at them and abruptly stopped and backed away. Both times Natalya felt the surge of power and knew Vikirnoff had silenced the animals.

She had made the decision to save Vikirnoff's life and

that meant she would have to donate blood whether she wanted to or not. She was practical about it once she made up her mind. She was part Carpathian and she had to have blood to survive. She didn't take blood that often, but when it became necessary, she had no qualms about it. Natalya left Vikirnoff nearly unconscious beside a sheaf of hay and she approached a farmer, calming him with a mage spell and taking his blood.

Unlike full-blooded Carpathians she couldn't remove the farmer's memories. She attempted to dim his memory and make it feel like a dream, but, no doubt, rumors of vampires would sweep the countryside. The only thing that mattered, though, was getting Vikirnoff into her room, out of the sun and away from people as quickly as possible.

Near the inn, she laid him down in the shelter of several bushes, shape-shifted and hastily dressed. "Don't make a sound. Last night, there was a suspicious man in the bar. I don't know why he's here, but he made my alarm bells go off and I never ignore them. I don't want to take a chance on being seen when we go in. Let me just take a look to see if everyone's still in bed."

His hand fumbled for hers. "You don't have to do this."

Her heart did a funny little fluttery thing she found annoying. "Just don't move." Natalya pulled her hand away and wiped her palm on her leather pants, trying to erase the strange electrical tingling he seemed to cause whenever she touched his skin.

"It's getting light," Natalya's voice turned unusually

husky. She cleared her throat. His fingers on her bare wrist felt too intimate. "We have to get inside before the sun comes up. It took us too long to get here. The farmers were already working, remember? We had to hide. Just rest while I take a look around."

She knew she sounded gruff, but her emotions were so unfamiliar and intense around Vikirnoff. She certainly didn't want to feel compassion for his terrible wounds or admiration for his stoic refusal to complain. She needed to keep an emotional distance at all times. Just saving him made her feel like an utter traitor to her brother.

But she *had* saved him and now he was her responsibility. Natalya didn't take her responsibilities lightly. She sniffed the air cautiously, searching for signs of anyone up, but she found only Slavica's scent in the kitchen, so she pushed open the door with stealth and studied the large room.

Slavica stood at the sink peeling potatoes for breakfast. Natalya stole up behind her. "You work too hard."

The innkeeper swung around, potato and knife in hand. "You! Natalya, you frightened me." Her eyes widened with concern as she took in Natalya's appearance. "What happened to you? Are you injured?"

Natalya realized she had blood smeared all over her. Most of it belonged to Vikirnoff. "I'm fine. I have someone with me I need to get up to my room, but I don't want anyone to see us. Will you help me? He's injured."

"How bad?" Slavica was practical.

Natalya grinned at her. "You're so great. Thank you.

He's in bad shape. He's lost way too much blood but I can't take him to a hospital."

"There is a hidden stairway," Slavica confided. "This inn was built on the site of an old monastery and part of that building was retained and incorporated into the inn. Only our family uses the stairs and rooms for our living quarters."

"If you wouldn't mind keeping a lookout, I'll go get him," Natalya said. The relief sweeping through her was tremendous.

Natalya hurried out the kitchen door and ran down the path leading to the dense shrubbery where she had left the hunter. She skidded to a halt when she saw him, slumped, his eyes closed, his face pale, almost gray and small dots of blood beading on his brow. Her heart jumped and her stomach rolled. "Vikirnoff? Do you think you can walk the last few yards to the room?" She couldn't very well become a tiger again, but he looked so worn and pale it frightened her.

He opened his eyes and managed to climb to his feet with her aid. He stood swaying unsteadily until she slipped her arm around him. "Just a few more minutes and you can lie down." Natalya encouraged him.

"This place is dangerous," he told Natalya as they entered through the kitchen. He offered a tentative smile to Slavica when she gave an alarmed gasp. "I didn't mean to startle you."

"I'm honored to have you, sir. My home is your home." Slavica curtsied, her hand going protectively to her throat. "This way, quickly. The workers will be here any moment to prepare the food. You must hurry."

Vikirnoff stiffened, holding up his hand for silence as he glanced toward the kitchen door. Muted voices drifted toward them. He waved his hand and the voices faded, the workers moving away from the room.

Natalya felt the shiver of pain rippling through his body as he expended energy to send the kitchen help away. She took a better grip on his waist and urged him toward the back of the room where Slavica pulled open a panel in the corner. The stairs led both to a door into the private residence and upward to the second story.

"Just a few more minutes," Natalya whispered. She wished he'd complain just once. Her ankles and side throbbed and burned and her injuries weren't nearly as severe as his, yet Vikirnoff was silent, not even grunting when his battered body was jarred as they went up the narrow stairs. He barely leaned his weight on her, careful of her side, but every once in a while his palm settled over her injury. Each time he did she felt warmth and the pain lessened, but she noted he became weaker and much paler.

"Stop it," she hissed. "I mean it. I've had a hundred wounds like this. I know when they're bad and mine isn't. The vampires were being careful not to inflict any grave injury on me. I can deal with it later." She pushed open the door to her room and halted, inhaling deeply. "Someone has been in here."

Slavica shook her head. "The maids clean in the morning hours. You left in the evening. They would have been finished."

"There is no one here now," Vikirnoff said, "but a man has been in this room recently. He smells of pipe tobacco and cologne."

"The man from the bar last night," Natalya said. "What is his name, Slavica?" She helped Vikirnoff to the bed.

"Barstow, Brent Barstow. He comes through our village several times a year. He says he's on business, but . . ." The innkeeper trailed off shaking her head.

Vikirnoff glanced at her sharply. "But he makes you uneasy."

"Very uneasy," Slavica conceded. "And he's asked questions of my daughter Angelina. I didn't like his questions."

"Questions about . . ." Vikirnoff prompted.

Natalya felt his pain as if it were her own as he stood there swaying, probing the innkeeper. She had the urge to just knock him unconscious, throw him on the bed and be done with it.

"He wishes to know about the people residing in this area," Slavica answered.

The moment Vikirnoff sank down onto the soft blankets he turned his face away, but not before Natalya caught another much sharper ripple of pain he couldn't quite hide. She couldn't prevent herself from brushing strands of black hair off his brow. "Slavica's a nurse, a healer. She can help you."

"She must attend your injuries first," he decreed.

Natalya snatched her hand away. "There you go again." She was angry with herself for the silly melting sensation touching him produced in the pit of her stomach. Could she be any more pathetic? "Don't be giving me orders." She winced at the harshness in her tone and turned away from him to fuss at pulling the heavy drapes over the windows and balcony door to block out the morning sun.

Slavica sat on the edge of the bed. "He will need other things, Natalya. In the kitchen there is a wooden bowl in the cupboard. Take that and fill it with the richest soil you can find in the garden." She leaned forward and swept the strands of hair that had so bothered Natalya from Vikirnoff's forehead, her fingers lingering against his cool skin. "You've lost far too much blood. I must send for your prince. He'll want to know you require aid."

Vikirnoff caught her wrist. "You know what I am." He could read that she did. Few humans knew of their existence, not only for the protection of the Carpathian people, but also for the humans. If Slavica had knowledge of their species, she was under the protection of his prince. "Who are you?"

"I'm Slavica Ostojic. My mother's name was Kukic. And you are?"

Before answering he took a long, careful probe of her mind and was shocked to find she had a friendship with the prince of his people. He had heard rumors that

Mikhail Dubrinksy had friends in the human world, but it was a rare occurrence to trust humans with the secrets of their species. "Vikirnoff Von Shrieder." He gave his name reluctantly, unable to fully overcome his natural reticence. He believed in few words, keeping his own counsel and taking action when necessary. This was an unfamiliar situation and he was feeling his way.

"This inn has been in my family for a hundred years. Mikhail Dubrinsky helped my mother to keep it when things in our country were complicated. He has always been a friend to our family and we have treasured that friendship."

Vikirnoff had trouble focusing on the woman's explanation. Hunger nearly overwhelmed him. The heartbeat of the women reverberated through the room and echoed through his head. The scent of blood nearly overwhelmed him and every instinct he possessed demanded he feed to save his life and that of his lifemate.

Slavica bent close to him and his gaze immediately riveted on her pulse. It beckoned and seduced, that small throbbing rhythm. His mouth watered and his incisors lengthened. He leaned toward her neck for a long moment, needing. Simply needing. Abruptly he pulled back. He would not take from one under the protection of his prince. To shut out the terrible hunger, he tried to concentrate on his lifemate.

Natalya fussed with the curtains, but all the while her confused emotions battered at him. The room shifted and whirled as he listened to the ebb and flow of blood moving through veins. His every instinct was to protect her, to claim her. His body and soul roared for hers, yet she tried to stay closed off to him. Her scent drove him to a fever pitch.

"I must send word to the prince," Slavica repeated. "He would be annoyed with me if I did not."

Vikirnoff closed his burning eyes in weariness, realizing his injuries might prevent him from keeping Mikhail Dubrinsky safe for some time. "The prince is in danger. Send him that message. It is far more important than worrying about my wounds. I will heal. I have had worse and will again no doubt."

Hearing the tired note Vikirnoff couldn't hide, Natalya glanced at him. She had been studiously avoiding looking at him, but now she saw the lines of pain etched deeply in his face, the blood on his chest as Slavica cut away his shirt. Her heart seemed to skip a beat and then go crazy as she viewed his terrible injuries. She knew his back would have rake marks, long deep furrows where her claws had rent him from shoulder to waist. She was ashamed of herself. She'd been too slow in stopping the attack when he had dropped from the sky between her and the vampire, yet she could find no blame or resentment in Vikirnoff's mind.

His body was hard and muscular and ravaged with pain. Everything in her cried out to touch him, to ease that pain. She became fascinated by the way Slavica's hands moved over Vikirnoff's bare skin. Soothing him. Examining. Touching. Natalya's breath caught in her throat. The hands mesmerized her. Infuriated her. Something dark and ugly stirred inside of her.

The curtains slipped from her hands so that the early morning light spilled over her. Vikirnoff, sensing sudden danger, turned his head, eyes wide open to see Natalya fading into the wall, the streaks of light camouflaging her body so that it was difficult to see her without straining. In spite of the pain movement caused, he turned on his side, gaze narrowing to focus more fully on her.

Natalya's entire demeanor had changed. She no longer appeared fully human, instead she had become a dangerous, powerful predator. Even her sea-green eyes had changed color, taking on a pearlescent appearance, fixed and focused on Slavica as if on prey. There was a stillness to her that spoke of a tigress on the hunt, muscles locked into position, gaze intent and fixed on the nurse.

"Mrs. Ostojic, Slavica," Vikirnoff said, his voice quiet, his tone commanding. "Move slowly around to the other side of the bed. Do it now."

Slavica glanced at Natalya as she rose. A small rumbling growl emanated from the corner where Natalya had faded into a blurred image. Hand to her throat, the innkeeper shifted her weight carefully, easing to her feet and putting the bulk of the bed between her and the woman.

Ainaak enyém, *what has you so upset?* Vikirnoff had little understanding of women, and even less of his lifemate. It was easy enough to understand that emotions were intense and neither understood exactly what was happening to them. He was fighting the battle of darkness and intellect had little to do with primal instincts. With Natalya so near and yet still not anchoring him, he was far more dangerous than he had ever been. Her chaotic emotions bombarding him were a recipe for disaster. Was the same thing happening to her? Were they both too close to animal instincts because neither understood what was happening to them?

Why are you allowing her to touch you like that? The accusation should have been ludicrous, but he sensed the way she held herself so tightly under control. To Natalya, the accusation was very real. She saw a woman's hands smoothing over the body of her lifemate. The emotions ran too strong, too intense, possibly fueled by his own terrible hunger, by his own rising beast.

Vikirnoff touched her mind. A red haze spread and gripped her. Instincts as old as time, hot with passion, animalistic. There was something buried deep in her he had yet to encounter, something she protected, but it was rising to the surface and it was every bit as dangerous and as powerful as a predator on the hunt.

He fought to keep the intensity of their emotions from affecting him. It was his duty to protect his lifemate, to see to her well-being. He had to find a way to defuse the situation until she could get herself under control.

"Slavica, perhaps you would get the necessary soil and herbs. You know what we need. Natalya will watch over me." Vikirnoff never took his gaze, or his mind, from his lifemate. He didn't dare. The effort was draining, but the alternative was unthinkable. Natalya should have been not only healing him, but as his lifemate, anchoring him. Instead, she was triggering his every animal instinct so that not only did he have to fight himself, but he had to provide the anchor for Natalya.

"Are you certain you'll be safe?" Slavica whispered the words.

A growling hiss of displeasure came from Natalya's direction.

"Thank you, yes." A soft growl of his own accompanied the words and he kept his face averted from Slavica, his gaze holding Natalya locked in position.

Vikirnoff needed desperately. The heartbeats were so loud it was almost a roar in his head. He needed blood and a way to control the danger emanating from his lifemate. He willed the nurse to get out before disaster struck. Trying to hold Natalya in check was difficult when his life was ebbing away from the loss of blood.

Slavica moved slowly, intelligent enough to sense the danger, and courageous enough to walk around the bed and make her exit, pulling the door closed behind her.

"Come here to me," Vikirnoff ordered, his tone dropping an octave until it was velvet soft and hypnotic.

Natalya shook her head as if trying to clear the haze from her mind. Unlike others Vikirnoff called to him, his lifemate was well aware she was under compulsion. Strangely she didn't fight him as she could have, instead she took a reluctant step forward, compelled by his black, black eyes and the stark hunger she couldn't define. The same hunger was in her, clawing with very real pain and power, threatening to consume them both.

She was acutely aware the appetite was mixed with desire, with lust, a passionate need that bordered on obsession. Fascinated by the intensity in his eyes, she emerged from the shadows, one slow step at a time, almost in freeze-frame.

She looked ethereal, her muscles moving suggestively beneath the bands of skin glowing strangely in the faint light. Not quite real. Definitely not human. Vikirnoff tried for a moment to probe deeper into her mind, to uncover the secrets that lay hidden behind her strange brain patterns. Hunger beat at him without mercy. Hers? Or his own? He couldn't separate the two. He couldn't tell which were his emotions, so intense, swirling out of control. Was she jealous? Or was that his own beast rising with a ferocious need?

Women were of the light. Did they feel the razor-sharp clawing at their gut? On the verge of killing? Unblinking, he watched the way she emerged out of the faded bands of light coming toward him. Her strangely colored eyes focused on him and stared as if he were the prey, not the other way around. The tigress was on the hunt and the tension stretched to a screaming point. Danger thrummed in the air between them.

Natalya couldn't stop moving forward. She felt in a dream, one she wasn't in control of, standing off to the side, watching the action with a pounding heart and screaming at herself to wake up. She honestly didn't know if she intended to kill him. She feared him. She sensed the darkness in him rising and self-preservation was strong in her, yet she was unable to stop each step forward.

Vikirnoff's fingers shackled her wrist. Enormously strong. Incredibly gentle. His touch set her heart pounding and her knees inexplicably turned to rubber. She sank down onto the edge of the bed. His hands slid up her arms, fingers tunneled through her hair and settled in a frame around her face. His black gaze burned over her, held her captive. She couldn't look away from him even as he forced her head toward his.

Natalya felt her stomach turn over. Every nerve ending leapt to life. She *felt* but she couldn't move. He lay injured, a hole in his chest, bleeding from the deep rake marks she'd made in his back and countless other wounds, weak and seemingly vulnerable, yet she went to him like a willing sacrifice.

His lips touched hers. Cool. Firm. Velvet soft. Her heart jumped in her chest. He trailed kisses from the corner of her mouth to her neck, tiny pinpoints of flames dancing over her skin. In her mind she screamed at herself to run, yet no sound emerged and she leaned closer to him, lifting the hair from her neck.

She wanted his touch. Needed to feel his hands on her. He belonged to her. No other woman had the right to touch him, to smooth fingers over his bare skin and be so close as to exchange air.

Fire raged in Vikirnoff's veins and stormed through his mind until thunder roared in his ears and the need to assuage his terrible hunger, a hunger that was mixed with sexual need, with possessive lust, was near frenzy. He inhaled her scent, took it deep in his lungs. Listened to the ebb and flow of life sizzling through her veins. She was calling to him, a timeless, haunting call of female to male, an aphrodisiac that enhanced his every sense. His tongue tasted her pulse. He felt her reaction, the swift intake of her breath. Her breasts brushed against him, a soft enticement that added to the strange roaring in his head.

Natalya felt his tongue swirling over her pulse and her womb clenched in anticipation. There was white-hot pain that gave way instantly to erotic pleasure. Her blood flowed into him like nectar. He shifted her in his arms, holding her close to him, one hand sliding up her body to cup her breast, thumb teasing her nipple into a taut peak.

Her body went into overdrive, weeping with need, hot with excitement, coiling tighter and tighter until she was nearly pleading with him for relief. Clothes hurt her too-sensitive skin. She wanted to be under him, his body ramming into hers hard and fast, filling her emptiness. She clawed at him, trying to get closer, arching into him, deliberately rousing him further.

Vikirnoff felt the power and lust sweeping through him, soaking into his injured body, supplying him with heat and excitement and strength. His body raged at him for a fulfillment that would be impossible in his present state. His demon rose fast and ferociously, roaring for his mate, demanding he claim her, that he tie them together for all eternity. She tasted like nothing he'd ever experienced and he knew he would need to return again and again and he'd never get enough.

In defiance of the roaring beast, he forced himself to pull back and deliberately swept his tongue over the pinpricks in her throat. A part of him wished he'd taken from the swell of her breast, but he wouldn't have been able to stop himself from possessing her body. He didn't altogether trust himself. In his aroused state, he would have died to possess her. Taking her would have cost him his life, and he was far too close to the edge for clear thinking. Better to take precautions than indulge his instincts.

He shifted her until she lay across him, her green eyes staring up at him, mirroring the same lust that had taken control of his body. He bent his head to her side, holding her still while he examined her wounds. It took only minutes to separate himself from his body and go into hers with his spirit to heal her wounds from the inside out. He paid particular attention to the puncture wounds on her ankles. The scent was unlike any he'd encountered and he wanted to be able to recognize it anywhere. The wounds were deep, all the way to the bone, yet she had never said a word and had insisted Slavica attend to him—until her jealous nature had overtaken her. She felt the pull of a lifemate every bit as strongly as he. She didn't want it. She didn't understand it, but it was fierce and strong and their souls were nearly already united and he hadn't yet bound them together.

Vikirnoff pulled her closer still, holding her head in the palm of his hand as he slashed his chest. He urged her close to him, until, of her own accord, her mouth moved, tongue tasting delicately. He groaned under the sensual assault. Natalya moved against him, her tongue swirling over his skin, healing the long thin line, just as his had closed the pinpricks.

Vikirnoff swore softly in his own language, prepared to try again when her teeth sank deep. The pain flashed through his body like lightning, gave way to pure erotic pleasure. His head lolled back and his eyes closed. He gave himself up to the magic of the moment, the true blood exchange between lifemates. He would always be able to find her, touch her mind at will, summon her, call to her, share her body and mind and soul. There was ecstasy in the sharing and a promise of passion.

She flicked her tongue to heal the small pinpricks and kissed her way up his chest and throat to find his lips. She was hot with need, her mouth demanding, tongue dueling with his, seeking more.

His hands crept their way under the leather camisole, kneading her breasts, his own demons taking hold. Natalya was a powerful anesthetic and aphrodisiac rolled into one. Pain disappeared as hot blood rushed to his groin, as his need to have her overcame the last coherent thought. He was crazy to want her when he was so near death and if she couldn't find the will to stop him, he just might perish, but he couldn't pull back. His body was a hard knot of desire, his veins sizzling, awareness settling in his groin with painful need. His beast roared, unleashed and leapt to claim her.

Natalya moaned softly, giving herself up to the sudden command of his mouth. Hot. Hungry. Wet. His teeth tugged at her lip, his hands busy at her breasts. Persuasive. Rough. Insistent. She slid her fingertips over his chest and felt him wince as she touched his open wound. *His wound. What the hell was wrong with her? She was practically raping a badly wounded hunter!*

Natalya pulled away from him with a soft cry of alarm. His arms slid away from her body leaving her bereft. Wound so tight she thought she might scream. Needy and aching. She backed away from him, her palm pressed to her neck. Her pulse throbbed in tune to the frantic pulsing in her womb, the wild sound drowning out the echo of her name as he whispered it. She could taste him in her mouth. His scent was on her skin. Worse, her body was alive with a need and hunger of her own, every bit as sharp and terrible as his. She blinked rapidly, trying to quiet her rioting heart. The dreamlike state was dissipating, confusion lifting. *He was a hunter.* Guilt and shame burst over her, struck at her like a heavy fist.

She wanted him. No, it was worse. She *needed* him. The idea was insane—and entirely unacceptable. He had to have done something to her. No vampire had ever succeeded in trapping her or taking over her mind, but *he* had. She hadn't felt his invasion, but she knew she would *never* have allowed him to touch her body. To kiss her. *And he had taken her blood and, oh, God, she had taken his.* She had been prepared to be a donor. But not like this. Never like this.

Natalya drew a knife from the sheath strapped to her calf and advanced on him with purposeful steps.

Vikirnoff watched her calmly as she approached the bed.

"You did something to me. You forced me to accept you." Her eyes blazed fury at him, once more going from green to a strange swirling of pearlized colors. "I *despise* your kind, yet I was willing to harm Slavica, a woman I consider my friend. You did that to me. Why? I could have left you to the vampires."

"You could not have left me to the vampires," Vikirnoff said. Even with her angry at him, unable to accept their relationship, even though he didn't understand her at all, he knew she was a miracle. A gift. He was shockingly happy as he lay there, waiting for her to see reason. He tried to repress the silly smile that kept wanting to slip past. He knew what happiness was. Finally. After so many centuries. He felt the emotion and it was exhilarating. He had been so close to turning vampire and she had arrived and saved him.

She didn't want to save him. The thought had him puzzled. Women were supposed to want to be with their lifemates, to see to their every need. He had only dim memories of his parents, but he was almost certain that was the way it worked. Unless he could no longer remember how it been between his mother and father.

Natalya's small white teeth came together in a snap of temper. That smirking little smile hovering near his mouth made her want to slap him. "You belong with the vampires. Do you think I can't feel the darkness in you? Smell it? It reeks; a stain there is no way for you to remove. You *deserve* death."

"Perhaps I do, but not at your hands. I will admit the darkness is strong in me and I cannot overcome it, but you can. And you will. It is your duty as my lifemate. I will not absolve you of your duties merely because you do not know what is expected of you. It is a situation we both are unfamiliar with, but we will learn. I may not be the lifemate you expected, but you are not what I expected either. We will learn together."

Why did the things he said hurt her? No one, other than her beloved brother, had ever been able to say things to hurt her. She kept those sensitive emotions locked away, yet Vikirnoff's words were almost as sharp and painful as the blade in her fist. Just because he didn't expect her wasn't a rejection of her, was it? And why did she care?

"Damn you to hell," she snapped. Her fury had dissipated abruptly and tears—*tears* burned in her eyes. She wanted the anger back. She needed it to shield her. Why didn't he fight back? Why didn't he say or do something to give her back her rage?

Natalya clutched the knife handle until it was in danger of becoming a powder in her hands. She forced air through her lungs. "I'll just wait until you're asleep and your body is lead and I'll open the drapes and let the sun fry your worthless ass." She kept her voice low, her words harsh, but inside she was weeping.

She wanted to kill him. He deserved death. Every hunter needed to die along with the vampires they kept in check. None of them had hearts or emotions. Yet, when she looked at him, she saw that faint light of happiness shining for her. *For her.* No one looked at her like that. And desire blazed in his eyes. How many times had he stepped in front of her to prevent injury from a vampire? He'd tried to send her away from the battle. As much as she wanted to be annoyed by that silly gesture, she felt protected.

Natalya shook her head, refusing to let her brain defend him. He had used some kind of mind control on her. There was no other explanation for her behavior. She would never have voluntarily touched him intimately or allowed him to touch her. Her breasts still ached and felt swollen and painful without his touch. She detested herself. Detested that she was such a weak woman around Vikirnoff Von Shrieder.

She had been jealous. *Jealous.* The sight of another woman touching him had been more than she could take. Her animal nature had overtaken her. What had ever possessed her parents to give her the nature of a tiger? And why hadn't she been warned about the deadly peril, so very real, a hunter could use on a woman?

She pressed fingers to her throbbing temples. She was wading in quicksand, sinking deeper and deeper the more she struggled against him. Vikirnoff said nothing. All the while he lay simply watching her, propped up on one elbow, his gaze never leaving her face. She was beginning to hate his eyes. That black, fierce gaze, so intense and so hungry for her. His eyes drew her like nothing else ever had—or would. No matter how much she told herself it was wrong, it was a betrayal, she was still drawn to him. Mesmerized by him. In lust with him. *And it wasn't natural. It couldn't be.*

Her inability to break his hold on her fed her temper. "I certainly have no *duty* to you. You have such gall to even suggest it."

"You cannot deny you are my lifemate. Our souls call to one another." His voice softened to a mesmerizing cadence. "Give yourself a little time, Natalya. You will get used to the idea. All of this will work out as it is meant."

She shoved the knife back into the scabbard, her hand shaking. He was seducing her with his eyes and his voice. How could she be so susceptible? She needed armor. How could she be so confused and raw and edgy? She was never like this and yet she didn't seem to have any control over her emotions.

"I want to smother you with a pillow," she lied, hoping to draw a response she could work with. "I can't believe you. No one could *ever* stand being your lifemate." She could rage all she wanted but he knew he was pulling her in. She closed her eyes and allowed truth to pour out. "I will never be your lifemate. You killed my brother. My twin. The only person in this world that meant anything to me. Do you think for one moment that I'd save you, let alone have anything to do with you?"

Vikirnoff was silent, touching her memories lightly, seeing the man she loved, feeling her love for him. He shook his head. "I did not kill this man. I have no memory of his face and I remember each of the men I had to destroy."

She turned away from him. To her horror, the tears she'd been fighting blurred her vision. The humiliation was unbearable. Her heart twisted with pain at the thought of her brother's death. "Not you, personally, but a hunter. One of your kind."

"Why would a hunter take the life of your brother?"

There was no inflection in his voice. He wasn't calling her a liar, nor was he admitting such a thing could have occurred. He merely looked at her with his intense black eyes, his face etched with pain and it tore her insides out.

Natalya jerked the leather away from her abdomen to reveal the birthmark that had condemned her brother to death. "I have the same mark. You can't be my lifemate when I bear this mark. It's a death sentence. All hunters will kill us immediately when they see the mark of the wizard on our skin." There was defiance in her voice, expectation in her eyes. She meant to shock him and readied herself for his attack on her.

Vikirnoff stared at the intricate dragon, low on her left side. He let out his breath slowly. "That is no mark of the wizard, Natalya. That is the birthmark of one of the oldest and most respected of Carpathian families. That mark is Dragonseeker. No hunter would kill a man or woman marked as Dragonseeker. It is not possible."

Her chin went up. "Are you calling me a liar?"

Vikirnoff didn't answer her verbally. He invaded her mind. He gave her no warning and no time to stop him, pushing past her barriers so that he shared her life, the love of her brother, his laughter, his caring, the way the two of them were forced to live, hiding and running from place to place, always ahead of the enemy.

Natalya didn't take the merging lightly. She tried to fight him off, to put up blocks, but there was a ruthless quality to Vikirnoff. He pushed further, uniting them together until he saw what he was looking for. She hated the invasion of her mind. To her, it was almost worse than if he had invaded her body. She lifted her hands and gracefully sketched symbols in the air between them, an attempt at erecting a shield to protect her memories, her thoughts, the very essence of who and what she was from him.

The symbols burned brightly in the air for a brief moment, orange and yellow and gold, then slowly faded, leaving her vulnerable.

Her resistance to their merging surprised Vikirnoff,

but he ignored it, intent on finding the memories that had shaped Natalya's distrust of Carpathians.

Natalya's grief over the death of her twin was wild and without end. Totally immeasurable. It was still as sharp-edged and painful as the day she had learned her brother, Razvan, was dying. Vikirnoff caught the echo of her brother's name in her cry of sorrow. Her brother had connected with her on a private mental path, in pain, laboring for breath, reaching out one last time with a warning for her to avoid the Carpathian hunters. To run while she could and stay hidden from the scrutiny of that dangerous race. They were liars. Deceivers. And they would kill her the moment they saw that mark. The dragon was the mark of death.

Razvan had been in agony, but he had held on long enough to send the warning to his beloved twin sister. Abruptly, before she could tell him she loved him, he was gone from her. She had never found his body—or his killer. He had not shown her the battle, or the face of his murderer.

"It had to be a vampire," Vikirnoff said, totally shaken as he pulled out of her mind. Her emotions were so raw, so intense, he felt them, too. He took several deep breaths to stay in control. "There is no other explanation. You know they are deceivers. Every one of them."

"It was no vampire," she hissed back. "Razvan knew the difference. Your people waged war on my people simply because a Carpathian cannot stand to lose his woman to another man. My grandmother left her lifemate and it started a war. If Carpathian males can go to war over such a thing, they are perfectly capable of murdering my brother."

"Your grandmother, Rhiannon of the Dragonseekers, was kidnapped and her lifemate murdered. She was murdered. That is the truth, Natalya, and somewhere deep inside of you, you are very much aware of it or you would have killed me when I stepped between you and the vampire."

"Shut up!" She pressed her hands over her ears, but she couldn't stop the way her mind tuned itself to his. The way her heart sought the rhythm of his. Or the way her body burned for him.

And she couldn't bear to be reminded she had nearly killed him. She had allowed the tigress freedom and her claws had shredded his skin from neck to waist.

He closed his eyes in weariness. "I am sorry for the death of your brother. In truth, we all have lost loved ones in the battle against evil."

The knock on the door saved Natalya from having to answer him. Slavica opened the door cautiously. "May I come in?"

"Yes, do," Natalya said. "You're welcome to take care of him." She had to get away, get her wild emotions under control. She had never felt such an emotional roller-coaster and never wanted to again. Exhausted, trying to hide tears, she snatched up clean clothes and ran for the bathroom. "I'm going to take a shower."

4

"Natalya seems very upset," Slavica said as she lit several candles to fill the room with the soothing aroma. "Is it always so difficult for your women to accept another woman helping you? Even when I am a nurse and you are so gravely injured?"

Vikirnoff gave her a faint, humorless smile. "I have only met two other woman of my species in recent years and it seems to me they were both difficult. I have little memory of those who came before."

"Natalya is a sweet girl," Slavica said. "My husband, Mirko, is sending word to the prince, Mikhail Dubrinsky, that you are injured. I told him that one of our guests had broken into Natalya's room while she was away. That really worries me." She frowned as she studied the deep hole in his chest. "This worries me as well. The muscle and tissue are shredded right down to your heart. Your artery is exposed and there seems to be infection already forming."

"Vampires are nasty creatures. They like to leave their mark behind."

Natalya leaned against the bathroom door and listened to the conversation, ashamed of her unreasonable jealousy. She wasn't a sweet girl. She was a grown woman much older than Slavica and she should be in total control at all times. Her flippant attitude was carefully cultivated to keep people at a distance, but as a rule, she was in complete control. Meeting Vikirnoff had her emotions ping-ponging all over the place. She didn't much like the feeling—or herself at the moment.

Of course the hole in Vikirnoff's chest was worrisome. A vampire had attempted to tear out his heart. What did Slavica mean by that? Was it a mortal wound? Slavica hadn't even gotten to the tiger claw marks down his back. Was Vikirnoff going to die after all? Natalya had been so busy climbing all over him, she'd nearly forgotten what he'd suffered in her defense. She was completely disgusted with herself.

Natalya thumped the back of her head against the wall in frustration. *What is wrong with me?*

Nothing is wrong with you. You were given a version of a story and you believed it. You think I am your enemy and yet you are the other half of me and your soul recognizes me. It is no wonder you are confused.

Vikirnoff's calm voice intruded into her mind. The voice of reason. Purity. Truth. So in control—as if giving her permission to be upset. And it annoyed the hell out of her. *Don't make excuses for me. I'm perfectly capable of making up my own mind. Everything about you annoys the holy hell out of me.*

Everything? His tone was mild, but the inflection was suggestive.

Natalya squeezed her eyes closed tight as warmth flooded her body. If his voice could make her weak with wanting him, she was terrified of what might happen if he touched her. She was vulnerable right now. That was the trouble. She longed for a home and a family. For someone to share her life and he came along, all handsome with those eyes and that mouth and body, and she'd tripped. That was all. A small stumble.

Slavica spoke again. "I'll need your saliva. Mine has no healing properties."

Natalya's stomach rolled and her muscles clenched in protest. "Damn it," she muttered as she flung open the bathroom door. She hurried out, grabbing the wooden bowl filled with rich, dark soil, not daring to look at Vikirnoff. "I'll do it," she announced, exasperation coloring her tone. *If you know what's good for you, you'll keep your freakin' mouth shut. And you won't dare smirk, because in all honesty, I have no idea what I'll do if you are that stupid and insensitive.*

I have never been accused of being insensitive. Vikirnoff wasn't certain that was altogether the truth. His brother's lifemate, Destiny, had definitely made a few pointed remarks about his lack of knowledge about women.

"Of course, Natalya," Slavica encouraged. "I'm grateful for the help. Healing a Carpathian is quite different from healing a human."

"Have you done it before?" Natalya asked, curious. It just didn't seem likely that the Carpathian race would share such vital information as their way of healing with humans.

Natalya glanced at Vikirnoff, unable to help herself. Her heart shifted uneasily. Had he always been so pale? There were dark circles under his sunken-in eyes. White lines around his mouth were the only real external signs of pain, but she *felt* it. And she knew he was, in some way, shielding her. That irritated her as well.

She was every bit as powerful and capable as he was. Just because he knew that you had to incinerate vampire hearts in order to kill the undead did not make him more powerful or dangerous, only more knowledgeable. She risked another glance at him as she worked on the soil, trying not to notice the way Slavica touched him. It was impersonal, she could read Slavica's mind, knew there were no inappropriate thoughts, only her need to help heal Vikirnoff's wounds. There was also a very real worry that she would not be able to save him. Still, watching another woman's hands on his body was disturbing.

"Tell me what else he needs," Natalya said before she could stop herself. A slow hiss of exasperation escaped, but she grimly kept up with her task. She knew the soil was all important, that it would be packed into Vikirnoff's wounds.

"He needs blood, lots of it. And he needs the earth and someone to enter his body and heal him from the inside out."

Natalya pressed her back against the wall. Damn the man. *I sure as hell do not want to crawl inside your mind and body.*

I would not ask it of you.

She ground her teeth together. Of course he wouldn't ask. If he'd asked, she would have told him to go to hell, but no, he had to be all stoic and heroic on her. He didn't ask her to bring him back to the inn, but he'd looked at her with his intense black eyes and left her no choice.

I was unconscious.

If you knew what was good for you, you'd be unconscious now. She fumed at him, glaring, but he kept his eyes closed. And that brought her attention to his black lashes and their incredible length.

"I've healed myself from the inside out, Slavica. It requires a great deal of concentration and if he stays quiet and doesn't say anything stupid and make me so mad I want to add a few extra wounds to him, then it may just work."

Vikirnoff's mouth curved into a faint smile. "She sounds so loving."

Slavica laughed. "She does at that, Mr. Von Shrieder."

"Vikirnoff," he corrected. "I don't think now is the time to stand on ceremony. If you are under the protection of our prince, then you are under my protection and a friend."

Natalya snorted derisively. "You couldn't protect a wet hen right now, Mr. Charm, so knock off the flirting and let me work."

Vikirnoff looked confused. "Why would I want to protect a wet hen?"

Slavica covered her mouth with her hand and coughed delicately.

"You're deliberately missing the point," Natalya said and sank down onto the mattress, her thigh brushing his.

"I do not understand how or why you are comparing Slavica to a wet hen," Vikirnoff said with a small frown. "I do not see the resemblance."

Slavica's giggle slipped out from around her hand. She hastily sobered and sent Natalya a quick look of apology. "Just lie back, Vikirnoff, and stay still. Natalya, you must teach me the chant that all Carpathian healers use when working."

"I don't know it," Natalya admitted, feeling guilty and ashamed. Why, she didn't know. She had no reason to know the silly chant. "I'm not full Carpathian and have never lived with their people. I know very little about them."

Vikirnoff's fingers caught her chin and raised it. Her gaze flew to his and held there when she wanted to jerk away. For all the severity of his injuries, he had surprising strength. *I do not like you feeling ashamed. Why should you know something without ever being taught? Few know the heart of the vampire must be incinerated or he will rise again and again. Even fewer know how to separate mind and body to heal. And the number who know the sacred words of healing is even smaller.*

His voice soothed more than his words, brushing over her like silk, enveloping them with an intimacy that brought unexpected tears to her eyes. She choked back a lump burning in her throat and dragged her gaze from his. He was touching her in ways she couldn't comprehend and her reaction to him frightened her. She was terribly ashamed of her shrewish behavior toward Vikirnoff when he lay on the bed with his chest, thigh and back ripped open, all the while trying to soothe her.

I am having trouble keeping chaotic emotions at bay, why should it be any easier for you? You have no reason to feel shame.

His confession nearly brought on another rush of tears. Natalya bent over his chest, pressing the mixture of healing soil and saliva into the hole so close to his heart. Beneath her fingers, she felt his muscles grow tense. Flicking a nervous glance at his face, she saw tiny beads of blood on his brow. Her stomach protested with a quick rolling lurch. Her breath hissed out between her teeth.

"It's good, Natalya," Slavica encouraged. "Vikirnoff teach us the words so we can help when Natalya attempts to heal you."

Hurry. It slipped out, breathless with anxiety. Natalya bit down on her lip, but it didn't stop the worry in her mind from betraying her. She hated causing him pain, even when she knew she was helping him with the soil pack. *Tell me the words and I'll relay them to Slavica. And tell me what the words mean.*

Kuńasz, nélkül sivdobbanás, nélkül fesztelen löyly. *It means, "You lie as if asleep, without beat of heart, without airy breath."* Vikirnoff coughed and there was a fleck of blood at his lips. He turned his face away from her to continue. Ot élidamet andam szabadon élidadért *means "I offer freely my life for your life."* His gaze flicked over her briefly. *You may not wish to continue.*

Just give me the words.

O jelä sielam jörem ot ainamet és sone ot élidadet. Vikirnoff coughed again and dragged his torn shirt to his mouth. Natalya could see it was instantly stained with blood. *"My spirit of light forgets my body and enters your body."* O jelä sielam pukta kinn minden szelemeket belső.

Vikirnoff paused when she took the shirt from him and gently wiped his mouth. Her eyes met his. "What does that mean?"

"My spirit of light sends all the dark spirits within fleeing without." His hand fumbled for her wrist to hold her still. *Thank you, Natalya.*

"You're very welcome. Give me the rest of it before you lose consciousness."

Pajńak o susu hanyet és o nyelv nyálamet sivadaba

means *"I press the earth of my homeland and the spit of my tongue into your heart."*

"Basically the chant covers exactly the procedure for healing," Natalya said.

Vikirnoff nodded. Vii o verim sone o verid andam *is, "At last, I give you my blood for your blood." This is repeated while the healer is inside the body. It is a ceremony that has been handed down through time and has much power.*

Natalya repeated the words slowly several times to Slavica. The nurse nodded and began to chant, picking up the accents and murmuring the words in a soft, melodic voice.

Natalya took a deep, cleansing breath and let it out. She had often healed small wounds on her own body with the technique of separating spirit from body, but never on another person. It was dangerous and difficult to allow the body to drop away and become the healing energy needed. And to enter Vikirnoff's body . . . What if she made a mistake? What if she did something wrong and made things worse?

There is no making things worse, ainaak enyém, *I cannot hold on much longer. If you do not enter my body and heal it, I will oblige you by dying and save you the necessity of finding new ways to kill me.*

Natalya had no idea if he was attempting humor or if he meant it, but his words steadied her resolve. She flashed him a quick glance. *Good riddance, too. You make me crazy.*

I know.

There was far too much satisfaction in his purring answer. But there was also an underlying echo of pain. He was finding it more difficult to shield her from the tearing agony that made him sweat blood. Natalya closed herself off from confusion and guilt and doubt. She needed to shed her own skin, put aside her ego and her doubts, the frailties of self and become only pure energy, the essence of life, a spirit so light it could travel without flesh and bones.

She began to chant as well, the rhythmic words helping her concentrate and focus on her task. She felt the separation and, for a moment, panicked as she always did. She forced herself to push through her awareness of self and let go. She knew Vikirnoff was with her, a shadow in her mind. She wasn't certain if he was there for support, for aid should she need it, or because he feared she might try to kill him.

She found herself back in her own body. Faint color stole up her cheeks. She couldn't look at Slavica and admit failure. *What did I do wrong?*

Nothing. You became aware of my presence and allowed it to distract you. It happens with all healers attempting to enter someone else. Try again, Natalya. You seem to be a natural.

I've only done this to myself.

But with no training. No one showed you how, but you managed on your own. You must be a powerful healer as were all the Dragonseekers. I am staying with you to ensure your safety. If you wished me dead, you would not be attempting this.

The utter weariness in his voice became her strength and determination. She let her breath out slowly again and freed her mind and spirit from her body. She narrowed her awareness to Vikirnoff, to his broken, bleeding body, the terrible injuries wrought by a vampire, the most evil of all creatures.

It was necessary to stay out of his brain, ignore his memories and his thoughts. She found it was a struggle to separate herself from him. Somehow they were already intertwined and some instinctual, emotional and alien part of her feared his death. She took another steadying breath and once more concentrated on the chant. It was there for her, focusing her energy, drawing her into Vikirnoff's torn body so that she floated through him, pure white healing light.

The damage was tremendous. Worse than she ever expected and far beyond her healing accomplishments to date. She wondered at his ability to continue when he was so completely torn up inside. The deep claw marks down his back were mere scratches in comparison to the damage done by Arturo.

Natalya began the meticulous work of healing from the inside out. After a time she became aware whenever she hesitated, it was Vikirnoff who directed her, helping her close off torn, jagged muscle and tissue, repairing the damaged organs and carefully removing infection and, in several spots, poison.

The volume of chanting increased as other Carpathians joined in from a distance, both male and female, their voices rising together to aid in healing one of their own, in spite of the sun climbing higher in the sky. If the work hadn't demanded all of her attention, the voices merging together would have made her nervous. She had never been in such close proximity to the Carpathian people and they were touching her mind, just as she was touching theirs.

She had no idea how much time passed before she finished with the repairs to Vikirnoff's chest, but by the time she pulled back into herself, her body was swaying with weariness. Slavica held a glass of water out to her. Natalya took it gratefully and drank it down in one gulp.

"How do you know how to do that?" she asked Vikirnoff. "I don't think a doctor could do what you just did."

If it were possible, Vikirnoff was even paler, his skin an alarming color of gray. Natalya gripped Slavica's arm. "Look at him. I made him worse."

"I don't think so," Slavica consoled. "He needs blood. We must find a way to give him blood." She took a deep breath. "I gave my blood once before to a Carpathian, although I don't remember what it felt like. I can give him mine."

The protest rising in Natalya was sharp and ugly. She forced herself away from the edge of danger. She flatly refused to make a fool of herself a second time. And she was *not* about to tell Slavica an exchange of blood with Vikirnoff was the most erotic thing she'd ever experienced.

"I will supply him with blood," she said. The thought of touching him, tasting him so intimately was frightening. The more she wanted to run from him, it seemed the closer they became.

"She is too weak," Vikirnoff objected.

His voice was so faint, Natalya bent over him to hear the whispered words. His breath was warm against her ear. She could see the weak flutter of his pulse. "Put yourself to sleep and conserve energy," she ordered. "I mean it, hunter. You're not going to die on me and mess up the best work I've ever done."

I am beginning to like the way you talk to me and that is frightening. There was the faintest of smiles in his voice.

She was *so* susceptible to him. "Just hibernate, or go into your suspended animation, or whatever you people do when you're underground." She looked at Slavica with too much desperation, but she couldn't help herself. "Can't you do something? Don't you have a shot of something that will knock him out so we don't have to listen to him anymore? He's so busy trying to be the boss he's going to die on us." She hated that she was betraying her concern for him.

"Unfortunately he is right about the blood," Slavica said. "You have to work on him more and you need your strength. The hours are slipping by and soon you will be too tired to do this. There is no way for us to get him into the healing earth without everyone seeing us either."

"I don't get as tired as the Carpathians do in the sun," Natalya said. "I'm only part Carpathian." She'd never really thought about that side of her and the gifts she'd inherited from her grandmother.

She stared down at Vikirnoff with a small frown on her face. He definitely needed more blood. She doubted her nature could stand him taking what he needed from Slavica. How could she explain to the nurse when she didn't understand it herself?

Slavica seemed to divine the problem. "Why don't I do the best I can to treat his remaining wounds and you give him blood? If I think he needs stitches, you can go back in just for that part. None of his other wounds is life threatening. You can probably do a quick inspection of them to make certain no bacteria have gotten into his system. That way you will conserve strength and you can provide for him."

Natalya helped Slavica roll Vikirnoff to his side, exposing his back. The rake marks were long furrows dug out of his flesh, several inches deep in places. Slavica glanced at Natalya. "I'm sorry, you will have to do this. I would have to give him stitches, the cuts are far too deep. I'll clean it to give you a chance to rest."

"Tell me how you came to know about the Carpathians. Do you see them often?" Natalya didn't want to think too much on how those rake marks had gotten on his back.

There is no need for guilt.

Please just go to sleep.

Slavica smiled. "Mikhail and Raven Dubrinsky are regular visitors to the village. They have many friends here and help out a great deal. I doubt anyone else knows they are not simply another human couple living in this area. Not long ago, two other Carpathians made themselves known to me. They brought with them small human children. Angelina and I often look after the children during the day."

Slavica worked while she talked, washing the wounds and pouring something that obviously burned on Vikirnoff's back. He broke out in a blood sweat. Natalya's stomach churned in protest. "I'm okay now. I'll see if I can't heal those injuries, Slavica." Wounds she'd made. Natalya closed her eyes briefly wishing she could take back that moment in time. Warmth immediately flooded her. Vikirnoff's touch. She recognized it now, so light it almost wasn't there, yet strong and incredibly tender.

It wasn't fair that he could do that. He had so much confidence in himself. With him in her mind so much, she couldn't help but catch glimpses of his character. *The strong silent type, although you don't seem to be all that silent around me. I can only wish.* Deliberately she teased him, wanting the pain to recede from his body if only for a brief second.

She felt his faint smile, but he didn't speak, not even in the more intimate way of lifemates. She let out her breath, unaware until that moment that she'd been hold-ing it. Vikirnoff was weak and the leaden state that in-vaded the Carpathian race was beginning to grip him. Even with the heavy drapes drawn the light hurt his eyes. She felt the burning as if it were her own.

"Cover his eyes, Slavica, while I finish this." Natalya said between gritted teeth. The thought of him being in such pain, pain that *she'd* caused was totally disconcerting.

Csitri. *You have not caused me pain.*

There was that tenderness that turned her heart over. How could his voice be so velvet soft and gentle? How could it stroke through her body like silken heat leaving her so weak-kneed and vulnerable? And what was he call-ing her?

Slavica added heavy tapestries over the drapes so that no light could possibly get through the window or door.

"Thank you," Natalya said. The darkened room made it easier to shed her body and regain her spirit form, trav-eling through Vikirnoff to reach the long furrows the ti-gress had carved out of his back. She closed the wounds, removing the bacteria, checking and rechecking that she had fused together every bit of torn flesh, muscle and vein. How he had managed to walk into the inn and up the stairs in such a condition she had no idea. She didn't want to admire him, but she did.

"I think I'm done," Natalya announced, leaning heav-ily against Slavica. She was exhausted. Vikirnoff lay un-moving. Between his wounds and the time of day, his body was already leaden. She had the most unnatural desire to lie down beside him, her body curled protectively around his, and go to sleep.

"Will you be all right if I leave you?" Slavica asked. "Mirko has been handling the inn alone and I would very much like to check on the whereabouts of Brent Barstow."

"I'll have to set safeguards on the door, so don't try to come in unless I call you," Natalya cautioned. "I'll call if we need anything. Thank you so much for your help, Slavica. And I'm sorry if I was a little strange."

Slavica patted her arm. "No need for that. Mirko and I will do our best to keep an eye on Barstow."

Natalya shook her head. "You've done enough for us. I don't want either of you in danger. We'll sleep until this evening and we can sort it out then."

She followed the innkeeper to the door to check the hallway. Uneasiness was growing in her, but it could have been fear of being alone with a hunter. Not just any hunter . . . Vikirnoff. She began to weave the intricate pattern of safeguards at the door and windows. Anyone disturbing their slumber would be in for a few nasty surprises.

Excellent job. I could not have done better myself.

His concession pleased her, even if the fact that he wasn't asleep made her uncomfortable. *I have been studying since I was a toddler. My family is from a very ancient lineage and the spells have been handed down for centuries.* She frowned when she realized she was using the much more intimate form of communication between them. Mind to mind rather than spoken aloud.

I am sorry if this form of conversing makes you uneasy. I do not have the strength for verbal conversation.

"I know you don't. I didn't object. If you'd stay out of my head, you wouldn't be hearing things you weren't meant to hear. People need privacy. Especially me." She drummed her fingers against the mattress. "You need blood. And I need to wash you up. Frankly, you're a mess." She surveyed him, hands on hips. "I don't see how you managed to make it even traveling on the back of a tiger."

The tiger was a wonderful experience. My brother has said, on more than one occasion, that I am stubborn.

"What a shocker that is." Natalya flashed him a small grin as she dragged towels, washcloth and a bowl of warm water out of the bathroom, pleased by his compliment. "I can't imagine anyone ever calling you stubborn."

You are very brave when I am seemingly helpless.

Natalya's eyebrow went up. "Seemingly?" She was gentle as she wiped his face clean, smoothing back his hair with the washcloth.

You do not have to do this.

She frowned at him as she patted his face dry. "Yes, I do. I'm sleeping on the floor and you're a mess." That was exactly what she planned to do. Sleep on the floor in front of the door with several weapons at her fingertips.

She longed to lie down and sleep in the soft bed for a couple of days, but it wasn't going to happen this day.

He was silent again and she finished washing him, smoothing the cloth over his heavy muscles, washing away all traces of blood from his chest and belly. Natalya tossed the rags left from his shirt into a corner. She hesitated, tempted to go further, but she was worn out and she still needed to give him blood. Besides, she didn't want to see anything too tempting.

His soft laughter brushed inside her mind. *It is not likely I could do anything about the ideas you would have in your head.*

Don't flatter yourself. I'm not easily impressed. Mortified that he was reading her thoughts again, Natalya hurried into the bathroom. Many of the rooms shared the same bathroom, but Natalya had specifically requested one with a private bath. She'd felt a little guilty when she knew she'd be away for several days at a time, but now she was grateful she had reserved the room.

The hot water felt like a miracle as she took a shower, hoping to revive herself for the long watch. She was sore everywhere. She hadn't even noticed until that very moment. Every muscle ached, her head pounded and her eyes burned enough to remind her the sun was climbing high. She could hear the buzz of conversations throughout the inn, the laughter out on the street, the clip-clop of the horses as the carts went by, interspersed occasionally with a car. She was a solitary person, but she enjoyed the sounds of humanity and usually sought out friendships in the towns and villages she passed through. It was the only way she saw herself fitting into the world when it was a place not meant for someone like her.

She was part Carpathian. She was capable of some feats, yet not all. She had the drawbacks, yet not the severity of them. She didn't belong in their world, she didn't belong to a species that had murdered her brother and waged a war over a woman, even if that woman had been her grandmother.

Mage blood ran strong in her. She was from ancient lines gifted with the ability to wield magick, to use the harmony of the earth, to harness the energies and spirits around her. She was adept at it, capable of weaving powerful spells, combining ancient text and her own inventions with astonishing results, yet there was nowhere for such things in the modern world.

The thought triggered a flash of memory, or perhaps a nightmare. *I don't want to do that. It's too dangerous. Razvan, tell him what will happen if I call on that spirit. I won't. Razvan, he's hurting me. Make him stop!* A shadowy figure stepped out of the darkness and loomed over her as her brother rushed to her aid. Gasping, Natalya pulled back . . .

What is it? There was alarm in Vikirnoff's voice.

Natalya closed her eyes, tears slipping past her lashes as she caught the vision of her brother lying on the floor, his face already swelling and blood seeping from the corner of his mouth. As always a door in her brain slammed down, effectively stopping the replay of the distressing memory.

Natalya? Shall I come to you? What has upset you?

She leaned against the shower stall wall. There was such caring in his voice. She hadn't had caring or affection in a long, long time. *Don't be silly. I'm just tired.* Could he see all the way into her mind? Into the places that were so dark and shadowed and beyond her own ability to see?

Her father, Soren, had been half Carpathian and half mage. He had married a human, her beloved mother, Samantha. Natalya closed her eyes tight and tried not to think about her mother and the mess the vampires had made of her. Her father had gone a little crazy and left his children, Razvan and Natalya, alone while he went seeking to find his wife's killers. He had never returned and Razvan had become her only family.

Her eyes burned at the thought of her brother. So gentle with her, so careful to make certain she used every safeguard, dead at the hand of a hunter. She put her palm on the shower door as if she could feel Vikirnoff through the partition. The hunter was alive because she had chosen to save him.

Sighing, she stepped out of the shower and dried her body, wincing a little when she touched bruises. Natalya sagged against the wall, covering her face. What would Razvan say to her if he were alive? Would he be disgusted and ashamed of her? Or would he understand? She pressed her hands over her ears as if shutting out whispered recriminations.

She didn't understand why she was so drawn to the hunter, why she even considered the possibility of being his lifemate. In the past, she'd been a witness to a woman being drawn to a hunter in spite of her intentions not to be, but Natalya was not fully Carpathian or fully human. She was also wizard, with the blood of the dark mage flowing in her veins; few had her power. She did not believe she could be successfully bound. How could she expect Razvan to believe it if she did not? And how could she expect his understanding? She had the fear that he might reach out from his grave to condemn her.

Opening the bathroom door, she stood across the room from the badly injured hunter and wondered why she had been so determined to see him live. Natalya pulled on a pair of soft drawstring pants and a long sleeve shirt and stood watching Vikirnoff. He appeared to be dead. She couldn't detect the faintest breath of air moving through his lungs, but she didn't want to get that close to him yet. She still had the task of giving him blood.

You do not have to do anything so abhorrent to you, kišlány. *It is not necessary. I will survive.*

Natalya stiffened. Had he been awake the entire time, a shadow in her mind? Why couldn't she tell when he was merged with her?

"What are you calling me? What is *Kish-lah-knee*?"

The emphasis is on the first syllable. Kish-lah-knee. It means "little girl."

Natalya sucked in her breath, anger rising instantly. "What else have you called me?" She was no little girl, no baby, and she damned well wasn't afraid of him. Well, maybe that wasn't altogether true, but she refused to be intimidated when the hunter was so gravely wounded. She pushed up her sleeve in a business-like manner and forced herself across the room.

I called you my "little slip of a girl" and "forever mine."

The weariness in his voice tugged at her heart in spite of her anger. He was using too much energy when he needed desperately to conserve. "I am not a 'slip of a girl' or a 'little girl,'" she declared. "I'm a grown woman and I expect you to treat me with respect."

As you do me?

She slashed her wrist and pressed it to his mouth. Pain knifed through her, but she stuck her chin in the air and accepted it. She wasn't going to feel guilty. He was a hunter, for heaven's sake. One of her greatest enemies. She'd saved his life, that should have been enough.

You are not a "little slip of a girl." But you are ainaak enyém, *"forever mine." I thank you for taking care of me when you are uncertain if it is the right thing to do.*

"Don't thank me. I don't want your thanks. Just hurry up and get better so I can throw you out. Maybe your prince will come and take you home with him and get you out of my hair."

And this night she dared not summon her dream of Razvan as she did each time she slept. She loved to go to sleep and call on her childhood memories of her twin so she could spend time with him. They had always met in their dreams and exchanged whatever each of them had been taught. It was all she had left to her, but not this time. She didn't dare face him, not with a hunter sleeping in her bed and her blood flowing in his veins. Not even when Razvan was dead.

I do not belong with the prince. I belong with you.

Natalya sighed and waited until he politely closed the gash on her wrist with his tongue. His touch was a velvet rasp that sent heat right up her arm. "I don't think we're right for one another. You don't even like me, Vikirnoff. My grandmother couldn't have been a true lifemate to her Carpathian if she fell in love with my grandfather. I was told the binding words only work on a true pair. I do not think we are true lifemates. We aren't compatible."

Vikirnoff opened his eyes. She had forgotten how black his eyes were. How intense his gaze was. Even in the darkness she could see that he had night vision, just as she did. "Rhiannon was with her true lifemate. Xavier murdered her lifemate and imprisoned her."

"She was in love with Xavier. I've heard many stories about their life together. Their time was short, but they lived every moment together happy."

His tongue moistened his dry lips. Natalya's heart jumped. She couldn't stand to see him in pain. "There was a war, Natalya. People were being killed. Do you believe she would have been happy? Would you have been? Xavier wanted immortality. He had longevity, but only

Carpathians could live on and on. He was a powerful wizard but he couldn't find a way to live forever as he wanted." His voice trailed off.

"Don't talk anymore. We don't need to do this now." She didn't want to think about Xavier or her troubled nightmares of him. She didn't want to think about her father or mother. Most of all she didn't want to think about Razvan. "Please, just go to sleep and do me the courtesy of staying out of me mind."

His eyes closed. *That is an unreasonable request. If I do not share your mind, how can I see to your health and safety and happiness? It is my duty as your lifemate to provide these things.*

Natalya sat with her back to the wall, knees drawn up, guns beside her, knives and sword within arm's reach. She laid her head on her knees and closed her eyes. "It isn't unreasonable at all. If it makes me happy to have privacy, then it stands to reason you should honor my request."

There was a long silence. So long she didn't think he was going to answer. *You are confused about what is between us and you are emotional. It can be difficult at first adjusting to what seems an intrusion in your life.*

Natalya allowed herself to relax. She needed sleep desperately and couldn't understand why Vikirnoff hadn't fully succumbed to the leaden state that took the Carpathian people when the sun was high. She preferred to sleep in the afternoon, and the sun burned her eyes, but she could push past the discomfort and go outside as long as her skin was protected. She probably should have gone out and found blood for herself, but frankly, she was too tired.

"I'm an intrusion in your life as well," she pointed out. "We don't have to give in to this thing." Whatever the thing was.

Vikirnoff was silent even longer. She didn't understand and he couldn't really blame her. He had to admire her, going against her beliefs to aid him. Guilt surrounded her, ate at her along with her complete bewilderment. The pull between lifemates was extremely strong and she felt it every bit as deeply as he. *It is not a choice,* ainaak enyém. *Without you the darkness would take me. I cannot allow that to happen and neither can you. You know how evil the vampire is. I have fought such creatures most of my life. I will not become the undead. Not even for my misguided lifemate.*

Damn him. He had a way of turning her words around on her. She bit at her knuckles to keep from ranting at him. He believed what he was saying. Worse, she believed it as well. She let her breath out slowly, waiting until she was calm. "You would become a vampire? Why?"

A Carpathian male cannot exist for all time without his lifemate. We are two halves of the same whole. You are the light to my darkness and without you, I have two choices. To seek the dawn or to succumb to that darkness. I have waited too long to make the first choice.

She detested the honesty in his voice. She detested

everything about the situation. "So Carpathian males turn into vampires. That's where vampires come from."

This was not taught to you?

"Who would teach it to me?" Natalya sighed. "No wonder you hunters are a such a murderous lot. That's why I feel the darkness in you. You are very much like the vampire."

Yes and no.

"This is just great news. My intended is the undead waiting to happen. Do I have a neon sign stamped on my forehead? If you're a bloodsucking evil monster, willing to murder and wreak havoc, please apply."

She felt his faint amusement and tried not to smile when she was so exasperated with the situation. "Go to sleep. And Vikirnoff, I have my own darkness in me. I cannot be your light. There's been a mistake. I just haven't figured out what to do about it yet."

5

"Natalya! Hurry. You're late again. Grandfather is going to be angry with you."

"I don't like going to see him. He has scary eyes."

Razvan puffed out his chest, his mop of tawny hair falling into his eyes. "I'll protect you. If he is mean to you, I'll tell him we're going to leave."

Natalya sucked in her breath and skidded to a halt, her silky hair flying in all directions. She shook her head solemnly. "No, Razvan, he gets very angry when you stick up for me. I don't want him to punish you. I know he was mean to you the last time you got mad at him for making me cry. You were too quiet and you didn't tell me what he did to you."

"I don't care what he does to me. I won't let him hurt you. Not now, not ever."

"Why won't Father come back? I don't like being all alone.

Mother is dead and Father went off and left us and now we just have Grandfather. I don't like him. You know Father wouldn't want us to live with Grandfather. He didn't like Grandfather either."

"Ssh." *Razvan looked around, his too-old eyes suddenly wary as he threw his arm around his sister's shoulders.* "Don't say that. He might hear you. He always knows what we talk about unless we meet in our dreams. We have to be careful, Natalya. Don't trust anyone. Don't trust Grandfather and don't be alone with him. Something bad could happen."

Natalya spun around as something thudded against the door. When she turned back, Razvan was gone. Alarmed she ran down the familiar steps leading to her grandfather's workshop and pounded on the door. It was locked and no one came to let her in. She slid down the door to the ground, tears running down her face. Razvan would be punished because she hadn't obeyed. He would suffer the wrath meant for her.

Through the sound of her sobs she heard her twin's voice. He sounded far away from her. "Natalya? Where are you? I can't see you? Something's wrong with me. Am I dead? Did you kill me? No, no, the hunter killed me . . . Where are you, Natalya? Tell me where you are!"

Razvan's plaintive cry wrenched at her heart. "I'm here, Razvan. At the inn."

Natalya woke with a start, tears running down her face. Her legs were cramped from staying in the same position for so long and her heart was pounding. Adrenaline flooded her body.

She and Razvan had been ten years old when their father had disappeared. She hated when reality or nightmares intruded into her precious memories of Razvan. She had no recall of her grandfather. She could only think that the events of the day had brought him into her dreams. Guilt weighed heavily on her mind and in her heart. Razvan was dead, killed by a merciless hunter and her guilt had entered her beloved dreams and twisted them, giving her a bad taste in her mouth and making alarm bells chime like crazy.

What had awoken her? She glanced at Vikirnoff. He remained still, no hint of breath moving through his lungs. No discernible heartbeat. She was still suspicious. She had seen him like that before yet he had been reading her thoughts.

Uneasiness spread through her mind. Her stomach churned and the hair on the back of her neck stood up. Something was wrong. Something was terribly wrong. She snatched up her guns and stood listening at the door. Nothing. She ran her hands over the door. The safeguards were intact, some of the strongest she'd ever woven. Still, the feeling wouldn't go away. Something was not quite right. She glanced nervously at the bed.

Vikirnoff lay as if dead and then suddenly, without warning his eyes snapped open and his breath hissed out in a deadly snarl. Natalya nearly jumped out of her skin. His gaze shifted immediately to her face.

What danger has awakened me from my slumber?

So you feel it, too? She turned in a circle in the center of

the room, trying to become a tuning fork to ferret out the
threat.

Get out of here. Go now, Natalya.

She crossed to the window and ran her hands over the
drapes. She had no idea what she was searching for, but
she didn't find anything. The feeling of dread was overwhelming. *It's a good thing I have a big ego or you'd crush
me with always wanting me to go away.* She shot Vikirnoff a
quick assessing glance. Should there be need, he would
not be able to fight physically. He couldn't move at all,
paralyzed by the time of day. She was tired and sluggish
herself, but she had her weapons and whatever threatened
them was going to get more then it bargained for.

She faced the door again. She felt a terrible dread each
time she turned in that direction. Her gaze shifted
around the room. The danger was palpable, but she
couldn't find the source.

*Natalya, get out. You must go. You can make it out the
window. Protect your eyes and leave this place.*

It isn't after me. It's after you. She was certain she was
right and she didn't even know what *it* was.

She stepped back toward the bed, and positioned herself between Vikirnoff and the door. Her hands sketched
an intricate pattern, while she murmured an ancient revealing spell. Whatever stalked the hunter was cloaked
and it had to have known how to slip past the safeguards
woven around the door. She didn't want to think of the
possibilities of what that would mean.

Vikirnoff watched Natalya through half closed eyes.

Even in the darkened the room, his eyes burned, but he couldn't look away from her. Natalya seemed to glow. Power radiated from her, surged in the air around them. Electricity snapped and crackled. Natalya's hair flowed around her, rising upward toward the ceiling. Her hands pressed forward, her voice never ceasing.

Something shimmered in the room. Transparent. A shadow, bent over and creeping along on the floor. Natalya could barely see it as it inched toward the bed. Insubstantial, the shadow was made of ever-moving black and gray smoke. Fierce flames burned in the eerie red eyes. For a moment her heart ceased to beat, then it went into overtime, pounding so hard she was afraid it would leap out of her chest.

Vikirinoff. This is a shadow warrior. There was awe in her voice and ragged horror. Better to face three vampires and a legion of humans.

You must leave now.

She wanted to leave. She was so frightened it amounted to terror. *You cannot defeat a shadow warrior in your condition. Even if you weren't so badly wounded, it's full day. The sun alone would put you at a terrible disadvantage. I can't leave you defenseless.*

Listen to me, Natalya. This thing is legendary. I have only heard of them and their skills. I have never faced one. But even if you were a seasoned hunter at full strength it is said that no one can hope to win a battle with a shadow warrior. We thought them long gone from this world.

Natalya watched as the whirling cloud of vapor stood

fully upright. Most of the time, the creature appeared to be nothing more than smoke, but there were moments she caught a brief glimpse of armor. The flames in the sunken eyes burned madly as the creature looked around the room. All the while the smoke was in constant motion, swirls of gray and black that seemed no more than a vague transparent film.

Self-preservation was strong in her and Natalya looked longingly at the drape-covered window. *Why isn't he attacking?*

Vikirnoff could lie passive, conserving his strength in order to have one chance at saving Natalya. There was no sense in wasting time arguing with her. She was strong-willed and he doubted if the bond between lifemates would even allow her to leave on her own. That bond, coupled with her personality, would make it impossible. He had to wait for an opportunity to use everything he had to save her life. *Legend says movement attracts them. He is not paying any attention to you, but he searches for me.*

The shadow was moving through the room slowly. Once, the gray smoke passed over Natalya and the thing hesitated, but moved on. *Only the ancient wise ones used the shadow warriors.*

There was only one ancient wise one capable of commanding the shadow warrior, Natalya.

Her heart sank. Xavier. She was well aware of the legendary rumor that she knew was a fact. Xavier, her grandfather, the dark mage, had been the one to create the weapon. Unfortunately she didn't know how they could be destroyed. She lifted her chin. Perhaps she was some-how responsible for this attack.

Taking a deep breath, she reached for her sword and in one smooth motion, stepped in front of the near-helpless Carpathian.

What do you think you are doing? His breath left his body in a rush of fear. His chest lifted and fell and that small ac-tion combined with Natalya's movements caused the shadow warrior to swivel its head directly around toward him, the flaming eyes glowing with fervor for the kill.

Don't talk. I can't be distracted. She was already sweat-ing, not a good sign.

Natalya watched the insubstantial shadow closely. The warrior raised its sword in the traditional manner. She raised hers in answer.

Vikirnoff watched her, his heart in his throat. She ap-peared perfectly balanced, her body light and graceful. Rather than a linear pattern, she moved with circular, gliding footwork, deflecting the warrior's sword as it arced toward Vikirnoff. Metal clashed on metal and sparks flew. Natalya danced away, slicing at the shadow as she glided once more directly into the path between Vikirnoff and the warrior. Her sword sliced through empty air.

The warrior turned directly toward Natalya. He grew in stature and substance, taking on a much more solid and powerful form. He towered over her, the flickering red of his eyes, tracking her every movement.

Vikirnoff forced his body to move. It took every ounce

of discipline he possessed, every bit of strength of will to overcome the gripping paralysis in order to bring his arm up and wave it in the air. It only lasted a few seconds and the arm flopped lifelessly across his chest, but the warrior turned immediately toward him, drawn by the movement.

The shadow glided with astonishing speed, sword whistling toward Vikirnoff. Natalya deflected the strike and answered, a blur of motion, her hair crackling, the color going as black as midnight and her eyes burning a bright blue, as she spun around the warrior, sword slicing completely through the shadow at least three times.

This isn't working. He's worse than good old Freddie. Think, Natalya, you're good at this sort of thing. Think of what to do, she admonished herself.

He's gaining strength with the energy. Do you feel it?

There has to be a way to defeat them. I refuse to believe they're invincible. She would not believe it. There had to be a way. In truth, she hadn't felt the growing power in the warrior, she was too busy trying to keep Vikirnoff alive. The shadow warrior wasn't trying to kill her. It merely saw her as a nuisance in its way. She continually intercepted the warrior's killing blows, preventing him from destroying Vikirnoff. The hunter was right, though. As the swords came together, her arm and body nearly went completely numb from the force he was generating.

You cannot kill what is already dead.

What did the legends say, Vikirnoff? She stepped in front of the bed again, fending off the flashing sword.

This time when the blades met, she stumbled under the sheer vigor of the blow.

Stop all movement.

If I stop, this father of all Freddies kills you. That's unacceptable. And before you get too excited by that and think I don't want you dead, I just plain hate losing.

It is too many hours before sunset. I cannot aid you with physical fighting.

Natalya parried another blow and took several slices at the armor-plated warrior. Her blade moved through smoke. *Physical fighting.* The words repeated over and over in her head. It was impossible to fight a shadow warrior and win.

What are they made of? Vikirnoff, hurry! What are they made of?

They have no substance. They are like Carpathians when we turn to mist. Small molecules, vapor, air. Even water. Dust. Whatever is around to form the particles is used. But he is dead, Natalya. Already dead. You cannot kill him.

It has to be more than that. It has life, essence. A spirit. Natalya parried another blow and sliced futilely through gray and black smoke.

The spirit of a lost warrior, taken from the grave without permission and forced to obedience without rest. That's what a shadow warrior is, right? she asked.

Vikirnoff again made a supreme effort to redirect the shadow warrior's attention back to him and away from Natalya. *If it slays me, remain absolutely still. It will ignore you and leave.*

Natalya deflected the blade of the shadow warrior from Vikirnoff's throat and sliced through the transparent body once again, whirling away from the bed so that the warrior tracked her across the room away from the hunter. *Stop being so noble. You set my teeth on edge. This thing is really making me angry. Trust me, that is not a good thing. They're already dead. Think, Natalya. Call on your skills.* She continued to instruct herself, staying very focused on the warrior.

I'm telling you it feeds off energy. The more you move, the more emotion you give it, the stronger the thing becomes. It's growing in stature, but not form.

I have a plan. Close your eyes and keep them closed. You'll have to trust me.

Vikirnoff immediately merged his mind with hers as she spun in a graceful circle, a blur of motion as she kept the warrior's attention fully focused on her. Even in the dire circumstances, Vikirnoff found her a beautiful, deadly combination. Grace and power, perfectly balanced, she moved with blurring speed, spinning in circles across the room, blade flying as she gained the covered balcony door. Her gaze shifted once to him, even as she parried another blow from the warrior. Vikirnoff saw her entire body vibrate with the force of the shadow warrior's strike.

Your eyes! It was the only warning Natalya was going to give him. If Vikirnoff wouldn't listen to her, even in the midst of a dangerous situation, that was on him. She gritted her teeth and caught at the drape, jerking the heavy covering down. Bright light spilled into the room through the glass of the French doors.

Instant agony seized her, abruptly cut off. She deflected another blow, her feet dancing in an age-old pattern, whirling and slicing as she glanced toward Vikirnoff. She could feel the light eating at her flesh, burning her eyes, but it had to be a million times worse for him. Cursing, she abandoned her plan and fought her way back to his side. Inwardly she damned herself for a fool. The shadow warrior gained strength with every moment while she grew weary. The hunter was going to die anyway. She was dumb, dumb, dumb, to keep fighting for his life.

Her sword whistled through empty space when she should have decapitated the warrior. His answering blade narrowly missed her waist and jarred her arm when she deflected it. She grabbed the quilt with one hand and yanked it over Vikirnoff's body to cover him completely.

The shadow warrior went after the movement of the quilt, drawn by the scent of the hunter. The deadly sword thrust into the quilt and a fountain of blood erupted. Natalya's breath hissed out in fury from between her clenched teeth. She lunged at the warrior, trying to drive him back with her shoulder, but she fell through his body, staggering to keep her balance and whirling to face him.

Stop your heart and lungs! It was a demand, accompanied by a strong push of compulsion at Vikirnoff. Her fear for Vikirnoff amounted to terror. She slammed her sword again and again against the warrior's, preventing his renewed attack on the hunter.

Her heart sank. They were both dead. She'd killed them with her confidence. What had she been thinking? She knew the effects of sunlight on the Carpathian race. Blisters were forming on her skin. She knew Vikirnoff would be fried even with the small exposure he'd suffered. And all the while her strength was draining. She couldn't fight the shadow warrior forever.

You need the door opened. With every ounce of his last remaining strength, Vikirnoff used telekinetic power to undo the safeguards and the locks to thrust the balcony door wide open. *Your plan is a good one. A warrior's luck to you.*

She recognized the words from somewhere as a formal ritual between hunters. Somehow the words calmed her mind and allowed her to think clearly again. She began a graceful, spiraling attack, constantly in motion, drawing the shadow warrior across the room, away from Vikirnoff and towards the open door. Her voice began a soft murmur as she drew on her legacy, the powers of earth, wind and spirit. She needed luck, more than luck. She needed a miracle.

"Hear me now, dark one, great warrior torn from your resting place, while I call on earth, wind, fire, water, and spirit."

The shadow warrior lowered his sword and was still for the first time since he had been revealed to her.

"I call each to me and bind them to me and with them, I invoke the right of shadow law. The dark mage's blood runs in me. Heed what I say. I command the wind"—she flung her arms into the air and brought the wind howling into the room—"to come to me, to carry my warrior home."

The shadow warrior remained standing, sword at ready, his glowing eyes fixed on Vikirnoff. Well, at least she had his attention. She knew spells, thousands of them. She just had to come up with the right combination.

She faced the warrior and seemed to grow in stature. Her hair crackled with electricity as she lifted her arms toward the shadowy figure. Most things were bound by blood. She could do this if she just thought it through. "By shadow law, through ancient's blood, I claim my right by mage's blood."

The warrior jerked as if she'd struck him. His fiery eyes shifted from the bed and focused completely on her. Natalya's heart rate increased dramatically. She wanted his attention, but he was intimidating. Her hand tightened around her sword as she sorted through ancient spells for words that might release him. "That which was brought forth, I now return, by power of air and fire that burns."

The wind increased, tugging at the gray smoke that made up the shadow warrior's form. The flames in the eyes leapt and burned, so that sparks actually flickered in the swirling smoke. The sight was terrifying.

It is working. Vikirnoff, holding the merge, saw her

brain functioning at high speed, sorting and discarding spells, turning words over and over in her mind, rearranging them and putting them together. He was astonished and awed by her amazing ability with so many ancient teachings.

Natalya swallowed hard and pressed on. *I need to send the warrior back to the nether world and seal him there for good.*

I feel your power. It is alive in the room and surrounding him.

Natalya took a deep breath. She could do this. She was born to do this! "Shadow and dust shall be reclaimed, earth sealing the tomb from whence you came." She was gaining confidence. This was her realm of expertise like no other in her. "Dust to dust, ashes to ashes, warrior return, breathe your last." Her voice swelled with command. "Air, earth, fire, water, hear my voice, obey my order, thrice around your grave do bound, evil sink into the ground. I now invoke the law of three, this is my will, so mote it be."

The shadow warrior stared at her a long moment with his fiery eyes. He bowed slightly and gave her a small salute with his sword. The wind rushed through the room howling, reaching for the warrior, dragging the smoke and dust out the door into the air.

The shadow warrior was carried away, his spirit set free at last, his insubstantial form blown into a million molecules and scattered across the sky.

"May you find eternal peace in another realm while the wind takes what is no longer yours to the four corners of the world so your rest may never again be disturbed."

Natalya dropped her sword and sagged against the wall, her arms aching, eyes streaming, skin burning in the glare of the sun. She found herself sobbing, her chest tight and painful, throat raw. Her body felt leaden, on fire, stretched beyond all physical boundaries. Worse than that was the emotion churning through her. Everything was all mixed up, swirling in a black eddy and clouding reason.

Natalya.

She closed her eyes at the sheer intimacy he gave her name. *Ainaak enyém, why do you weep when you have destroyed what no one else has ever defeated? You are an amazing woman. A true warrior and I can give you no higher praise.*

His tone held admiration, respect, but most of all a dark, purring sensuality that turned her insides to mush. She couldn't look at him without feeling weak-kneed and stupid. She hated to be so confused and emotional and weeping in front of him like the little slip of a girl he had called her.

You need to shut your heart and lungs down. She wiped at the tears on her face and forced herself to her feet. "I'm not giving you any more blood and you're losing it everywhere."

I cannot shut down my heart when you are crying like your heart is broken.

"I absolutely refuse to play Juliet to your Romeo. It's just adrenaline overload, that's all." She pulled the balcony door closed and locked it, trying to find her normal bravado and rid herself of the emotional storm.

It is impossible to lie to me, although perhaps you are good at lying to yourself and do not really know your own mind.

Natalya yanked the drapes over the door, once again blocking out the light. The relief was tremendous. She stood briefly, eyes closed, gathering her strength. She had never been so tired. She wanted to lie down and sleep forever. "How bad is the wound this time?"

He cut my thigh. I was grateful his aim was not a few inches higher.

"Which means you're bleeding all over the place again, aren't you?" She hurried to his side and pulled back the quilt, ashamed that she had taken so much time to recover from her fight with the shadow warrior.

Vikirnoff was covered in blisters, his skin raw and angry-looking. Blood bubbled up from the wound on his thigh. Natalya didn't give herself time to think. She was already on automatic, pressing her hands to the wound, looking around for the wooden bowl with the remaining soil Slavica had left to refresh the packs.

"You're a mess," she said.

So are you.

She ducked her head, preparing the soil, avoiding his too-intense gaze. She knew she looked like Frankenstein's bride. And he didn't have to sound so gentle. She was going to cry again if he kept it up. It was easier to be angry. She didn't even know what the hell she was crying over, but she couldn't seem to stop.

Why would you think such thoughts? You are a beautiful woman and you must know it. Look at yourself through my eyes.

She tried to crush the sudden thrill his observation

caused. She was so confused. So upset. Her world had turned upside down. Everything feminine in her responded to her greatest enemy.

You are angry with me because you think I did not trust you enough to stop my heart and lungs. That is not so, Natalya. I have relied on my own judgment for well over a thousand years.

"Yeah, I loved your judgment." She rolled her eyes, both hands on her hips. "Your big plan was to die so the 'little slip of girl,' who, by the way, saved your ass yet again, could turn tail and run! I can't imagine how you managed to survive on your own all that time. It's a miracle."

You did not allow me to finish. I could not leave you without my protection, little though I had to give. It is impossible for me. Your skills are apparent, but I have never heard of a shadow warrior being defeated. I could not go quietly to sleep and abandon you to such danger.

She swallowed the sudden lump in her throat. He sounded so sincere. So caring. Thinking of her when he was ravaged by the sun and had suffered yet another wound. She didn't answer him. She worked on his leg in silence, stopping the flow of blood before separating her spirit from her body and healing him from the inside out. She concentrated wholly on the work, welcoming the chance not to think about what was happening between the hunter and her.

When she came back to her body, she was swaying with weariness. "That's the best I can do. Sleep now, Vikirnoff. We have a few hours until sunset."

Before Natalya could move, he whispered something soft, nearly indistinguishable in her ear. Tired, unprepared for an attack, Natalya felt him grip her mind, hold her in his enthrallment. She knew she was succumbing to sleep, her body stretched out beside his, but there was nothing she could do about it. The last thing she comprehended was his mouth moving over the blisters on her face and neck, healing the raw burns.

"Natalya, you didn't notice I had my hair cut today."

Natalya laughed. "I noticed. You're just so vain I wasn't going to say anything to make your ego bigger. You're so busy watching the women watch you, it's too funny."

"Since you give me no encouragement, I have to find it on my own. I fear for any man who falls in love with you."

Natalya tossed her tawny hair and made a face at her brother. "I don't care if a thousand men fall in love with me, I have no intention of falling in love with them. I see how you are once you know a woman has fallen under your spell. That is not for me."

Razvan hugged her. "Don't worry, you'll always be my favorite sister."

"Ha! I'm your only sister. Fat consolation that is."

Razvan laughed and sprang away from her, a young colt running fast over the slight hill. "I'll race you home! Come on Natalya, don't be such a girl. You have to run faster than that."

Natalya heard Razvan's voice calling her in the distance. She ran and ran, but she couldn't catch up. He sounded like he was laughing. She loved the sound of his laughter, but she was getting upset that she couldn't catch him. Razvan could rarely outrun Natalya. She had been gifted with incredible athletic skills. And when it came to casting magick, she was often ahead of him in their studies. She knew she had a competitive streak and right now, she was annoyed that she couldn't reach him.

"Stop!" Natalya looked in every direction. "I can't see you."

"I am dead. You cannot follow me to this place. The hunter murdered me and you have not yet avenged me."

Her heart pounded in alarm. "I don't know which hunter killed you."

"It doesn't matter. They are the enemy and they wish us dead. You are my beloved sister. I cannot save you from them, you must save yourself."

Natalya wrenched herself awake. She had to push through layers of haze and it took every ounce of discipline and control she had. Every muscle in her body felt sore, but her skin was clear, the blisters and the red, angry burn gone as if it had never been. Her neck throbbed, right over her pulse. She covered it with her palm and felt warmth tingling through her body.

Her neck ached. She rolled out of bed and hit the floor running, dashing for the bathroom to stare at the mark on her neck. "Damn, damn, damn it!" She dressed hastily and shoved her things into a pack. "You took my blood again, you demon spawned from the devil. I know you did."

Hunger hit her. Sharp. Terrible. Biting. It crawled

through her body and overwhelmed her mind. The whispers intruded, soft and sensuous, beguiling with temptation. Her mouth ached, teeth wanting to lengthen, saliva collecting. She turned her head and her stomach dropped away. Vikirnoff's black eyes watched her and there was hunger in his dark gaze.

Without hesitating, Natalya yanked flex cuffs from her pack and bound his wrists tight. He made no move to stop her, just watched her with that disconcerting, focused stare.

"I'm sorry. Glare at me all you want, but you're dangerous. Even when you're like this, you scare the hell out of me. I'm going to leave and I'll just make certain I have a good head start before you follow me."

Vikirnoff attempted to move and discovered the binding spell she'd added to hold him helpless. His features hardened perceptibly and his eyes grew a fierce black, but he didn't speak. *You think I will allow you to leave me?*

"I'm not willing to give you a choice. I'm not having you take my blood whenever you feel like it." Her eyes mirrored the gathering storm in her mind. "Do you think I'm so stupid I don't know blood is power?"

I know I will not allow this.

She tossed her hair and shrugged. "Too bad you don't have a say. I'm sorry you're angry, but I'm not lifemate material. Even if we're supposed to be together, and I'm not convinced we are, it wouldn't work out. I annoy you. You irritate the hell out of me. We'd be in counseling all the time." She patted his head, a gesture meant to add to his annoyance, but it turned into smoothing his hair back. Her fingers lingered, stroking the silky strands. The moment she realized what she was doing, she snatched her hand back as if he'd burned her.

Vikirnoff said nothing, but he looked more dangerous than ever. It was amazing to her how much power he seemed to exude, even wounded and tied up.

Natalya didn't know why she couldn't stop trying to defend herself, but she made one more stab at it. "Look, I could have left you in the forest. And I could have let the shadow warrior get you," she pointed out. "I'm tying you up for both our protection. I don't trust you."

"You are the one who attacked me," he said.

Natalya blinked rapidly. His voice was low and compelling. Her stomach did a peculiar little flip. "That was unintentional and you know it. You dropped out of the sky between the vampire and me. I was attacking him, not you. In any case, I've made up for it by helping you. Had I left you there, the wolves would have returned along with the vampires and you'd be dead or captured."

He glanced down at the flex cuffs. "It appears that I am *your* prisoner." His voice was sensual, a deliberate implication.

She felt faint color stealing into her neck and face. Her temper went up a notch. "You'll be able to get out of the cuffs once the binding spell wears off. I'm leaving now and that will give me a good head start. You should be fine."

"I will not allow this. Ask me for anything else and it is yours, but not this, Natalya. I am warning you. I will not let you walk out on your responsibilities."

Natalya tossed her head, eyes flashing at him. "Who would have guessed the hunter is a sore loser? Talk is cheap, *little slip of a boy!*"

He still hadn't blinked and his predatory stare kept her heart pounding. She knew he could hear it and it only increased her resolve to get away from him. If it were possible, his eyes deepened into a black that made her shudder with sudden anxiety. He had formed a barrier in his mind, most likely to prevent her from feeling his pain, but it also shielded other emotions, such as anger. Or rage. His eyes were turbulent and as black as the stormiest night.

"*Te avio päläfertiilam. Éntölam kuulua, avio päläfertiilam.*" He whispered the words in his ancient language, his eyes never leaving her face. "*Ted kuuluak, kacad, kojed. Élidamet andam. Pesämet andam. Uskolfertiilamet andam. Sívamet andam. Sielamet andam.*"

"Stop!" She pressed her palm hard against her heart. Whatever he was saying was affecting her. She knew spells. She knew almost all spells, but she didn't recognize the words. She knew Hungarian, but she didn't know his language. It was more ancient even than Hungarian. It didn't seem to matter. She felt every word in her heart and soul.

Vikirnoff's expression never changed and he didn't

take his gaze from hers, holding her captive with his eyes and his voice, in spite of the flex cuffs on his wrists. *"Ainamet andam. Sívamet kuuluak kaik että a ted. Ainaak olenszal sívambin."*

As he spoke, each word he uttered in that soft, mesmerizing whisper of sound seemed to penetrate deep into her body and mind, wrap around her heart and go deeper still, finding something inside of her that rushed to meet him. "Stop," she pleaded again.

"Te élidet ainaak pide minan. Te avio päläfertiilam. Ainaak sívamet jutta oleny. Ainaak terád vigyázak."

A spell. It had to be a spell. She pressed her hands over her ears, but nothing stopped that insidious whisper. Worse, she was beginning to think she was catching some of the words, although she was certain she'd never spoken the language. "What have you done?" She pressed against the wall, tried to make herself smaller as if by doing so she could escape his magic.

She was so certain she'd held him prisoner with physical and otherworldly bonds, but his words had done something irrevocable to her. She felt everything in her reaching for something in him. Needing him. Wanting him. Somehow those ancient words had bound her soul to his for all eternity, as if they really were two halves of the same whole and his words had somehow put them back together.

"What have you done?" she demanded again when he only watched her through his too-black eyes. "Something about giving me your body and soul and heart. You said that, didn't you? Answer me, Von Shrieder. What have you done? What did you say?"

"I claimed what was rightfully mine."

"Translate it."

Vikirnoff studied her pale face. Her eyes were enormous, her lips trembling. "Do not be so afraid. It is a ritual as old as time and no one has ever been harmed by it."

Natalya gnashed her teeth together and opted for a blatant lie. "I am *not* afraid. I'm *angry*. Whatever you did is some kind of binding spell, isn't it?"

"You mean like the one you used on me?" His tone was mild.

She felt color flooding her face. "Maybe I went too far," she conceded. "I'll take mine off if you'll remove yours."

"It cannot be done."

He didn't sound remorseful. There was no inflection at all. Her breath hissed out. "I would very much like you to translate what you said into a language I can understand. All spells are reversible if you know what you're doing. And I know what I'm doing."

Vikirnoff studied her face. She was lying through her teeth. He could smell her fear. She might not know, but she *felt* he had said something that was irrevocable, that her life had been changed for all time. "I cannot translate exactly but this is close. The words are said in our language first and then translated aloud for the woman in a language she can understand, although it is binding without doing so. It is roughly this. I claim you as my lifemate."

Natalya gasped. His voice was sensual, mesmerizing, just as powerful as when he spoke the words in a language she didn't understand.

Vikirnoff continued. "I belong to you. I offer my life for you. I give to you my protection, my allegiance, my heart, my soul and my body. I take into my keeping the same that is yours. Your life, happiness and welfare will be cherished and placed above my own for all time. You are bound to me and always in my care. That is the closest of translations. Males of my species are imprinted with the ritual binding words before they are born. They are given the ability to bind their lifemate for just the very reasons you have shown this evening." He lifted his bound hands to her eye level. "You should have more respect for your lifemate."

"Okay." She paced across the room. "Okay, hands down. You win this round. Now take it off. Undo it."

6

Vikirnoff couldn't pull his gaze away from the angry confusion on Natalya's face. With every step she took, her entire appearance underwent a change. Her skin began to glow and her tawny hair took on a strange banded quality, almost as if there were stripes he couldn't quite make out. Her hair moved with energy and light, even in the darkness. Her eyes were also peculiar, the color ever changing. One moment sea-green and vibrant, the next going opalescent and stormy. She actually looked feral, eyes focused on his face, her body all flowing muscles, her steps utterly silent.

"I would not do so, Natalya, even if I had the power." He could feel very real power building and crackling in the room. She was furious, and maybe, he conceded, she had reason to be. He was not about to allow her to walk out on him, but he'd forgotten she had the nature of a tiger. She was wild and impossible to tame. He should have kept that knowledge close to him and acted more carefully. She was dangerous, he could see and even feel it in her. He waited, expecting anything, breathing away his own rising emotions in an effort to be calm for both of them.

She stalked him across the room. The tension rose between them until it was nearly electric. "I don't think you're in any position to say no to me. I could cut your throat right now and there isn't much you could do about. I've killed vampires. To me, you aren't much different."

"If that is your wish."

"You're such a bastard." She swung away from him, angrier than she'd ever been in her life. Deep inside her, the tigress fought for freedom, demanding the freedom to rend and tear and remove Natalya's enemy for all time. "Take it back."

He sighed softly. "I cannot."

"I should have left you in the forest to bleed to death or fry in the sun."

"You could not. You did not want to take me with you, but you could not leave me. That is the truth." He said it with a mild tone, yet she felt the lash of a reprimand.

"I owe you *nothing*. I didn't ask you to interfere and I would never have been injured in the first place if you hadn't been whining so loud the entire world could hear you." Her heart was pounding so hard she was afraid it would burst through her chest. She'd fought vampires, yet this man, tied and lying so still on the bed, terrified her in ways she couldn't hope to comprehend. Her lungs burned for air and her throat felt raw.

Understanding dawned. She wasn't afraid of him, she was afraid *for* him. She was terrified of the power and anger rising up together deep inside of her in a furious meld. The tiger unleashed could do things she could never undo. She would not be caged by this man. By anyone. If —*if* she ever chose a mate, it would be one of *her* choosing. She forced air through her lungs. Forced her heart rate back to normal. The dark mage blood in her ran deep and strong. She could undo what he'd wrought. In all her years of study, no other had accomplished the things she had. Still, she would not stoop to murdering a helpless man.

"What you did was wrong, Vikirnoff. Whatever reasons you have, they are not good enough to try to take away my freedom." Looking at him, seeing his dark eyes so filled with pain, she realized the tremendous pull between them had allowed her emotions to become so intense she honestly couldn't tell his from hers. Almost as if they fed one another everything from anger to passion in one long chaotic roller-coaster ride. He seemed calm, yet when she touched his mind, he was feeling everything just as strongly as she was. And his confusion ran just as deep as hers.

She tilted her chin. "I am not going to discuss this any further with you right now. There is no point." And there wasn't. She had faith in herself. He didn't know how strong she was, but she did. She was certain, with time, she could come up with a reversal spell, once she knew the exact words. He had given her a rough translation, but she would figure it out from what he had said.

"Natalya," Vikirnoff began. He had no idea if he was attempting an apology, or even why he would want to say he was sorry. He'd upset her, but it was natural for him to stop her from leaving him. "I am not human, nor mage. My species has instincts that must be met."

"You had a choice, Vikirnoff. Don't let yourself off the hook by claiming instincts. You're a thinking person. I was doing something you thought was wrong and you stopped me. That's imposing your will on me whether you want to think so or not."

He frowned. "Tying me up and putting a binding spell on me was not imposing your will? I would not have bound you to me without your consent had you not decided you were leaving me."

There was a sudden silence between them as they both felt the earth shudder. Natalya's eyes met Vikirnoff's in understanding. "The sun has set."

"Yes, it has and the earth is protesting as the vampires rise. I feel the presence of more than one of them." Wincing, Vikirnoff sat up gingerly.

As if there had never been a binding spell. "As if I spent ten minutes weaving air." She watched the flex cuffs fall away to lie useless on the floor. She shook her head. What was the point in summoning up anger? She should have known he couldn't be trapped that easily. She was smarter than that. He was an ancient hunter and far more powerful than she'd given him credit for. Let him underestimate her. She wouldn't make the same mistake with him again. "Why didn't the binding spell work on you?" Better to find out. Knowledge was power and she could see, with Vikirnoff, she would need every edge she could get.

His eyebrow rose at her mild tone. "I was in your mind. As fast as you wove it, I unraveled it," he admitted. Both hands went to the hole in his chest and pressed tightly. The blood drained out of his face, leaving him pale and sweating tiny beads of blood.

She put her hands on her hips. "Maybe you should lie back down. Do you have the least idea how truly irritating you can be when you're acting all heroic?"

"I'm beginning to. The vampires have risen and at least one is heading our way. We cannot allow them to come to the inn. You know I will draw them here, just as you will. I am much stronger than I was last evening."

"Last evening you were near death so that's not saying much." She gave a small sigh when she saw him swing his legs over the edge of the bed. He was going to get up and watching him suffer in silence was heartbreaking to her, despite her earlier anger with him. "Please tell me it isn't that jackass, Arturo, or worse, Henrik. He is dead and gone this time, isn't he?" She attempted to interject humor into the situation, hoping to distract him.

"Henrik can not rise again. His heart was incinerated."

"Henrik was a true Freddie. I'll probably miss him."

"You seem obsessed with this Freddie person." Vikirnoff's gaze captured hers.

Natalya shot him a quick grin. "You sound jealous. Freddie Kruger is a lovely man, king of the late night movies."

Something in her tone warned him he was being teased. It was an unfamiliar situation for him, but one he thought he'd better get used to. "He isn't real?" She was trying to get past their argument and he was grateful. His entire body was screaming in pain and he knew he was more than likely headed for battle.

"No. He's a character in a string of horror movies. I can't believe you haven't watched him. What else is there to do at night when the rest of the world is asleep?" Natalya turned away from Vikirnoff's too-intense gaze. He could melt a woman at fifty paces and sharing a bedroom with him was just too intimate, especially with his shirt off. The man had a chest on him. Even with a hole in it.

Natalya was rather shocked she noticed his chest. And his eyes. And his mouth. He flashed a small grin at her. His smile made him look younger. She desperately wanted to see it again. The unexpected yearning was so strong she fell back on her cultivated flippant attitude and made herself remember she wasn't about to accept his claim on her. "Your mouth would be perfect if you kept it closed. *And,* just so you know, the moment the vampires are away from us, you will remove this binding spell, or I will, and you might not like how I do it." She dragged fresh clothes from the drawers. "I take it we don't have much time."

"I do not want Arturo to realize you are friends with Slavica and her family. Vampires take great delight in killing the families and friends of their enemies." He did not want to start another argument with her over the ritual words. She had been furious, her righteous anger blazing with a dangerous fury. He wanted a chance to think things through before he broached the subject again.

She poked her head around the bathroom door as she wiggled into her jeans. "You sound like that's said from experience."

"I have had many experiences with the undead, Natalya, and none of them have been good. This place is overrun with vampires."

"That's because I'm here. They always follow me now. They have a for a while, which is strange, considering they left me strictly alone for years."

"Which would explain why you didn't know you had to incinerate the heart."

"It was rather annoying."

"I can imagine. Do you have any idea why they are after you?"

Natalya pulled her close-fitting shirt over her head and came out to find him immaculately attired. She instantly felt disheveled in comparison. Even his hair was neat and tidy and there was no sign of blood or even a wrinkle on his shirt. He was hunched over, favoring one side, but his clothes were perfect. She shoved her feet into her thick socks and shoes and dragged on her shoulder harnesses for her guns and extra clips. "Arturo said he wanted me to perform a small task." More than anything she wanted Vikirnoff to lie back down or find a resting place somewhere to heal. She knew it was futile to argue with him so she didn't bother to try.

Vikirnoff watched her slip a multitude of weapons into loops and compartments in her clothes. He couldn't help but admire the efficiency of her movements and the familiarity with the weapons. She knew what she was doing and was obviously skilled in the use of each weapon on her person. She was especially skilled with the sword. "You have no idea what the particular task is?"

She shook her head. "But a short while ago, I suddenly developed a compulsion to go to the mountains and find a particular cave." She said it as matter-of-factly as she could, not with the heart-pounding terror she often felt.

His gaze narrowed on her. Dark. Intent. Speculative. "Compulsion is a very strong word."

"It's a very strong compulsion." She hadn't told anyone other than Razvan, and then, only in her dreams. From the moment she realized she was under compulsion, she had been terrified of who or what had managed to slip under her guard and take control of her. She studied Vikirnoff's face. He was in and out of her mind often, yet she was barely aware of him when he shared her mind—and that was disconcerting. She was powerful and she had barriers. What had happened to dull her psychic senses so that Vikirnoff could get past her shields into her mind? It was a question she intended to answer when vampires weren't hunting her.

He shook his head. "I did not do this thing to you. Allow me to search for the hidden threads. There is always a path back to the sender."

She gasped and took a step back. "No. I've searched and found nothing. I don't want you running around in my head."

His expression hardened. "I asked as a courtesy."

She snapped her teeth together. "Do you do it on purpose?"

"What?"

She yanked her pack to her and added two water bottles. "Irritate the hell out of me?"

"Perhaps it is a gift."

She shouldered the backpack and stood up, trying not to smile. His tone was teasing, a blend of smoke and sensuality that definitely had melting possibilities, but it was the fact that he tried to tease her that set her pulse pounding. "I'm heading for the mountains. They'll follow me and stay away from Slavica and her family." She looked at him. "Are you coming?"

"Of course."

"Are you strong enough to pack me out of here?" Her chin was up, but there was worry in her eyes. More than worry. Anticipation. Hope.

At last. Something he could give her. He steeled himself for the torment, his answering grin slow in coming. "You want to fly."

"If you plan on following me around, I may as well have fun and make use of you." Natalya shrugged her shoulders, trying to look nonchalant, when she was so eager to fly through the sky she could barely contain herself. She had phenomenal athletic abilities, and she was able to shape-shift into one form, that of a tigress, a gift given as her birthright, but she had dreamt of soaring through the night sky most of her life.

Vikirnoff studied her averted face. It was a secret desire she was sharing with him, one she hugged to herself and felt silly for wanting. He stood up and held out his hand. "Well, let us do it then."

She hesitated before taking his hand. His fingers closed around hers, solid and strong and incredibly warm. His thumb brushed across the back of her hand. She was acutely aware of him as they flung open the door to the balcony.

"Your injuries can't possibly be healed," she said as they stepped up to the railing. "Can you do this? We can find another way to the mountain if we need to. The tiger can carry you."

He pressed a palm over the hole near his heart as he let go of his physical self to inspect the damages to his body. Natalya had done a good job repairing the injuries. His body was trying to heal from the inside out. The wounds were still there, raw and painful, but tissue and muscle were knitting quickly. A few days in the ground or utilizing ancient blood and he would be as good as new. He came back to his body and nodded. "I am much better, thanks to you, Slavica and the richness of the soil. How are your ankles?"

She considered misleading him, but didn't want to risk the humiliation of being caught in a lie. In any case, it might be important. "It's strange, but I can still feel the creature gripping me. Sometimes I feel as if he's pulling on my legs."

"I was afraid of that. I healed the wounds and I searched for poison and bacteria he may have injected into you, but he was more than the undead. I think he marked you."

She was silent, staring out into the night. She loved nights in the mountains. The air was always crisp and clean and when the weather was clear, the stars sparkled endlessly. "You mean he can track me? Or draw me to him?"

"He may think that, but I don't. He prepared a trap for you and he must have been studying you for some time before he sprang it. I believe he thinks he can draw you to him with his mark, but I believe he is wrong. I think you're too strong-willed and would fight with your last breath."

Although Vikirnoff sounded worried, Natalya couldn't help but be pleased with his assessment of her personality.

Vikirnoff glanced at the sky. Dark clouds spun and boiled to the north. "I must let Arturo know he has a serious rival for your affections." He jumped up onto the railing and crouched down. "Do you want to me to carry you, or do you want to ride?"

His choice of words made her stomach flutter. "Ride." She liked control. She was no baby to be held in his arms while traveling across the star-lit sky. She was going to have her eyes wide open and a smile on her face. She had been alive a long time and she believed in embracing each new adventure, each new opportunity to gain knowledge. And the threat of vampires hunting her was not going to diminish her joy in the novel experience one iota.

She climbed onto his back and circled his neck with her arms, laying her body down the length of his just as he had done when he rode the tiger. His muscles bunched, contracted. Warmth seeped into her body. Her breasts pressed into his back and ached with the need to be closer. She pushed aside the rising physical awareness of him. Nothing would mar this moment for her.

Vikirnoff let his breath out slowly. This was torture. Sheer torture. He could barely keep the beast in him leashed when her blood called to him, when every cell in his body demanded hers, when his lifemate was lying across him, her body imprinted into his skin, his flesh, his very bones.

The scent of her blood, the sound of the life moving through her veins called to him, tempted him when he was in such need. Hunger raged through his body and mind, but he forced control, called on a thousand years of discipline and emptied his mind of erotic images of her, filling it instead with the form of a giant bird.

A small sound escaped Natalya as his bones crackled and popped, stretching to accommodate his wings and the body of an owl large enough to race across the sky carrying a woman. Iridescent feathers covered his body and his hands curved into sharp talons to grip the balcony railing. Agony filled every cell in his body and flooded his mind so that he had to use every ounce of discipline he had learned over the centuries to hold the form of the owl. His body shuddered with the effort and for a moment his lungs burned for air as he came to grips with pain.

"This is fabulous!"

The uninhibited joy in her voice was worth the terrible agony in his body. It was worth every wrenching tear of his injured muscles and organs. He knew nothing of women and even less of lifemates. He was aware he was making every mistake he could possibly make, although he didn't understand why. He had lived far longer, his experiences far exceeded hers, his nature demanded he protect her, yet she seemed to be offended when he attempted to impart wisdom or protection to her. But this—this simple thing he gave her and she was overjoyed. Her joy took away the pain as nothing else could.

Laughter bubbled up in her, spilled out as he sprang into the air and gained height, flapping his tremendous wings and circling above the inn. He cloaked them, preventing the townspeople from seeing them, although he was certain they would hear her laughing as bird and rider gained the skies.

He flew over the rolling hills dotted with a half dozen farms. The sharp eyes of the owl spotted a group of men heading back to the farmhouse, glancing uneasily toward the north. *We need blood.*

Natalya held on while the large bird swooped low and hopped from a hay sheaf to the ground. She slid off and watched Vikirnoff shift, entranced by the ease with which he changed. For just one moment she glimpsed pain in his eyes and then he was striding away toward the farmers. She kept an eye on the skies. The darker clouds spun and boiled but stayed far to the north. She could feel the continual pull of the mountain peaks calling her, drawing her to them. She couldn't turn back, no matter the danger. It was rather like being one of the too-stupid-to-live teens in the late night movies, going to the very place where Freddie waited with his steel claws.

There you go thinking about Freddie again. How many times did you watch these movies? Vikirnoff's voice held a gentle teasing note.

Natalya looked up at him with a quick grin. "That was fast. Have you heard the concept of savoring your food?"

He bent toward her until they were a breath apart. "Only when it is you."

Natalya gestured toward the mountains. "I have to get

there, Vikirnoff." She wasn't going to look into his eyes and get lost.

Maybe you are already lost and just do not know it yet.

"Dream on, buster." She snapped her fingers. "Where's my ride?"

It was easier the second time, especially with his hunger abated. Once in the air, Vikirnoff flew over the meadows and hills in a low flying pattern to allow Natalya to see the countryside from the air. She was a natural, fearless, moving with him, her body so tuned to his that she would begin to shift her weight at the exact same moment he needed her to.

He picked the cave coordinates out of Natalya's mind. She was so preoccupied absorbing the sensations of flight, she didn't notice his intrusion, nor did she have any barriers up against him. And that bothered him. Why was she utterly vulnerable to him when she was obviously so strong? It made no sense and set off an alarm in him.

Vikirnoff took advantage of the situation to delve for the source of her compulsion, to find why she had no barriers and to try to find the meaning of the marks in her body the dark creature had left behind. The compulsion to go to the Carpathian Mountains and find a particular cave was very strong, urgent, and had been planted years earlier. A recent event had triggered the compulsion to become active, to draw Natalya to the cave for some hidden reason. He tried to find the event that might have been the trigger, but if Natalya knew of it, he couldn't find evidence of it in her memories.

He found several places where it seemed her memories were wiped clean, as if she had suffered a terrible trauma and her brain had been damaged. He found threads of memories that led nowhere, suddenly ending abruptly in a dark void. He didn't dare stay too long and he was getting tired trying to maintain too many things at once so he pulled out reluctantly to concentrate on enjoying the flight with his lifemate.

Vikirnoff banked and plunged downward to give Natalya an additional thrill, pulling up at the last moment before hitting the surface of the water and skimming the canopy of trees. She laughed out loud. He could actually feel waves of happiness flowing out of her.

She leaned close to the bird's ear, but spoke telepathically. *This is wonderful! Thank you so much, Vikirnoff. This is one of the coolest things I've ever done in my life.*

He was grateful he was the one giving her the experience. Deliberately, he flew above the lakes and treetops, giving her a bird's-eye view of the beauty of the country. The ice and snow sparkled, the mountains glittered. Sheep dotted the meadows and farms and churches and castles stretched out below them.

It is amazing is it not? Seeing it all through her eyes brought back forgotten memories of his childhood, his first flight over the exact same area he was taking Natalya. Of course, it looked a lot different then, much more wild and uninhabited. He had wobbled a bit, but he had soared nearly all night. The freedom had been intoxicating. *I have you to thank for the memories. I have not thought of that in more centuries than I care to recall.*

Do you call up dreams when you go to sleep?

No, we shut everything down. Do you?

Oh, yes. Everything I love about my childhood and my times with Razvan. All the things we did together, the things we learned. I had a relatively happy childhood. My mother died when I was about ten and a year later my father left us and we had to live with . . .

She trailed off, a frown replacing her smile. She fell silent. Vikirnoff waited, but Natalya didn't continue the conversation. He touched her mind, but it was as if a door had slammed shut—or one of the damaged threads of memory had ended abruptly. He could feel her bewilderment.

I feel your distress. Is the memory of the loss of your parents so painful still that you cannot talk about it? He dropped low to skim through a meadow of wildflowers before circling around to fly back up toward the higher peaks.

Natalya bit down on her lower lip. She didn't want to admit the truth. She forgot things. Worrisome things. What could she tell him that would make sense?

Vikirnoff began quartering along the ridge of the mountain, searching for an entrance to the cave in Natalya's mind. *It is difficult to lie to one another. You may as well not try. If you prefer not to tell me the truth, silence is better than a lie.*

Natalya appreciated the sincerity in his voice. She

didn't know what was wrong with her and she had no way to explain it. She resorted to teasing in an effort to bring back the fragile camaraderie between them. *Oh, great, so if I take a few lovers, you'd know. That's what you're telling me.*

If you decide to take lovers, ainaak enyém, *be very certain they are men you consider enemies and wish destroyed.* He sounded very calm, but she felt the bite of his teeth as they snapped together.

I'm going to have to really work at understanding the concept of lifemates and how you were able to bind us together. I really am very good at turning spells around. The ritual words have to be a type of binding spell. There must be a way to undo what you did. I'm fairly confident I'll be able to figure it out.

Vikirnoff winced inwardly. It was evident that Natalya intended to be rid of him as quickly as possible, anyway that she could. She regarded him as an enemy of her family. Most of all she didn't like him. And that hurt.

He turned that piece of information over and over in his mind. He couldn't remember anything hurting him emotionally. Not a single incident. There must have been moments in his childhood, in his youth as a fledgling, yet this moment, this realization hurt deeper than anything he remembered.

What is it?

So she was tuned to him whether she wanted to be or

not. She wasn't touching his mind, yet she felt his sudden wrenching heartache.

I cannot lie to you either and I would prefer not to discuss it. He would prefer to do the things necessary for their survival. For Natalya's survival. He didn't need to turn into a pathetic romantic who expected his lifemate to be enamored of him. It didn't matter whether she was or not. They were joined, two halves of the same whole. That was all that mattered.

Natalya nibbled on her lower lip, trying to puzzle out what was wrong. In the short time she'd known him, she'd come to realize Vikirnoff rarely showed emotion. Not in his tone, not in his expression, not even in what he said. Only his eyes were alive, raw power, hunger, desire, an intensity that overwhelmed her. She was grateful she couldn't see them now. She didn't want to see hurt or sorrow. Her stomach was tied into knots at the thought of it.

Neither one of us is very good at talking things out, are we? she asked. Her hands smoothed the feathers at the back of his neck.

I guess that is so. I never had much need to discuss feelings when I had none. I relied on my own judgment in battle, in every decision, in every way. Who was there to discuss things with and what would I discuss? If it was an apology, he knew it was a poor one. He honestly didn't know what people talked about or how they did it.

You've spent a long time alone, haven't you?

There was a small silence. Natalya feared he wouldn't answer. She found she was holding her breath waiting.

Centuries. I have been cut off from my homeland and my people, sent out long ago to battle the vampire. When the darkness crouched too close, I found my brother and remained with him to ensure he did not succumb before I made the choice to end my life. That wait was long and the darkness spread until I was no longer certain who I was.

It was the simple truth. She heard it in his voice. A lifetime of honor and service told in three sentences. It did not convey the stark isolation, the emptiness of emotion and color, yet she felt it as surely as if she'd been there and she found herself weeping for him.

Do not think of something that will cause you sorrow, ainaak enyém, *look beneath us to the world below and enjoy this time.*

Natalya lifted her chin, allowing the wind to carry her tears away. *You'd better not be calling me a "little slip of a girl."*

His laughter was low and sensual. She felt it in the pit of her stomach, lower still, a curling heat that spread throughout her body and pooled into a throbbing ache. *I will certainly never make that mistake again.*

She looked beneath her to the wild countryside they were circling. There were deep gorges cut into the mountain and she could see several entrances to caves. The meadows were a vivid green even in the gathering darkness. Wildflowers bloomed everywhere, in the valleys, clinging to the sides of the rock and valiantly decorating the plateaus. As Vikirnoff swooped lower she could see in the deeper depressions where water filled the basins forming a peat bog. The beds of moss were a vivid green, enhanced by several shallow pools. The moss beds wound their way around stands of birch and pine.

It is so beautiful.

Yes, but I feel uneasy. Do you not feel the subtle warning in the air around us when I drop into the mist near the peak of the mountain?

Vikirnoff circled around once again, flying straight into the white mist hovering around the mountaintop. Natalya stiffened as she felt the subtleties of magick weaving a web of fear through her. *We must be close to the entrance.*

Vikirnoff landed on the nearest outcropping, gripping hard with his talons and extending one wing politely.

She slid off of the extended wing, landing on her feet. The ground seemed to shake as she adjusted to land again. "This is definitely the place. The feeling of wanting to leave is much stronger here."

Vikirinoff shifted shape a distance from her, knowing the wrenching of bones and muscle would be agony. He did it fast, not wanting to give himself time to think about it, clothing himself at the same time. Spots of blood dotted his white shirt and when he swiped his hand across his brow, his palm came away smeared with blood. Cursing softly, he breathed deep to ride above the pain and did another quick healing session to repair the damage the shifting back and forth caused. Once he was certain there was no trace of the blood on his body or clothes, he strode over to the boulder and paced around it, careful not to disturb anything should there be a trap.

Natalya watched him coming toward her. He staggered, his hand going to his chest in an involuntary gesture, but he recovered immediately, walking as if he were fit and strong. He carried an edge of danger without even being aware of it. Had she not known he was so severely injured, looking at him now, she would never have known.

She sighed. She had so many issues to settle with him. First and foremost, the ridiculous spell that bound them together, but she could set all that aside for later and work with him if she could trust him. Every instinct told her she could, yet her mind churned with turmoil, guilt ever present and the sound of her brother's voice continually admonished her.

"What is it, Natalya?"

His voice turned her heart over. That was the trouble. He had those eyes and that voice and she responded completely to him. "You looked into my mind to try to find who put me under compulsion, didn't you, Vikirnoff?"

"Yes." He wasn't going to try to deceive her. He saw no need for it, and no need to apologize. If he was going to keep her safe, he needed to know who had put her under such a strong compulsion and why. "I did not have much time to find answers, but I have not yet finished."

Natalya took a deep breath. What she was about to do might be worse than anything she'd ever done in her life. "Do I have memories of Xavier? My grandfather? Other than stories told to me by my father, I mean."

Vikirnoff leaned against a boulder and studied her face. His gaze was focused, sharp, missed nothing at all. "That is a strange question, Natalya. Why would you ask such a thing? How could you have memories if he is dead?"

"I don't know. I have disturbing dreams of him. He creeps into my dreams and when I try to remember my childhood with Razvan while I'm awake, I cannot. It's hazy and distant and pieces are missing. I have been afraid for some time that my memories of him are buried." She forced herself to look at him when she feared he might think she was crazy.

Vikirnoff was silent. She was nervous with him, attempting to trust him with something important to her, but more than that, he recognized the significance to his people. Xavier was a mortal enemy of the Carpathian people. He had murdered and kidnapped and waged war for one purpose, one end. He sought immortality. Should Xavier be alive he would be planning another strike against the Carpathian people. It didn't seem possible, but it had always bothered Vikirnoff that no body had been found to substantiate the claims of Xavier's death. Vikirnoff needed to choose his words carefully and not alienate her. He knew he didn't have the necessary skills to sweet-talk his lifemate. He only had the truth.

"Are you afraid Xavier is alive? That he is the one who placed you under compulsion? And that perhaps he tampered with your memories as well?"

Natalya sighed. "I don't know. I can't remember anything about him other than the stories told to me by my father, but I have dreams and they aren't pleasant. Worse, my father disappeared when I was ten. Razvan and I couldn't have lived alone, but I can't recall those days, or who took care of us. I dream about them and Xavier creeps into every dream."

"Do you suspect that he is alive?"

Natalya pressed her hand to her churning stomach. She did suspect Xavier lived, but that was crazy. She'd suspected it for some time. And she worried that he wasn't the wonderful man her family had portrayed to her. Her dreams were often disturbing and Razvan and she suffered greatly at his hands. She had flashes of memories during waking hours that made no sense, memories of a shadowy figure that terrified her. She was afraid that man was Xavier.

"I don't know," she admitted reluctantly. "I know he was a dark mage and capable of controlling memory, but if he is alive and he didn't want me to remember him and he was altering my memories, why didn't he completely wipe himself from my mind? And what would be the purpose?"

Vikirnoff's dark eyes moved over her face, drinking her in, devouring her. She was so beautiful to him with her strong will and her warrior ways. When she sounded so confused and forlorn, his heart turned over. "Maybe he could not. You have tremendous strength in you, Natalya. Could he have controlled your memory to some extent but perhaps found it impossible to wipe it clean?"

She looked so downcast, so vulnerable, he stepped forward and framed her face with his hands. "I think you are a surprise to everyone you meet. You have more strength of will in you, more power coiled in you, than even you are aware. I see it in you. And I feel it when I am close to you. It would not matter how powerful a mage your grandfather is, I doubt he could wholly manipulate you should he attempt such a thing, because you have too much strength of character."

Tears glittered in her eyes and tangled on her lashes. "That's the nicest thing anyone's ever said to me."

"It is simply the truth." He bent forward, his breath warm against her cheek. "You break my heart when you cry, Natalya."

Natalya's heart nearly stopped beating when she felt his lips, smooth, firm, velvet soft, brushing away her tears. She hadn't been touched in years and he was seducing her with tenderness. "I don't mean to."

"I know. That is what makes it so appealing."

He kissed the corners of her mouth. She knew she should stop him, but she didn't want to. She waited, lungs burning for air, her heart beating too fast. His mouth settled over hers with infinite gentleness. Warmth spread and erupted into flames, searing her from the inside out. His arms enfolded her close, brought her into the heat of his body. Against his heavily muscled chest, his wildly beating heart. His scent enveloped her and she opened her mouth to his, tongue stroking hers with sudden wanton abandon.

Vikirnoff's kiss went from gentle to rough the moment she responded, the moment she gave herself to him, deepening into a fiery tango of possession and hunger and sheer passion. His hands bunched in her hair to pull her closer still until their mouths fused together in heat and fire.

They devoured one another, Natalya seeking his skin through his clothes. It wasn't until she felt him wince that she lifted her head and looked into his black eyes. "You are one beautiful man."

"Men are not beautiful." He traced her mouth with his fingertip.

She bit at him, drew his finger into her mouth and swirled her tongue around it. "Maybe not to you, but you certainly are to me." She could see how pale he was. Stark hunger burned in his eyes—both physical and sexual hunger. Her womb coiled tightly. "You need to feed again. The flight and shifting took too much energy."

Her voice was sultry with invitation. His entire body clenched in reaction, every nerve ending coming alive.

"I need to be deep inside of you." His lips skimmed down her neck, her throat, lower still, nudging aside the neckline of her shirt so he could flick his tongue over the swell of her breasts. So his teeth could tease sensitive skin. "You have no idea how much I want you." His hands pushed at her shirt, moving it up to bare her stomach and her enticing navel. "What is this?" He bent her back so that she rested against the slope of a boulder while he inspected the small belly button ring she was wearing. He nibbled at it, played with it with his tongue, flicking small velvet strokes much like a cat against her bare skin.

"I think you like it." He was making her crazy with desire. Her body was hot and aching and heavy with the need for release. His fingertips rubbed over her skin, pushing her shirt up further until he was touching the undersides of her breasts. She thought she might go out of her mind. Just the simple brush of his fingers on her sensitized skin had her dizzy with need.

"It is the only thing you should wear." He kissed the sparking gold band and tasted his way up her bare skin to her breast.

Natalya shivered in reaction, her hands tightening on him, pulling him closer to her, urging him on. She had never wanted anything more than she wanted the feel of his hands and mouth moving over bare skin. His teeth scraped erotically and her entire body tightened, heat building until she was nearly crying for relief. His mouth closed over her breast, hot and moist and so unbelievably seductive, she felt her body dissolve into liquid. "Vikirnoff." She whispered his name, stroked his hair. "I'm not going to make it if you keep this up." She didn't want him to stop. She wanted to strip the clothes from her body and wrap herself around him.

We could be in deadly peril here. The reminder was punctuated with flicks of his tongue.

She laughed aloud. "You can't say *deadly peril*. In all those late night movies the stupid teens know they are in danger and they take time to kiss and touch just like this . . ." She groaned when his tongue flicked her nipple and sent waves of desire shooting through her bloodstream. "And then Freddie comes and kills them and they deserve it."

His mouth pulled strongly at her breast until her legs nearly gave out. *There are no vampires near so I do not think your Freddie will bother us right now. But if you are worried, we can leave this place.*

She groaned at the hopeful note in his voice, that deep husky aching note that tore her apart. Natalya smoothed his long hair. "I cannot leave." She said it simply, her throat raw, her heart breaking. It was the truth. She couldn't break the compulsion and leave the cave without entering it. "I'm sorry."

Vikirnoff nuzzled her breast once more and kissed his way higher until he found the pulse beating strongly right over the swelling curve. *Never be sorry for what you cannot change. I have you in my arms and that is enough.*

Natalya closed her eyes as his tongue swirled over her pulse. Her body throbbed and burned for him, but at the touch of his tongue, everything in her stilled. Waited, tense with need. His teeth sank deep and she cried out, clinging to him as the white-hot pain flashed through her and gave way to pure erotic pleasure. His hand cupped her breast, thumb sliding gently over her nipple while he fed from her pounding pulse.

He was nearly starved for her. For the essence of life. It all mingled together, his need of both. Hot. Sexual. He fought to stay centered when he wanted to lose himself in the lust and hunger. He heard the warning growl rumbling in his throat as the beast rose, fighting for supremacy, fighting to insist on the right to his lifemate. His body felt hard and painful but gloriously alive. He *felt*, his emotions and his cravings intense, so strong it shook him. He swept his tongue across the pinpricks at the top of her breast and pressed his lips across the creamy flesh.

They were bound together. Already his mind dwelt within hers. Their soul was shared, a complete bonding. He didn't want to wait for the joining of her body. Waiting went against every instinct, but he sensed she was not emotionally tied to him. If he lost himself in her body, could she call him back? Would she even try?

What is it? Natalya straightened, not bothering to drag her shirt over her exposed breasts. She felt dreamy, wanton, hungry to touch his skin, to taste him. Centuries old drive took over and she used the palms of her hands to inch his shirt up to bare his chest to her. She ran the pads of her fingers over his chest, traced his muscles, leaned forward to taste his skin. He cupped the back of her head and pressed her closer, his hips moving against her body in a slow seductive rhythm.

"I don't actually like to take blood. I do it only when necessary," she confided, her lips feathering against his chest. Her tongue stroked over his hammering pulse. Once. Twice. She heard him groan. "But I can't resist the way you taste."

Her Carpathian legacy demanded she survive by occasionally taking blood, but for the most part, she was able to resist the lure. Right now it didn't matter. Nothing mattered but the feel and taste of him. The lure of his body heat, the touch of his hands. She groaned softly and gave into the terrible addiction that seemed to have overtaken her. She *craved* him. She craved the feel and scent of him. His touch. His kiss. His body. She really wanted his body.

Her teeth sank deep and she felt him shiver with rising hunger. She wanted him. She would have him. She pressed her breasts against his chest, moved in a restless, enticing way, deliberately adding to the painful ache in his body. She felt him thicken, heard his breath leave his body in a rush. He tasted like nothing she'd ever experienced and it wasn't enough. She wanted it all. She flicked her tongue over the small pinpricks and stepped back, reaching to remove her shirt.

Behind Vikirnoff, the ground rippled as something raced beneath the dirt toward them. At once her ankles burned and hurt, just as if the creature that had dragged her below the surface had a hold of her again.

7

"**S**omething *moved under* the ground." Natalya jumped back and reached down to rub at her suddenly burning ankles. "Do you think it's that creature, the one that grabbed me?" She shuddered and backed up another step. "The ground did move, Vikirnoff, I saw it. Watch out. It might be after you. We *so* deserve this for acting like a couple of sex-starved teens in the late night movies."

Vikirnoff picked her up and settled her on the outcropping that had a half-inch crack zigzagging down the face of it. "I will be fine. You are obsessed with your movies, Natalya. I do not think viewing them has been a good influence on you."

"Well, I should have known better than to make out when *deadly peril* surrounded us. Please be careful. The

Troll King could burst through the ground any minute
now and take you to some disgusting lair. I'd have to rescue you again and . . ."

He shook his head, his faint intriguing smile capturing
her attention and wiping out all coherent thought before
she could finish. "Your imagination is running away with
you. Tell me what you want to do."

"I want to get the hell out of here, but I can't. I have to
go into the cave and get rid of this compulsion." She
caught at his shirt. "I know you're thinking of taking me
away from here, but I'd just have to come back and I'd
search without you. Please don't do that, Vikirnoff."

He studied the desperation in her eyes. "I know you
have this to do, Natalya. I am with you all the way. If
Freddie or Troll King try to bother you, I will keep them
off your back until this is finished."

Natalya let her breath out slowly, leaned forward and
brushed a kiss over his lips. "Get up on this rock with me
before that thing eats you alive."

His eyebrow shot up. "One of us has to be on the
ground to find the opening. I know it is here, somewhere
around this rock. We will have to be wary of traps. The
cave does not want us to enter it."

"Good luck to you then."

He laughed softly. "I thought you might say that."

"Yes, well, I'm the practical type."

Vikirnoff studied the niche and outcropping, pacing
back and forth around the front and sides of the boulder
several times. Natalya was right, not only was something

moving beneath the ground, but it was mimicking his every stride. The ground swelled slightly as if something large searched in serpentine motion just inches below the surface parallel to him each time he took a step. He also noticed, whenever he ceased to move, the creature raced to the boulder where Natalya was perched and remained still, melting back into the earth. The mist thickened around them, rolling in with cold blasts of air, but hovering to blanket the small peak, rather than continuing out in a path over the mountain as it should have. Voices howled and moaned and something dark and shadowy moved in the mist.

"Okay, this has gone way beyond spooky," Natalya said. "And I am *so* not putting my feet on the ground if there's a chance that hairy-armed, ice-pick-for-fingernails creature is anywhere near here." She looked around her, peered at the ground and rocks. "There has to be an entrance here. Why would it be so well-guarded if we aren't in the right spot?"

"The entrance is here," Vikirnoff agreed, keeping his eye on the moving soil. Small plants wiggled like worms as the thing beneath the ground disturbed them in its passing. "Do you see those rocks right there? The small ones? Do they look right to you?"

Natalya almost fell off the boulder as she leaned over the side. Vikirnoff steadied her with one hand at her waist. "They're set in a pattern, but . . ." Her voice drifted off.

"It's not quite right," he finished for her.

"Watch that thing," she pointed towards the shifting ground. "I think the rocks need to be put in a different order. More like this . . ." She reached down, still balanced on the boulder and nudged a rock out of the lineup to exchange with another three spaces over. She frowned in frustration, shook her head and leapt off the boulder to crouch down beside the smaller rocks. "This is it, Vikirnoff, the way to the entrance. I just have to rearrange the rocks into the right order."

Vikirnoff hunkered down beside her, close, where his body could shield hers, if necessary. He kept a wary eye on the churning, thickening mist, as well as continually scanning the ground.

"I've got it!" Natalya dropped the last rock in place with evident satisfaction.

The ground beside her hand erupted like a small geyser. A foul-smelling eel-like creature with spiked teeth bored straight at her fingers, emitting a high-pitched scream. Vikirnoff caught the serpent by the back of the neck, dragging the struggling body away from Natalya. The teeth snapped repeatedly, the body twisting frantically to get at her.

"Look out!" Vikirnoff warned as the ground around Natalya burst open in half a dozen places, the serpentine heads rocketing out of the holes straight at her from every direction. "Jump!" He flung the snake away from him and lifted his hands toward the sky. Lightning arced through the swirling mist, lighting the edges in fiery red tones.

Natalya didn't even care that his tone held both compulsion and command. She somersaulted onto the boulder and glared at the writhing creatures. "I detest snakes. Really, really detest them."

Lightning sizzled and cracked, a great whip slamming to earth, scorching the ground in a small circle. At once a stench rose, the foul creatures turned to ash. The blackened spiked teeth wiggled, as if alive, then disintegrated.

Natalya pressed her hand to her mouth and choked back a cry of alarm. "That was just gross. Totally disgusting. Never let those things near me again."

Vikirnoff studied her for a moment before realizing she was serious. He caught her in his arms and pulled her off the boulder. "You are shaking." Holding her close to the warmth of his body, he tightened his arms around her in an effort to bring her comfort. "You were not really afraid of those creatures, were you?"

"I *loathe* snakes." Natalya leaned in close, trying to get her knees to stiffen up. "I've always had an unreasonable fear of them."

"You kill vampires and destroy shadow warriors. You never even flinched when you faced either adversary." He caught her chin in his hand and bent his head to hers. "You are going to intrigue me for all time."

She put a hand on his chest with the idea of pushing him away. "And drive you to drink. Don't let's forget I annoy you." She couldn't afford to be distracted. And Vikirnoff was very distracting. "And we're in *deadly peril*. I refuse to be a too-stupid-to-live teenager necking while the snakes return."

He hadn't budged an inch, his skin touching hers, body heat warming her. "I had forgotten." His smile was slow and sexy and took her breath somewhere other than her lungs. "Completely."

She looked up at him with a small frown. "We're in the middle of a siege here. Those things were going after *me* this time, not you."

"I noticed. Why would that be, do you think?" He dropped his hands reluctantly and surveyed the crack in the boulder that was significantly wider. "We will have to do a little maneuvering to slip through."

Natalya recovered her pack and checked her weapons, avoiding looking at the blackened remains of the serpents. "I'm the one under compulsion. Maybe someone brought me here to kill me."

"Too much trouble, Natalya. Why not make it easy and kill you when you are asleep somewhere? Why lead you to the mountains, to this particular cave?" Vikirnoff stuck his head in the crack. "This is very narrow, but it widens a bit once past this section." He thinned his body and crawled inside the jagged crack.

Natalya glanced at the sky as the wind rose in a shriek of rage, of protest. Clouds boiled angrily and inside their depths she could see dark figures moving. Smoky. Gray. Transparent. She closed her eyes briefly and sent up a silent prayer the clouds were not spawning shadow warriors for her to fight again. She'd been very lucky in sending the warrior back to realm of the dead, but it didn't mean it would happen again. She knew in the realm of magick spells could be altered easily.

"Hand me your pack." Vikirnoff reached back for it.

"I'll carry it. I prefer to have everything I need close." Natalya followed him into the cave. It was so narrow, the sides scraped her back as she slipped through the opening and made her way into the slightly larger hall. Although the tunnel was wider, she had to stoop, then crawl, as she followed Vikirnoff deeper into the cavern.

Behind them the rocks rolled out of the pattern and scattered around the cave entrance. The jagged crack slammed closed with a grinding of rock, leaving them trapped inside the mountain. Natalya treated Vikirnoff to a litany of curses.

"Can you see?"

"I have excellent vision in the dark," she replied. The ceiling dropped lower and lower until she had no choice but to move forward on her stomach. "Those snakes had just better stay outside." She was so thankful he was there with her. Her nerve endings still prickled with awareness of the spiked teeth coming so close to her hand.

"We will be all right," he assured.

"I didn't say anything," she objected.

"Your heart is pounding. Listen to the rhythm of mine and match the beat."

Natalya did so, allowing her heart to settle into a more natural rhythm. "You didn't tell me what you found in my memories. I dislike not being in control and I can't overcome the compulsion to come to this cave. Believe me, I've tried. I'm a firm believer in avoiding trouble if at all possible and this place is definitely trouble, but I couldn't stop myself from coming here. That really disturbs me."

"I have to agree, I do not like it either, but I feel the need very strong in you. It is why I did not forbid you to do this."

She ground her teeth together. "If I were you, I'd choose my words very carefully. I'm behind you with a knife in my hand. If you plan on spending any time at all around me, strike words like 'forbid' and 'allow' from your vocabulary."

"Those words offend you in some way?"

"You know very well they do and you probably use them on purpose just to get a rise out of me."

"It works very well."

"Well, stop. I'm being serious. We're crawling through this mountain with mutant snakes with big teeth coming through the ground at us, so how about a truce."

"I can feel cool air," he reported. "It has to be coming from a subterranean chamber."

"Is it cold enough to freeze snakes?"

"I will not *allow* a snake to attack you again. Should one try I will *forbid* it to do so." There was laughter in his voice.

She felt a tug on her heart. She'd never heard him really laugh before. "Ha ha, you're suddenly a comedian, and not a very good one at that." She could listen to his voice forever when he sounded like that. She cleared her throat. "Are you going to tell me what you found in my memories? Or was it too awful?"

Vikirnoff heard the small note of fear. "The memories of your grandfather are very confusing, Natalya. I cannot tell if they are dreams, or actual memories any more than you can. There is little doubt someone has tampered with your memories, but I cannot tell why or how. Any trail of Xavier is dull, veiled or ended abruptly in a dark void. I found little of your childhood with your brother. In fact all of your younger years are fragments of memories. I do not know what it means, but we will find out." He projected confidence into his voice, knowing she had been disturbed by her lack of recollections for some time. "What happens when you try to remember things?"

"I feel upset, nervous, you know, and that's just not like me. I get an instant headache and my stomach hurts." She knew it was a planted reaction, she had known all along, but it was good to be able to confirm it with someone. More than that, there was comfort in being able to discuss her fears with someone else.

Vikirnoff paused and glanced back at her. "You have obviously been suspicious that your grandfather has been alive for some time and you believe that he has something to do with your memory loss." He chose his words carefully. "If he has deceived you and tampered with your memory, why do you persist in believing the Carpathian people are just as evil as the vampire?"

"I've been told all my life Carpathians would murder me just for bearing the symbol of the dragon."

"*Who* told you?" Vikirnoff persisted. "You say all of your life, yet your memories are fragmented. Is it possible the warning is something that was planted in you as well?" He kept his voice as neutral as possible.

"I am certain my father is the one to tell me this first."

"But you do not know, Natalya. The symbol on your body is of a very old and revered *Carpathian* lineage. No Carpathian would harm a Dragonseeker." Vikirnoff ducked his head and made his body smaller and more compact. "This tunnel has sharp angles making it difficult to maneuver," he warned. "Watch your head."

Natalya pulled her head out of the way of a low hanging rock. "They wouldn't? Then why would a hunter *murder* my brother?"

"It had to be a vampire posing as a hunter. No Carpathian would harm someone bearing the mark of the Dragonseeker," he reiterated hoping if he said it enough times she would at least begin to entertain the idea that the warning could have been planted.

He whistled softly as the hall opened into a larger chamber. "This opens up into a much larger gallery. You'll be able to stand up straight." He turned back to help her. The drip of water from every wall was constant. Almost with the rhythm of a heartbeat, as if the caverns were alive. Vikirnoff felt uneasy, feeling the weight of eyes on them, yet scanning, he could find no danger to them. Something guarded the caves, yet he could not ferret out the unseen sentinel with his increasingly powerful probing.

"My memories," she said again as she studied the finger-like formations surrounding a large abyss that yawned open in the middle of the chamber. "That looks a long way down." She lifted her gaze to his face with some dismay. "We're going down there, aren't we?"

"You are the leader of the expedition," he pointed out. "What direction does your tuning fork indicate?"

She heaved a sigh. "Down. We have to go down. Into that." She pointed to the black hole below them. It was icy cold and she shivered. "I need to know now, Vikirnoff, what else did you find?" If Vikirnoff had recovered valuable information that in some way was damaging to her family, she could always remove his memory of it.

"You believe you can erase *my* memories?"

The distaste in his voice was a severe chastisement. Natalya hadn't meant for him to catch that thought, and it really bothered her that she couldn't always feel him merged with her. "I don't mean it like that."

"How else if not disrespect? You want my help. You are willing to use me, but you have every intention of tampering with *my* memories."

"I shared my misgivings with you. I haven't shared that with anyone else." Natalya sighed. "In all honesty, Vikirnoff, I don't know what to think anymore. I feel like someone has been running around messing with my head and now you're there, too. Why can't I block you out if I'm so powerful and strong? Why am I so vulnerable to invasion?"

There was real fear in her voice and he didn't blame her. She was powerful and she should have been totally protected, but something had left her mind open to attack. In spite of the fact that he was angry with her, his heart went out to her. "Have vampires ever been able to draw you to them?"

She shook her head. "No." She frowned. "Wait. I've noticed I've had a much more difficult time with their voices, hearing their real voice and seeing past the illusion they wear recently."

"About the same time the compulsion to find the caves began?"

She looked confused. "I don't know. My head is beginning to ache again and I'm freezing." She rubbed her arms in an effort to get warm. "You don't even appear cold."

"I am sorry. I should have been paying attention to your comfort." Before she could protest, he gathered her into his arms, equipment and all, and breathed on her. At once warmth stole through her body, surrounded her like a great cocoon so that the shivering stopped and her teeth ceased chattering.

"Much better, thank you," she said and circled his neck as he stepped off the cavern floor into the dark abyss below them.

Vikirnoff was acutely aware of her soft body pressed

tightly against his, and her misery over their conversation. She was very distressed over her lack of memory and she'd been holding her fears in for years, unable to discuss them with anyone. He brushed a kiss on top of her head in a gesture meant to reassure her.

Vikirnoff settled them onto the floor of the chamber. They had descended close to two hundred feet. The sound of the dripping water was even louder, a pulsing heartbeat that felt more ominous than right. His gaze slid alertly around the ice-cold chamber, probing every possible place of concealment. He kept a cloak of heat around Natalya to help regulate her body temperature. "I do not like the feel of this place."

"Me, neither, but it's beautiful, isn't it?" Natalya said. She dug a glow stick from her pack and held it up. "I swear there are veins of gold in here." She turned in a circle holding the stick high to help illuminate the large gallery. "I've never seen such beautiful ice formations. All of these openings lead to halls and more galleries. This is amazing. Like a great crystal palace."

Vikirnoff went still. He had heard those words long ago to describe the great cave of the dark mage. *A great crystal palace with a burning flame in the center of one room, a palace of gemstones and gold.* He stared at the ice formation rising up in the center of the room. Depending on the angle, the formation appeared polished diamond bright, or looked exactly like a brilliant red-orange flame. When Natalya played the light over it, scattered gems seem to glow from the very center of it.

"Natalya." There was warning in his voice. He waited until she looked at him. "I think this is the cave of the dark mage. The one used for study and experiments. I think this is his place of power." *There would be guards. Powerful, deadly guards.* He listened to the sound of the water again, the relentless pulse taking on new meaning.

She bit her lip hard. It wasn't hard to believe that he was right, and that meant the caves would be strewn with what would amount to landmines. "Even in death, Xavier would never leave his cave unguarded. It would hold too many of his secrets. So what you're saying is, we've stumbled into the lion's den."

"That would be about it." He moved to cover her, keeping his body between hers and the walls of the cavern. "If he is alive and he was the one to tamper with your memories, why would he lure you here? What would be his purpose?"

"That is the burning question, isn't it? The vampires want me, you want me, maybe my dead-or-alive grandfather wants me. I'm just a popular woman." She shrugged and sent him a faint grin, using humor to keep her courage up.

His heart reacted, shifting and melting in his chest. He frowned. It was uncomfortable being so susceptible to her. He could not remember a time in his life when sentiment or emotion swayed his judgment. Right now, his every instinct screamed they were in danger and he needed to scoop her up and run for the surface. He could read fear in the depths of her eyes, but she had steel in her and she wasn't about to leave until she had a few answers.

He forced down his natural protective inclination and tried to find a way to aid her, one that might get them out of the trap as soon as possible. And he was very certain the cave was a giant trap. "What can you do aside from the obvious charms and skills you have, that might make you so valuable to the vampires? Or to your grandfather?"

"I have no idea. I'm good with spells. I can find things. I honestly don't know, Vik." She sent him a quick look from under long lashes.

"Vik?" He winced visibly and his eyebrow shot up. "You are not going to call me Vik. I am considering using one of the words you have stricken from my vocabulary."

Her eyes sparkled at him. She turned her body in the direction she could feel the strongest tug. "We have to go that way." She indicated a hallway that was little more than a tunnel.

He groaned. "How did I know you were going to choose that one?"

She reached for his hand with obvious reluctance, but needing the contact. "I feel the subtle vibration of power. Do you feel it?" Her voice trembled.

"Yes," he answered tersely. "Let us get this done." He squeezed her fingers in reassurance. "Be careful, Natalya. I will follow you." He didn't want to tell her he was certain there were a couple of vampires stalking them. The undead were still a distance away, but he feared she was somehow imprinted with something that drew vampires to her. "Have you been here before?"

"No, never." She frowned, searching her memories. "It's so frustrating to remember bits and pieces. I've studied thousands of spells. I've read ancient text, and can remember all of it, but I can't remember *where* I studied. In my dreams, Razvan would protect me from the teacher. He would be punished when I refused to go work. In my dreams I remember what my grandfather looked like, but I couldn't describe him to you now. How do I know what is real or not?"

Frustrated, Natalya turned back to the tunnel to keep him from seeing her expression. What did she know about her childhood? What if everything was a lie? Memories removed and others planted. The idea of it sickened her. "Great." She couldn't help feeling humiliated and ashamed that Vikirnoff had seen the inside of her mind and the trauma of a blank void. "I'm a freakin' robot."

"With a beautiful backside," he pointed out when she dropped to her hands and knees, head disappearing into the ice hall.

She wiggled her bottom suggestively and grinned back at him, grateful to him for giving her something to laugh about.

His heart nearly stopped beating and the air left his lungs in a burning rush. She could have lit up the entire cavern with her high wattage smile. Thunder roared in his ears. Deep inside, his demon struggled for release and unexpectedly, desire shot through his body. Not the intense lust he experienced earlier, but something bright and passionate and deep that came, not from his groin, but from his heart.

"You don't have to come with me," Natalya said, forcing the words out as she looked back at him. He had gone so still, his expression carved in stone. How could he want to be mixed up with whatever was happening? The fact was, she was terrified of the cave. Something she couldn't even remember from her childhood warned her she was in danger and the increasing volume of the dripping water was nearly driving her out of her mind. Every instinct told her to run, but her body and brain refused to obey the command.

She had longed for a partner, someone to share her life with, but for the first time she *needed* to be with someone. And not just anyone. Vikirnoff. Not just for his fighting skills, but for the sheer comfort of his presence. And that was almost as frightening as the situation she was in.

Vikirnoff exuded power and confidence. She couldn't imagine anyone defeating him, not when he was at full strength. *But he wasn't at full strength*. The thought came out of nowhere. She realized that not once had she worried about his physical condition since they'd been in the cave. He wasn't fully healed. She had seen the agony on his face on more than one occasion earlier, yet he carried himself as if nothing was wrong. Had he been subtly influencing her or was she really that selfish? She groaned softly.

"I am with you because I want to be. I am not under

compulsion, Natalya. And I am fit enough to protect you should there be need."

She turned away from him before he could see her re-action to his words—his voice. There was just something about the man that called to her. She crawled through the twisting ice tube until it began to widen and opened into another series of galleries. The ice formations and columns were impressive. Following her instincts she chose one chamber and discovered streaks of old blood along the ice wall. Her own blood ran cold and she stood gaping at the thick, frozen clots clinging to the wall. "This doesn't look good, does it?"

Vikirnoff put a hand on her shoulder. She wasn't used to being touched and she trembled in response, but didn't shrug him off. "You can see where they put ice picks through him to hold him to the wall." He touched the frozen blood. "There was a Carpathian being tortured in this chamber." He examined the entire room. "It was not within the last week. Someone rescued him, human I think, and at least one vampire died here." He sighed. "Why would a vampire risk coming into the cave of the dark mage?"

"Secrets? Power?"

"Maybe. But is it worth the risk? There have to be traps scattered everywhere. The vampires are looking for something. There is no other explanation." He glanced around warily. "I can feel something watching us, can't you?"

She wanted to deny it, but the back of her neck prickled with alarm. "Yes. The vampires think I can help them find whatever they are looking for, don't they?" Natalya said. "That's why Arturo said he had a small task for me. He wants me to find something, probably something the dark mage left behind."

"Anything Xavier had of power would be deadly to the entire world, not just our species, if a vampire wielded it."

"Can you tell where the others got out? The ones that killed the vampire?" She pointed to a solid wall of ice. "Because I want to go there."

Vikirnoff examined the wall. "A Carpathian closed a slide tube behind them. I still feel the power lingering."

"Can you open the slide?"

He studied the bluish wall of ice. "Yes." He knew he sounded grim. He felt the weight of the ice over them, the pressing of their enemies closing in and more than all of that, the certainty that they were going somewhere far worse than where they were. He hesitated, the need to get his lifemate to safety hammering at him. He actually settled his fingers around her wrist in protest.

Natalya shook her head. "I really have no choice, Vikirnoff."

Swearing under his breath, he found the original opening, the tube slide that led to the lower caverns, and commanded the ice to bend to his will. Even within the cave of the dark mage, he wielded power over the things of the earth. The ice shifted, parting, to once again form the slide leading to the lower chambers.

"Thank you," Natalya said. She didn't have words to express how grateful she was that he didn't fight her on the issue. She had the same warning bells shrieking at her and she sensed he was forced to fight age-old instincts. His protective nature simply did not allow him to see her in danger without shielding her. And without him, she had no idea how she would have made her way through the ice to the lower chambers.

"We go in together," he decreed.

She sent him a black scowl, just to warn him to back off with the orders, but didn't mind in the least when he wrapped her in warm, safe arms and climbed into the cold of the ice chute. Vikirnoff pushed off and they slid deeper into the freezing world of blue and crystal ice, spiraling fast down the long, cold tube. His arms kept her from ice splinters and the thicker, jagged crystalline protrusions that hung above their heads. It was breathtakingly beautiful, yet utterly frightening in that she knew the formation was unnatural.

Natalya felt a little dizzy by the time they reached the bottom and she held onto Vikirnoff until she knew her legs would support her. In a narrow hall of ice they both were able to stand up straight without fear of hitting their heads on the ceiling.

"Are you all right?" Vikirnoff kept his arm around her until her legs stopped shaking.

She shook her head. "I feel strange. Afraid. I'm not

usually afraid all the time. My heart is pounding so loud it's hurting my ears. And I feel sick to my stomach. Worse"—she looked up at him as she pressed her hand against her body, low, to the left, just below her stomach— "the dragon burns. A vampire is close."

"Ahead or behind us?" He was already scanning, as he had been since they'd entered the ice caves and was dismayed to find he couldn't locate the vampire. And that meant it wasn't Arturo. Arturo couldn't hide his presence from the hunter. He sent up a silent prayer that he wouldn't be facing a master vampire when he was already wounded.

"I can't tell." She began to jog, hurrying through the tunnel.

The hall ended abruptly, the floor dropping away to a great abyss. Vikirnoff caught her before she ran off the edge of the precipice. He held her against him. "That was close."

Natalya stared at the ice bridge glittering so invitingly. The structure was made of ice and stone, very narrow and had several holes in it. The bridge appeared to be the only way across. She frowned, gesturing toward the gaping holes. "I'm not going to set one foot on that thing." She grinned up at him. "I knew you were going to come in handy."

"Are you expecting me to carry you?" He lifted an eyebrow.

"Without a doubt. We go to the other side."

Vikirnoff reached for her, gathered her close. Natalya

wished it felt impersonal, but his touch was electric, heat coursing through her body, making her acutely aware of him, aware of the definition of every muscle in his body as she leaned into his strength. It seemed natural to be in his arms and his body was familiar. Perfect. She fit exactly. She closed her eyes and savored the feeling of him being so close as they moved together through the air to the other side of the cave.

Vikirnoff was careful, holding her even as he settled onto the ice floor, looking cautiously around before allowing her feet to touch the ground. "I feel the level of danger elevating. Hurry, Natalya. Find what you must and let us leave this place."

Natalya didn't need him to prompt her. She wanted out of the cave more than he could possibly know. She hurried through the chamber, past a small alcove and turned back abruptly. She held a glow stick high so that it shone on the wall of ice. Her breath caught in her throat. "Vikirnoff," she whispered. "Look."

Scales covered the body of an enormous creature. A long serpentine neck supported a wedge-shaped head. The extended tail ended in a spike and the wings were folded in close along the body. Sharp claws, made for rending and tearing, looked as if they had been digging in the ice as if trying to scrape free. One beautiful eye, a sparkling vivid emerald green stared at them hopelessly through the thick wall of ice.

"A dragon, Vikirnoff. How would a dragon be trapped in the wall like that?" She wanted to weep for the creature. She put her hand on the ice, fingers spread wide, right over the claw as if to hold it close to her. "Who would do this to a dragon?" She couldn't look away from that one, brilliant eye.

"Not one, but two." His voice was grim. He peered closer. "There is a second one, side by side with the first. You can see the outline of the leg and claw."

Natalya pressed against the wall, until her nose turned blue. Unconsciously, her fingernails dug at the ice, trying to get to the mythical creatures. "This isn't right, Vikirnoff." She wanted to weep. Her chest burned and felt too tight. "Can we get them out?"

His hands were gentle as he pulled her away from the wall of ice. "Is this what you are after? More than one vampire are now seeking us. I feel the presence of Arturo and several others. Unfortunately, I worry more about the ones I cannot feel. I sense the presence of evil, but cannot tell where it is. We cannot take a chance of removing a wall of ice this thick without the entire mountain coming down on us and even if we could, we do not have the necessary time."

"I wish I had come for the dragons. This is just not right. I had no idea dragons were real."

"They are and they are not." He turned her away from the ice tomb. "You are much too sensitive. Your grief is as strong as it is unexpected." And her compassion only endeared her to him more. He tugged on her until she followed him. "Which way?"

Natalya took the lead again. The hall opened into a

gallery. Tall columns of intricately carved, Gothic-style architecture rose to the high cathedral ceiling. Crystals and ice pillars formed two rows of columns down the room, each holding several round globes of various colors.

Natalya stopped abruptly. "This is the place. I'm supposed to come here, to this room. Don't touch anything, Vikirnoff. There are traps everywhere. I can feel them." She paced a distance down the wide-open room and then returned to him. Mythical creatures rose up from the floor in life-size sculptures made of clear crystal. Blood red pyramids made of stone gleamed from chiseled archways in the walls. If she stared too long at one of the many spheres, it came alive, swirling and changing color, trying to draw an unwary victim to the intense beauty.

On the floor, beneath the ice were strange squares, pyramids and starburst patterns of stones. In the center of each shape were hieroglyphics, pictures carved deep into the rock. "This is the way out," Natalya said. "They had to have an escape hole and the shapes have to be stepped on in a certain pattern to open the stone above the stairs."

"You have really never been here before?"

Small lines appeared around her mouth and across her forehead as she tried to reach into her memories. "I may have dreamt of this place. My father told me of the cave and the ice stairs leading the way out. He warned me not to touch anything until I was certain . . ." she trailed off, her gaze suddenly meeting Vikirnoff's. "It was my father.

He set up the compulsion for me to come here. He must have."

"Why would he put you in such danger?" Vikirnoff watched her pace restlessly through the huge room, examining objects on display. A tall rack of weapons in a shallow alcove caught her eye, but after a moment she moved on, as if driven to find a single item.

"I don't know, but it must be important." Distracted, she moved slowly up and down the room, trying to tune herself to the right direction. She didn't have a clue what she was looking for and her dragon birthmark was burning with alarm. She pressed her hand over it, trying to stop the warning. "I think the vampires are close."

Vikirnoff scanned continually throughout the network of caves, looking for anything that would tell him where the vampire was. It was close. He had an instinct for the undead, and right now his warning system was blaring an alert. The sound of the water was even louder. Normally he could tone down the volume, but the continual dripping was a drumbeat, echoing throughout the network of caves. Calling to something. Awakening something. The deeper they had come into the caverns, the louder and more insistent the dripping water.

The sound of water swelled until it was a booming pulse, a constant irritating reminder they were trapped beneath hundreds of feet of ice. Vikirnoff glanced toward the small pool forming at the base of one of the columns. The pool should have been a clear liquid, but it was discolored, a faint rusty-brown. Like mud. Or old blood. Drops of water ran down the column and fell into the puddle. With each drop the surface shook. The shock waves seemed to travel outward to encompass the chamber itself so that cavern shook slightly with each drop.

Something glittered in the depths of the puddle, something dark and lurking just below the murky surface. Peering down into the oily mess, Natalya thought something stared back at her with red, glowing eyes. A dark shadow slithered through the rusty-brown waters. She jumped back. "That can't be good."

"Get away from there," Vikirnoff warned. "Whoever or whatever the water is calling, we want no part of."

Natalya moved closer to the collection of spheres. One glittering crystal globe, a full foot in diameter, rested on a tower of black obsidian. Natalya held out her hands, palms not touching the crystal, but shaping the curve of the globe. At once she felt the tremendous drawing as it leapt to life at her close proximity.

Can you feel that? The heat? She tried to pull back, but couldn't look away. Mists swirled inside, pulling her—drawing her—commanding her to take hold.

Natalya, no! But Vikirnoff's warning was too late. Even as he leapt forward to pull her away from the crystal ball, she grasped it in both hands.

8

Natalya screamed, the sound of agony ripping through the long ice cavern. Her fingers welded to the crystal ball, burning until she thought her skin would peel back to the bone.

Vikirnoff leapt to pull her back, but her voice protested in his mind. *No! You cannot touch me. It is consuming me. It cannot take you, too, or I have no way back.*

Swearing aloud he dropped his hands to his sides. It took every ounce of discipline he possessed to keep from yanking her into his arms. Breathing deep, ignoring the constant sound of the water booming and echoing through the chamber, he concentrated on holding Natalya's essence to him.

I can't do this. It burns, Vikirnoff. I can't think because of the pain.

He felt agony sweeping through her body, the wrenching at her bones and flesh, as if the ball drew her out of the world she inhabited and into the turbulence of the crystal globe itself. Setting his teeth, he took the brunt of the pain from her. Immediately his skin beaded with blood and it dripped from his brow into his eyes. *You are both Carpathian and mage. You command the earth and the air and you are unusually strong. Get what you came for and get out.*

Natalya took a deep breath as the pain lessened. It was the confidence in his voice, the respect he afforded her, that allowed her to go beyond her physical body and reach for her mage training. Her body was nothing, a shell, no more than that. Her spirit was stronger than the whirling winds tearing at her flesh. She rose above the pain, above the terror and found her strength.

Colors swirled around her, midnight blues, glittering stars, streaks of light like comets trailing across the sky. Galaxies and star systems shot by her at a dizzying speed, twined together briefly and arced apart with a shower of sparks falling like rain. She found herself staring in wonder, in awe, aware the future lay in that direction. She could find a thread, one that was hers and follow it and know what was waiting. The temptation was strong. It was dazzlingly beautiful, impressive and the idea of knowing what lay ahead was difficult to resist.

Throughout the midnight blue sky lightning forked repeatedly, flashing like a neon sign, drawing her attention. She realized she was being pulled in that direction, her spirit traveling along one of the zigzagging threads. She pulled back. At once the draw fought with her, tugging and tugging, beguiling her with glimpses of her future. She steadfastly refused to look, instinctively fearing once pulled into the realm of the future, she might not find her way back. And what she sought could not possibly lie in that direction.

Ropes of various colored pearls whirled around her, carried by the power of the winds. One in particular caught her attention because of the unusual color, the same cloudy hues that glittered in her eyes when the tigress in her was rising toward the surface. She watched them even as she fought the strength of the wind. Her father had often compared her eyes to sea pearls.

Natalya reached for the strand that resembled the color of her tiger eyes. A turbulent vortex gripped her, sucked her into the whirling mass. Clutching the rope of pearls tightly, Natalya clung to the merge she held with Vikirnoff. He was her anchor and wherever her spirit traveled, he traveled with her holding guard over her physical body.

Scenes of battles rushed past her. Dark, ugly visions of blood and death. She wept, overcome with the useless deaths as men fought for religion or power or land. Natalya fought to keep from sliding farther into the vacuum of the past. Small, black shadows tugged at the edges of her spirit in an attempt to consume her. The voices of mages whose souls had been trapped in the endless cycle of the past wailed at her in warning, in sorrow.

She might have lost herself in the terrible pain of reliving so many deaths, seeing the mistakes made over and over throughout history, but Vikirnoff was always there, murmuring encouragement, holding her tightly without physical form.

Soren. She'd nearly missed him in all the history swirling around her, but there he was. Her father, tall and handsome with his black hair and vivid green eyes. Her heart turned over and she reached for him. She couldn't touch him. Natalya realized she was looking at him through a reflection. He turned and her heart nearly stopped. He was ravaged and worn with pain. Burned on one side, encased in ice on the other. He had been tortured, yet kept alive, his blood draining from his body in a long tube.

Father! She screamed it—tried frantically to reach him, but he shook his head and looked straight at her. His eyes clouded and she could see a knife reflected there. It was obviously ancient, ceremonial, the handle studded with gems, the blade slightly curved. The knife spun, pointed at her, turned again so that she could see it from every angle. *You want me to find the knife.* For a moment the vision held and then the knife wavered and was gone. His gaze dropped to his hands. She saw that he was holding a huge tome. An ancient spell book. It was closed, the cover etched in dark reddish brown stains. *The book is important.*

A shadowy figure, the man she recognized from her childhood nightmares loomed over Soren. Instinctively Natalya pulled back. Movement must have caught the eye of her father's tormenter, because she saw the dark shape turn toward her and heard a slow hiss of rage. She felt the icy breath of death on her and her spirit trembled.

Graphic images of her father being tortured overwhelmed her. Vivid details of her mother being devoured by vampires followed. Of her father finding her mother, his grief so deep he was nearly insane. Each explicit vignette was in horrifying detail, each worse than the one before until she was paralyzed with grief and horror. She felt the darker shadows tugging and pulling and drawing her to them, but she couldn't move, couldn't break away. Evil laughter echoed. Something clawed at her mind, raked at her.

Natalya! Come to me now! Vikirnoff issued the command with every bit of power he possessed. Her body had begun to fade. It started on her arms, as if something was taking bites of flesh from her, replacing her skin with a thin opaque shell. She was becoming translucent, a ghostly image rather than a flesh-and-blood body.

Fear nearly consuming him, Vikirnoff plunged his mind into hers. Ainaak enyém, *I will not let you go. They cannot have you. You are* ainaak sívamet jutta, *forever to my heart connected. Come to me now, Natalya, your lifemate commands this.*

Guilt and fear warred with self-preservation, but the power of her lifemate was incredible, even there in the realm of past and present. In the midst of a living storm, with the fury of the wind tearing at her, Natalya turned to Vikirnoff. The reassuring warmth of his presence enveloped her, his memories, his character, the way he thought and acted. His integrity and strength of purpose. She focused on his steadfastness. For the first time she was happy that they were connected, that his strength of will could be added to her own.

I can't make myself leave my father.

She couldn't find her way back. She was too exhausted, too tired of being alone. Her father and mother and Razvan were all here, in this place. She could stay with them, be with them. So many years had gone by with her moving from country to country with no one to talk to, no one to share with. What awaited her but endless loneliness if she returned?

It is another lure, Natalya, an attempt to cloud your thinking. You belong with me. Your father would not want you trapped here with him. You cannot save him. What was done cannot be undone. Come with me, ainaak enyém, *merge and become one with me.* Vikirnoff used every art he possessed. Beguiling her. Compulsion. Seduction. Commanding— all wrapped together in his softly spoken words, dragging her back up the strands of time through the sheer strength of character and will he had come to possess over so many centuries.

She heard a roar of fury as she moved away from her father and his tormenter, from the tearing claws of the smaller dark shadows, climbing ever higher. The shadows streaked after her, reaching with hands and claws in an attempt to stop her and as she approached her own time, dazzling white orbs spun and beckoned, attempting to lure her with glimpses of the future.

Natalya clung tighter to Vikirnoff, crawling deeper into his mind where she knew she would be safe. Vikirnoff would never abandon her. She closed her mind to the all too-vivid memory of her father's tortured death and embraced life in her own time, whatever that might be. She didn't need to stay in the past. She chose the here and now.

Natalya found herself back in her own body, so weak she would have collapsed onto the floor of the ice cave if Vikirnoff hadn't caught her to him. They clung to one another, Natalya shuddering violently and Vikirnoff trembling with the knowledge he'd nearly lost her.

Tears poured down her face. "My father." She could barely get the words out, her throat was so raw with grief. "He was tortured."

"I know, *ainaak enyém*." His voice was tender as he stroked her hair, seeking a way to comfort her. "I am so sorry." She hadn't just seen her father's torture; she had experienced it. "I would give anything to prevent you having to go through that." He framed her face with his hands and kissed her tears away.

Natalya looked up at his face, the smears of blood on his forehead, the tracks of blood-red tears on his face. He'd shared the same experience and he'd also shared her wild grief and outrage. She wiped his brow with gentle fingers, touched the tear tracks and leaned into him. "Thank you for being with me."

"Always, Natalya." All the while he was comforting her, he was aware that the boom of the water had grown frantic, so loud the ice chamber shook. He eyed the rusty pool that was growing with each drop, not deeper, but spreading out like a giant stain. "We have to leave this place now, Natalya." Attacking the pool without knowing what he faced in a cavern full of magick could be suicide.

She took a breath, her fingers digging into his arm for support. "I have to find the knife. You saw it. You were in my mind. I have to get the knife." She glanced around the ice chamber. "The alcove has a huge cache of weapons. It's the most likely place."

"You have got to hurry. The vampires are nearly on us. We are going to have to fight our way out of here," he cautioned.

He clamped down hard against his natural protective instincts to snatch her up and get her away from danger. He was beginning to realize having a lifemate was difficult. Living with her wasn't about what he wanted, or even needed. Being a lifemate was about supporting Natalya even when everything in him wanted something else. Her personality required a certain amount of freedom and it didn't always matter what he deemed best.

He knew she had to complete this task. And now, when it was apparent her father had been tortured and murdered, it was more important than ever. He guarded her back, moving with her across the floor of ice, eyes scanning the great chamber.

"My heart is beginning to beat with the same rhythm

as the water dripping," Natalya confided in a whisper. "And that's just freaky." She kept her gaze fixed on the small alcove containing the cache of weapons. She knew the vampires were close. The dragon on her body seemed to be burning a hole through her skin.

"My heart is doing the same thing, Natalya," Vikirnoff said. "And when I pulled you away from the shadows, the bubbling in that puddle took on an entire new meaning."

Natalya glanced at the thick rusty puddle. "It looks like a witches brew." Her gaze went right back to the weapons, drawn by something outside of herself. Her breath caught in her lungs and she stopped abruptly. "I see the knife."

"Can you get to it?"

"Yes, but doubt I'll just be able to grab the thing."

Vikirnoff shifted his attention to the west wall down near the floor where the ice was melting at an alarming rate. Insects poured into the chamber, a mass exodus of crickets and beetles and every cave-dwelling bug imaginable. "We are going to have company any minute, Natalya, do what you have to do and let us leave this place." He positioned himself between his lifemate and the rapidly melting ice.

"Keep them off of me for a few minutes," she replied. "I have to figure this out." Unlocking the safeguards around the ceremonial knife required concentration, something difficult when the steady drip of the water was echoing through her brain and jangling every nerve. Even her blood seemed to jump as each drop fell into the ever-widening puddle. The insects would have been a terrible distraction, but they were rushing through the chamber to get away from something far worse following them.

Natalya moved her hands in a complicated pattern, murmuring a simple uncloaking spell her father had taught her in her early childhood. Knowing her father had drawn her to the cave made it easier to solve the puzzles. He would use safeguards specific to her. And the uncloaking spell was one of the things she recalled from her earliest memory of him. The invisible barrier shimmered into view. She studied it from every angle.

Vikirnoff hissed a soft warning to Natalya as mud and water burst through the west wall, spilling onto the floor carrying a wiggling mass of spike-toothed serpentine creatures. Right behind them Arturo and a second vampire stepped into the ice chamber. As if sensing the presence of fellow evil, the rusty puddle on the floor of the cavern erupted into a boiling mass of noxious, thick bubbles.

Vikirnoff whirled into motion, calling on fire, fashioning a whip of flames to snap at the serpents racing toward Natalya. The fire whip whistled through the air, a dazzling orange-red messenger of death, lashing the creatures in a display of expertise. The smell of burning flesh added to the putrid brew of the puddle.

You don't believe in niceties, do you? Natalya asked.

Get it done. More are coming.

Natalya forced her attention back to the barrier. Vikirnoff had dealt with the snakes in a rather spectacular and efficient way. After sharing such a deep mind merge with him, she had absolute faith that he'd hold off the vampires until she had what she'd come for. There was no give in Vikirnoff. He'd fight for her with his last dying breath. As strong as the compulsion was for her to complete her task, his protective instincts were stronger. If necessary, he would get to her safety.

Natalya took a deep, calming breath and let it out, focusing wholly on the box the uncloaking spell had revealed. The box seemed solid. A transparent rectangle surrounding the knife. Cautiously, she put her palm close to it. Heat and power blasted her skin and she hastily pulled her hand back.

Vikirnoff cracked the flaming whip at the vampire Arturo had thrust in front of him. The whip curled around the lesser vampire's neck and as Vikirnoff tugged hard, the whip dragged him closer.

The vampire screamed, the high-pitched sound shattering several stalactites so that they dropped like spears from the ceiling, straight at Vikirnoff. He dissolved, throwing up a hasty shield around Natalya as he streamed past the lesser vampire and went straight for Arturo, shifting back into his natural form immediately.

"Get the woman, Cezar!" Arturo ordered, stumbling backward at the sudden attack.

Natalya felt the protective cloak surround her on three sides and sent up a small prayer of thanks that Vikirnoff, in his haste, hadn't closed her off from the knife. She pressed her palms together tightly, raised them in ceremony, murmured a short, but powerful spell of protection and pointed her fingers straight at the exact middle of the box. With her hands pressed tightly together, she pushed forward resolutely, straight into the center of the barricade, pulling her hands apart as she did so to part the obstruction and allow her access to the ceremonial knife. She felt the incredible heat close around her, but the protection spell held and she reached for the gem-studded handle.

Vikirnoff drove his fist straight through Arturo's chest, slamming hard, fingers going through the bony shield toward the shriveled heart. The vampire howled, bent his head and sank his teeth into Vikirnoff's neck, slicing through skin and tissue, artery and nerves. Vikirnoff grasped the blackened heart, ripping it from the vampire's chest just as Natalya gripped the ceremonial knife.

The moment Natalya's fingers settled around the handle, she felt the walls of time shape and curve. She knew at once she'd made a terrible mistake. She should never have touched the object without a barrier between it and her skin. *Vikirnoff. Link with me now! Help me. Merge with me.* She screamed for his help telepathically as she was sucked down—deep into the violent past of the knife.

Vikirnoff merged his mind deep into hers. His spirit ripped through the curving tunnels with her, his mind divided in both the past and the present. Having the presence of mind to keep a grip on the vampire's heart, he dragged his fist from the evil one's chest and flung it onto the floor. To his astonishment, the organ flopped, not toward Arturo, but toward the bubbling rusty puddle.

Arturo's scream was one of rage and pain. He leapt across the room toward the rolling heart, calling it back, his commands going unheeded. As Arturo fell to the ground and clawed his way across the ice in search of his heart, Vikirnoff slammed the flaming whip directly across the path leading to the puddle. The heart ran right into the dancing flames just as Arturo's hand slammed over the top of it.

You may kill me Xavier, but you will never destroy my people. My blood may run in the veins of my children, but it will not provide you with the immortality you seek.

Vikirnoff whirled around shocked to hear the voice of Rhiannon of the Dragonseekers. It was so clear, so real, he expected to see her standing behind him. It took a moment to realize he was sharing the past with Natalya.

Arturo took advantage, dragging his burned hand from the flames and gleefully restoring his heart to his chest. Blood was pouring down both the front of the vampire, and Vikirnoff's neck. Arturo reached out and smeared the ancient hunter's blood on his hand and licked at it. "You should have joined us. Your prince is injured, his hunter in the ground, nearly dead and now you and your woman will die."

Vikirnoff was already in motion, whirling away from the attack as both vampires rushed him. Blood loss weakened him and it was disorienting to be in two places at one time. They needed help and other Carpathians in the vicinity should have felt the presence of evil. He had wondered why Mikhail Dubrinksy, the prince of the Carpathians had not come to their aid in the earlier battle with the vampires. Vikirnoff could only think Mikhail must have been injured and in the ground not to have felt the battle in the forest.

Cezar slammed into the protective barrier shielding Natalya. He clawed at the shield with sharp talons, then crawled up the side of the ice cave, his body shifting into the form of a dark furred creature with talons and a spiked tail. He launched himself at Vikirnoff as Arturo's body contorted, his face elongating into the muzzle of a wolf.

Natalya. Drop the knife now.

Vikirnoff's voice was steady, but she caught the underlying sense of urgency. Natalya wanted to let go. She tried to open her fingers, but it was impossible. The aftermath of violence attached to objects always trapped her for a time. The more violence the object held, the more difficult it was to escape. The ceremonial knife had been used often. *Xavier was trying to gain immortality by consuming Rhiannon's blood.*

It was impossible to look away from the scene. Her grandmother was beautiful in spite of the bruises darkening her too-pale skin. She lay paralyzed, bound by not only powerful spells, but some type of poison Xavier had used to hold her prisoner. Tubes ran from Rhiannon's body, draining blood from her, just as Natalya's father had been drained. The same shadowy figure approached the bed, knife gripped in hand.

"I no longer need you, my dear. You have served your purpose and have given me a son and two females to take your place. Your blood runs in their veins. I will use the females' blood and allow my son to give me grandchildren that I might continue to live." He laughed, the sound evil even as it traveled through time. "You will never know them and they will never know you. Go now, join your precious lifemate."

Rhiannon smiled. "My children know me, even as babes, they know me."

Xavier raised the knife high and plunged it deep into Rhiannon's heart.

Natalya screamed, both hands going to cover her heart as Xavier dug deep with the blade in Rhiannon's chest. She watched her grandmother's death in horror. Xavier collected the blood from the heart and put it in a small vial, carrying it over to a table where a large book lay open.

Xavier closed the book, satisfaction on his face as he glanced back at the dead woman. "I have what I need from you, Rhiannon. At last. You will be the instrument of destruction of your race. When I am done, there will be no Carpathians, no Jaguar, and only one dark mage ruling what always should have been mine." He closed the book and ran his hand over the cover.

Natalya held her breath as she watched him set the vial of blood beside two others. He chose one and lifted it high. "Sealed with the blood of the dark mage." He poured the second. "Sealed with the blood of the jaguar." He picked up the third. "Sealed with the blood of the Carpathian. Sealed with blood of the three, opened with blood of the three."

A chill went down Natalya's spine. What was he doing? What did it mean? She tried to move into a better position to hear the spell he was using, but her attention shifted when she felt Vikirnoff falter.

Natalya. I have need of you now!

The urgency in the hunter's voice overrode the enthrallment of experiencing the past. Something was terribly wrong and she had to get to him. In the past, when she'd accessed violent scenes from objects, she had always relived the entire vignette, not breaking free until it played out, but Vikirnoff wouldn't ask for help unless he was in dire straits. Natalya concentrated on the knife. Her fingers around the knife, the feel of it in her palm. That was real. In the here and now. She was standing in an ice chamber with the ceremonial knife in her hand. All she had to do was open her fingers one by one to release it. She focused on her fingers and pried them loose, allowing the ceremonial knife to clatter to the floor.

At once she was back in the present, the walls shaping around her and the bitter cold stealing into her body. She knew the vignettes from the past often played out in seconds, even when she felt wrung out and exhausted as if she'd relived hours of time, but it was the intensity of the violence rather than time passage.

She had little time to orient herself to the present. Horrified by the blood on Vikirnoff's neck and the sight of the two vampires closing in on them, she flung several throwing stars at Arturo, racing toward him as she did so. The small missiles sank deep into the chest of the vampire as he attempted to shift into the form of a wolf.

You're losing too much blood, Vikirnoff. The sight of him nearly shook her confidence. If they didn't stop his bleeding their chances of escaping were down to zero. She somersaulted over Arturo, kicking him in the thick muzzle as she did so to keep his attention centered on her. As she landed behind him, she caught up her pack and dragged out a shirt. He whirled around to face her, snarling, showing a mouthful of teeth.

You'll have to cauterize the wound, Natalya. I cannot shut down my heart and lungs at this moment and there is little chance they will wait for me to heal myself. Vikirnoff caught the furred creature in midair as Cezar landed nearly on his head, claws raking, teeth and tail slashing. Vikirnoff staggered under the weight as the vampire struggled, using the agility of its animal form.

"Arturo, I'll just bet you missed me." Natalya was already in motion, whirling in close, just out of his reach, her knife slicing across his chest as she moved past him to scoop up the ceremonial knife, using the shirt, and jamming it deep into her pack. *I don't know if I can do it, Vikirnoff.* The idea was so distasteful, she felt sick.

Vikirnoff threw Cezar off, whirling and slashing with his own talons, fighting past the razor-sharp claws in an attempt to penetrate the vampire's chest. Cezar fell back to avoid Vikirnoff's attack, only to spring at him a second time, this time cloning himself so that three creatures sprung forward, all teeth and claws, instead of one.

Blood sprayed from Vikirnoff's neck now and he was far weaker. *You are a strong woman, Natalya. You will do what needs to be done.* He resorted to the fire whip to keep the creatures at bay. *Watch Arturo. He is up to something.*

Natalya stuck the blade of her knife into the orange and red flames of the fire whip until the blade glowed with heat, all the while watching Arturo. He stalked them across the ice chamber, still half-wolf and half-man. *The knife is hot enough, Vikirnoff.* Her stomach lurched. He was counting on her. He thought her strong, but the idea of pressing the hot blade of a knife against the terrible wound in his neck was barbaric.

Now, Natalya. I am too weak to keep this up and the other is near. I cannot feel his presence, but Arturo and Cezar are both suddenly excited. Can you feel the difference in them?

The air vibrated with electric excitement. *Whatever they are expecting can't be good for us.* "Arturo, your fur is looking a bit moldy." She inched closer to Vikirnoff, the blade of her knife glowing with heat.

Arturo's muzzle gaped wide, exposing the huge canines.

"What big teeth you have, grandma," Natalya said,

steeling herself to cauterize the wound on Vikirnoff's neck. She took a deep breath. *I'm sorry.* Natalya pressed the blade of her knife to Vikirnoff's neck before she could lose her nerve. She stayed firmly in his mind, even when he tried to throw her out, clinging tightly, wanting to shoulder the pain. He shuddered with agony, his body breaking out in a sweat. The smell of flesh burning was sickening. Natalya fought back bile. *I'm so sorry, Vikirnoff.* She felt the sting of tears in her eyes.

You do what is necessary. Take Arturo, but stay out of his reach. He is strong.

"Arturo! Baby! Come dance with me." She crooked her finger at him.

Arturo shifted fully into his human form. "I do not think it would be fair to do so when the hunter is recovering from his wounds. Cezar, what do you think? Perhaps a five minute truce to allow him to rest?"

Natalya forced a carefree laugh. "Sorry, big boy, five minutes is way too long to spend in your company." She drew the guns from under her arms and shot him repeatedly, firing rapidly as she dove to his left away from Vikirnoff and toward the patterned stones on the floor of the ice cave. The sound of gunfire reverberated throughout the cavern. She aimed over the head of the vampires and shot at several stalactites so that they broke loose and crashed to the floor of the cave. She skidded to a halt directly over the patterned squares.

It was difficult to study the pattern and keep her eye

on the vampire at the same time and she wanted an alternate escape route planned. Arturo was furious, his face contorted as he flew at her, slamming large ice blocks around her in an effort to cut her off from Vikirnoff.

She leapt on top of the ice wall as a third vampire emerged from the hole the first two had made. He was tall and thin, his hair long and his eyes red-rimmed. An eerie silence greeted his arrival. No one moved. She sensed Vikirnoff's sudden stillness and shifted her gaze to him instinctively for guidance.

Vikirnoff's features remained completely expressionless, but his heart sank as he recognized one of the Malinov brothers. *Natalya. This one is nearly indestructible. He is a master and will be very hard to destroy. I helped to kill his brother not so long ago, and it was a difficult battle, one we nearly did not win and there were two experienced hunters. We must get out now.*

They needed a miracle. Three vampires, one a master. Not just any master, but a Malinov. *We are in trouble, Natalya, be prepared for anything.*

"Vikirnoff, it is long since I have seen you," the tall vampire greeted.

"Maxim, it has indeed been long." *Do not draw his attention. It is imperative we escape, Natalya.*

Normally Natalya might have defied him, just because she disliked orders, but something about the newcomer was terrifying. She could see Arturo trembling. All three of the creatures that were Cezar cowered to make themselves smaller. She had a sudden desire to do the same when the vampire flicked his cold gaze in her direction.

"I met Kirja recently in the United States." Vikirnoff deliberately brought the vampire's attention back to him.

Maxim's expression hardened. "You were there when my brother was murdered?"

"I do not recall a murder, Maxim. I believe Kirja was attempting to kill a hunter and his lifemate." *Find the way out, Natalya.*

Natalya jerked her mesmerized gaze from the vampire and began to work on the pattern she knew had to be in the stones on the floor. The dark mage would have had an escape route known only to him, one easily accessible. He couldn't fly the way the Carpathians could, so he would have had a way to flee from the cavern.

"Have you seen your precious prince?"

Vikirnoff forced himself not to react when his gut rolled in protest and his heart wanted to accelerate. "I have not had the honor as of yet."

"I fear he has been gravely injured, as was Falcon, the hunter guarding him. So sad, but Mikhail's death will benefit so many."

Vikirnoff's heart sank but his expression remained the same. An injury to the prince was the only reasonable explanation for the lack of aid to either of the battles. Still, Vikirnoff had held out hope only to have it dashed. "He will not die, Maxim. His people will not allow his death."

"Oh, I say he will, Vikirnoff. He is surrounded, under

siege, wounded and without protection. We outnumber him and he cannot escape us. When he falls, so will his line fall and the people will scatter and we will pick them off one by one." Maxim tapped his long fingernails against his arm. The rhythm matched the water dripping steadily into the ever-widening puddle.

Vikirnoff risked a glance at the bubbling water. It had grown and was beginning to overflow onto the floor, the brownish liquid spreading like fingers out over the ice, running along unseen grooves, following several paths all leading toward Natalya. Vikirnoff's heart jumped when he realized it was within striking distance of her. He couldn't afford to wait much longer. Natalya had to find them a way out of the cave. If he took her and tried to escape using the route they'd entered, the vampires would kill them before they ever gained the entrance of the cave. He had been in desperate situations over the centuries, but never quite like this—and never with a lifemate to protect.

I think I can open the escape route, Vikirnoff. Say the word and I'll give it a try.

There was little point in stalling. Malinov intended to kill him and Vikirnoff didn't want to wait until the three vampires were in position to do so. Arturo was already inching his way closer. The two clones and Cezar growled and showed teeth. Malinov simply smiled, his eyes cold and alert.

Vikirnoff whirled into motion. *Now, Natalya, open it and be ready. You cannot allow them to see what you do.* He snapped the fire whip across the backs of the three creatures snarling at him. One howled and he lashed it mercilessly, driving it back, sending flames dancing over the dark fur. Cezar immediately shifted shape, dissolving into a greenish vapor and streaking toward the small alcove where the cache of weapons beckoned enticingly.

"No!" Natalya called out the warning, Vikirnoff's voice echoing her.

It was too late. Cezar caught up a heavy sword and turned to face Vikirnoff. Wind rushed through the chamber, rising to a howl of fury. The tall columns of ice trembled and within the spheres, clouds and mist swirled angrily. Something moved in the corner.

The floor cracked, a long jagged streak, several inches deep running the length of the room. Ice crackled overhead and along the walls surrounding them, shifting with creaks and groans so that cracks appeared overhead. Black and gray smoke poured from the cracks in the ice. Above their heads, a gray smoke swirled in the wind. More gathered near the columns until the chamber was filled. The smoke separated into individual pillars, continually moving, red fiery eyes glittering dangerously. They caught glimpses of suits of armor and large menacing swords.

"What have you done?" Maxim Malinov demanded of Cezar, staring around the huge chamber at the tall, daunting looking figures taking shape around the chamber.

"He touched what did not belong to him," Vikirnoff said.

"You fool," Maxim snarled. "You have summoned the shadow warriors."

"*She* touched things." Cezar defended himself. "She has something in her pack right now. I didn't bring them to us."

I have the blood of the dark mage running in my veins. I can touch objects others cannot.

And you can command them, Vikirnoff pointed out.

Maybe.

Maxim gestured toward Natalya. "Kill the hunter and take the woman prisoner now before it is too late. And bring to me what she has in her pack."

Cezar raced at Vikirnoff, sword raised for the kill. Arturo remained frozen in place. At once the shadow warriors went on the alert, glowing eyes trained on Cezar, converging on him from all directions to surround him.

Movement attracts their attention. Do not move if you can help it, Natalya. Can you send the warriors back to their resting places as you did the one at the inn?

I honestly don't know. There are so many of them. Hopefully he used the same spells to draw and bind them.

What else can go wrong? Vikirnoff remained locked in place, calculating the distance to Natalya and whether he dared chance taking the form of mist to reach her.

Hold on. The male voice came out of nowhere, shockingly on the common mental path used by most Carpathians. *I am coming to your aid.*

Mikhail Dubrinsky. Prince of the Carpathian people. Vikirnoff's heart jumped into his throat. Even injured, the prince had come for them. He knew Maxim had caught the message. The vampires, in spite of the shadow warriors, were excited.

"He comes! Kill him. Call the others. He is alone, without aid. Surround him and kill him," Maxim demanded.

It is a trap, Mikhail. Get out. I have no need of you. Go now.

I will not leave a wounded hunter trapped. There was iron in the voice. Steel. Implacable resolve.

"Of course not," Maxim sneered gleefully. "He is invincible."

9

As they had never exchanged blood, Vikirnoff had no way to get a private message to the prince. When he spoke telepathically he had to use the common path even the vampires could hear. It mattered little. He wanted help. He *needed* help. But . . . *You cannot endanger your life, Mikhail. You are too important to our people and I cannot adequately protect you. It means much that you would come to our aid, but you cannot.* He glanced at Natalya and there was sorrow in his eyes. He switched to their private, more intimate path so only she could hear. *I must close the only other way in.*

Do it. She injected complete confidence into her voice when she didn't feel it. She was still touching Vikirnoff's mind and she could feel how torn he was, between his need to protect his prince and the need to keep her safe. *We don't need another burden down here. We can do this together*.

He sent her warmth, an incredible flooding of every sense, as if he were touching her intimately. *Maxim Manilov is the master vampire*. As he spoke to Mikhail Vikirnoff inched his way in freeze-frame motion toward Natalya and the dark mage's secret escape route. *He is part of a greater conspiracy. He has called other vampires to hunt you. Do not enter this place*.

The nearest shadow warrior reached within striking distance of Cezar, swinging his sword in a classic attack. Cezar's sword parried the blow, sparks showering down across the ice floor as the blades met. He sliced at the warrior, but the shadow was already gone, stepping to the side to deliver a second blow meant to kill.

Several shadow warriors surrounded the vampire, swords at the ready. Cezar shrieked to Arturo for aid. Natalya waited for her moment to seize control of the warriors. It was a risky plan. There were several of them and it was possible the dark mage had used more than one binding spell. Often, if the caster made a mistake, especially in dealing with dead spirits, the repercussions were deadly.

You are injured. I will aid you. The prince spoke with grim finality.

Vikirnoff sensed Mikhail inside the cave, moving toward the great abyss in preparation for the descent to the lower chambers. If he sensed the presence of the prince, so did Maxim. He glanced at the master vampire, certain he was up to something.

Maxim remained still, watching dispassionately as Cezar fought for his life. A small smile hovered on his thin lips. It was that small smile that made up Vikirnoff's mind for him. Maxim cared little whether Cezar lived or died, but he would give anything to see Mikhail Dubrinsky dead. Vikirnoff was not willing to risk whatever plot was going through the mind of the undead.

Forgive me, Natalya. Vikirnoff spoke Natalya's name in a soft whisper in his mind and heart. He was risking her life as well as his own. Vikirnoff could feel the prince's wounds, every bit as raw and painful as his own. Mikhail Dubrinsky was far too important to his people to allow the risk. *My prince, I cannot allow you to sacrifice yourself. Your duty is to all of your people, not to a single pair.* With every bit of power Vikirnoff possessed, with all of his ancient knowledge and strength, he slammed his command to earth, building a tower of ice that rose like a mountain, thick and impenetrable, wedging solidly in the sinkhole and blocking all ability to descend into the main chamber from the surface.

A warrior's luck to you and your lifemate. The prince murmured softly.

The cavern shook with the force of Vikirnoff's power. All around them ice cracked and groaned. More stalactites fell to the floor and shattered. There was a small silence. Even the shadow warriors ceased movement.

Maxim hissed his anger, his teeth snapping together,

lips drawn back in a snarl. "That was foolish. You have succeeded in trapping us all in this place. And for what, Vikirnoff? The prince is already dead. He just does not know it yet. We have made certain of that. You cannot stop what is happening here. It was begun long ago and will come to pass whether you interfere or not." His cold, dead gaze fell on Natalya. "He has traded you for his prince, my dear. You made a poor bargain when you chose this one."

Vikirnoff winced. Natalya hadn't chosen him. He had forced the bonding.

Soft laughter brushed against his mind. *If I have the choice between that cold-blooded reptile of a vampire and you, trust me, babe, you win hands-down.*

That is no compliment.

I know. From her precarious position on the blocks of ice, Natalya blew him a kiss. In spite of himself, his heart grew warmer. Natalya's small gesture sent the shadow warriors into another frenzy of sword display. With each frantic movement of Cezar, the warriors grew in form and stature. They pressed the lesser vampire hard, slicing deep cuts into his skin as he tried to fight his way to Maxim.

If I can command the warriors to go after Mr. Reptilian big shot there, we'll have a chance to escape through the hidden passage.

Vikirnoff eyed the dark stains that had spread across the floor of the ice cave. The thick rusty colored liquid had taken on the appearance of a bony hand with long heavily knuckled fingers stretching out toward Natalya. At the end of each finger appeared to be a sharp talon and as the liquid spread, the talon seemed to grow longer. *How are your ankles feeling?*

Natalya looked startled. *How did you know? They burn and they feel weak, like I might not be able to trust them to hold me up.*

Look at the floor.

Natalya glanced down. Her hand went to her throat. *The Troll King has found me again. Great. Just great.*

Arturo and Maxim, like Vikirnoff and Natalya, remained utterly still to keep the shadow warriors from turning on them. Natalya felt it was a standoff of sorts, all of them watching Cezar being hacked to pieces. It was a terrifying scene, the vampire desperate and the shadow warriors relentless.

Get us out of here, Natalya, before your Troll King reaches you. Vikirnoff was more worried about that hand inching across the ice floor than even Maxim. And Maxim hadn't yet begun to show his power.

Natalya waited until Cezar had ceased all movement and it was no longer possible to tell what the warriors were slicing with their great swords. She looked away from the mess and inched her arms into the air, careful to keep her movements slow and measured so that she wouldn't draw down the shadow warrior's attention.

"Hear me now, dark ones, great warriors torn from your resting places, I call on earth, wind, fire, water and spirit." Natalya heard, or maybe just felt the master vampire's shock. She sketched him a small salute before continuing. "I call each to me and bind them to me and with each I invoke the right of the shadow law. The dark mage's blood runs deep in my own and I command thee."

Wind swept through the ice chamber, clarifying each individual warrior. They straightened slowly, one by one, and turned to her, swords raised toward the ceiling, once again motionless awaiting her orders.

You did it.

If only it was that easy. Natalya racked her brain for the proper wording to countermand their long-buried commands, for a way to set them against the vampires when the undead knew not to move and draw the shadow warrior's attention.

On the floor of the cave, Cezar's mangled body began to wiggle. The head jerked, then rolled. Natalya's stomach lurched and she couldn't pull her horrified gaze from the sight.

Concentrate.

You concentrate. That is just gross.

Vikirnoff's fire whip snapped out again and again, reaching parts of the lesser vampire, raining fire, incinerating everything it touched. He searched out the heart with the flames, wanting to at least ensure Cezar could not rise against them again.

Natalya took a deep breath and let it out. She had the attention of not only the shadow warriors, but also the master vampire. She had to bind the warriors to her fast. "Hear me warriors of the ancient past, warriors of the an-

cient law. Whose blood was shed, who died with honor."
As she chanted, she studied the squares with symbols embedded in the ice on the floor, grateful it was hidden from the others. If she could figure out the pattern, she was certain she could unlock the hidden door.

They are paying attention. Keep going!

Her gaze shifted to Vikirnoff. *This isn't exactly easy!*
She had to go through thousands of spells she had learned to pull out the right words, all the while trying to figure out how to escape. "Hear me warriors of old, whose souls are lost, this night I call you, this night I summon you to my aid. Hear me, warriors, a new cause has arisen, your body gone, now spirit be . . ."

Maxim struck without warning, thrusting his mind and will hard against Natalya's mind, pushing to break through any shields. She felt the thrust of his mind, ugly, oily, a filthy abomination touching her, oozing inside and spreading quickly like a cancer. Every evil thought and deed, the countless murders, the depravities, everything Maxim had been and was, poured into her mind.

Vikirnoff. She screamed his name in desperation. The sickness flooding her mind drove her to her knees. She gagged, clutched her heaving, protesting stomach. She was unclean. She would always be unclean. Nothing would take away the dark poisoned stain of evil.

I am here.

Vikirnoff was. Calm. Surrounding her with warmth when she was so utterly cold. Filling her mind with a radiant light, the sun bursting through her mind. How had she ever thought there was darkness in him? She saw darkness, evil of the worst kind and it was nothing like Vikirnoff. He entered her mind with confidence, his every thought, past and present, open to her. As he moved with purpose, he built a reflective light, a mirror turned onto the vampire, forcing him to see what he was. The dark shadows retreated before him, so that Maxim had no choice but to reluctantly flee. Inch by slow inch, Vikirnoff drove the master vampire from her mind. Behind him, Vikirnoff built high, thick shields, weaving them from the strongest safeguards he'd learned over the centuries.

Natalya didn't leave it at that. She wouldn't. She could protect herself. She knew things others didn't know and nobody was going to walk in her mind. "Shield of smoke, earth and fire, come to me, hear my desire. Mold to form, both front and back, protecting me from attack." She had no idea why her shields weren't holding, but she wasn't going to let her guard down again around the vampire.

Maxim hissed his displeasure, the sound loud in the hush of the ice chamber. Throwing out both hands, he slammed his palms forward, toward Natalya. The chamber shook with the force of his blow, driving the bitter cold air straight at her, a fist to her solar plexus. The air left her lungs in a rush, doubling her over so that stars danced in front of her eyes, but he could not penetrate her mind.

Heat seeped through the terrible cold, warming her. A

soft wind fluttered over her face, pushed into her lungs. Vikirnoff breathed for her. In and out. She felt him surrounding her, holding her up and it gave her the strength to straighten her body and face Maxim, her gaze cool and hard.

"By your spirit I summon you. Each of you I enlist. I call you, warriors lost, come to my aid."

Maxim's face twisted with fury. He blasted Natalya a second time, raining sharpened stalactites down on her head. Vikirnoff answered with an umbrella of ice.

He does not want you dead. He is stalling. Anxiously he studied the hand stretching to the ice wall where Natalya stood. The rust colored fingers were already creeping up the side of the wall, reaching for her. *He is waiting for whatever the puddle hides to reach you. I am coming over to you.*

Wait! Don't move until I order the warriors. They will attack you. Natalya couldn't quite catch her breath, even with Vikirnoff's steady breathing, her lungs burned and felt squeezed of all air. She had to figure out the pattern. "Hear me, fight at my side. Protect me from harm. Come to my side, protect me from harm."

The shadow warriors moved, tall and ethereal, cloaked in clouds of whirling gray smoke, ghosts really, insubstantial one moment and dressed in armor the next. They formed a lose circle around Natalya giving her a reprieve from Maxim's smoldering hatred. She kept her eyes on the patterns. *I've got it, Vikirnoff. I can open the floor.*

"Hold this circle, give no ground, battle that which is still, but cannot be bound." Natalya couldn't help the triumphant smirk she flung at the master vampire. "Be it vapor or foggy mist, hold it fast though it turns and twists."

Maxim roared with rage and raised his hands toward Natalya. The low ice wall Natalya stood on obeyed his shouted commands, shifting, sweeping through the circle of shadow warriors, brushing them aside as though they were feathers in the wind. Icicles spears hurtled toward Vikirnoff, the sharp ends spinning with flames straight toward his heart. Maxim leapt at Natalya so fast he was no more than a blur.

Already the shadow warriors were reforming their protective circle around Natalya and just feet from her, Maxim saw he had no chance to take possession of her. In midair he turned, choosing to kill Vikirnoff instead.

Vikirnoff picked an ice-spear from the air and used it to deflect the barrage coming at him. *On the ground, Natalya!* Before he could give any more warning to remind her of the creeping puddle of water, Maxim had landed behind him and reached for his throat with piercing talons. A sword slammed between them and the master vampire shrieked with rage, fingers falling to the floor of the ice cave. Even as Maxim turned to meet the attack, digits were already growing back. He caught the head of the shadow warrior and twisted sharply, flinging the warrior away from him and turning toward Vikirnoff.

Shadow warriors surrounded him. Maxim waved his hand and both he and Arturo were replicated over and over, a hundred clones whirling like madmen between the shadow warriors.

The rust-colored fingers reached Natalya, creeping up her boot in silence to circle her ankle. Vikirnoff sprang off the floor, using dizzying speed, vaulting over the ice floor crowded with fighting shadow warriors and vampires. For a moment bright, blinding light flashed in the cave as lightning forked, slamming into the wall just above his head, evidence that Maxim would not be defeated easily. Vikirnoff didn't hesitate or look back at his enemy. He caught Natalya in his arms and landed on the first squared pattern, the ice wall momentarily hiding them from the shadow warriors and the vampires.

"It burns," Natalya said, trying to reach for her ankle.

Vikirnoff held her hand away from the spreading stain. "Leave it," he said harshly. "Open the floor fast."

"It's burning into my skin." Natalya choked back another protest and concentrated on the pattern she had figured out already. She led the way, hopping from one square to the next, trying desperately to ignore what amounted to a bloody handprint wrapped around her ankle and burning through her clothes to her skin. "I can't leave my pack." She clutched it with both hands to keep from reaching down to her ankle. It was difficult to think when it felt like something was branding her flesh.

The ice walls exploded all around them, showering down large blocks of ice along with sharpened ice spears. Vikirnoff covered Natalya's head with his arms as they stepped over the squares, following the pattern in her mind. He shielded her body with his as he retaliated, the fire whip unfurling to send flames dancing over the vampires, driving them back. It passed through the shadow warriors who ignored the fiery lash, still fighting clones of the undead.

The floor beneath Natalya trembled and a large square slid away to reveal a stairway leading further beneath the earth. She hesitated. *We're going down not up. What if the Troll King is down there?*

We have no choice. This is the only way out of the chamber that we have left to us. We must take it. He reached out to brush tears from her face with the pad of his thumb.

Natalya hadn't realized she was crying. The burning in her leg was bad, but it was more the idea that the unknown thing was attached to her. Just as Maxim had managed to slip inside her head. It was humiliating to think that the master vampire had gotten into her mind and Vikirnoff, not she, had driven him out. Now she had some parasite attaching itself to her body, boring into her flesh.

Turning back she gave her warriors a last command. "Hear my commands though I be gone. Continue to hold. Stand straight, stand strong." She gave the shadow warriors a small salute, wishing she could give them peace and send them back to their resting places.

"We have to go now," Vikirnoff urged.

She turned away from the chaotic scene and took the narrow stairs chiseled from ice leading below the chamber of the dark mage.

Vikirnoff followed her down, down deeper still, closing the hidden panel behind them and weaving safeguards against the vampires in the event they found a way to escape the shadow warriors. Once the panel slammed shut an eerie light gleamed along the twisting stairway. It was carved with care, very narrow steps that seemed to go on forever.

They ran down the long staircase for several minutes. It was strangely silent as if they were the only two people in the world. "I don't think they can follow us using that escape route, do you?" Natalya asked, stopping abruptly.

"Not unless Maxim has hours to figure out the safeguards I used."

"Then get this thing off of my leg," Natalya said. "I can't stand knowing it's on me."

Vikirnoff nearly smiled at the demand in her voice. She was totally confident that he could and would get it off. "Sit down and rest. Let me take a look at it."

"Take your time, it's only burning a hole through my leg and grossing me out, but hey! Just look at it." Natalya scowled at him.

His dark eyes ran over her face and made her shiver. She bit her lip. "I'm sorry. When I'm scared I tend to be a little flippant."

"Do not apologize to me. I am well aware of your need to make light of the situation." He crouched beside her and took her leg in his hands, pushing the material away from her skin so that his fingers brushed intimately against her calf. "I am attempting to develop a sense of humor where you are concerned."

He bent his head to study the grotesque fingers circling her ankle. His dark hair spilled around his shoulders, wild and disheveled and far too appealing for her liking. His breath was warm on her skin. It was all Natalya could do not to reach out and touch his hair. His neck was a mess, the burn hideous and painful looking, yet he seemed detached from it as if the only importance to him was helping her.

"It's alive, isn't it?" She asked the question to distract herself. There would be no more kissing in the midst of *deadly peril*. She absolutely refused to be too stupid to live. Her gaze dropped to his mouth. He had a sinful mouth and that was the problem, not her. It was all Vikirnoff.

"Yes." His voice was grim. "This leaves the same scent as the one you named Troll King. I think this is his work."

She swallowed hard. "Xavier?" She would *not* call him grandfather. She didn't want to think he was related to her. She couldn't think about him without seeing him murdering her grandmother.

Vikirnoff frowned. "I do not think the dark mage. This one feels vampire yet not. I cannot tell yet what we are dealing with. I'll have to go inside to push the parasites out."

"Parasites? Are you telling me I have freakin' parasites in my leg? Get them out of me now. Right now. Hurry, Vik, or I'm going to lose my freakin' mind." Natalya shuddered, her skin suddenly feeling as if bugs were crawling all over her.

"I am uncertain just what *freakin'* is but it cannot be good." He thought it best not to mention the *Vik*. She really was distressed, her lower lip trembling and giving his heart a small shake-up.

"No, it isn't good and my butt is going numb with cold sitting on this block of ice." Oh, lord. She was complaining. Whining. Sitting there like a sissy when he was covered in blood and had his throat nearly torn out. The tigress had deserted her leaving her vulnerable and shaky. She covered her face with her hands too humiliated to face him. "Just please, please get them out of me."

He murmured something soft to her in his ancient language. It sounded tender and gentle and made her want to cry. She sat very still watching as he separated himself from his body, his spirit moving through her with warmth and a far too intimate touch. He did is so easily, not at all like her clumsy attempts. There was no fighting for focus or concentration, just a brief closing of his eyes and she knew his body was an empty shell.

She felt his presence the moment he was in her, touching her mind with reassurance and much more. He made certain not one shadow of the master vampire lingered behind, hidden and waiting to spring from the corners of her mind. He added more safeguards to keep her shields strong before moving through her to her leg. She felt his quiet confidence and she leaned heavily on it. Too many things had gone wrong and Natalya was no longer certain she could handle alone the task given to her. Just the revelations about her grandparents were enough to shake her to the very core of her existence. She tried to stay still, to appear as confident as Vikirnoff when she was really very distressed.

Vikirnoff studied the tiny microorganisms clinging in clusters to the original puncture wound. They wiggled like little worms and around the wound, the area appeared inflamed and swollen. He had seen such things before. His brother's lifemate, Destiny, had been infected with such microorganisms. The imprint of the hand itself was branded deep into Natalya's skin and blisters formed in small clusters around the bony-looking fingers.

The parasites tried to hide or run from the white light of his healing spirit, but he was relentless, ridding her body of every single one, taking more time than they comfortably had to ensure her bloodstream and her every cell were free of the microorganisms. Only when he was certain he had eradicated every one of the intruders did he turn his attention to the original wound. What kind of mark had been branded into her flesh and bone? He had thought he had healed the injuries earlier, but the puncture wounds had reopened deep in her ankle.

He was not a master healer but he should have been able to repair her body. She should have had extraordinary shields to keep out the vampire and, to some extent, him, but her mind was vulnerable. It didn't make sense. He was missing something important and it could cost them both their lives. Again, he repaired her ankle, paying particular attention to the tissue around the wound, inspecting it carefully to make certain he had closed and sealed the wound properly after removing all infection.

The brand seemed to be an entrance for more microorganisms, but he couldn't figure out how. This was very complex and alarms shrieked at him. Maxim or one of his brothers might have the brains to figure something like this out, but he doubted they'd have the patience. This took experimentation, time, endless time. Someone had worked in a laboratory and combined old magick with modern science.

Healing the brand on her skin required more time and energy than exterminating the parasites. The blisters and burn marks disappeared easily, but the brand itself was stubborn, refusing to give way before the white light. In the end, Vikirnoff managed to erase a small part of the palm only.

He pulled back into his own body swaying with weariness, worry on his face. Natalya studied his expression and looked down at her leg. "It's still there, isn't it? What exactly is it?"

"The original puncture wound is the host, I think. The brand allowed entrance for tiny parasites, very small, microorganisms. They are difficult to detect and there's something strange about them. Someone developed them, cultivated them in a lab and mutated them using some sort of chemical."

Natalya stiffened. "Chemical? A chemical was attached

to the parasite? As in a potentially explosive chemical?" She rubbed her temples and shook her head.

"What is it, Natalya?"

The gentleness in his voice warmed her. He looked so tired, lines etched into his face, his skin pale. She brushed his jaw with her fingertips. "One of my memories that doesn't quite connect. I thought of that. In an experiment once, but I can't remember what I was doing."

"And you are getting a headache."

She smiled at him. "One more ache among many. Thank you. I know it wasn't easy trying to get those things out of me."

"We will remove any that linger as soon as we can, Natalya. And we will find a way to get your memory back if at all possible. This practice of marking with parasites is something fairly recent the vampires seem to be using to identify one another." His fist bunched in her hair, fingers rubbing silken strands. For a brief moment he rested his brow against hers. "We will make it out of here. You know that, right?"

Natalya stayed close to him, skin to skin, her hand on his face, his in her hair. They were both exhausted and hurting, physically and emotionally. "I'm glad you're with me, Vikirnoff."

His smile was slow in coming, but it reached his eyes. "It has been a fun adventure, has it not?"

"Oh, you're funny. Now you think you're a comedian. Adventure my butt. Let's get out of this place." Natalya stood up and looked around her. The stairs seemed endless, giving off a strange translucent glow that only made the effect creepier. "Do you think we're going to run into something worse?"

"Worse than the vampires or the shadow warriors?"

She shook her head. "Worse than whatever is tracking me beneath the ground."

Their gazes locked. Vikirnoff had such compassion in his eyes, Natalya looked away, afraid she would cry. The idea of parasites clinging to her body or even just the hand branded on her skin, sickened her.

"We will get rid of it, *ainaak enyém.*"

The way he said the endearment turned her heart over. "What does that mean *exactly*?" She tried to interject suspicion into her voice, as if he was still calling her slip of a girl or something equally obnoxious, but she recognized the word *ainaak* as forever. More than that, it was the way he said it, the look in his eyes.

"Forever mine." His fingers curled around hers. "Which you are."

She gave an inelegant snort of what she hoped would sound like derision. She felt a little foolish walking down the stairs holding his hand, but it was comforting. "How was he able to get into my head, Vikirnoff?"

"Maxim?"

"He was able to crawl *inside* of me." She shuddered and he felt the revulsion rippling through her mind as well.

"I am not certain," he replied carefully.

"But you have an idea."

"Shields are safeguards. Blocks. We weave them automatically and we expect that no one will come into our minds and tear them down." A muted sound distracted him, divided his attention. It was hushed, stealthy, as if someone or something was nearby. Even with his extraordinary night vision he couldn't see beyond the ice pack of the walls bulging around them and overhead. The staircase wound downward, but now was leveling off and curving toward the south.

Natalya chewed at her lower lip, frowning, concentrating on what he was *not* saying. "Why would my safeguards be destroyed?"

"I do not know. How did the shadow warrior get into the room at the inn?" He sent his senses seeking around them for any hint of danger. Something was definitely moving in the darkness off to their left. The wall of ice was thick between them, but the unknown stalker kept pace with them. *We are not alone. Keep talking, but do not say anything of importance.*

Natalya let go of his hand and dropped back two stairs to give both of them room if they should have to fight. The feel of her knife was familiar and even comforting as she laid the blade up along her wrist to conceal it. "It's cold down here. You aren't even shivering." She allowed the tigress to rise toward the surface just enough for her to utilize the superior senses of the cat. At once she scented something peculiar.

It smells like something wild. Not a vampire, but not human. Not Carpathian. I don't recognize the scent . . . yet I do.

She uttered a small shriek of frustration in her head. *I detest having my memories so fragmented.*

"I can regulate my body temperature," Vikirnoff responded aloud. "You can, too." *Does it smell the same as the creature that caught your ankle and tried to drag you beneath the ground?*

At once he heard her heart begin to accelerate wildly, but she was game enough, snorting derisively. "If I could regulate my temperature, *Vik*," she smirked at him when he threw her a warning glance over his shoulder. "I'd be doing it."

Keep an eye on the walls. He gave her the warning as he searched the wide expanse of ice.

Not the walls! She stared at the steps below her feet frantically. *He's below us now. Vikirnoff, we have to get off the steps.*

No, he's pacing along beside us.

I'm telling you he's below us.

Vikirnoff simply turned and dragged her into his arms, taking to the air to get her feet off the stairs. He was certain he was right. The creature was not below them, but instead was stalking alongside them, obviously aware of some break in the wall they had no knowledge of. He moved fast, using preternatural speed, racing through the twisting, narrow hall, staying as far from the left wall as possible. Even using his supernatural speed, the creature kept pace with them and then suddenly it was ahead.

He is moving into position to strike.

My ankles are burning. Which side? She gripped the knife.

Left.

Natalya shifted closer to Vikirnoff's left shoulder, knowing her knee was digging into the wound on his chest and her elbow had to be hitting his neck. He didn't wince, but she *felt* his pain. Not in her mind, but in her body. *I'm sorry.*

Vikirnoff heard the soft whisper in his mind, felt her lips brush his temple. His gut clenched, a curious roll that was unfamiliar to him. She was combat ready. A part of him admired her, thought her extraordinary and another part of him was outraged that he was allowing her to be in harm's way.

She growled a warning. He had no idea whether it was meant for him, or for the creature stalking them, but the knife flashed as the opening yawned to their left and the narrow cavern erupted with a wild howl of pain and rage.

Blood splattered across Vikirnoff's face and Natalya's arm. It burned like acid. Natalya swore in his ear. *I can't make it out, did you see it?*

He glanced behind them, momentarily slowing down. Natalya gasped and jerked on his hair. *Don't you dare! I mean it. We're getting the hell out of Dodge this time. I'm not tackling that thing when you're hurt and shadow warriors could be on us at any moment. Kick it up a gear, Speed Racer, and get us out of here.*

He knew he was too badly injured to fight anything with the kind of speed and strength the creature displayed, but he wanted to get a look at it. *We are not in Dodge nor am I Speed Racer. Is your Troll King a vampire?*

Natalya had excellent night vision as well as olfactory senses. Even the tiny hairs on her body acted like radar, much like a cat's whiskers, yet she couldn't identify the creature through scent or sight. She had tried to look at it, but her impression was of something tall and very muscular. *Like a very blurry Godzilla. And it smells familiar yet not. I can't explain it. It's very frustrating.* And she was getting dizzy as they hurtled around narrow corners, just barely missing crashing into the walls. *He stopped following us and is throwing a bit of a tantrum, digging in the ice. I think I scored a really good hit on him, there was a lot of blood.*

Vikirnoff had no idea what or who Godzilla was, but it didn't matter. She couldn't identify the creature as vampire and it was going to come after her again and again until he destroyed the threat to her. He wasn't at all certain the creature was that injured. It was very possible he was trying to bring tons of ice down on top of them. They needed to get out of the cavern immediately.

The hall encasing the stairs widened and Vikirnoff increased his speed, moving so fast he nearly missed the small tunnel that seemed to lead upward.

Wait! Natalya tugged at his hair again. *That's it. The hidden entrance. I know it is. I feel it.*

You are certain? He was already backtracking, feeling

her certainty. She had mage blood in her and it had to be directing her.

Vikirnoff allowed her feet to touch the ice floor. At once she looked down, her eyes searching the floor around her. "I no longer feel his presence. Do you?"

Vikirnoff didn't believe she *had* felt his presence. Whatever was beneath them coming down the stairs had been no more than an illusion—and one she shouldn't have fallen for.

Natalya shook her head. "The entrance is here, Vikirnoff, we just have to find it."

"What happened to Vik?"

She glanced up at his droll tone, a small grin hovering around her mouth. "I wouldn't want you to think it was endearing or anything like that."

"I doubt there is reason to fear." He stood directly behind her, his body shielding hers, his hands reaching around her, caging her in, as he pointed out faint marks in the ice. "What are those?"

"Ancient symbols."

"Can you read them?" It had been long since he had seen such things and his memory wasn't to be trusted unless it was necessary.

"Of course." She moved her hands with confidence, touching various symbols to arrange a pattern. "He loves patterns."

Vikirnoff dropped his hands on her shoulders. "Who loves patterns?"

Natalya tilted her head back to look at him with a frown. "What?"

"You said *he* loves patterns. Who loves patterns, Natalya?"

She rubbed her pounding temples. "I don't know. I *detest* not being able to remember things. I hate it, Vikirnoff."

His fingers massaged the nape of her neck, easing the tension out of her. "Do not worry about it now, think only of opening the entrance for us. We will work it all out."

10

Natalya hurried through the progression of symbols to open the exit. She wanted out of the cave more than anything else. Keeping her back to Vikirnoff, she glanced over her shoulder at him then looked quickly back at what she was doing. "I should never have considered the idea of removing your memories. Whether I could have or not is irrelevant. It's offensive. It's not right. The idea that someone tampered with my brain, deliberately removed my childhood and who knows what else, is so disturbing I can't even tell you. I have flashes of things I can't remember and it's maddening."

The door creaked open and light spilled in nearly blinding both of them. Natalya covered her eyes with her hands. "Is it morning already?"

"No, but it is close to dawn and we have been underground for hours. Give your eyes a moment to adjust." His arm curved around her shoulders and for a moment, she rested against his body.

"How are we going to get this thing completely off of my leg?" She ran her fingers over his arm, breathing in fresh air.

"In a day or two I will be at full strength. If I still cannot remove it, we will take you to a strong healer. In the meantime, you must be very careful."

His fingers continued working at the nape of her neck, a small massage to ease the tension out of her. It felt amazing, a gift she couldn't remember having before. It was such a small thing, but she'd been alone for so long without someone to comfort her, to talk with her, laugh or argue.

She acknowledged the longing with wariness. She and Vikirnoff had shared too much too fast and Natalya didn't trust it—him—or herself. Emotionally she was battered and bruised with reliving the past and witnessing the murders of her father, mother and grandmother. She was too vulnerable and she wasn't about to give herself away on those terms. She needed distance from Vikirnoff to regain her perspective and strength.

Natalya forced her spine to stiffen and stepped out into the predawn open air. They were on the mountain, but nowhere near the peak and certainly nowhere near the entrance they'd used. The breeze ruffled her hair and touched her face as she drew the fresh air into her lungs. Mist hung heavy above them, but at the lower elevation, the air was free of any preternatural warnings. She glanced over her shoulder to Vikirnoff and her breath caught in her throat. Out in the open she could see the damage done by the vampires, the scores of cuts and claw marks, the streaks of acid burns, and the terrible chunk out of his neck that had been cauterized and was black with burned blood and flesh. His chest wound stained his shirt red and his skin was unbelievably pale.

"You look awful."

"Let's get back to the inn before the sun rises," he answered.

"Can you get us back there? The tiger could carry you, but we're a long way from home."

Dawn would be breaking within minutes. Both of them were already exhausted and needed shelter as soon as possible. "I can get us to the inn. Come here."

Natalya had put distance between them, pacing restlessly, her mind turning over and over, trying to remember the shadowy figure that was so elusive. The one that liked patterns and who must have tampered with her brain so she couldn't remember most of her childhood. Xavier.

A thought came unbidden. Had the dark mage disguised himself as a hunter and murdered her brother? Again her gaze flicked to Vikirnoff. She had walked in his mind—saw the darkness crouching close, the bleak endless years of serving his people, saw, too, his joy in find-ing her. His puzzlement in who and what she was. Noth-ing like he thought. That hurt. Really hurt. And she didn't like that she'd allowed him into her mind and soul enough to hurt her.

Vikirnoff gathered her unresisting body into his arms and took to the air. He wanted to get them away from the mountain, away from the unknown creature that was using the mark on her ankle to track them. *What is it? You are suddenly quiet and that is very unlike you.*

She was so close to him, so close to his body. He was shielding them from eyes, not aggravating his injuries further by taking a different form. Heat poured off his body and into hers. His chest was hard and his thighs gripped her tightly. She became aware of her own body softening and fitting even closer to his. Desire shot through her, unexpected and piercing and totally out of place. She was being drawn, in spite of herself, into his world and she was terribly confused.

He whispered something in his language, something low and sexy, breathing it against her throat. She was vul-nerable to his voice, to his accent, to the feel of his mouth moving against her skin.

What is it? Tell me?

Natalya shifted just a little to circle his neck with her arms, to weave her fingers into his hair while she told him the truth.

I looked into your mind, Vikirnoff. All this lifemate stuff you keep preaching is a bunch of crap. Part of her, some treacherous, lonely, feminine part of her desperately wanted it to be true. *You want June Cleaver. Or Donna Reed. That's who you want. Some little yes woman with her apron on cooking you meals and saying "Yes, dear." Instead you're stuck with* . . . She pulled her head back to look into his eyes. She knew she was showing him she was hurt. It didn't matter right then. She needed to belong somewhere. If only for a moment. He wanted a lifemate, but he didn't want *her*. She kept her gaze locked with his. *You're stuck with Xena, warrior woman, who you don't want, can't conceive of and don't understand.*

She felt his confusion. Puzzlement. His eyes changed color, deepened, darkened with such intense emotion he robbed her of breath. *I do not know these women, Natalya. I do not hear jealousy as much as hurt and it is unacceptable to me that I would cause you sorrow. I do not desire them nor would I ever. I prefer not to eat food so I do not expect nor want cooked meals And I have no other lifemate, only you. I have never met this Xena you speak of.*

Part of her wanted to laugh and the other half wanted to cry. *I'm Xena warrior woman, you dope. You don't know anything, do you?* She rested her forehead against his. *This lifemate thing wasn't your choice any more than it was mine. You didn't want me. I want to be wanted for who I am.*

There was such sadness in her voice, in her mind, it echoed through Vikirnoff's heart. *How can you think I do not want you? You are a miracle to me.*

Natalya turned her head away. She'd been in his mind and she knew his thoughts. He wanted a submissive woman who would hang on his every word, not someone with a smart mouth and an attitude. For one moment she thought about trying to change, trying to be what he wanted, but she could never mold her personality or drive the tigress out of her. She was passionate and fiery and entirely too impulsive. She didn't wait for someone to lead her, she took her own path and she couldn't imagine being any different.

She watched the ground below them, inexplicably sad, the vivid shades of green, the riot of colors from the meadows of flowers and the stacks of hay dotting the rolling hills, all blurring together until she blinked away the tears swimming in her eyes. There were people down there, people with lives far shorter than her life, but so happy. People with families and children and someone to talk to. She had Vikirnoff. She knew he wasn't going to leave her, he believed he was tied to her for eternity, but he didn't want Natalya Shonski, with the blood of the dark mage running in her veins and a tigress crouching deep within her soul. He didn't want the woman who fought vampires and watched really bad movies on late night television.

Vikirnoff pressed his body tightly against hers so that she could feel what she did to him, the tight, painful ache that never seemed to entirely disappear, not even in the midst of danger. How could she think he didn't want *her*? There was no other woman for him, there could be no other woman. *I have much to learn about women, Na-*

talya, it is true, but do not doubt that I want you. His hands shifted on her body, a subtle difference, but she felt it all the way to her toes.

She wanted to smack him one. It just welled up, a tight hot ball of temper that raced through her bloodstream and came spilling out in a low warning growl that vibrated through both of them.

There was a small silence. His body rippled, muscles flexing and his knee pushed between her legs, forcing her into contact with his hard thick erection. *Did you just warn me off?*

If there was a suspicion of laughter in his voice, she couldn't catch it, but she felt it, as if the idea was amusing to him. His tone was pitched so low she shivered. It had gone from soft to black velvet, dark and mesmerizing and oh-so-confident. He knew she was drawn to him, that her body ached for his. He was in her mind and he could glimpse her fantasies. As much as she tried to keep sexual thoughts out of her head, they persisted, crowding in when she least expected it and the tigress in her reacted, rising with heat and need and hunger. *Yes, I did*. There was a challenge in her voice. What could he do, after all? She was safe and she knew it.

Because you think you are safe.

She tilted her chin. *I know that I am*. She let her gaze move insolently over his body. *You aren't exactly in shape to win wars*. Was she challenging him? Deliberately provoking him? She wanted to feel his mouth crushing hers again, his hands on her body. She wanted to belong, just once, to lose herself in another person when her whole world had come crashing down.

You should never underestimate your lifemate.

Her feet touched the balcony just outside of her room at the inn, but he didn't release her. His arms held her close and his knee was still wedged between her thighs. Natalya found herself caged between his body and the wall. His eyes glittered dangerously, and she recognized the predator. She felt the rush of heat spreading fast, the quickening of her pulse in answer to his sudden aggression. He'd been so gentle with her, she'd almost forgotten how dangerous he could be. He had the same animal instincts, the same possessive nature, the drive to be dominant.

Her heart pounded and her body pulsed with sudden hunger. He could drive away every demon she had, replace it with pleasure. There was no give in Vikirnoff and by challenging him, she brought out his every predatory instinct. She wanted to be mindless, to forget everything, only to feel.

Vikirnoff framed her face with his hands, the pads of his thumbs sliding over her soft skin. He studied her upturned face, the tears so close, the weariness. A small sigh escaped and his features softened. "You have gone through trauma witnessing the events of the past. In effect, you lived those events. There is sorrow and rage in you and your emotions are all mixed together so you cannot separate one from the other. I will accept your challenge another day, when you are not so confused and I know that any decision made is real and not because you are vulnerable. I took away your choice when I bound us together, I will not do so twice."

Natalya stared up at him shocked that she was so close to tears. She had never felt so raw in her life. He pulled her into his arms, enfolded her against him, his palms at the back of her head, this time without even a small hint of aggression. There was comfort in his strength as he stroked caresses down her hair.

"I am sorry about your parents, Natalya. It is a terrible thing to have family betray us. There were times I thought hunters needed the loss of emotion in order to hunt friends and family who became the undead."

Vikirnoff hadn't needed to share the deaths of her parents with her, but he had chosen to do so. He had stayed in her mind through it all, reliving those dark moments with her, sharing the emotional outrage and grief right along with her. He had fought beside her, healed her, teased her and shared his mind when she needed an anchor. Now, grievously wounded, his eyes and skin burning in the morning light, he still offered her comfort.

She pressed her lips to his chest and straightened her spine. "We need to get inside where you can lie down." She felt his hesitation and a dark dread began to take hold of her. She looked up at him. "What is it, Vikirnoff?"

"My injuries are very severe, Natalya. You still have to

access the scenes from the past and complete your task, whatever that task may be. The prince and Falcon are both wounded. I need to be at full strength with a master vampire in the area. I have no choice but to go to ground this rising to heal." His voice was grim.

There was a small silence. Her fingers curled tighter in his hair. She couldn't breathe, couldn't find enough air to drag into her lungs. The thought of being separated from him was terrifying. Her emotions swirled up violent and chaotic and totally without sense, so unexpected she couldn't hide it from him. "Why can't you stay here? I can watch over you while you sleep. You know I will." Was that really Natalya Shonski? Pleading with a man to stay with her? Not just any man, but a hunter who had bound her to him by reciting an ancient spell? It didn't bear thinking about.

A part of her wanted to take back the plea, to say something flip and make them both laugh, but the dread was too close and too overwhelming. He was going to leave her and she was going to be alone again.

"Only Mother Earth can heal these wounds, Natalya," he said, regret in his voice.

"Well, let's not forget good old Mother Earth also gives the Troll King a nice little hideaway. What if he decides to come burrowing up under the ground to your resting place and I'm not there to save your butt again?" Her nails dug into his arm. She was pathetic, trying to hold him to her.

"I do not want to leave you, *ainaak enyém,* but you cannot yet come with me and sleep our rejuvenating sleep."

"How can I be forever yours if the Troll King is going to drag you into his lair while you're sleeping?" She would *not* beg him to stay. She wouldn't. "I'll go with you and just sit on top of your resting place."

Vikirnoff shook his head. "You cannot and you know it. I do not want to leave you to face the separation of lifemates, but I have no other choice." One hand slid to the nape of her neck, his thumb brushing over her chin in a small caress as he bent his head even closer.

"I am capable of looking out for myself," Natalya reminded him, squaring her shoulders. His mouth was so close to hers. A temptation. She knew he wanted her. That his body was full and aching. It was in every beat of his heart. It was in the hardness of his muscles and fullness of his groin. Most of all, in his eyes, diamond hard, glittering with such intensity as he stared down into her face. The erotic images she'd glimpsed in his mind took her breath away. He was no shy lover, but everything the tigress in her craved—needed—dreamt of and fantasized about. It wouldn't be difficult to change his mind, to keep him with her. The thought was there, unbidden, but strong in her mind. She didn't want him to leave her.

Vikirnoff lowered his head to kiss her. A small taste to get him through the separation, a mere brush of his lips against hers, but his will melted away as unexpected fire raged in his veins and his heavy erection pressed painfully against the material of his jeans. He heard a strange roaring in his head and every injury his body had suffered, every pinpoint of pain came together at the point of his groin. He needed. He hungered. He couldn't think anymore, only feel, pleasure and pain mixed together until he couldn't tell them apart. Until he knew this woman in his arms had to belong to him, *did* belong to him in spite of her denials. Not anyone else, only Natalya.

His mouth crushed hers, rough and demanding, teeth tugging on her lower lip, tongue sliding on the seam to thrust deep with his own claim. She realized he didn't want the separation any more than she did. He was more than willing to succumb to seduction. Wounded, in pain, it didn't matter, he would give everything up to claim her body, to be a part of her. Hunger seemed insatiable, hers, his, she couldn't even tell the difference, only that her fingers fisted in his hair and her head tilted back to give him a better angle while her mouth fed at his.

He dragged her closer and her arm knocked against his neck. He tensed, his body shuddering, breaking out immediately in a blood-beaded sweat. Natalya pushed away from him, shrinking back against the wall, pressing the back of her hand to her swollen lips. "This is crazy. You're making me crazy. Go away, right now. The sun is climbing, your eyes are burning, the next thing I know your skin will burst into flames."

A reluctant smile tugged at Vikirnoff's mouth. It felt like flames were already dancing over his skin, but she was right. He was weak, needed blood and healing soil. It was only the fact that he was an ancient, well experienced with grave injuries that allowed him to stay on his feet. His strength couldn't last forever and she would have need of him in coming battles.

"Go, Vikirnoff, I mean it."

"I will see you safe first. Remove the safeguards and enter your room."

She couldn't think straight, her blood so hot and her body tight and uncomfortable, begging for release. She took a breath and forced her scattered mind to work again. If she concentrated on the safeguards and not on the fact that he was going away, she would be all right again.

The room was just as they'd left it. She flung her pack into a corner and sat down in the small chair just in front of the television set. She'd paid extra for the television set and it was covered with the same colorful tapestries as the walls and bed, so much so that she could barely see the screen. "I'll be fine. You can see no one is in here or has been here."

"It will not be easy. Being separated from a lifemate is extremely difficult. I, of course, have not experienced it, but am told grief is overwhelming because our minds need to touch. I will be asleep and you will not have access to me."

"Don't flatter yourself, Vik." She crossed her arms over her churning stomach and managed a smile. "I've been without you for a century or two, I think I can manage."

"The doubt will creep in, Natalya. You will think I am dead. Emotionally you have already been through a storm. It will be difficult not to give into wild grief."

Her eyebrow shot up. "Grief? Not just grief but *wild* grief? I think I'll manage just fine. The sun is climbing and you're wasting time. Just go now before . . ." Her voice trailed off. She *wanted* him to go.

"Do not try to access the past by touching the ceremonial knife, Natalya," Vikirnoff cautioned.

"I do have a perfectly good mind and I've been able to use it all this time by my little old self," she answered. "You're stalling."

"Give me your word."

She was beginning to feel desperate. "I give you my word, but you tell me the first line again."

His eyebrow shot up. "The first line?"

"Of the binding spell. I want you to say it again in your language." Her chin shot up. "You aren't the only linguist. I can speak several languages and I'm very good at figuring things out."

"So you are still determined to undo what I wrought."

"Yes." She didn't know how true that was anymore, but damn him to hell, he was leaving her and she was already acting out of character, a whiny baby ready to cry for him. She'd tried to seduce him into staying and she'd pleaded with him. She had no shame and that just wasn't okay with her.

His eyes went diamond hard again. *"Te avio päläferti-ilam."*

"That one isn't so difficult. When languages regress words are often dropped. There would be no 'are'. Literally it would be, 'you wedded wife-my.'" She looked at him triumphantly. "You literally married me, bonded with me, tied us together in the way of your people."

"That is so."

"I'm ready for the next line, unless you're afraid I can undo it," she challenged.

He suddenly leaned forward, one hand on either side of her head, effectively caging her in. "It would not matter to me. You are my lifemate, *ainaak enyém,* forever mine, and that is all there is to it. I do not give up what is mine. If trying to find a way to undo the ritual words occupies your mind and allows you to get through the hours of these next few risings without me, please feel free to work to your heart's content." He kissed her. Hard. Deep. A fierce claim meant to shake her up, to brand her his, and it did.

Natalya couldn't stop her response, opening her mouth to him, feeding on him, devouring him with the same edgy hunger. Vikirnoff broke the kiss and lifted his head, his gaze holding hers captive. "You are mine. Your body doesn't lie, Natalya."

"Oh, go away." She pushed at him. "I belong to myself. I don't care what you say . . ." Her voice trailed off as her gaze lifted to his. "Next few risings? What does that mean? You won't come back tonight?" Fear was the first emotion followed closely by anger. She shoved at him again. "You did this thing to me. You made me dependent on you, but I refuse, absolutely *refuse*, to waste one moment of my time grieving when you're walking out on me. You shouldn't have tied us together if you were going to do this. Get the hell out of here, Vikirnoff, and don't you worry. I'm not going to look back. Not at all." Was she prodding him again? Challenging him? She couldn't think straight with her mind in such chaos.

"I can take you with me, Natalya. We have exchanged blood on two occasions. It would be my pleasure to do so again." There was seduction in his voice. A threat. A warning.

She studied his face. He was riding the edge of his control. There was too much feeling, too many emotions crowding in and they were feeding each other, back and forth. Natalya took a deep breath and drew back from the edge of the precipice she had nearly rushed over. "I'm sorry, Vikirnoff. I'm very shaken. Thank you for all you've done for me. I'm not acting like it, but I really appreciate it."

He pressed his lips to her forehead. "*Éntölam kuulua, avio päläfertiilam,*" he whispered. "Good luck, *kislány,*" he added deliberately with a small grin.

She feigned outrage. "I know you didn't just call me a little girl." There was a lump in her throat, but she forced her gaze to meet his. She could watch him go and never look back if she had to. She was no little girl, but a grown woman with a mind and heart and will of her own. "Go ahead and mock me. You won't be smirking when I find the spell to unbind us."

"Weave your strongest safeguards, Natalya. No matter what, I will come back. I want you to remember that. I will come back to you."

He straightened and she caught the slight wince. There was fresh blood leaking onto his shirt. Ashamed that she was holding him there, Natalya waved him away. "Go. I'm going to sleep for two days. That should give you plenty of time to heal, Superman." It sounded impossible, but small cuts on her own body could heal nearly instantly and Vikirnoff was full Carpathian.

Vikirnoff pulled open the balcony door. The early morning sun was climbing fast. Light spilled over him and into the room. "Do not forget the safeguards, Natalya."

"I won't."

He took a step into the burning sun, hesitated and turned back. He hated leaving her. It hurt. A bone-wrenching, gut-churning pain that persisted in spite of the fact that he knew he would find a way to make her safe. She wasn't the only one to deal with separation. He had been alone too many centuries and the idea of being apart from her, unable to protect her, or hold her when she was so upset, bothered him more than he cared to admit. She had crawled under his skin and was entwined around his heart in spite of the fact that she was bold and flip and knew little of respect.

He still didn't know if he approved of her. She didn't act anything like the woman he had envisioned for himself or at all for that matter. When he'd thought about women, they were all gentle and peaceful and sweet. He turned back to her. She looked small and vulnerable, nothing like the little tigress out on the battlefield. Her knees were drawn up and she rested her chin on them, arms drawn tightly around her legs. She looked utterly alone. His heart stuttered. Swearing, he turned back to her, closing the doors firmly. "We are going to need the heavy tapestry."

"What are you doing?" She kept her gaze fixed on his face. She could look at his face forever. There were lines that shouldn't have been there, but it was a strong face, beautifully male, sculpted with clean, firm edges. Her heart was doing crazy little somersaults at his words.

"Staying. I am staying."

Natalya took a deep breath, let it out and crossed the distance between them, taking his hand. "No, you're not. It's enough that you want to stay for me."

"Not for you, Natalya," he said. "For me."

"Where will you be? Tell me where. *Show* me where and I won't worry."

His palm cupped the back of her head, brought her to him for a long, searing kiss. Her mouth scorched his, every bit as hungry, her body melting into his, fitting to his form, so that he slid his hands down her back to her bottom and lifted, pressing her pulsing core tight against his heavy erection. He felt desperate, not wanting to let her go. They were both too raw with the emotions they'd relived through the past, with the newness of feeling emotion. He didn't just want to bury his body deep inside hers and stay there, he wanted to hold her forever.

Just stay merged. Inhale her, share her skin as well as her body. It was a fierce, intense desire that shook him to the core of his being.

She loved his mouth, his taste, his smell, everything about him, especially the way he kissed her, as if he could devour her and it still wouldn't be enough. She could have kissed him forever, but the sun was climbing and he was feeling it. In a short time it would be too late, they would have no choices left to them. Maybe that was what he was banking on, but Natalya wasn't willing to allow him to sacrifice his strength and energy. She pulled away from him.

"Go. Show me where you plan to rest and go. It's best for both of us and you know it is. I'll double my safeguards and wait for you." She knew it was necessary to reassure him and she looked him in the eye, opened her mind to him so he could see she meant it.

He showed the cave with mineral rich soil that he remembered from his childhood. It had been a favorite place, although quite remote. Sharing the coordinates was easy enough with their mind merge. He caught her face in his hands, leaned his head onto hers. "Do not let anything happen to you."

"You just look out for yourself and remember the Troll King. He's freaky. I'll be really, really mad at you if you get one more scratch on you." She stroked his cheek. Her hand was trembling so she put it behind her back. "Please go, Vikirnoff. For me, take off now." Because if he didn't, she was going to cry and then he'd stay and she'd feel guilty and angry with herself. "Please. For me."

Vikirnoff turned abruptly and launched himself into the air, shifting into the form of a bird, uncaring that it ripped his wounds and droplets of blood dripped from the sky. *Mikhail. I have need of you.* He sent the call. Imperative. Demanding.

I am here.

I go to ground to heal.

I felt the wounds. I will send aid to your lifemate. The brother and sister of Traian's lifemate are here. I will send them and they will make certain she survives the separation. Let her know to expect them.

Vikirnoff sent Natalya the information. Immediately he received the impression of a snarl. *I do not need a baby-sitter.*

Nevertheless. Vikirnoff broke the connection between them, unwilling to argue with her. It served no purpose when he intended to send her help regardless of her posturing. He didn't want her to be alone. Natalya had the mistaken idea that the ritual words were a binding spell. Both Carpathians and the wizards, those schooled in the power of the elements, were used to using what others deemed magick, but the ritual binding words were so much more elemental. Imprinted on a male Carpathian before birth, the binding ritual ensured the continuation of their species.

He found himself smiling, deep within the form of the bird. If it helped her get through their hours of separation to work on undoing the binding between them,

then he would put aside his hurt feelings and be happy
there was something to aid her.

*Mikhail, there are many vampires in this area. I believe
they seek to destroy you. You must be very careful.*

We have been under siege for some time. Mikhail answered. *Traian was attacked by a master vampire. He did
not recognize him, but it was without doubt an ancient and
well versed in all the powers. Traian had no choice but to leave
us. The vampire drank his blood and connected them. Traian
feared he could be used to spy against his own people. He has
gone with his lifemate to meet the rest of her family.*

Who is left to protect you? Vikirnoff stifled the alarm
shooting through him. Maxim had seemed utterly confident in his ability to destroy the prince of the Carpathians. He had said Mikhail was without protection. Where
was everyone? Their people were few and scattered over a
wide range, but surely the prince was well guarded.

*Falcon lives close and Manolito has returned from South
America. You are here as well. In any case, I am capable of
protecting myself.*

Vikirnoff was silent, mulling it over as he winged his
way toward the old cave. *I think there is a well-orchestrated
plot against you. How is it all of the hunters are gone?*

*My brother and Gregori have been in the States. Byron is
in Italy and I believe Tienn and Eric are traveling with their
lifemates. Gregori and Jacques are on their way back, but they
travel slowly as Shea is pregnant. Gabriel is not too far. Should
there be need, they will come with all speed.*

Vikirnoff didn't like it. There was need. Great need

right now. *Forgive me, but perhaps you are being too complacent. I was in the States with Rafael and we encountered Maxim's brother. It took both of us to kill him and Rafael nearly died doing so. They have grown powerful, Mikhail, and they are developing strange weapons against us. The vampires are banding together and they mean to assassinate you. Maxim told me it was their goal. If they have sufficient ranks here, we may be in trouble. You said Falcon was wounded. You are wounded as am I. We do not know the full extent of the army they have in place against us. You are used to battling fledgling vampires and those of lesser skills. You have never faced an ancient of great power. With some of our most experienced hunters such as Traian or Falcon injured, perhaps we need to reassess what is going on.*

Vikirnoff was never much of a talker. He preferred action and it hadn't been his intention to get into a confrontation with his prince before actually meeting him, but twice now they had disagreed on a course of action. The prince was necessary to sustain their species. It was possible his daughter, Savannah, carried the necessary gene to ensure the survival of their entire species, but Vikirnoff wasn't willing to gamble with the prince's life to find out.

Heavy vines and a pile of rocks covered the entrance to the cave he sought. The area looked as if it hadn't been disturbed for several hundred years. The opening was very slender, hidden behind mere cracks in the boulder. Vikirnoff and his brother, Nicolae, had discovered the entrance as children. Magma, deep below the surface, heated the narrow tunnel and the caverns and springs. The double chambers were rich in minerals and the brothers had often carried the soil home to aid the healers.

Thank you for this information, Vikirnoff. I will take it under consideration. Do not worry about your lifemate. My friends will protect her.

Vikirnoff didn't snort his derision. It would have been rude when talking to royalty, but in truth, no one was going to protect his lifemate. If there was any protecting going on, Natalya would be the one doing it, he didn't care how distraught she might be over the separation. On that thought, came pride. Respect. Natalya might not be the woman he'd dreamt of, or fantasized about, but she was extraordinary and reliable. Utterly, absolutely reliable.

Deep within a chamber he opened the healing earth. His body was tired and he desperately needed to feed, but he had waited too long and the sun had climbed too high. Floating down into the warmth of the rich soil, he allowed the soothing properties to wash over him. *Are you all right?* He reached for her because he had to touch her. To know that she was alive and well.

Yes. What about you? You sound exhausted. Why haven't you gone to ground?

I was having a discussion with the prince.

There was a small silence. *You were ordering him around, weren't you?*

Why would you think that?

I just know you. Diplomacy and tact aren't exactly your strong suits.

The dirt began to fill in around and over him as he laughed softly, the sound echoing through her mind.

11

" I love the way you laugh, Razvan, but it isn't going to get you the spell. You were supposed to study."

"I did study." Razvan grinned at her, his hair falling into his eyes the way it always did.

Natalya knew he believed all the girls thought he looked intriguing that way. She thought he looked like he needed a haircut, but she refrained from saying so.

"Just not spells. You know I think they're archaic. What's the point? No one believes in magick and I don't have the affinity for it that you do. Besides, you always tell me in the end, so stop stalling.

Natalya put her hands on her hips. Of course she was going to tell him. She always did, but she wasn't going to give it up that easy. "What do you have for me in return?"

"*You're supposed to give it to me because you adore me,*" her twin pointed out.

"*Adoration went out the window a long time ago when I realized I had to do all the studying. Safeguards are important, Razvan. What happens if I'm not around and you need to be safe?*"

"*I can always reach you, Natalya.*" He hugged her to him. "*It's never made sense for both of us to study the same thing. We share information.*"

"*But you aren't retaining the spells,*" Natalya argued, the smile fading from her face. "*That worries me, Razvan. What happens if you need safeguards and you can't reach me? You protect me all the time, the only real thing I have to give you in return is knowledge and you don't take it seriously.*"

"*Believe me, Natalya, I take it very seriously,*" Razvan corrected. He ruffled her hair affectionately. "*You're so much smarter than I am, and maybe I take advantage of that by not studying as hard as I should, but never think I'm not aware of how much you help me. I'm proud of you.*"

"*Did he hurt you this time or did the safeguards hold against him?*" Natalya lowered her voice and looked around them. A shadow fell between them. Razvan's arm slipped from her shoulders and all at once he was a good distance away from her. He seemed to fade and Natalya reached out a hand to him, but she couldn't touch him and she dropped her arm.

"*He was very angry. I think you're stronger than he is. If you keep working and learning things like you are, he can't touch us. Maybe his power is diminished, I don't know, but it worries me that you may be in danger. He doesn't like that he can't control you. If he can't hurt me, he can't get to you."*

For a moment Natalya's hair and skin banded with stripes and her eyes glowed a stormy opaque. "He was able to get through the safeguards and he hurt you, didn't he? To punish me because I won't come to him when he insists."

"Show me the new one. Show me what you're using now."

Razvan was fading from her and Natalya couldn't stop him. Grief intruded. Not for her brother but for Vikirnoff. Her need to touch Vikirnoff's mind, just to know he was alive, was safe. She ached for him, her mind reaching. . . . reaching . . . but he wasn't there—only a dark pitiless void she seemed to be tumbling into.

"Natalya! The safeguards." There was desperation in Razvan's voice.

"I told you to take them." She was so distracted. She needed Vikirnoff. Where was he? Why wasn't he answering her call? Could he be dead?

"No! I'm dead. The hunters killed me and you haven't made me safe. Why won't you make me safe, Natalya? I need the safeguard . . .

Natalya woke with a start. Her head was pounding and she looked around trying to remember where she was and what she was doing. Past and present always seemed to come together with a vengeance in her dreams. It was disorienting. She sat in the middle of the floor, knees drawn up, rocking back and forth, with tears streaming down her face. The television was on, but she had no idea what she'd been watching. She didn't remember summoning a dream of her childhood, but she must have just before she'd succumbed to exhaustion. Swearing under her breath, annoyed by her lack of control, she forced herself to look around the room. She should have remained alert, not given in to sleep when enemies surrounded her.

Rubbing her ankle, Natalya looked at the heavy drapes drawn to block out the light. Her eyes and skin still burned, so she was certain the sun hadn't set yet. She tried to focus on the television, but she couldn't seem to think straight. She loved really old movies with bad special effects and she'd found a channel that played them, but she couldn't seem to keep her mind from straying to Vikirnoff. And that was just plain making her angry.

She gave it up with a little sigh, switching off the set and kicking at the rumpled bed. There had been no maid service in the room and it was still a mess from when Vikirnoff was there. The pillow held his scent and she buried her nose against its softness, inhaling deeply before hugging it to her. "Damn you, Vikirnoff Von Shrieder." She felt better condemning him out loud.

Usually dreams of her childhood with Razvan soothed her, but grief was inches from her, clawing at her, threatening to choke her. Not grief for her twin brother, long gone from her, but grief for a man she'd barely met. But she knew him. She'd been in his mind and she knew what kind of man he was. Her soul had touched his. *Where was he when she needed him so desperately?*

"I'll be damned if your stupid binding spell gets the better of me." He was alive. She knew he was alive. It didn't matter that she had reached out to touch his mind a hundred times over the last few hours and found a dark void, she would not give in to such fantasy. He was merely sleeping the rejuvenating sleep of his kind. She knew what it was, she'd actually studied the healing properties of the various soils in one of her many frenzied periods of gathering information to fill the long, empty hours of her life.

"Maybe I'll have to go to your cave and sit there waiting for you to wake up while I work on the spell to unbind us. Because I don't like this feeling." Emptiness was a hole eating her alive. "*Éntölam kuulua, avio päläfertiilam*. I can figure this out. It isn't that difficult." She pressed her hands into her churning stomach.

A soft rap on the door startled her. Natalya spun around, looking wildly for her weapons. They were always at her fingertips. Was she so far gone that she'd let her guard down? Vampires might not be able to attack during daylight hours, but they were masters of puppets, ghouls created to do their bidding. And there was always Brent Barstow skulking around. She wasn't in the least bit fooled by his casual attitude. The man was up to no good and that put him in league with the vampires as far as she was concerned.

"Who is it?" She stood to the right of the door, gun in hand, finger on the trigger, safety off. The safeguards should hold, but she believed in being prepared. The tigress rose close to the surface, allowing her to utilize the incredible gift of scent. A man and woman, no sweat to indicate fear or danger, but she didn't let down her guard.

"Jubal and Gabrielle Sanders, ma'am. Your lifemate sent us to watch over you."

Natalya let her breath out in a long, slow hiss of annoyance as she sagged against the wall. *You're an idiot, Vik, sending them here. You know damn well I'll be trying to take care of them instead of the other way around.* He couldn't hear her, but it gave her satisfaction to say it. "I told him I didn't need a baby-sitter, thank you very much. He's flattering himself to think I might miss him."

"Ma'am. We can't very well stand out here in the hall talking through the door." There was a small silence. "Well, okay, we could, but we're going to attract a bit of attention eventually."

"You could just go away," Natalya said hopefully.

"We have orders from the prince, ma'am. We can't leave."

"If you call me ma'am one more time, I may just shoot you right through the door," Natalya said. She sighed. "Just a minute." It took several minutes to remove the safeguards from the door. Staying to the side, gun rock-steady she took careful aim at the entrance. "Come on in."

The man entered first. He was tall and stocky with wide shoulders and dark wavy hair. He grinned at her and raised his hands into the air, stepping aside for the woman to enter. Natalya noted he stepped to place his body between the gun and his sister. "This is my sister, Gabrielle. I'm Jubal Sanders. Basically, we're human in-laws to Traian."

Gabrielle closed the door and slid the bolt into place. "Slavica, the innkeeper and her husband can vouch for us. Slavica and her daughter sometime help us watch Falcon and Sara's children. The children are human and can't go to ground so they need caretakers during the daylight hours."

"I don't need Slavica to vouch for you, I can read your mind." It was a lie. The brother and sister had very strong barriers, shields Natalya was certain the prince or Falcon had helped to construct.

Jubal's smile widened at her as if he knew she was lying. "Are you going to shoot us, because I'm beginning to feel like I'm in one of those gangster movies?"

"I'm still deciding," Natalya said. "I haven't killed anyone today and I don't want to make that a habit. I have to stay in practice."

"Well at least introduce yourself before you shoot me," Jubal said, looking around the room, his eyebrow arching upward.

Natalya followed his gaze to all the scorch marks and blackened pieces of cardboard. "Natalya Shonski." She slid the safety into place on the gun and waved them to chairs. "Thanks for coming, but I'm fine. I don't fall apart all that easy." She was turning into a first-class liar. Her insides were raw with grief and there was hole burning its way through her throat. She managed a smile. "Vik tends to worry over the silliest things."

Gabrielle looked around the room, trying to ignore the burn marks everywhere and focus on the brightly colored tapestries. "When we first came here, we stayed at this inn. Our room had beautiful woven rugs, all in earth tones. This is very red."

"Isn't it though? I wanted the television and the bathroom so I went with bright," Natalya explained. "I really feel uncomfortable with putting the two of you out by making you stay with me."

Jubal shrugged. "You're much easier than the kids. Sara has a million of them. They run me ragged. Okay, the question has to be asked. I'm sorry if this isn't considered polite, but what have you been doing in here?"

She tried to look innocent. "I have no idea what you're talking about."

"It looks like you're the world's worst smoker, leaving old stogies burning while you fall asleep. *Or,* you're a closet pyromaniac and we'll have to be shot after all for discovering your secret. What gives?"

Natalya made a face. "I was working on a project, not smoking." She shrugged when he kept looking at her. "I was experimenting. I don't have a flamethrower so I was making one. I needed to see how close I'd have to be to use it effectively."

Jubal and Gabrielle exchanged a long stare. Gabrielle

cleared her throat. "You were practicing in this room with a flamethrower?"

Natalya looked at all the blackened marks. "Well, yes. I was careful. I burned paper and old clothes and things. I kept water handy so if the fires were bigger than I expected, I could put them out immediately."

"You were burning objects here in the room?" Jubal repeated.

Natalya scowled at him. "Don't be such a prig. I was experimenting. It's not like I was trying to set the building on fire. Do you think I can just go out and buy a flamethrower? They aren't that easy to come by."

Jubal cleared his throat. "Why the obsession with a flamethrower?"

"Vik informed me I have to incinerate the heart of the vampire to kill it. I killed Freddie the vamp like twenty times, but he wouldn't die. He just kept getting back up again and again. It was downright annoying and a spooky and when I complained, Vik said I needed a flamethrower. Well . . ." She hedged. "He said I had to incinerate the heart and I can't just call down lightning or throw fireballs, so there you go."

Jubal swept a hand through his hair, clearly agitated. "Let me get this straight. You've been *inventing* your own version of a flamethrower?"

"What the heck did you expect me to do? It isn't like I can go down to the local market and pick one up cheap. A can of hairspray and a lighter works, although I have to be way closer than I'd like. The good news is, it's easy to carry."

"Do you have any idea how dangerous that is?" Jubal demanded.

"It was actually fun."

Gabrielle burst out laughing at the expression on her brother's face. "Go, Natalya. You and my sister Joie will get along just fine."

"Don't encourage her, Gabrielle," Jubal chastised. "What does . . . er . . . *Vik* have to say about all this?"

Natalya's eyebrow shot up. "*Vik* doesn't say anything because it isn't his business how I choose to kill vamps." She shrugged carelessly. "Whatever works. He has his methods of dealing with the undead and I have mine."

"You don't think it's just a little bit weird that you're in your hotel room burning things up?" Jubal asked.

"The burning things up is a by-product of testing. I was testing out distances. And, by the way, you can't hold down the trigger because the flame comes back to the can and the can will blow up."

"I'm surprised you didn't blow out a window."

Natalya gave him a cool look. "I'm very good at what I do. I only blow up things I want to blow up." She was becoming distracted again, unable to focus on the conversation. She turned away from her visitors, wanting to pull on her hair. Claws were dangerously close and she flexed her fingers several times to ease the aching.

The need to reach out and touch Vikirnoff's mind shook her with intensity. She could feel her heart pounding and sweat broke out on her body. He wasn't dead. He was asleep. Just asleep. And when he woke up she was going to make him dead. She wanted to strangle him slowly for putting her through hell.

"Do you blow things up often?"

"Jubal!" Gabrielle objected.

"I'm just curious. She's just like Joie. I swear, I'm always surrounded by females who think they can take on King Kong."

A reluctant smile found it's way to Natalya's face. "I love that movie."

"What were you watching?" He indicated the television set.

"I don't remember." And she didn't. She loved the wonderful old television shows and B movies with their old-time special effects. It didn't matter what language they were in, they always provided entertainment, but now she couldn't remember a single thing she'd watched all day. "But it wasn't King Kong."

She couldn't make small talk with perfect strangers. She had learned how to appear friendly and never give anything of herself away, but somehow her life had changed. In any case, when she was so distraught, which was *never,* before Vikirnoff, the tigress roared for supremacy to protect her and that meant Jubal and Gabrielle Sanders might not be entirely safe.

Natalya felt empty without Vikirnoff. She twisted her fingers together and slid back down the wall to sit on the floor in the midst of her weapons. She wasn't afraid of the brother and sister; in such close quarters the tigress would make short work of them if the weapons proved useless, but she felt vulnerable. She'd never been so vulnerable and raw and exposed. *Damn Vikirnoff and all Carpathian men!*

"Natalya." There was compassion in Gabrielle's gray eyes. "Raven Dubrinsky told me that one time years ago, Mikhail had to go to ground without her. He was wounded and she had not yet been converted. She said it was one of the most difficult periods of her life and she wanted me to tell you that if she could be with you right now, she would have come."

"How bad are the prince's injuries?" Natalya asked, desperate to latch onto something that would keep her need of Vikirnoff at bay. If needing a man was a by-product of being a lifemate to a Carpathian, she was more determined than ever to find a way to break the binding ritual. Not only did it suck, but it was humiliating to think she couldn't be without Vikirnoff for a couple of days. She'd been around the world several times by herself. Most of her life had been solitary. She did *not* need a man.

"His injuries were pretty bad. I didn't see him, but Raven was very upset. He was led into a trap," Jubal said. "Both he and Falcon were attacked by several vampires in two separate instances. I think the vampires are trying to wear them down, to keep them injured and weaken them from blood loss rather than go in for the kill."

"Vikirnoff thinks the vampires are gathering to kill the prince. Maxim, that's the master vampire, told Vik they would kill Mikhail and the entire race would be doomed." Natalya drummed her fingers on the floor. "Is that true?"

"I haven't been here that long," Gabrielle answered, "but Gary told me the prince is a major link between all Carpathians."

"Gary?" Natalya prompted.

"Gary Jansen is one of those geeky guys who can do anything, know everything and talk so you can't understand him," Jubal said, grinning at his sister.

"He is not." Gabrielle flicked a chewing gum wrapper at her brother. "He's the kindest, most wonderful man around. And even Shea thinks Gary has the best chance for figuring out why the Carpathian women miscarry so often." She smiled at Natalya. "He's brilliant."

"A brilliant geek," Jubal pointed out.

Gabrielle wrinkled her nose at her brother.

At once Natalya felt alone. She used to joke and tease with Razvan. The closeness between the Sander siblings reminded her of how much she'd lost. "I had a brother once." She leaned her head back against the wall. "We were twins. He was handsome, Gabrielle, much like your brother. And a terrible flirt. Women chased after him all the time—and he liked it."

"Jubal likes women, just not his sisters," Gabrielle said.

"I like my sisters, especially when they don't talk. And you have to admit, they both are crazy." Jubal grinned at her. "Like you. Did you make your brother crazy all the time?"

Natalya thought it over. "Probably. Yes. I only remember bits and pieces of my childhood with him, and we had to separate when we were older. After that, we met at night, in dreams, and exchanged information."

Gabrielle frowned. "Why would you have to separate? We all live different lives but we see each other all the time."

Natalya fought for the memories. More and more she was having flashbacks and piecing together bits of information. "It wasn't safe. We went opposite ways. He didn't know we could communicate in dreams."

"Your brother? I'm confused," Jubal said.

Natalya shook her head, frowning. "Not my brother. A man. I think he may have been my grandfather. In any case, Razvan and I were apart out of necessity. He was different toward the end. He wanted children. It was a big deal to him, more than having a wife. He was with a woman in California and later I found out there was a child; of course she's grown now. He also had a woman in Texas and one in France." Before either of them could comment, she looked up. "Not at the same time, he was a wanderer and he never could stay in one place with one person. I have no idea if he had any more children. He never told me, but he wanted a child so much, it wouldn't surprise me. He was killed before he ever saw his child in California. She didn't even know who he was."

"I'm sorry, Natalya, that must have been terrible for you to lose him. I wonder why he wanted children if he couldn't stay in one place. That would have been hard on children to have their father leave them all the time," Gabrielle said.

"Are your parents still alive?" Natalya asked.

"Oh, yeah," Jubal said with a grin. "Very much alive and I imagine they are grilling Joie and Traian about why they didn't wait to be married with the parents in attendance. Mom will be really upset, won't she, Gabrielle?"

"That's a nice way of putting it. Traian's in for a little surprise. I wish I was home this time, just to be a fly on the wall."

Natalya liked the way they teased one another. It was obvious they were very close and it made her long for a family again. Even though she felt close to Razvan, she had been unable to spend time with him. Their hugs were in their dreams, rather than in flesh and blood real time. They had spent their very long lives in fear of the dark shadow stalking them. Razvan had deliberately taken the brunt of it in order to free Natalya, but she had been alone.

"You look so sad," Gabrielle said.

"I miss my brother." Natalya rubbed her chin on her knees. "And that lunkhead Vik." She was used to being without Razvan, but Vikirnoff had wound his way into her heart and she seemed stuck with him.

Gabrielle exchanged another amused look with her brother. They had spent time with the Carpathian males and the idea of one being labeled a lunkhead or even using a nickname such as "Vik" was humorous to them. "You're really angry with him, aren't you?" Gabrielle asked. "Joie talks like that when she wants to throttle Traian."

"If he's anything like Vikirnoff, he probably deserves throttling. And Vik's so *serious* all the time. And all about the orders. He can't just say something in a pleasant voice, he has to give me the big order. He's really a throwback to the dark ages. You know what I'm talking about, the big caveman pounding his chest."

"He didn't like you fighting vampires, did he?" Jubal guessed.

Natalya rolled her eyes. "That's putting it mildly, but at least I know when to run and fight another day. He just wants to take on the world."

A slow grin spread over Jubal's face. "This is good. Too bad Gary isn't here to witness this one. He loves watching the interplay between the Carpathian male and their women."

"Where is he?" Natalya asked. She wanted to weep. To claw at the walls and floor. She was not going to fall apart in front of strangers.

"Gary's in the States at the moment, but he's returning soon," Gabrielle said.

Natalya was beginning to feel desperate. She had to

work at staying focused on the conversation. "Does he fight vampires, too?"

"In his way, but not physically," Jubal said. "The society"—he frowned—"you have heard of them, haven't you? Humans dedicated to destroying all vampires, but they don't seem to be able to discern the difference between a vampire and a Carpathian. Anyway, the society hates Gary. He's on their hit list."

"Do you fight vampires?" Natalya asked curiously.

Jubal spread his hands out in front of him. "I'm not the best at fighting vampires, but I'm learning. I didn't know they existed until a short time ago."

"Do you use a flame thrower?" Natalya asked. "Do you have one? If I could get my hands on carburetor cleaner, I bet that would work better than hairspray."

"You're obsessed with flamethrowers."

"Do *you* have to kill a vamp a hundred times before he stays dead?" She flexed her aching fingers again. Her muscles were beginning to contract painfully.

Jubal noticed Natalya's eyes changing color, going from a beautiful sea-green to a strange cloudy opaque. Her tawny hair darkened to a deep black with strange bands beginning to appear through it. He nudged Gabrielle with his foot. She nodded. She'd already seen the signs of agitation and felt the growing danger in the room.

"Since most of the locals use horse carts I think the chances of you finding a good supply of carburetor cleaner is practically nil," Jubal said.

"That's such a bummer," Natalya said with a small sigh. "But I did call Slavica earlier and asked her if she'd find me several cans of aerosol hairspray, so I should have a good supply."

"Has Vikirnoff seen your invention?" Jubal asked.

Natalya sent him a look promising retribution. "Make fun all you want, but if you're in a battle with the undead and they get up thirty-seven times after you've put them down, a can of hairspray and a lighter are going to be looking really good to you."

He groaned. "Unfortunately, that might be true. I don't want to have anything to do with those creatures. In fact, I don't even want to know about them."

Natalya smiled wearily. "Neither do I."

"Natalya," Gabrielle said. "You keep rubbing your ankle. Are you hurt? I could take a look at it for you. I've actually gone through med school so I might be able to help if you're injured."

Natalya glanced down at her ankle. She hadn't even realized she was rubbing it. She pulled her leg closer to her. "Unfortunately we couldn't heal it all the way. I don't know how dangerous it would be for you to touch it."

"I've dealt with hot viruses, Natalya," Gabrielle assured. "Why are you worried about it being dangerous to me?" She sank down onto the floor beside Natalya, gingerly pushing aside a gun and a very sharp knife. "Let me see."

"This is really an entry wound. I was punctured first,

all the way to the bone, and then this happened. Vikirnoff said parasites were able to enter my system through this." Natalya pulled up the cotton pants and showed Gabrielle and Jubal what was left of the handprint branding her leg. "He went in and removed what he could. He said there were microorganisms and he thought he was able to get rid of them, but he couldn't remove this. It aches."

Gabrielle studied the handprint carefully. "It looks like . . ."

"Skin," Natalya said. "Cloned skin. It appears to be about approximately one one-hundredth of an inch thick and it has attached itself to the host skin, in this case, my ankle and calf, in the manner of a skin graft."

"It normally takes five days for grafting to complete," Gabrielle pointed out.

"That's what is so extraordinary. My blood vessels grew very fast from the underlying host skin tissue to the handprint, bonding the two layers together." She looked at Gabrielle. "That's why Vikirnoff couldn't remove it, because it has become my skin, breathing, perspiring, performing all the functions of skin; it's part of me."

"Why wouldn't your body reject it?" Gabrielle was moving closer, bending her head to examine the area.

"You already suspect."

"Your bone marrow was taken when your ankle was punctured. Your own stem cells were used; that's how it was done, wasn't it?" Gabrielle asked. "All potential immune system rejection is eliminated because any material cloned from the host will be host's exact genetic match."

Jubal held up his hand. "Wait a minute. What are you saying? Someone attacked her and scooped up her stem cells to clone her skin? I thought you could only use embryonic stem cells for that kind of thing."

"No." Gabrielle shook her head, but she was watching Natalya closely. "The latest research tells us adult stem cells work just as well and, of course, one of the most successful sources of stem cells is bone marrow."

"This is just bizarre. Why would anyone want to do that to you? Just to mark you? I can't buy that when the technology has to be very sophisticated," Jubal argued.

"It's my technology." Natalya's voice was very low.

"What?" Jubal demanded.

"It was my idea, my experiment. I was given challenges all the time, things to accomplish through a blend of science and other skills I have. I had to find a way to inject microorganisms into a host without detection of the parasites and without rejection at the site." She stared down at her hands. "I did this. The vampires can mark people, track them through the parasites."

"How are the microorganisms injected into the body?" Jubal asked.

"Through the hand, although I didn't do anything so dramatic as branding a hand onto anything. It works on the same principle as a mosquito bite." Natalya rested her head against the wall and wiped at the small beads of sweat dotting her forehead. She had known the moment

Vikirnoff explained to her what was going on in her leg. Her own research had been used against her. "The parasites are injected into the host. The thing is this. I wasn't simply experimenting with putting parasites undetected into a body, I was using those parasites as weapons. I was able to bind highly dangerous chemicals to the parasite. I was able to bind several different things to the parasite and get it into a host undetected."

Jubal looked at Gabrielle. "Is this possible?"

Gabrielle nodded. "Yes, of course it is. The research into stem cell and grafting and even binding chemicals onto microorganisms is very advanced. Yes, it can be done."

"How would the vampires get ahold of my research?" Natalya asked the question out loud. She had no idea why she hadn't confessed to Vikirnoff when she told two perfect strangers, but somehow it had been much easier.

There was a small silence. Gabrielle sighed softly. "Where did you do your research, Natalya, and why haven't I heard of you? This is a field I'm very interested in and I keep up with all the latest."

Natalya hesitated. Her body was rocking back and forth without her knowledge again and when she became aware of it she wrapped her arms around her knees tightly in an effort to regain control.

"I don't remember a lot of things about my past. There are gaps, but I love knowledge and when told to do challenges, I couldn't resist." Especially if it meant Razvan wouldn't be harmed. How could she explain her life?

It didn't make sense to her, and with the gaps in her memory she couldn't figure it all out.

"Who knew about your research?"

"I don't know."

There was another silence. Natalya read the suspicion in their eyes and couldn't blame them. "Obviously someone who betrayed me to the vampires. Which means someone I know is in league with them." Her grandfather. It had to be Xavier. She couldn't remember him ordering the experiments, but from her dreams she knew Razvan protected her and she tried to protect him. Even after accessing the crystal globe, she couldn't remember what Xavier looked like. And that was truly frightening.

She rubbed her hands up and down her arms in an effort to warm up. "Are you cold? Is it cold in here?" She was shaking she was so cold. The tiger was rising in an effort to protect her, to keep her from being so agitated, and it was looking for a target.

Natalya dug her fingers into the floor of the bedroom, nails gouging the wood before she could stop herself. She wanted to weep again, to claw at something until the wild grief in her was gone forever. It was sharp and terrible and took over when she least expected it. Even the tigress was weeping, deep inside, a stark loneliness that seemed to eat her from the inside out. The wood came off the floor in long narrow strips. She looked down at the slender splinters with horror.

"Maybe you should go. I'm not certain it's safe anymore. I seem to be having a very difficult time." She swallowed the lump in her throat that was threatening to choke her. "This lifemate business is very uncomfortable."

Jubal nodded. "So I've heard. He's really asleep, healing in the ground. He isn't dead, you know."

"Intellectually I know he's not dead. And right now, I don't even like him all that much, but my mind *needs* to touch his for reassurance. He said some words, like a binding spell and I could feel the difference immediately. Even if you don't believe in that sort of thing, which I do, the binding works. I'm working on a way to reverse it."

Gabrielle's eyebrow shot up. "You think there's a way to reverse it? I thought lifemates *wanted* to be together. You don't want to be with Vikirnoff?"

Natalya opened her mouth to emphatically deny it. Of course she didn't want to be with him and he certainly didn't want to be with her. It was a chemistry thing. Lust maybe. She loved kissing him. But to spend her life with him? For eternity? Did she want that? With a man who wanted June Cleaver?

She was so distracted by her fears for Vikirnoff, she nearly missed the footsteps stopping outside her door. Natalya held up her hand for silence and inched her gun closer to her. Jubal took the knife.

The knock on the door was tentative. "Natalya. It's Slavica with your nightly chocolate."

Not cans of hairspray. Chocolate. Natalya didn't order

chocolate on a nightly basis. She signaled Gabrielle to go into the bathroom and Jubal to stand to the left of the door. She took the right, gun rock-steady and every trace of agitation gone.

12

"**P**lease come in, Slavica," Natalya called out. "Can you get the door?"

"Yes, I have my key." Which was unusual. Slavica would never enter a guest's room uninvited. She would knock and expect the guest to open the door.

Natalya inhaled. Brent Barstow. She'd known all along he was something other than a guest. He was too observant and he'd visited her room once, which meant he was either a very creepy pervert, or he was up to no good.

The key turned in the lock and Slavica pushed the door open. Heavy drapes covered the windows and doors, and night was falling. Natalya knew it would take a moment or two for eyes to adjust from the brightly lit hall to the dark of her room. Slavica stepped into the room carrying a tray with a steaming mug on it. Her eyes were red-rimmed and there was a faint bruise on her cheek. Anger flashed through Natalya and she pushed down the tigress before it could rise and wreak vengeance.

Directly behind Slavica, Brent Barstow followed her, matching pace for pace, the muzzle of his gun pressed tightly against her neck. Natalya swung the door closed and pressed the muzzle of her gun against his neck. "Here's the thing, my man, I've had a really bad day. You don't even want to know about my day. And I think I'm PMSing on top of everything else. That's just wrong, you know? I'm betting that you care more about your own life than I do about a total stranger's life. What do you think?"

"You're not going to pull that trigger," Brent said.

"Actually, I *want* to pull the trigger. You threatened the innkeeper; it's not like I'm going to get in a lot of trouble. Take a look around my room, darlin'. Do I look like a sane chick to you?" She jammed the muzzle harder into his neck. "Cuz, I'm not. Quite sane that is. I like blowing things up."

"I've got her family downstairs and if anything happens to me, they're all dead."

"All the more reason to cap your ass and go take care of the problem downstairs."

Brent lowered his gun and Jubal pulled Slavica to safety behind him.

"They hit Mirko several times in the head. They wouldn't let me take care of him. And they have Angelina." Slavica set the tray down and pressed trembling fingers against her mouth. "There are three of them downstairs."

Natalya slammed the barrel of her gun against the back of Brent's head, staggering him. "That's for being such a jackass. You kidnapped a little girl? I swear if there are any stray vamps hanging around, I'm going to offer them you for dinner."

"Don't kill him, Natalya," Jubal said. "We need to know what he's doing here."

Gabrielle poked her head out of the bathroom. "I remember him from when we stayed here before, Jubal. He was hanging around in the bar. He had a peculiar look on his face when he saw us come in and I noticed him because of it."

"So you are in league with vampires," Brent said, his features twisted with fanatical hatred.

"Sorry pal, you got that wrong. I kill vamps, I don't run with them. They're freaky little devils and damned hard to kill. You have to have the right technique . . ."

"*Don't* start on the flamethrowers, Natalya," Jubal warned. "You're obsessed with the subject."

"That's impossible, we've had you pegged as a vampire for a long while now."

"What a shocker. You can't even get your information straight. You're not very bright, are you?" Natalya asked

"Back off, Natalya," Jubal warned. She was shaking again and he noticed her fingers curling into the shape of claws. "Go breathe for a while. I can't let you shoot him until we get more information from him." He winked at her as he caught Brent by the collar and shoved him into a chair. "You picked the wrong room. She's got a damned arsenal in here and she knows how to use it. Why did you target Slavica's family?"

Natalya listened to Jubal question the man with only a small part of her attention. She concentrated on touching Brent Barstow's mind, feeling him in the way of the tigress. He stank of fanaticism. *Vikirnoff. Wake up!* She used every ounce of telepathy she possessed to reach him. *Can this situation get any freakin' worse? I've got vampires and Troll Kings and now some nutcase kidnapping little girls and threatening innkeepers. I'd let you stay in your comfy little bed to get your beauty sleep but you sent these people to babysit me and now they're all in danger. Get your butt up and come help me sort this out.*

She held her breath waiting for anything from him to indicate he was alive and well. She needed his response, even if he just yawned and went back to sleep.

Natalya felt him first. He said nothing, but his awareness was in her mind. And then his warmth began to spread through her cold body. She felt him accessing her memories and thoughts so that he knew everything that had happened. He stretched, a great predator unsheathing his claws and flexing his muscles. The impression was strong in her mind. Relief swept through her. Not just relief. *Tremendous* relief and on the heels of that, anger.

While she'd been suffering, he'd been snoring away without a single thought for her.

I appreciate the loving greeting, ainaak enyém, *and it is good to know you have not found a way to separate us. What have you been doing?*

Saving the world while you're sleeping, what do you think?

I am getting the distinct impression of fire. Over and over. Clothes burning, your room filled with smoke so that you had to open the windows and balcony door for a short while. There was a definite reprimand in his voice and the sensation of exposed fangs.

Try to focus on what's important here. This idiot thinks I'm a vampire and he and the three stooges have kidnapped Slavica's family.

Half the time you talk in riddles. I will be there shortly. Do not burn down the inn while you are waiting for me.

Who said anything about waiting? I'm not leaving that child down there unprotected. As it is Slavica is beside herself and I feel somewhat responsible. And you should, too. If I hadn't been so distraught I would have heard the whisper of conspiracy and I could have prevented it.

Ah. There was a moment of silence. *I see now.*

You see what? She was suspicious of his gentle tone.

Xena, warrior woman. You are Xena warrior woman. She must be in the movies and you were identifying with her.

Shut up. Sheesh. I so do not want to get into the Xena discussion with you right now. I'm still very much aware you want Susie Homemaker for your lifemate. And believe me,

Vik, you're not worth the suffering. Susie is more than welcome to you.

He was rising. She felt him burst through the earth into the sky. The power surged through him to her as if there was so much strength in him he couldn't contain it. She didn't see how he could possibly be healed already and at full strength, yet the energy sizzled in the air like an electrical charge. In spite of herself, joy rose up in her right along with her sheer physical awareness of him.

You feel a little pale, like maybe you're not quite up to par. I'll hold the fort while you go feed. She couldn't let him think she was ecstatic that he was coming to her.

Where do you get these sayings? And I thought I would feed on you. She received the immediate impression of strong white teeth snapping together, and a flood of very erotic images.

Pervert. She was not going to admit to the excitement racing through her or the heat in her bloodstream.

She turned her attention back to Brent Barstow. The man reeked of fear and violence, a very dangerous combination. He kept shaking his head and insisting that Slavica and her family consorted with vampires, enabling them to acquire victims to fill their ranks.

Sickened by his unnatural hatred and his closed mind, she leaned down, her face inches from his, allowing the tigress to rise, so he could see the urge to kill in her eyes. "You count on people being civilized when you're not, but this time, buddy, you made a bad mistake. When my friends are threatened, I don't do civilized."

"Natalya," Jubal warned. "He's a fanatical imbecile. Let's turn him over to the authorities."

"If you kill vampires as you claim," Barstow said, "then we're on the same side. There's no need for this."

Natalya's eyebrow shot up. "No need? When you have Slavica's husband and daughter, a young innocent girl who couldn't possibly have anything to do with vampires, tied up in their own home? I'm not on your side and I never will be."

"In any war there are sacrifices. And we are at war," Barstow declared.

Slavica had been silent, but a single sound escaped and it went straight to Natalya's heart. She wanted to rip the man to shreds. She could feel her hands curling into claws and a wildness rose up in her.

Gabrielle slipped between them and put a gentle, restraining hand on Natalya's arm. "This man isn't the problem right now. His friends are. The most important thing to do is to figure out how to get Slavica's family back safely."

"They are in league with the vampires," Barstow reiterated, glaring at Slavica. "Her entire family hangs out with vampires."

"Hangs out? You just said hangs out," Natalya repeated. "Do you have any idea how utterly stupid you sound? Vampires do not hang out. They tear your throat out and drain every drop of blood from your body. They do not hang out. Where do people like you come from?" She turned away from him unable to stomach looking at him

She could feel Vikirnoff. He was close, feeding, his manner respectful, even gentle as he ensured he didn't take enough blood to make the farmer dizzy. She liked that trait in him, that old-world courtesy and the care he seemed to take with others. With her. She ached to see him. She told herself it was only because he could read minds and extract information as well as becoming invisible.

"He's got a knife!" Jubal yelled.

Slavica screamed. Gabrielle gasped. It was that sound, so telltale in Natalya's world, that small breathless gasp of utter shock, that had her whirling around. Gabrielle stared at her, eyes wide, the blood draining from her face. She reached out to Natalya, her hand trembling. Natalya caught her, felt her collapsing and tried to ease her to the floor.

Vikirnoff! She screamed for him. This couldn't be happening. Gabrielle with her bright smile and intelligence blazing in her eyes. She had even stepped protectively in front of Barstow to keep the tigress from a kill. It made no sense. None. She wept inside even as rage grew into a monster roaring for release.

Jubal was already on the floor, fighting for the knife. He took a slash across his chest before pinning Brent's wrist and slamming his hand repeatedly against the floor, forcing him to drop the knife.

Slavica leapt into action, helping Natalya lower Gabrielle to the floor, turning her to see the extent of the injury. "He stabbed her several times." There was a catch in her voice. "Look at the blade. It's notched all the way down."

Natalya looked into her eyes. There was sorrow. Resignation. Three times in the kidney and, as Gabrielle turned, he stabbed her repeatedly in the chest.

Vikirnoff! I need you now!

"I am here." He came striding through the door, tall and powerful, wearing that mantle of authority and complete confidence that usually set her teeth on edge, but now sent relief flooding through her.

She sat on the floor, holding Gabrielle in her arms as both Slavica and she tried to stem the flow of blood.

Vikirnoff reached down and wrenched Barstow's head. The crack was sickening, but he finally lay still.

Jubal crawled off the man. "Save her. I know you can save her. She's psychic. You can make her like you if you have to." Tears poured down his face. "Why didn't I tie him up? I didn't even search him once I took the gun."

Can you save her? Please, please, Vikirnoff, say you can save her. I was careless. This is my fault. She is so sweet and innocent. She doesn't deserve this. Please save her. Natalya couldn't look at him, couldn't look at the others. Gabrielle lay on the floor with blood running in streams from her body because Natalya had been too confident.

Another voice broke into their minds. *You must save her if possible.*

Vikirnoff recognized the voice of the prince. *I will do what I can.*

He bent over Gabrielle and looked into her eyes. Her spirit was fading away. There was no way, even with their healing skills they could save her as a human. "Hear me, kin to one of my kind. If you wish me to attempt a conversion I will do so. It is your decision. Can you live as one of us?"

"Gabby, please." Jubal's voice broke.

Gabrielle nodded and closed her eyes, the breath leaving her body in a long, rattling sigh. Blood bubbled around her lips.

Natalya heard Vikirnoff swear softly to himself. She touched his arm. *Please do this. I know it seems impossible, but she is special.*

I will be tied to this woman for all time, Natalya.

She met his gaze. Knew he was asking permission. Was warning her of things she couldn't know. She didn't fully comprehend what he was trying to say, nor could she grasp the explanation from his mind, but it didn't matter. It couldn't matter. *Please do this.*

For you, although not because you are responsible, you are not, but because you asked me. Others come. Keep them off of us. He had to surround her spirit—her soul and leash it to his to keep her from sliding away from them. Vikirnoff took a deep cleansing breath and sent himself seeking outside his body to enter Gabrielle's, leaving himself vulnerable to attack. There would be no healing Gabrielle fast and easy.

Natalya swallowed fear and guilt and shoved her guns into her holsters, added knives to the loops on her belt and extra clips. She stepped over Brent's body. "Slavica, take care of Jubal's chest wounds, while I cover us." She had no idea why, but Vikirnoff's absolute faith in her ability to guard his back left her glowing inside.

Jubal held out his hand. "Give me a gun. I can shoot."

"I think Mikhail is on his way, Slavica," Natalya reassured her as she handed her spare gun to Jubal. "Once he gets ahold of these idiots, you'll have your husband and daughter back." She glanced at Vikirnoff. He was attempting to repair the wounds enough to give him time for the first blood exchange. She knew it would be important to get his ancient blood into Gabrielle's body to speed healing.

It took a moment to sink in that ever since Vikirnoff had risen, she had been touching his mind, living in it as a light shadow, afraid to let go of him. Now she could feel his sense of urgency, his concern that he could not do what was asked of him when the time was so short, the task so large. She could hear the soft whispers of other Carpathians, a woman's voice, Joie: *Please. Please.* A man's voice, Traian: *I offer freely whatever you need, whenever you need, keep her alive for us.*

There was so much pressure. Why didn't they leave him alone? She wanted to put her arms around him and keep him safe from the demands of so many others, but she had been the one to put him in the position. She had been the one to ask him. She swept her hand down the back of his head, a light brush, before taking aim at the door.

Vikirnoff sealed off the wounds in an effort to stem the flow of blood. The heart was in bad shape. Blood was pumping through several deep tears in the left ventricle. The artery leading to the chamber was severed and blood filled the chest and lungs. The kidney and heart were nearly destroyed by the twisting motion her attacker had used and the jagged notched edges on the blade of the knife. To try to work fast and efficiently in so many areas was nearly impossible. He couldn't allow doubt to enter his mind, but the problem was so vast, so complex, he was finding it difficult to know which direction to turn first.

Mikhail Dubrinsky, prince of the Carpathian people strode into the room. Immediately, a second white light of energy entered Gabrielle's body. Vikirnoff recognized the immense power instantly. *I have the heart, you take the lungs.* Vikirnoff directed, grateful for the other's swift presence.

Falcon is here. He will join us when he has helped your life-mate dispose of the enemy. Raven and Sara are on their way.

Tell them to hurry. We need someone working on her kidney.

Vikirnoff reached out immediately to include Natalya in the circle of information. He didn't need her trying to cut off Falcon's head with her sword. *He will come up behind them and they will not see him. Neither will you, but he will be there to assist you.*

If I can't see him, it isn't likely I'm going to chop off his head. Don't worry about me, I know what I'm doing. Take care of Gabrielle.

Vikirnoff worked meticulously to repair the damage done to the heart. This was a human woman, not a Carpathian. He didn't see how her body could go through the rigorous process of conversion when her heart was so badly damaged. She was barely alive. Mikhail was breathing for her as he drove the blood from her lungs. Vikirnoff contained her fading spirit, speaking softly, soothingly, whispering for her to stay with them. From afar a woman's voice joined with his, begging her sister to stay with them. It was heartbreaking. He had felt nothing for so long that now, when he needed to be strong, emotions choked him. This could have been Natalya.

Be careful Natalya.

Natalya allowed her gaze to rest briefly on Vikirnoff. There were lines of strain etched on his face. Whatever was taking place in the fight for Gabrielle's life was difficult and Vikirnoff was identifying, worried something might happen to her. Deliberately she brushed her mind against his in reassurance, and then turned her attention back to protecting him.

The door handle twisted with infinite slowness. Natalya resisted the urge to fire through the door, fearing the intruders might have a hostage as a shield. She inhaled, in an effort to catch the scents of anyone out in the hall. With the blood and so much fear and adrenaline, it was more difficult to distinguish individual scents, but far from impossible. There were four men and one woman. One very scared man and woman. It had to be the three accomplices and Slavica's husband and daughter.

Signaling Jubal to stand to the left of the door, she took the right side and waved Slavica into the relative safety of the bathroom. The idiots were coming in and they had to suspect that she had either taken Brent prisoner or killed him.

They are coming. She sent the warning to Vikirnoff. He didn't even flinch or turn around, certain she would hold them off.

The door burst open. Shots exploded into the room, reverberating loudly, the sound deafening in the small space. The only people exposed to danger were Mikhail and Vikirnoff, but at her warning, Vikirnoff had obviously thrown a barrier around them to protect the prince and Gabrielle.

The attackers remained in the hall, shielded by the hostages. Mirko held his daughter's hand as they stood side by side, forced to obstruct the doorway and ensure the safety of their captors.

Natalya didn't want to risk hitting them and signaled to Jubal. He reacted instantly, throwing Slavica's daughter, Angelina, to the floor as Natalya yanked Mirko down. Even as she dragged him down, she embraced the change, clothes ripping into tatters and falling away from the fur-covered body. The tigress rose, roaring with rage, exploding from a crouch to full attack leaping over the top of the innkeeper's husband and knocking the three gunmen backward. Teeth buried deep into one throat while claws raked and tore at the other two bodies. The tigress ripped and mauled with relentless fury until there was no sound but the satisfactory death rattle in throats.

Natalya gave one last swipe of her paw to the man closest to her, the one who had held Angelina, and she turned and went back into the room, ignoring the way Jubal raised his eyebrow and the Ostojic family cringed a little as she padded back to the bathroom. Neither Mikhail nor Vikirnoff looked up from their work as she brushed past them.

Natalya dressed hurriedly. She had to get back out in the hall and clean up the mess before the inn emptied of the guests. They had to have heard gunfire, screams and the roar of a wild, enraged animal. It only took a moment to collect her weapons from the middle of her shredded clothes before she stepped out of the room into the hall.

A tall man with a wealth of black hair stood in the hall surveying the damage. "There was very little for me to do," Falcon said. "You seemed to have everything under control so I just directed the guests elsewhere and held down the volume."

Natalya gave him a small shrug. "I was really pissed at them. I'm Natalya."

"Falcon. I understand you are of the Dragonseeker

line. You have Rhiannon's eyes. She was well-respected and much loved. It is an honor to meet you."

Two women materialized just to the left of Falcon. One had dark hair and incredibly blue eyes. She smiled at Natalya. "Thank you for your help. I'm Raven Dubrinsky." She indicated the other woman who had a wealth of thick chestnut hair and enormous violet-blue eyes. "This is Sara, Falcon's lifemate. I wish we could have met under better circumstances. Gabrielle is dear to us and we don't want to lose her."

"Vikirnoff isn't about to let her die." *Because she'd asked him not to.*

"It takes three blood exchanges to convert her," Raven said. "I am very afraid we'll have to space out the exchanges to give her the strength needed for the conversion and I'm not certain we have that kind of time. This is very risky."

"They have need of you inside, Raven," Falcon said. "Gabrielle is bad. Vikirnoff is holding onto her by a thread. You will have to see what you can do to help. Sara, they want you to work on the damage done to her kidney."

"What about the mess?" Sara looked around the blood-spattered hall. "We can't just leave it. Mirko and Slavica will lose all of their business."

"I will take care of this," Falcon assured her. "Perhaps, Natalya, you and Jubal would be willing to escort the Ostojic family to their residence and make certain they are safe. I will remove the memory from the daughter and distance the trauma of it for Mirko and Slavica. Mikhail will want to speak with them after he has finished with his task."

"Sure, no problem," Natalya said. She waved the Ostojic family past the carnage on the floor. Jubal led the way down the stairs while she guarded them from the rear. "Is everyone all right?" she asked.

Angelina bit back a sob and nodded, her eyes enormous. "I'm just scared. They didn't hurt me."

Slavica kept her arm firmly wrapped around her only child. "They beat Mirko, but he told them nothing." Anger crept into her voice. "They put a gun to our Angelina's head."

"Falcon will make certain she doesn't experience any permanent trauma," Jubal said. "You know they can do that. I'm so sorry this happened, Slavica."

"It is not the fault of our friends, or you. These people are madmen and they came to our inn to spy."

Natalya reached out to rub Angelina's arm, distressed by her quiet weeping. She hesitated, patted the girl and dropped her hand abruptly. "You were very brave. We have to walk downstairs and go through the big hall to get to your residence. Can you act like nothing is wrong? I'm sorry, I don't have the ability to make people look the other way."

Angelina nodded her head. "I can do it."

Jubal glanced over his shoulder at the girl's silent father. "Mirko, are you all right?"

"I am very angry."

"I'm angry, too," Jubal agreed.

"I'm sorry about Gabrielle. I hope they can save her life."

"I'm sorry about what they did to Angelina," Jubal replied. "I hate that we all have to worry every minute of every day that some psycho is going to try to kill us because Mikhail and Raven are our friends and Joie and Traian are family."

"We accepted the risk when Mikhail gave us a choice to know him for what he is," Mirko said. "I still cannot believe they threatened my daughter." His fingers curled tightly into fists. "They threatened my family."

"Well, they're dead now," Natalya said cheerfully. She gestured toward the few people wandering through the downstairs room and lowered her voice, keeping a smile firmly in place. "Slavica, thanks for the warning earlier. If you hadn't mentioned nightly chocolate, I might have opened the door without being prepared."

"I was about to take the hairspray to your room and just as I opened the door to go into the hall, they shoved me back inside. Fortunately they didn't realize the package was for you and I could tell them I was about to go to the kitchen for your chocolate."

"You got my hairspray for me? Thank you! I hope you got as many cans as you could find."

"I bought out the store, just as you instructed."

"You can't wait to play with that stuff, can you?" Jubal laughed.

She grinned at him. "Well, okay, maybe that's true. I want to see if it really works. It isn't like I'm going to go looking for trouble."

"That's exactly what you're going to do," Jubal objected.

"What are you planning to use the hairspray for, Natalya?" Mirko asked.

"She's developing flamethrowers to use on vampires," Jubal said. "Can you believe that?"

Natalya abruptly moved passed Slavica and Angelina to touch Jubal's arm, the smile fading from her face. "I need to make certain there aren't any nasty surprises waiting for us. Why don't you take them to the kitchen and let Slavica tend to Mirko's face?"

"I don't want you to go into their quarters alone. Vikirnoff will kill me. Literally."

She snorted. "He won't do any such thing, Jubal. Take them to the kitchen now."

Jubal's brows rose in sudden comprehension. "Because you think someone's in there."

"Slavica, take Angelina to the kitchen," Mirko ordered, his voice hard. "We are going with Natalya."

Natalya snapped her teeth together, irritated at the men's manly egos. She couldn't very well tell them they were going to be in the way. She preferred to fight by herself. Besides, some*thing* was in that residence, not some-*one*. The birthmark of the dragon burned hot on her body and she knew *nosferatu* waited inside.

"Please explain to me what you think is in my home," Mirko said.

Natalya exchanged a glance with Jubal and shrugged. "I believe the undead, the vampire is waiting inside for you and your family to return."

He stared at her face for a long moment. "And you were planning to go in alone, unaided to fight this thing?"

"I've fought them before." She patted her weapons and the single can of hairspray she had left in her bag. "I'm prepared."

"And this is what you use the flamethrower for? To kill the vampire?"

Jubal groaned and shook his head. "Do you have any idea how crazy this sounds? Have you seen a vampire? You're not going to kill one with a can of hairspray."

"I plan on bringing them down and then incinerating their hearts with the can of hairspray," she explained.

Jubal shook his head. "No vampire would dare come to the inn with so many hunters here. That's crazy."

Natalya shrugged. She was not about to argue when she was totally sure of herself. Something was in that residence. And she was beginning to think vampire weren't only in the Ostojic home, but perhaps in other parts of the inn as well.

She touched Vikirnoff's mind. The battle for Gabrielle's life raged on, but it wasn't going well. Vikirnoff was literally forcing her heart to beat while Mikhail breathed for her. She could hear the ancient healing chant, the voices swelling as Carpathians joined from a distance. She could hear a woman, most likely Joie, Gabrielle's sister, weeping as she tried to join the others in the chant.

For a moment Natalya was there with Vikirnoff, seeing the overwhelming task, the terrible damage done to Gabrielle, her body torn and drained of blood. Vikirnoff never faltered, never gave up. She could feel his determination, the endless strength and power he poured into Gabrielle's failing body.

Vikirnoff was a man of steel and compassion. There was something in him that drew her in spite of her every determination to hold him at bay, to be angry with him for binding them together, for making her so aware of him as a man and herself as a woman.

The task she'd asked of him was enormous and required every ounce of his will to keep Gabrielle alive, but he was doing it for her. And she was going into that room filled with vampires for him. She didn't exactly believe in putting herself in danger unless it was for a great cause. Keeping vampires off of Vikirnoff was an *excellent* cause. She blew a kiss toward the stairs.

"*Natalya!*" Jubal demanded. "Let's get this over with. I'm getting nervous thinking about going in there. Let's just do it."

"That's a vampire in there, Jubal," Natalya said. "You'd better be very sure you want to do this."

"I said I was going in."

"I just said, be sure." She didn't wait for his comment, but pushed open the door with caution. The lights were out. A lamp was overturned and lay on the floor, the bulb broken. Cans of hairspray were strewn across the floor and over by the window, a vase with wildflowers lay on its side, water forming a small puddle. Natalya drew her sword and stepped into the room, gliding in silence, her senses flaring out to "feel" the room. She signaled the two humans to stay back as she went farther into the residence.

She knew something was there. She couldn't find the telltale "blank" spots that might indicate the presence of the vampire, but she *knew* it was there.

Vikirnoff. It was a terrible thing to disturb him when he was working so hard to save a life, but she was beginning to feel a trap had been sprung. Real fear was intruding. Why had Brent Barstow attacked Gabrielle? It made no sense. Not even a fanatic would think she was in any way a threat to him. There was only one reason. *Barstow had to be under compulsion. There are vampires here and they must be after the prince.*

She felt the jolt of awareness that sent him back into his own body. *Natalya, get out of there.* He didn't question her judgment, although he scanned the building and surrounding areas and found nothing to indicate the presence of the undead. *They could be after you.*

It is the prince. They drew him to the inn and with all of the hunters are wounded, I'm betting they think this is the perfect time to strike. Get the prince out of there.

He will not go.

Natalya kept to the edges of the room, moving in a circle, calling the tigress to the surface enough to use its superior senses of sight and smell. The room appeared to be empty, but the tigress went on alert, stilling inside of Natalya. Her muscles locked into freeze-frame stalk. *They are here, Vikirnoff.*

I am coming to you.

No! You would never forgive yourself or me if something happened to Mikhail and you have not prevented Gabrielle's death. I can do this. Trust me as I'll be trusting you to keep everyone there alive.

Vikirnoff swore in three languages. She could feel his frantic need to get to her, to see to her protection. In truth, she was frightened. The adrenaline was already pumping through her body with her heightened alertness, but she could deal with fear.

Vikirnoff, I know what I am asking of you.

Do you? He bit the words out. *If anything should happen to you. . . . One scratch, Natalya, I will be most angry with you. You do not want to see me angry.*

She snorted for his benefit, but somewhere deep inside, someplace she kept secret, she was pleased. He made her feel like she counted. His concern was for her, not the prince and not Gabrielle, yet he trusted her enough to stay and do what needed to be done. And that respect and trust meant everything to her.

I will be with you at all times.

She recognized he didn't want her thinking he wasn't safeguarding her. *I know. You like to make things difficult. Do your thing, Vik, and I'll do mine.*

Teasing him helped ease the fear. She stilled near a

long, low-slung couch, listening. Waiting for information she knew was there. And then she heard it. Air moving in and out of lungs. Not one set, but several. She looked around her and saw multiple pairs of eyes staring back. They had ringed her as best they could with her staying against the wall. The eyes glowed red in the dark. It took a moment to make them out, the long, muscular bodies and powerful jaws of the wolves. This time the vampires were using the animal form rather than using the animals. She faced a pack of the undead.

13

"We are in trouble. Natalya is certain vampires are inside the building. She believes they are coming to kill the prince and she does not make mistakes." Vikirnoff didn't look at Mikhail, but at Falcon. It was their duty to see to Mikhail's protection and whether he wanted protection or not, the prince was going to get it.

Without waiting for a reply, Vikirnoff bent his head to Gabrielle's throat. "I am sorry, sister kin, but I do not have the luxury of waiting to see if we can accomplish this task without conversion." He murmured the apology and sank his teeth into her throat, taking only enough blood for an exchange. She needed volumes and his ancient blood would speed the healing process.

They had only minutes before they would have to move both Mikhail and Gabrielle to a safer place. She would not survive without his blood. He was uncertain whether she could possibly survive the trip even with the infusion of ancient blood. They dared not stay and jeopardize the lives of the humans staying at the inn and that was the one powerful argument they could use if Mikhail insisted on fighting the undead.

Vikirnoff exchanged a long, knowing look with Falcon as he forced Gabrielle to consume his blood.

I do not detect the vampire near us.

Vikirnoff could see Falcon was worried, his gaze moving restlessly to the balcony and the hall. *They are here.*

Mikhail took a cautious look around. "That is enough blood for a first exchange. We must do this slowly. If you are certain there are vampires here, we have no choice but to move her. We can't risk the innocent people here at the inn." A flicker of a smile appeared briefly at the looks on their faces. "I am the prince, not a child. I do not put others in danger in order to feed my ego. We must transport Gabrielle now. We can take her to my home where we can better protect her."

"She isn't strong enough," Raven objected. "We can't keep her alive. All of you are already overseeing the functions of her body. How can you possibly do that while we transport her and fend off vampires at the same time?" She stroked back Gabrielle's hair, tears in her eyes. "This will kill Gary. And Jubal and Joie."

My love. Mikhail reached out to his lifemate to comfort her.

"Sara, I need you to take over Gabrielle's heart. Natalya is downstairs alone and I feel the danger to her. I must go to her at once." Vikirnoff indicated his spot. "If we can give the vampires the illusion that Mikhail is downstairs, we can buy more time for all of you to make an escape. I will take Mikhail's form and he can take mine."

Mikhail looked up sharply. "I do not allow others to place themselves in danger for me. I know what you think to do and I say no."

"You do not have the luxury of saying no to me," Vikirnoff replied. "Our people cannot afford to lose you. I cannot provide proper protection. Vampires surround us. We are trying to save this woman's life and keep the humans in this inn safe. It makes sense to exchange forms and you know it. There is nothing more to discuss."

Mikhail's eyes flashed with anger, but Raven put a restraining hand on his arm. "He is right, my love. We have no time to argue. Go Vikirnoff. Sara and I will keep Gabrielle alive while you hunt."

"You will need blood," Falcon said, tearing at his wrist with his teeth. "Take mine, I offer freely."

Vikirnoff took the rich ancient blood without protest, his gaze meeting that of the hunter. Falcon knew what he planned, because the hunter would have done the same thing. He closed the wound respectfully and stood up, shifting shape as he did so, assuming the form of their prince. He strode out into the hall, rather than shifting to vapor, wanting all eyes to see him as Mikhail. *I am coming to you, Natalya. I will look like the prince, so do not stick a sword through my heart.*

Why does everyone think I'm going to kill them? Sheesh!

Vikirnoff could hear the determined lightness masking her growing concern and fear. Pride swept over him. Respect. She had such an indomitable spirit and he couldn't help but admire her. *Perhaps because you take after Xena, warrior woman.*

Don't bring that up. And stay there. I've got this under control. Natalya fought down the sudden surge of fear. If the vampires thought Mikhail was in their grasp, they would go into a fighting frenzy, doing anything and everything they could to kill him. Vikirnoff never seemed to think of himself in battle. She touched his mind and found concern uppermost for her. For the prince. For Gabrielle. Raven and Sara. The humans and finally the other hunters, but most of all for her. She could not find concern for his own well-being. She had no intentions of sacrificing him, even if he did. Someone had to watch out for him.

Natalya was certain only one or two of the vampires masquerading as wolves were real, the others had to be clones. She couldn't tell the difference, but the tigress could. She leapt into their midst, shifting as she did so, the predatory cat instinctively going for the nearest vampire hiding deep in the wolf's body. The flexible, much heavier muscles of the cat allowed her to use her weight to knock the wolf off its feet and the tigress went for the exposed throat. She sank her teeth deep, clamped down and held on, shaking with tremendous force, claws ripping at the other wolves as they leapt on her.

The tigress refused to let go, would not be dragged down. Natalya was determined that at least this one vampire would not rise to fight Vikirnoff if she could help it. She ignored the wolves tearing at her and went for the chest, exposing the heart.

"Step back, Natalya," Mirko's voice came out of nowhere. "I've got that one now."

She turned her head and saw the innkeeper had crept up behind the wolves and held a can of hairspray and a lighter in his hand. Jubal was shoulder to shoulder with him. She instantly scented a second vampire and, shaking off the wolves, leapt at the undead, slamming the tigress's shoulder hard into the wolf's body to drive it to the floor. At once she went for the kill, teeth clamping onto the throat.

Twin columns of fire sent the wolves scattering in all directions, fur smoldering and the smell of burnt flesh filled the air. As the tigress clamped down hard on the vampire's throat, Natalya spotted a third vampire shifting, leaving the wolf's body to leap at the humans. Horrified, she roared a warning, praying she was understood.

"Catch, bat breath!" Jubal calmly tossed a can of hairspray at him so that the undead automatically caught it.

Mirko sent a column of concentrated flames straight at the can and Jubal added a second intense streak as well. As the vampire rushed them, the can exploded like a small bomb.

A wolf leapt on Natalya's back, powerful jaws clamping on the nape of the tigress's neck and ripping. The tigress whirled around, the flexible muscles and spine allowing her to reach back and rip at the attacker.

"The heart, Mirko!" Jubal shouted, pointed to the exposed heart of the vampire as it tried to burrow deeper into the safety of the burned chest. "We didn't destroy the heart."

Mirko caught up another can of hairspray and directed the flames at the heart. Immediately several of the wolves rushed him. He stood his ground holding the incinerating flame steady until the heart turned to ashes. One wolf drove into his chest, back feet tearing at his skin, jaws open and teeth boring straight for his throat just as the can of hairspray ran out. Mirko dropped the useless can and caught the wolf with his two hands, holding him off as they toppled to the floor.

Jubal threw his empty can and lunged for another one, kicking one of the wolves as he did so. "Natalya!"

She rose up with three wolves biting at her sides and back. She shook them off and rushed the wolf attacking Mirko. It was far worse than she'd first thought. She had been unable to detect all of the hiding vampires even through the tigress. They had come in full force, determined to kill the prince.

The door to the residence slammed open and a tall, wide-shouldered man filled the doorway. Everyone froze. Natalya could hear the pounding hearts, the rushing of blood through veins. She growled in annoyance as two more vampires shifted into their natural forms. The remaining wolves lifted their heads and howled, breaking the sudden silence.

"Mikhail Dubrinsky. Welcome." One of the vampires inclined his head. "Maxim will be so pleased that we have accomplished our task."

Natalya, bleeding from half a dozen wounds, turned her head, her opaque eyes glittering as she met Mikhail's gaze.

"Behind you!" Jubal warned.

The beat of wings, the thunder of feet, the brush of paws sounded overly loud on the wooden floor as the vampires and their clones attacked. Mikhail dissolved into vapor and streamed over the heads of the creatures. He slipped through the main entryway door, beneath the crack and streamed out into the night toward the forest with bats, birds and wolves rushing after him.

Natalya turned on the nearest wolf, her mind racing. She would have recognized Vikirnoff in any form. The clone wolves still remained behind and she "felt" the presence of evil in the inn, probably stalking those upstairs, but the vampires had charged after Vikirnoff and she was certain there would be more of them. Snarling, she whirled to face the wolves, wanting to dispose of them quickly so she could follow Vikirnoff.

"Cover Natalya, Mirko! I'm going to protect my sister." Jubal picked up two more cans of hairspray and raced out the door.

The few people crowding close to see what was happening, ran when Jubal burst out of the same room where several hideous creatures had just emerged from. No one was in the hall, but the walls seemed to expand and contract as if the building itself was breathing heavily. The door to Natalya's room was ajar and Jubal skidded to a halt wanting the lighter out in case he needed it to defend himself or Gabrielle.

"I'm coming in," he warned just before peeking his head around the door.

His heart stuttered when he looked at his sister. She was white, almost gray, the life gone from her face, and both Raven and Sara looked pale, their expressions focused as they concentrated on keeping Gabrielle alive. Mikhail, in his Vikirnoff disguise, and Falcon moved carefully around the room, examining the walls and floor.

"We are taking Gabrielle out of here, Jubal," Falcon explained, his voice calm. "Mikhail is leading them away to give us time to get Gabrielle to safety." In the very likely event vampires were near, Falcon wanted to preserve the masquerade as long as possible that Mikhail had left the inn.

"Is she dead?"

"I will not lie to you. We are keeping her alive, but we do not know if what we are doing will work. She is mortally wounded. Vikirnoff holds her spirit to prevent her from passing now. We can keep her body functioning, but we cannot contain her essence. He was the first person here and her spirit is sealed to his until she dies—or completes the conversion."

"We must go now." Mikhail mimicked Vikirnoff's voice perfectly. There was urgency in his tone. "I feel the presence of the vampire, but cannot locate his exact position."

The tigress pushed its way into the room, ignoring the others as she caught up her pack in her teeth and went into the bathroom. Natalya emerged a couple of minutes later, still shoving weapons into the loops on her pants.

"Sorry it took so long, but there were a few of them. You have to go now." Her birthmark was burning painfully. "Another vampire is close."

"Jubal, bring the car around," Vikirnoff/Mikhail instructed as he lifted Gabrielle into his arms. "Hurry, we do not have much time."

Raven and Sara crowded close to him, protective of the woman as the prince started for the balcony.

Without warning, pieces of the ceiling rained down in sharp spears. Raven threw her hands into the air, creating a shield as they raced for the balcony. Jubal tossed the can of hairspray to Natalya and ran out of the room and down the stairs, using the front entrance to get to the car.

Natalya and Falcon separated, each moving to an opposite corner of the room. Natalya lifted her sword in preparation. The ceiling gaped open, and something dark and shadowy dropped into the room. She recognized the vampire immediately. Knowing Falcon had the better chance of killing him quickly, she stepped out of the corner to draw his attention.

"You're too late, Arturo," she greeted. "And you look a little worse for wear. Did you and your master have a bit of trouble with the shadow warriors, because, honestly, you look like you've been sliced and diced."

He snarled, flexing his hands into claws. "You. The hunters deserted and left you to your fate."

"The hunters didn't think you were worth their time. I told them I could handle you no problem. I've already killed you, sheesh, let me think"—she tilted her head to study his face, lined now with hideous scars— "at least four times, maybe more. The battles with you seem to blur together."

Falcon glided in silence to stand directly behind the vampire.

"I'm really going to miss you, Arturo, but all good things must come to an end," Natalya said and took a step toward him, sword at the ready.

Falcon struck from behind, driving his fist through skin and sinew and bone, grasping the heart and wrenching it from Arturo's body. Lightning forked across the sky and slammed through the hole in the roof hitting the heart as Falcon dropped it, incinerating it immediately.

"Nice work," Natalya said. "You don't fool around. I hope you can repair the place for Slavica and Mirko," she added. "I'm going after Vikirnoff."

"He is an experienced hunter. He will not want his lifemate to place herself in jeopardy." Falcon directed the lightning to the body. "He expects me to guard the prince." It was the only apology he could give her.

"I am well aware of what he expects." Natalya raced for the bathroom again. She'd changed her clothes so many times in one day she was beginning to get annoyed with the whole thing. "Go. You do what you have to do and I'll do what I have to do."

"Good hunting."

"Same to you." Vikirnoff had drawn off a pack of vampires and he might lead them in circles just to buy the prince and Gabrielle time, but eventually he would have to fight them. She was damned if he was going to do it alone.

Natalya undressed once again. It took seconds to shove weapons, ammunition and clothes in her pack before slinging it around her neck and shifting back to her animal form. She could always put out the rumor of an escaped circus animal or let the Carpathians worry about a cover story. The roof was repaired and Falcon already gone when she reentered the bedroom. There was no body and no singe marks on the floor, not even from her practicing with the hairspray cans.

The tigress leapt from the balcony to the wraparound deck and then to the ground. She sprinted through the town, keeping to the shadows as best she could, avoiding humans whenever possible. She heard a few murmurs as people caught glimpses of the tigress moving fast through the bushes and trees. With all the events at the inn, there would soon be many frightening tales that would grow with each telling into large legends and her tigress would become a part of that.

She stayed connected to Vikirnoff, reaching past his persona of the prince. He was thinking thoughts the vampires might pick up, thoughts of his people and how it was so important to stay alive to protect them. She considered Vikirnoff's impressions of what Mikhail might be thinking idiotic. . . .

Idiotic? These are princely thoughts. What do you think you are doing?

Following you. Watching your back. You're leading them deeper into the forest, aren't you? Where he would have to deal with them alone. Natalya wasn't about to let that happen, whether he wanted help or not.

Yes. I want them away from the inn, but in a place of my choosing to fight. Far away from where his lifemate would be in danger.

Arturo is dead. Falcon killed him and he's guarding the prince. He said it's what you'd expect of him.

Of course.

Natalya sighed at the perfect calm in his voice. He had gone into his battle mode and put aside his feelings, relying on centuries-old warrior instincts. *They said only you could keep Gabrielle alive. What did they mean?*

I am the keeper of her spirit. They will continue to try to heal her body and Falcon will give her blood next. They will try

*to heal her again and Mikhail will give her blood. She will go
through the conversion at that time. If she is strong enough, if
my will and her will are strong enough, we will see that she
lives.*

Natalya increased her speed, cutting through a
meadow and bounding over a hill. She took every short
cut she could find as she raced to find his chosen battleground. *Can you do that and fight, too?*

Of course.

Of course. She repeated it sarcastically. *Why did I bother
to ask? You're invincible. How many do we face?*

We?

*Yes, we. And don't argue with me. You're already in
enough trouble with me.*

She received the brief impression of his teeth snapping together. *Five. But not Maxim.*

At the name, Natalya's heart gave a jump of fear.
*That's a relief, but I'd like to know why. If he went to the
trouble of springing a trap, why isn't he here with his little
minions? You might be heading into an ambush.*

*Feel to the north. There is a battle taking place. The night
sky is alive with lightning and the earth is groaning. I believe
Maxim was on his way and ran into a hunter of great skill.
Look to the sky.*

There was something in his voice. Expectation. Caution. She couldn't put her finger on it, but she paused as
she loped up the hill and looked toward the north. In the
distance, lighting forked across the sky, not in long
jagged whips, but in the shape of a glowing dragon

breathing fire. Her breath caught in her throat and she felt the birthmark throb on her body, even beneath the thick pelt of the tigress.

That is the mark of the Dragonseeker. No other Carpathian uses that image in battle. To my knowledge, only you and Dominic remain. Of course the world is a big place and maybe more still live.

In spite of herself, in spite of the situation, racing across the hills to guard Vikirnoff's back, Natalya couldn't help the thrill rushing through her at the sight of the dragon in the air. It took her a moment to realize Vikirnoff's voice was coming from a much greater distance than she had first realized. He was diverting her with the truth, with something he knew would throw her off his trail, if even for a few minutes so he had a better chance of leading the vampires away from her.

The tigress took off at a ground-eating lope, going for higher ground and the safety of the trees. *Why are they called Dragonseekers?* She was not going to give away the fact that she was on to his little plan. He was leading the vampires to a specific location. She had a vague idea of where it was from reading his mind, but he was doing his best to shadow his thoughts. She increased her speed, moving as quickly as possible without draining her strength.

Dragons represented celestial and terrestrial power, wisdom and strength to the Dragonseekers and they sought the power and wisdom of the dragons. It was not so much the elusive creature they sought, but the code, what the dragon repre-

sented. We believe in ancient times, a dragon bestowed gifts to the first Dragonseeker, or perhaps, there is dragon in the bloodline. Who knows which is truth?

The ground shook beneath the tiger's paws and she snarled, gripping the earth with claws as she looked warily around. Overhead the sky darkened, clouds blotting out the stars one by one, spreading across the moon in a reddish-brown stain. The wind began to pick up around her, small at first, blowing through the trees so that the leaves rippled with strange life. She crouched lower and moved with more caution, weaving through the dense brush and timber.

She sniffed the air and sent the senses of the tigress along with her own out into the night, seeking information. A few miles ahead, another battle had begun. Vikirnoff had made his stand and, just as she feared, he refused to show the vampires he had tricked them, continuing the illusion of being the prince and making no further attempt to outrun them.

You're an idiot. She murmured it more to herself than to him, but damn him all the same. He just didn't have good sense when it came to fighting. She believed in the old adage "Run away to fight another day." She covered the last couple of miles with relative ease and under concealment of thick brush shifted back to her natural form. She dressed hastily and readied her weapons before sitting a moment to recover her strength and breath.

Lightning flashed continually and there was a noxious odor that indicated Vikirnoff had scored against at least one vampire. Natalya crept stealthily through the thick foliage to get a better view of what was happening. She pushed aside leaves and her breath caught in her throat.

Vikirnoff glided with grace and power, his body as graceful as any dancer's, his features hard-edged and free of all emotion, sculpted in masculine lines and set with intense concentration. She could see him clearly beneath the illusion, his determination, his focus. He moved with blurring speed in the circle of vampires, striking fast at one, retreating before they could touch him, only to strike at another.

Natalya stared at him, utterly mesmerized by him, by his masculine beauty as he fought a battle against so many. She had never seen such a demonstration of power or skill. He flowed like water around them, always moving in a circular pattern, his feet barely skimming the ground. Admiration and respect welled up and spread through her.

Natalya crouched there, unable to take her eyes off of him, fascinated by him, proud of him. Muscles rippled beneath his shirt and he looked both elegant and a warrior. His long hair swung with each motion, looking like fluid silk. She could barely see Mikhail superimposed over Vikirnoff, he was that strong to her. The tigress moved inside of her, recognizing its mate. The dragon, her birthmark burned from the close proximity to the vampires, but it throbbed with a different kind of heat as she watched him fight.

She would never forget that moment, that sight of him

blazing with power and energy, moving with fluid grace and absolute merciless resolve. "You *are* my lifemate." She whispered it aloud, awed by the fact that her body knew him long before her mind made the acknowledgement.

She watched in amazement as he literally ripped the heart from a chest, while two vampires collided in the air where he had been a split second earlier. She felt she was watching a choreographed battle, every move pre-arranged and rehearsed.

Vikirnoff kept the vampires off center using his blurring speed, not wanting them to realize he was not the prince. These were fledgling vampires, pawns Maxim used as fodder to inflict as much damage as possible to weaken the lines of defense. Vikirnoff was certain Maxim had sent the fledglings to the inn to fight and hopefully wound the hunters guarding Mikhail. Maxim would have planned to be right behind them for the kill, but he had not calculated or considered that chance would bring another experienced hunter into the fray.

As Vikirnoff dissolved into vapor to keep from being split in two by the most experienced of the undead, he glanced toward the north. By the look of the sky in that direction the Dragonseeker had Maxim on the run. The master vampire would never be foolish enough to fight such an experienced hunter without a clear advantage. At least the trap had been broken up before there were too many losses.

In the form of vapor Vikirnoff streamed behind a dark-haired vampire and reached out, shifting back into his form at the last second, catching the head between his hands and wrenching hard to break the neck. It wasn't a killing blow, but each wound served to weaken the enemy. He immediately was on the move again, running up the side of a tree to back flip over the top of the same vampire, kicking him as he did so to knock him to the ground. He had successfully destroyed two of the five vampires and so far had only minor scratches to show for it.

The vampires pulled back, dragging their injured comrade with them. As Vikirnoff approached them, they threw up a barrier between them. Vikirnoff settled to earth and studied their faces.

"I do not recognize any of you. How is that?"

"You do not recognize a childhood *friend*, Mikhail?" The one with the broken neck snarled. Spittle ran down his face and he wrenched at his neck, settling his head more carefully on his shoulders. "I am Borak, and you must remember Valentine and Gene. We ran with you in these very forests, yet you cannot even remember who we are."

Vikirnoff bowed, a simple courtly gesture from the waist. "Forgive me, Borak, it must have been that the years have changed you. I remember your youth and unmarked face, not the vision of evil you have chosen to become." He held up his hands and for a moment, crystal clear water swirled in his palms, reflecting back the faces of the three vampires.

They shrieked and hissed as they swirled long capes over their faces to hide from their repulsive images.

Vikirnoff dropped his hands to his sides. "You see why I do not remember old childhood friends."

"You have no friends," Valentine snapped. "Even Gregori has deserted you. All of them. They deliberately left you alone, knowing there would be an attack. Your own people have decided your fate. They want you dead."

The flutter of wings filled the air. The sky darkened overhead as a migration of large vampire bats flooded the area. They began to settle in the trees, ringing the battleground, hundreds of them, more even, folding wings and gripping with tiny claws. There were so many on some of the branches that the limbs drooped with the weight.

"Come and kill me, Valentine. I await your pleasure."

Valentine snarled, exposing his jagged teeth. He glared at Mikhail. "You mock me, but it matters little when I know you have no way out."

Vikirnoff spread his arms. "You are welcome to try, Valentine. You are stalling in the hopes that your master will tell you what to do."

Natalya could see a difference growing in the vampires. Where before they had been cowering behind the shield they had erected, now they were standing taller, eyes beginning to glow, taking on more strength of purpose. She was certain their master had begun to pour power into them as well as a battle strategy. She looked toward the north. The lightning dragon was gone and once more the skies in that direction were calm.

Over her own head, dark clouds spun and twisted, and a light rain had begun to fall. She couldn't tell if it was natural or not, or who might be controlling the weather. The vampires spread out, their bodies glowing with a ghostly light. Borak looked grotesque with his head skewed to one side. His head flopped continually and he muttered threats and spit curses as he readjusted it on his shoulders.

The bats fluttered and began to spread their wings. Some took to the air while others dropped to the ground. The way the creatures stalked Vikirnoff across the ground, using their wings in a stilted, crablike walk was so creepy Natalya shivered, goose bumps rising on her arms and legs. The bats formed two circles around Vikirnoff and the vampires, the inner circle moving clockwise, the outer circle moving counter-clockwise. Her heart began to beat faster and she took several deep breaths to slow it, not wanting to give her presence away. She had to trust him. She *did* trust him, yet it took tremendous self-control to keep from shouting out a warning. Natalya shoved her hand into her mouth and bit down hard.

Borak shimmered, was nearly transparent. The other two vampires followed his example. The forms shortened, contorted, took on the shape of a woman. A smaller woman with long dark hair. Vikirnoff found himself facing three Ravens. He knew it was to throw Mikhail off, that they counted on him hesitating before striking at her. Already the vampires were rapidly cloning their forms, so that a hundred Ravens stood across from him looking vulnerable and innocent.

It wasn't difficult to distinguish which of the shapes were Borak as his head didn't stay in place, but the others were perfect replicas of Raven. Some were weeping. Others pleading. All of them held out their arms to him as they began to walk toward him. Vikirnoff's own form shimmered, dissolved, streaked into the army of Ravens and contorted into the same image so that it was impossible to tell who was vampire, who was clone and who was the hunter.

Vikirnoff moved with the other clones, working his way slowly toward Borak. He was positive he had located the vampire in the midst of so many. The clone heads were slightly tilted, but one kept flopping to one side or the other as the vampire focused on the hunt and not on his image.

Vikirnoff moved within striking distance and at once the bats in the air began to dart at him and those on the ground made small noises. The rain increased and the wind picked up, blowing through the leaves on the trees so that they once again shuddered and twisted, dancing madly overhead.

Vikirnoff whirled gracefully among the clones, reaching for Borak as he shifted into the form of the prince, slamming his fist deep. Raven's face contorted into a malicious mask, the mouth yawning wide, teeth gaping. Borak shifted instantly, trying to dissolve around the burrowing fingers that drove through his body with the speed and intensity of a thrown spear. Vikirnoff yanked the heart free, still gliding in his flowing circle, taking the withered, blackened organ with him as he mowed down several clones.

Natalya couldn't take her eyes off of him. She wanted to move, wanted to at least get rid of the bats moving so dangerously close to him, closing their circles down to make the battlefield smaller, but she felt in a trance, unable even to blink or take her eyes off of Vikirnoff. She saw him so clearly beneath the image of the prince, moving in his warrior's dance, his hands strong, his face etched in lines of determination, of resolve. Her heart quickened to match his beat; her feet felt the same graceful rhythm.

Borak shrieked, his voice hideous as he raced after Vikirnoff, his clones of Raven's image falling to earth and disintegrating as if they'd never been. Dark acid blood withered the vegetation as Borak toppled to the ground. Lightning forked in the sky, lighting the gruesome scene before the bolt incinerated the heart the hunter flung to the ground. The jagged whip leapt to the body, burning it to a fine ash before flames engulfed the blood on the ground and the nearest circle of bats.

The second circle of bats took to the air to escape the intense heat. Natalya blinked rapidly as she watched the battle unfolding, feeling as if she were climbing out of a strange trance. Her mind refused to comprehend what happened at first, but then she was back to herself and she realized Vikirnoff's movements were hypnotic. He was able to enthrall his enemy with his flowing movements and dull the mind of his opponent enough to slow them down.

Valentine and Gene shifted shape a second time, working in unison, flying at Vikirnoff, directing the bats to attack him as well. Vikirnoff threw off the illusion of the prince and met them in the air, a force of power and skill unlike anything the two had ever encountered before. He burst through the flapping wings of the bats, knocking several out of the sky in his pursuit of the two vampires.

Gene broke off and turned tail, streaking through the trees in a run for his life. Valentine chose to stand and fight, dropping back to the ground and facing the hunter. Natalya tried to keep Gene in sight, not trusting that he would leave when they had so clearly been following the instructions of another, most likely Maxim. Gene had been swallowed up by the thick grove of trees, but Natalya drew her sword anyway, holding it at the ready should the vampire be attempting to ambush Vikirnoff.

"You are not the prince," Valentine snarled. He repeated it, shouting. "He is not the prince!"

If he was asking for permission to get away, it was far too late. Vikirnoff whirled around, catching the vampire by the nape of the neck and hurtling him to the ground. He was on him immediately, driving his fist into the chest to extract the heart.

Natalya felt the burn of the dragon and looked frantically around, scanning the trees, the bushes, everything near Vikirnoff. A small rock rolled just inches from his leg and her breath caught in her throat. She burst out of concealment as Gene rose up behind Vikirnoff, triumph on his face as he lifted the knife in his hand.

Natalya somersaulted across the distance, wielding her sword as she flew past, slicing through the vampire's legs as she did so. He screamed horribly, over and over as he fell backward. Vikirnoff was already turning, striking as he did so, his speed so fast, he had the heart before Gene hit the ground. Lightning flashed and flames raced from the blackened hearts to the two bodies. Vikirnoff lifted his head and looked at her.

14

"What the hell were you thinking, following me like that, Natalya? You could have been killed." He knew the moment he uttered the words, how ridiculous he sounded. Natalya might easily have taken care of the vampires and that just upset him more. He wasn't even certain why he was so distressed. Maybe it was the smear of blood along her shoulder and the bruise on her face from the earlier battles. He swore under his breath and rubbed a hand over his face.

Natalya smirked at him. "Just say thank you and we'll call it good."

He looked at his hands, held them up for her to see. "Look at this. I itch, actually itch to shake some sense into you." His palm slid over the top of her head, down her hair to the nape of her neck. He pulled her closer, bent his head and kissed her. It was brief, electric and not at all satisfying to either of them. "You terrify me. You make me feel things I do not want to feel. You are so courageous you terrify me." He took her mouth again. Hard. Possessive. A little brutal.

She tasted his terror. She tasted his need. There was so much hunger. So much resolve. Vikirnoff could be gentle, but he wasn't feeling gentle. She had scared him and that wasn't a good thing. "Let's get out of here, Vikirnoff. This place gives me the creeps. Can't we go somewhere and talk?"

"I do not feel much like talking."

She took a deep breath, let it out slowly and looked him directly in the eye. "Neither do I."

His body tightened at her words, but more than that, his heart turned over. He reached for her without preamble, gathered her close and took to the air. Deliberately, Natalya wound one leg around his thigh, allowing the damp heat of her body to tease him as he took them across the night sky.

"Are you afraid?"

"No." She tugged at his earlobe with her teeth. "Yes. I don't know. Maybe a little."

"You know what you are doing?" His hand was low on her spine, fingers spread wide, palm burning her right through her clothing. His voice was harsh with hunger. So much hunger. Her womb clenched and her nipples hardened into tight peaks.

"You're asking me if I'm committing to you." Her

body ached. Felt empty. She turned up her face to his, her arm circling his neck and kissed him, tongue licking his lips, her hand sliding down his chest to brush the thick bulge pressed so tightly against her.

"Be very certain. Because once you do, I will not let you go, Natalya. Even if you somehow managed to undo an ancient binding ritual as old as time itself, I will not let you go once you are mine." His beast was roaring for his lifemate. *Save me. Choose me. Be forever to my heart connected.* She was his. *His.*

She liked that he didn't close his mind to her. She wanted to feel the possessiveness of his thoughts. She wanted to be swept away so the small scared part of her wouldn't be able to think too much and she could just take what she wanted. Do what she wanted. Have someone for herself. Someone to talk with, share laughter, be angry, be frightened for. She wanted it all. Vikirnoff was offering all of those things.

"I am not an easy man to be with—"

She kissed him again, stopping him in midsentence. He tasted hot. Carnal. He tasted sweet and close to love. "I'm not an easy woman to be with either—" She broke off to kiss him a third time, her fingers sliding beneath his shirt to feel his chest. She was careful to avoid his still tender wounds, not quite healed from his earlier battles. "I think I'm going to be addicted to kissing you."

She circled his neck with her arms as he made the descent with dizzying speed into a small chimney in the mountain, closing her eyes and hiding her face against his shoulder. The entrance was narrow and long. They plummeted straight down into a wide chamber with cathedral-like ceilings. He set her on her feet, holding her steady until he was certain she wouldn't fall after their flight.

Natalya tossed her pack into a corner and surveyed the large chamber as Vikirnoff waved his hands to light the candles. Instantly the air was filled with the scent of soothing lavender. "Wow. This is wonderful. Our own hot tub." She pointed toward the natural pool surrounded by flat rocks.

"I used to come here when I was a fledgling. I spent a lot of time here studying. I covered the entrance before I left, but never expected it to still be intact."

She nudged him with her shoulder. "So you said, you have to see to my happiness. Didn't I hear that when you so rudely married us without my consent?"

He groaned softly. "I can see this is going to be one of those difficult days."

She tossed her head so that her tawny hair fell around her face in waves doing things to his heart he didn't want to examine too closely. Even her rude noises were becoming endearing and that was just plain frightening.

"I think you're going to have a lot of those."

"Difficult days? I think you are right."

"So answer the question. You have to make me happy, right?"

"I can do no other," he agreed.

A slow, wicked grin curved her mouth and set her eyes

sparkling. "I need lots of things to make me happy. And keep me happy. I'm that kind of girl."

"What kind of girl?" Suspicion crept into his voice.

"Needy. High-maintenance."

"I do not doubt that for a minute." His gaze drifted over her face and something in him shifted. Stilled. "Come here."

Natalya backed up. She meant to hold her ground, but his eyes had gone to a smoky gray and darkened with intense heat. With desire. A shiver of excitement went down her spine. She licked her lips and wasn't certain whether it was necessary or deliberately provocative.

"You heard me, Natalya." His voice was low. Utterly soft. A whisper of velvet stroking her body, stroking nerve endings. "Come here to me."

Excitement surged through her. He looked grim and forbidding, his face etched with lines from the battle, his hair flowing like silk and his body so hard with his need of her. But it was his eyes, the deep hunger, the way he looked as if he were starving for her body that set her pulse pounding. The way he looked as if nothing could or would stop his possession of her.

She needed that look. She craved a man who wanted her so much nothing could stand in his way. She didn't care if that made her strange, it was who she was, who the tigress was. She wanted that implacable resolve. She wanted that possessive mouth commanding hers, his hands rough and his body hard and painfully full.

She stepped closer. Just out of reach. Tantalizingly out

of reach. She wanted to prolong the moment. Heighten his desire. She wanted to see his eyes glaze with the same brutal hunger clawing at her.

Vikirnoff felt lust rising sharply, mingling with something far more potent. He caught her arm, pulled her the scant feet separating them so that her body fell against his. Her heat nearly melted him. Her skin was satin soft. Her breasts pushed into his chest so that he felt her hard nipples rise and fall against him with each breath she took. His fingers fisted in her hair, pulling her head back so his mouth fused with hers.

Natalya was certain electricity crackled in the air around them. Liquid heat poured through her body, through veins and muscle, nearly catching her on fire. She felt the harsh tug on her hair, his mouth crushing hers, eating at hers with a wild abandon and she needed more. Demanded more. She caught at his shirt, tore at it, desperate to get at his skin. All the while she devoured his mouth, kiss for kiss, exploring with teeth and tongue, making her own demands, deliberately pushing his need higher.

He brushed aside his clothing in the way of his people, with barely a thought other than he wished them gone. Catching the front of her camisole, he stripped it away, baring her breasts to his hungry gaze, the primitiveness of the action heightening his pleasure. She was beautiful, spilling out of the material, round and firm and good enough to eat. He bent his head and took her nipple into his mouth.

Her hips bucked hard against him, her belly contracted and a hot moan escaped. He held her there, suckling at her breast, her body on fire and her needs swamping him. With each swipe of his tongue and tug of his teeth, he felt her body rock, her muscles contract; he knew her body was wet and slick and welcoming. Her mind was wide open to his deliberately. She shared her desire, fed his needs with her own open abandon. Whatever he wanted, she was there to fulfill for him and she expected the same.

His hand slid down her belly to the little ring that had intrigued him so much. He touched it, slid lower to find her pants.

"Take them off of me," she ordered, bending forward to lick at his nipples. "Hurry, Vikirnoff. Get my clothes. They hurt my skin."

He stripped her, deliberately rough, arousing her further as he walked her backward until she was against the cavern wall, took possession of her mouth again as he pulled her naked body tightly against his.

She cried out, unable to stop the small sound, uncaring that he knew she wanted to sob with so much pleasure running through her body. She ground her hips against him, wanting more, seeking more. His hand cupped her breast in reward, thumb teasing her nipple, stroking and caressing so that waves rippled through her body and tightened her womb. "More," she whispered, greedy for it all, every experience.

His teeth nibbled at her chin, teased her throat and nipped the swell of her breast. He lifted her easily, his strength enormous, holding her pinned against the wall while he laved her belly button and pressed little kisses on her stomach.

Her breath came in gasps. She tried to wrap her legs around him, so hot and wet she needed relief, but he lifted her to a ledge, so that her bottom sank into a groove there. His hands were hard on her knees jerking her thighs apart. The cool air hit her hot core, but nothing could cool her, nothing could make the ache stop.

She heard her own heart beat. She heard the sound of her ragged breathing. Then his breath was on her. His peculiar brand. A claiming that would never go away. She felt it deep inside and her entire body tightened to the point of pain. She was nearly sobbing for him. His hand cupped her mound, pressed into her heat. She jerked, twisting with hunger. Her pulse pounded in her ears, throbbed in her womb. His finger slid through her heat, pressed deeper into her.

That easy she came, shattering into fragments, her body so responsive she couldn't hide her reaction if she wanted to. Her eyes met his. She loved his face, the masculine lines etched so deep there, a warrior's face. A lover's face. She brushed her fingertips over the lines, traced his lips, all the while staring into his eyes, reveling in the sheer intensity of his desire for her, the feel in his mind that he was on the razor thin edge of his control.

"I want *you*, Natalya." His voice was husky. His fingers pushed deep so that she couldn't stop the way her hips rode him, every muscle contracting with heart-stopping pleasure.

"I know you do, Vikirnoff. I want you, too." She could barely manage to get the words out, gasping as his fingers retreated and plunged deep again.

He shook his head. "I mean *you*. I want you to understand I do not want any other woman. Only you."

She cried out as his fingers withdrew. He caught her hips in his hands, his thighs wedging between hers. "Look at me, *ainaak sívamet jutta,* I want you to know who you are with."

She met his gaze steadily. "I know exactly who I'm with."

His erection was painfully hard, almost an agony he could no longer bear. He needed to be deep inside of her where he belonged. Where they would be connected for all time. He pressed against her feminine channel, so wet and slick and hot with hunger for him.

Natalya moaned and the sound was almost too much for him, vibrating through his body until it felt like fingers on his too-tight skin stroked and caressed up and down the length of his erection. He kept her gaze captive as he pressed into her, a slow, long stroke that pushed through her feminine folds so that she gripped him like a tight fist. His breath escaped in a long rush of air as he waited for her body to accept him, waited to push a little deeper. Again. And then again. He wanted to be so deep she would never get him out.

She shuddered with pleasure. His fingers dug deep into her hips, holding her into the seat in the ledge. He began to move, withdrawing, a long excruciatingly slow movement that robbed her of her ability to think. She could only feel, could only dig her nails deep into his arm and hang on as he plunged into her, thrusting hard and deep, driving through her velvet folds while she screamed his name. He didn't stop, but kept surging powerfully into her, thick and hard, pushing through her tight folds, tilting her to get a better angle, holding her on the edge of release until she sobbed for relief. The loss of control shattered her when she'd always had so much control. It was frightening to need so much, to feel helpless under the pounding beat of sexual hunger.

"Vikirnoff." Just that. His name. *His* name. The breathless plea sent him careening out of all control. Every muscle in his body tightened to the point of pain. Every nerve ending in his body was alive and shrieking for release. The sensation built like a volcano, a strong powerful rush that shook him. He had never felt such intensity, such a feeling of need and hunger and possession as he did at that moment. Lust and love seemed intertwined, inseparable. His fingers dug into her skin and fangs exploded in his mouth. He fought back the urge to take her blood as he neared the edge of his control.

Natalya's soft breathless gasps and moans drove him over the edge. Her body was like hot silk, her feminine channel as tight as a fist, squeezing and gripping until the friction and heat burst through him like molten gold.

His release was shattering and took her with him, so that her muscles convulsed around him, over and over, powerful contractions that kept them both gasping for breath, lungs burning and bodies on fire while the world around them fragmented. Even his powerful legs turned to mush so that he leaned over her, gripping her thighs for support.

She looked an offering, lying back so that her breasts thrust upwards invitingly, her legs sprawled open to allow him to stand between her thighs. Her hair was in wild disarray and her eyes were half closed, long lashes fanning against her cheeks. "I can't move."

"Neither can I." In truth he didn't want to move. He wanted to stay buried in her for all time. She was a haven, a secret refuge that offered glimpses of paradise. He stroked her thighs with the pads of his fingers, needing to touch her, needing the intimacy of being able to touch her so freely.

"You didn't take my blood." She didn't know if she was disappointed or relieved. In all honesty, the craving was in her veins, in her mind, so strong she felt the lengthening of her incisors and the taste of him in her mouth.

His gaze jumped to hers. Hot. Hungry. The intensity stealing her breath.

"I have not discussed such a thing with you, Natalya." His accent was much thicker than usual and set her heart pounding.

"Why?"

"I will not take that decision from you." He had made up his mind to honor her wishes. He wanted her acceptance of him as much as she wanted it of him.

She was all too aware of his body locked so deeply inside of her. Of his hands stroking her thighs, moving up her belly to brush her breasts. She should have felt vulnerable splayed out as she was, but she felt utterly sexy. Wanted. Needed even. It was in the heat of his gaze and the stroke of his fingers. In the way his body stayed hard and thick and throbbing with fire even through the catastrophic explosion between them.

Natalya reached up to run her fingers through the silk of his hair. "I have to find the book. If I were to make a blood exchange with you, would it affect the way I am able call upon the elements? My magick is a part of me, like breathing. If magick was lost to me, I wouldn't know who I was anymore."

He closed his eyes. He was wholly Carpathian, born a hunter, a shape-shifter, able to command the things of nature. He didn't have to give up his world or who or what he was. Would she still have all her abilities? He couldn't give her an answer. Vikirnoff groaned and bent toward her.

Natalya responded eagerly, fusing her mouth with his, delighted that the action drove him deeper into her and set aftershocks rippling through her body with enough force to start new ones. When he lifted his head, she kept her hands on his shoulders forcing him to look into her eyes. His hips moved in a gentle, almost lazy rhythm, sending spasms of pleasure through her body. She wanted to be a part of him. Of his life. But she wanted him to want her for herself. For who she was, not because some ancient words had bound them together, or because the universe had decreed they belonged.

"You look sad, *ainaak sívamet jutta,* what are you thinking?"

"Aren't you sharing my mind?"

"Not at this precise moment. I enjoy watching the expressions on your face. Right now, while we are connected and sharing the joy in our bodies, you are looking sad. I must endeavor to find better ways to please you."

A faint smile curved her mouth. "I think you're well aware that you please me. Stop fishing for compliments."

He moved to adjust his angle just slightly as he pushed deep with a hard stroke, heightening her pleasure even more so that a small gasp escaped and the sadness disappeared from her eyes to be replaced with something altogether different.

"Vikirnoff, what is *ainaak sívamet jutta?*" Another moan escaped as he plunged deeper again. "The *exact* translation."

"It means 'forever to my heart connected.'" He shrugged, a slight movement of his wide shoulders. "Or fixed. Forever to my heart fixed. The words are interchangeable."

Her gaze drifted over his face. "Am I? Am I connected to your heart?"

"How could you think otherwise?"

Natalya didn't have an answer for that. She had confidence in her intelligence, her courage and her abilities in most areas, but not that of a woman. Of a partner. She had never thought in those terms and the ideas in his mind of what a lifemate should be were very far from what she was—or could ever be. She wanted to be his *ainaak sívamet jutta,* but she had doubts he was seeing her realistically. She closed her eyes and gave herself up to the ecstasy of his lovemaking, unwilling to think too much about the future.

She lost herself in his body, in the absolute magic they created together. She craved the feel of his hands on her body, the feel of his skin and muscles, the power of him as he took her. There was an edge to him, as if he could be ruthless in his lovemaking, pushing her beyond any limit she had ever thought she had, all the while heightening her pleasure, keeping her wanting more. Always more.

Time slipped away from her. There was only Vikirnoff and his hands and mouth and body. Each time she thought it was over and they would rest, he was there again, demanding again, wanting her. Hungry for her. She felt the scrape of his teeth and swirl of his tongue. There wasn't an inch of her that didn't go untouched, untasted, unused, but all the while he was wringing gasps of pleasure, moans and pleas for more.

He carried her to the hot springs and settled her on his lap where he could bathe her. Limp with fatigue, deliciously sore, she buried her face in his neck. "Thank you for not taking my blood. I feel the need in you, but you were so careful." His pulse pounded beneath her lips, the strong ebb and flow of life that beckoned and called and tempted.

"I told you I would not."

"Still, I would have let you," she confessed. "I wasn't thinking straight."

"I told you I would not," he reiterated. "If it is important to you, I will always remember, even when I am not thinking clearly either."

She turned her head to lie against his shoulder so she could look up at his face. There was male beauty in the lines etched there as well as other traits she was becoming familiar with. Vikirnoff wore power and dominance as easily as other men wore clothes, yet it was so natural to him, so intrinsic to his personality, she had accepted it in him without much thought, because he tempered those things with integrity and fairness.

"I'm beginning to like you."

His smile was brief, but it flared in his eyes and her heart, as tired as she was, responded with a quick beat. She smoothed her fingertip across his lips.

"That is a start." He tugged on her wet hair. "You could be hard on a man's ego if he allowed it."

She laughed. She couldn't help it. She wanted to spend all night making love every way they could and feasting on each other's body. "I doubt anything could dent your ego, Vikirnoff. The water feels so good."

"I do not want you to be sore. I intend to make certain you are properly healed before you go to sleep."

There was a note in his voice, husky, sexy, a promise of something sinfully wonderful that sent heat spreading through her veins. "I'm all for that. Are we going to stay here?" She didn't want to be separated from him. She couldn't go through another day without him.

"I think it is best. The vampire cannot send human enemies against you and I can better protect us here."

"How is Gabrielle doing? Is she still alive?"

"Yes. I hold her spirit with mine. They have sent her to sleep. Falcon will give her blood on rising. If her body can wait, Mikhail will do the third exchange on the following rising. The wait will give her plenty of time for several healing sessions with the others and a chance for her body to adjust to the ancient blood."

"How will she be connected to you, Vikirnoff?" She stifled the small pang of jealousy she was ashamed of feeling. She hadn't had anyone for herself in so long and she wanted to be his *only*.

His teeth nibbled at her shoulder. "Not in a sexual way, or in the way of a lifemate, Natalya. She will have a private path to my thoughts, as I will to hers. Our spirits will maintain a connection, as she will have been in my keeping for over twenty-four hours. Gabrielle will awaken as one of us. She will not have a lifemate to turn to for support in her new world. Her sister and brother-kin are returning as quickly as possible to aid her, but she is half in love with Gary, a human. The males will not want her to continue a relationship with him as there are so few Carpathian women and they will hope she can be a lifemate to one of them. She will awaken to many problems and will need aid."

"And you have to be there for her."

"You wished me to save her life," he reminded gently, even as his teeth bit down over the pulse beating so frantically in her throat. "I could devour you, Natalya, and never get enough."

She laughed again because she could hear the truth in his voice and felt the stirring of his body against her. It reassured her when she felt so vulnerable. "I believe you. I'm exhausted. We can't possibly, not again. I need to sleep for a week or two. And so do you."

Vikirnoff lifted her with casual ease and carried her to the far side of the cavern where he had prepared a large bed on the ground. Candles were everywhere, the flames flickering and dancing, throwing shadows on the walls to illuminate crystals and give color to the walls. The spread appeared to be a midnight blue, velvet soft with a host of cushions. He laid her facedown in the middle of them, his hands gentle on her body, positioning her head on a soft pillow and bringing her arms out.

"We're wet."

"We're not." And they weren't.

Natalya allowed her lashes to drift down as his hands began a massage at the nape of her neck. He murmured to her in his own language, urging her to sleep while he attended to her sore body. He kneaded the muscles in her neck and shoulders, her arms and back, lower still to her buttocks and thighs and calves before turning her over to attend the front of her.

Natalya drifted in a haze of mind-numbing pleasure. She felt his tongue swirling over her pulse. Teasing the valley between her breasts. Her nipples ached from the sweet torment he had inflicted for hours, but this time it was as soothing as it was stimulating as his tongue flicked and laved and lingered. He suckled gently, before attending the undersides of her breasts and spending a great deal of time tugging on the small golden hoop in her belly.

"You like that, don't you?" She didn't open her eyes. She liked the feel of drifting while he explored her in such a slow, languid fashion. There was something to be said for the slow sensual buildup as opposed to the violence of their earlier hunger.

"Very much." He nuzzled the ring and kissed his way down to the tawny triangle. "I love your body, Natalya, all soft and firm and curved so beautifully." Deliberately he pressed a finger into her wet heat. "Mostly I love how you respond for me. I have had many years to imagine what it would be like. I've studied how to please a woman to be prepared. I wanted to know every way I could bring her pleasure and how she could do the same for me. But the imagination, when one has no feeling, cannot prepare for this."

Natalya lifted her lashes just enough to watch as he

dipped his head between her thighs. She had felt every emotion, yet she was unprepared as his tongue stroked and caressed, finding every sore spot and healing her. She was unprepared for the fire racing through her, and the edgy need that spread and built until she was gripping the blanket beneath her and lifting her hips to meet his marauding mouth.

"I thought you were getting me to sleep." She reached for his hair, anything to stay anchored when her body was so ready to fly away with her.

"I changed my mind. Do not move, Natalya. Just lie there and do not move."

"It's impossible."

Immediately her arms were anchored above her head. She couldn't see how he did it, but she lay stretched out on the blanket. He lifted her hips and placed pillows beneath her to make her more comfortable before returning to his ravishment. His mouth and teeth and tongue were everywhere, his hands possessive, demanding as they moved over her until she was sobbing for release. He took her to the edge over and over, but never quite tipped her over.

Natalya could feel the heat of his erection nearly burning against her thigh. He thought he had her helpless, tormenting her to the brink of insanity, but she had other ideas. Deliberately she merged her mind with his, sharing the terrible craving for him, the dark edgy need for relief. She built a picture in her mind of him kneeling above her, her mouth engulfing him, suckling and stroking and driving him to the same fever pitch. All the while she moved her thigh subtly, like a great cat, rubbing back and forth to create a friction against his most sensitive skin.

She heard his soft groan, felt the response as he grew harder and thicker and jumped in anticipation and need. He might think he could dominate and she would be submissive, but she was as fierce and as passionate as any tigress and she was every bit as capable of driving him out of his mind with pleasure as he was doing to her.

Vikirnoff kissed his way back up her body, rubbing his face against her soft skin, unable to get enough of her. He loved the feel of her, satin and silk, fire and flame. The candlelight played lovingly over her body, a temptation in itself. He followed the erotic picture in her mind, rising above her, knee on either side of her breasts, tight, so he could feel her against him.

Natalya teased him, blowing a breath over him, flicking her tongue, swiping with small curling licks as if he were an ice cream cone. Flames engulfed him, took him to a new hunger. She looked helpless, lying stretched out on the blanket beneath him, her arms still above her head, her eyes like jewels, but there was nothing helpless about Natalya.

Vikirnoff reached down to cradle her head in his palms, holding her to him. Her lips slid over him, the moist heat of her mouth taking his breath, setting his heart pounding hard. Her mouth was a miracle, tight and slick and so hot it seemed an inferno. He lost himself in the mixture of rising lust and power and sheer carnal desire. He knew she was feeding the intensity, deliberately stealing the control. He watched the way he slid in and out of her mouth, the taunting laughter in her eyes, felt the way she wanted him to feel the same pleasure he had given her.

Destiny had tied them together, but she was so much more than that. This woman, impossible to tame, had wrapped herself around his heart. He could not imagine any other suiting him, making him laugh, making him crazy with desire, just as he was right at that moment. Groaning, he pulled away from her, to blanket her, waiting a heartbeat as he pushed slowly against her entrance. He felt the initial resistance of her body, as if she might not open for him, and then he was inside of her, surrounded by her, buried deep the way he hungered.

He whispered to her in his language, unable to find another way to express the deep connection and commitment to her. He made love to her, slow at first, watching the way her pleasure built, feeling her body tighten around him until he could only thrust harder and deeper, surging forward to keep that connection forever. She had tears in her eyes when the powerful quakes rocked through their bodies and left them gasping for air, struggling to slow their hearts; they were limp with exhaustion.

Vikirnoff rolled his weight off of her, kissing her neck as he drew her against him. "It is nearly dawn. We must sleep."

Natalya struggled to find a way to talk without proper

air. Her lungs were burning and her body still rippled with pleasure. "Aren't you going to sleep underground? Shouldn't you? I'll sleep right here, over the top of you and protect you from all the gremlins," she insisted. "The only thing you have to worry about is the Troll King."

"I have provided intricate safeguards. Even your infamous Troll King would have to pause to unravel them and I would awaken. We will be safe here."

Natalya pillowed her head on his shoulder. "I really don't mind if you need to go to ground, Vikirnoff. I can handle it."

Vikirnoff wrapped his arms around her. "I prefer to sleep right here beside you," he said. "I like holding you. If you should wake and I appear dead . . ."

"I know, I know," she interrupted. "You're really asleep. Stop flattering yourself, I'm perfectly fine without you."

"You get into trouble without me."

"Every morning, when I finally am tired enough to go to bed after watching television all night alone, I call up a dream of my childhood with my brother, Razvan. I've been doing it for years. It was the only way I could feel like I wasn't so alone, as if I still belonged and had family. This is the first time in many years I will not feel as if I have to call him to me."

"You do belong," he said. He pressed kisses against the nape of her neck. "You belong with me, thanks to those binding words you disliked so much."

She frowned, snuggling closer. "Don't think I'm giving up on undoing the spell. I'm tenacious."

"It is not exactly a spell." His eyes were heavy and his arms were taking on the leaden feeling of his kind. "But did you figure out the first two lines?"

"Of course." She felt smug; she couldn't help it. She had always had a gift for languages and she had the advantage of speaking earlier languages before they had evolved into the twentieth century patterns. She was familiar with the way many words were considered unnecessary in the earlier languages. "The first two sentences translate more exactly to something like this: 'you wedded wife-my'. There is no specific word for the word 'are'. The second line comes out something close to: 'to me you belong, wedded wife-my.' I'm not certain of the exact phrasing, but it is far closer than the more modern form."

A slow smile lit his eyes. "Really?" He arched his brows at her.

"Yes, really," she said, undeterred. "I know you think it's funny, but I refuse to be trapped into something whether I want it or not. It's not good for you to think you've got me tied to you. I'm not a passive person and I wouldn't want you to think I am."

His laughter was soft, his breath warm against the nape of her neck. "Passive? You? I cannot imagine anyone, least of all me, making that mistake."

She grinned, closing her eyes. "Razvan said I needed

to curb my tongue and that if Shakespeare had met me, Kate wouldn't be the famous shrew, Natalya would."

"He said that, did he?" Vikirnoff was wise enough not to agree aloud. Not when her body nestled so comfortably next to his. "What else did Razvan have to say?"

"He said I needed to learn how to sew, to be more restful and soothing and to censor most of what I say." There was laughter and affection in her voice.

"I cannot imagine."

"I told him I did censor most of what I say. If he could read my mind . . ." Her voice trailed off, her lashes lifting so she could meet the amusement in his gaze. "Lucky you. You get to know the real me with no censorship."

"Good night, Natalya." He kissed her again and succumbed to the sleep of his kind, feeling very lucky to know the real woman.

15

"**R**azvan! Where are you? I'm so happy. Come to me to-night. Where are you? Why won't you answer me?" Natalya hurried down the cobblestone steps leading to the great garden. They always met in the garden if they'd been separated for the day, but she couldn't find her brother anywhere.

"Why are you so happy?" The voice came from a distance and Natalya spotted her twin seated on the slabs of slate overlooking the fountain. He looked glum, his legs drawn up, his elbows on his knees, chin propped in hand. "Where have you been, Natalya? Do you even realize you deserted me? I didn't know the safeguards and I had to see grandfather."

That brought her up short. They never referred to him as grandfather. Xavier was supposed to be dead. If they talked about him he would punish them, and his punishments were terrible. Xavier. Their Grandfather. They were forced to live with him after their father had disappeared. Natalya frowned. Why couldn't she remember Xavier when she was awake? She knew exactly what he looked like when she conjured up her dreams of her childhood, but not when she was in present time awake. How did that happen? "Don't call him that. We are to call him Uncle. He might hear you."

"Why didn't you give me the safeguards, Natalya? How could you leave me wide open like that?" Razvan stood up slowly, turning as he did so, lifting his shirt. "Look what he did to me."

Natalya halted instantly. "Oh, no! Razvan, why does he take it out on you when I make a mistake? I hate that. I hate that we're so afraid to be together we have to meet like this. Did he take your blood?"

"He always takes my blood. If not mine, then he would take yours. You know that. I don't care if he punishes me; he isn't going to get your blood."

"Why do we stay? Why are we allowing him to dictate to us and keep us small children? I have power. He can't control me. He wants me to believe he can, but he can't. You have the same power in you, Razvan. You've resisted him for years. Together we can break free of him."

"We have different strengths, Natalya. You're good at commanding the elements. You have a quick mind and can figure things out."

"You come up with the ideas in the first place, Razvan. Without you, we would have been dead a long time ago." The words caught at Natalya. She looked down at her hands. They weren't the hands of a child, but those of a grown woman.

Shock spread through her. She looked up at Razvan. "What happened to us?"

The form of the teenage boy shimmered, became translucent and a man's image superimposed itself over the child. "You betrayed me. You chose the hunter, my enemy."

Natalya shook her head, reaching out toward her brother. "I chose happiness, Razvan. That was something our grandfather didn't understand, could never understand. What was the point of longevity? I've watched people die over and over, but they led happy lives while I just lived on and on alone with no one to share anything with. Neither sorrow nor joy." Her arms dropped back to her side, empty.

"We have power beyond imagination."

"No, we don't. I've seen power beyond imagination, but it doesn't matter to me. Those people who are born, live their lives together as a family and die surrounded by family; they know how to live. What do we do? What does he do? He hides from the world with his malevolent schemes, drinking blood to stay alive—for what? Why live so long without happiness? I choose to be happy, to share my life. I will not apologize or feel guilty for that."

"Look at us, Natalya. You took our world and changed it. I'm no longer a boy and I'm fading. Would you really choose him over your brother? Your twin?"

"I will not leave him. Why would you think I'm trading one for the other? You're in my dreams, Razvan. I will never forget you, never." Her heart pounding, she studied the fading image of her twin, the harshness in the face of the man.

"*You don't need me. You have him.*"

Natalya refused to sound as if she were pleading. Or asking permission. "*He is alive and I am alive. I cannot sustain my life on dreams of a brother long gone from me. My love for him is different.*"

Razvan's face twisted with anger. "*I forbid this! He is a hunter, hated by our family. Choose another.*"

"*This is a dream, only a silly dream. I choose Vikirnoff. I choose happiness,*" *Natalya said, determined to wake up. She would not allow her dreams to take on the twisted nightmares that sometimes invaded them. Razvan would want her happy. He wouldn't be so angry with her over choosing to be involved in a relationship with someone who made her happy. Whatever occasionally crept into her dreams and corrupted them, she wasn't going to put up with it anymore.*

"*Wait!*" *Razvan called frantically.* "*The safeguards. You didn't give me the safeguards. I can't weave them myself.*"

Natalya turned back to him, frowning as she murmured the spell to him.

He smiled at her, beloved Razvan, already repeating the words to ensure he didn't forget them. Pain flashed unexpectedly through her head, a terrible pressure that increased without mercy, and then, just as abruptly disappeared, leaving her shaken.

He shook his head. "*It isn't right. That's not right. You aren't telling me the truth.*"

Natalya stared at her brother in sudden shock and dawning horror. "*My god, Razvan, it's you. It's been you all along.*"

She gave a low, tormented cry. Her heart felt as if he had literally torn it from her chest.

She jolted into full consciousness with the sound of her cry still echoing in her ears. Tears spilled from her eyes and her breath came in great anguished sobs. "This can't be happening. This can't be happening." She pressed the back of her hand against her trembling mouth. Her stomach lurched and she crawled away from Vikirnoff on her hands and knees and was sick in the corner of the cave.

He woke instantly, moving with his preternatural speed, kneeling beside her, hand on her back, his body pressed against hers. "What is it? Tell me what has caused this distress." Only an hour or so had passed, and the lethargy did not have him in its grip.

"A dream." She sank into him, shivering with cold, wanting his arms around her. "Only it wasn't my dream. It hasn't been my dream for a long time only I didn't know. I didn't understand."

Vikirnoff wrapped his arms around her tightly, pulling her into the shelter of his body. He rocked her gently, feeling her pain, a terrible hurt that couldn't be comforted. "Tell me, *ainaak enyém*." His voice was infinitely gentle.

Natalya was grateful he didn't probe into her mind. She felt raw. Betrayed. Ashamed. Was it the legacy of her mage blood? Was it possible her whole family was so tainted? A small sob escaped before she could choke it back. She huddled closer to Vikirnoff while he rocked her, stroking her hair and holding her close to him.

"He's alive."

"Xavier? We knew that."

She shook her head, tightened her fingers around his wrist, needing to hold onto his solid strength while her world shattered around her. "Not Xavier. Razvan. He's alive. He's the Troll King." Her hand crept down to rub her ankle. "And that means he's in league with Xavier and Maxim. He's in league with vampires."

Vikirnoff brushed the top of her hair with a kiss and rubbed his cheek against the back of her head in an effort to soothe her. "How do you know this?"

"Remember when we were in the cave and Maxim attacked me, was able to get into my head so easily? My safeguards were gone. You replaced them, not me. You wove a different thread through my mind, not one I've ever used."

"How does that make him alive?" Pain radiated off of her in waves but all Vikirnoff could do was hold her, feeling utterly helpless in the face of her anguish. All of his centuries of education, all of his vast power could not prepare him for this moment when she needed him the most. He could only hold her to him and feel her terrible grief.

"My dreams have always been of my childhood with him. It was the only time we were together. We separated to be safe from Xavier, but we'd meet in our dreams and share information. We did that for years. After he died, I summoned the dreams and they would repeat and it would comfort me. But somewhere along the line the dreams started changing. I don't even remember when. We would talk about things pertinent now, in this time. I just assumed it was because I was lonely and I wanted to share my thoughts about things so the dreams changed to suit me."

"That's logical, Natalya. Things occurring during the day that prey on our minds often will creep into dreams. At least that's what I've read."

She shook her head, her eyes dark with pain. "It wasn't like that. *He* would ask me questions about experiments just like in the old days, but these were new ones."

"The challenges. You said you were challenged to make things work. I thought Xavier challenged you."

"It was Razvan. Razvan has been using me, for I don't know how long. It's why I can't remember things. Not Xavier. He didn't have my blood." A sob escaped, torn from her throat, the sound piercing Vikirnoff like a knife. "When I was a child, Razvan protected me from Xavier. He took the punishments and he went to the laboratories. He came up with ideas, but I figured out how to do them and gave Razvan the information. It was how we prevented him from receiving Xavier's punishments. Xavier thought Razvan was the one who had the natural abilities. We tricked him for years into thinking that." She wiped at the tears running down her face; the pain was so deep she felt as if her brother had torn out her heart. She pressed her hand there, trying to still the agony.

"And you believe somewhere over the last few years, Xavier managed to recruit Razvan to his side?" Vikirnoff kept his voice strictly neutral. Natalya was so devastated and he was helpless in the face of her suffering. He snapped his teeth together hard, rage building in spite of his effort to be calm. His arms tightened. He wanted to take away all of her pain, protect her from any further hurt, but Natalya was not a woman to wrap in cotton. She would face this in her way. On her own terms.

"He had to have. I don't know how. I don't even know why. Living a long time without happiness sucks. Why would either of them want that?"

His arms tightened, sheltering her even closer to him. "I have no idea. But are you certain, Natalya? Is it possible you really were discussing your everyday thoughts in your dreams?"

"You provided the safeguards and he couldn't reach me. He couldn't track me. That's why the Troll King didn't show up when you were fighting the vampires. It was so strange that he wasn't there." She raked her fingers through her hair in sheer agitation. "That bugged me. He'd been there every other time. He didn't have the advantage of being able to read my mind. He couldn't find me."

"Because I used a completely different safeguard, one unfamiliar to him."

"That first morning, after the Troll King marked me and I brought you to my room, he knew. You were already able to get past all my shields, which by the way, are incredibly strong, but Razvan had removed them. That's how the shadow warrior was able to get in. I set the safeguards in the room, not you. And that's why I didn't sense him in the ground, even when he was attacking me in the cave." Again she rubbed her ankle. "I was only aware of the actual attack after the poison was already on my leg."

"And when we were running down the stairs in the cave, I sensed him running parallel to us, but he confused you, making you believe he was under us."

Natalya nodded her head, trying not to shake with the sudden cold settling into the very bones of her body. "He's alive, Vikirnoff. And he's orchestrating something very bad here."

"And he and the vampires want the book your father stole. Xavier and Razvan need the book to complete their plans."

"But my father hid it from them. And Razvan knows I can touch objects and see things so they've been waiting until the right moment to acquire the book in order to proceed." She pressed her fingertips into her aching temples. "I provided them with the way to do this." She tapped her ankle. "Razvan challenged me and I made it happen. He used my own work against me. How ironic is that?"

"I am sorry, *ainaak enyém*, I know how much you love

him." He held her tightly, breathing for her, feeling the pain knifing through her heart and praying he wouldn't have to be the one to kill her brother.

"I know I'm right, Vikirnoff. He'll come after us with everything he has now. He knows that I know. I didn't mean to give myself away, I was just so shocked." She spread her hands out in front of her. "I'm so sorry. If only I'd thought to play along with him. I could have gotten us information."

Vikirnoff took her hand, pressed a kiss into her palm, her knuckles, the tips of her fingers. "Do not apologize. Not now, not ever. Your reaction is entirely justified."

"But he'll try to kill you."

"He has been trying to kill me." He smiled against the nape of her neck. "You thought about killing me. I seem to bring that out in people."

She tried to smile, appreciating that he would make such an effort with her, but she couldn't get past how obtuse she'd been. "I should have handled it better."

"Betrayal is never easy to handle and there is no right way to accept it. It doesn't matter now. We are going to be okay."

Natalya was silent for a long time. He could hear the beat of her heart begin to accelerate. She turned her face up to his, one hand reaching back to catch him around the neck as she looked into his eyes. "Exchange blood with me."

His own heart began to pound wildly, matching the

rhythm of hers. "I thought we were not going to take any chances that you can't access the memories of the knife."

"If I won't be able to find the book, neither will they. Neither side will have it and that's probably a good thing. Anything Xavier made and sealed with the blood of three magical species is no doubt powerful, deadly and too dangerous for anyone to try to wield."

Vikirnoff took a deep breath and let it out. There it was. Total commitment. There would be no going back once she converted. She was tied to him now, but that last step, that important difference would seal her to him and his kind for all time. He wanted her to choose that path for herself. Not to escape from who she was.

"Natalya . . ." What could he say? He could deny her nothing, especially now when pain was her world and she was so shattered. "If we do not know where the book is, how can it be protected? What if they find a psychic woman with your talent to help them find the book? We need to destroy it."

"How can we destroy the book? If it could have been destroyed so easily, then my father would have done so."

"You have a good point. I do not know the answer to that, Natalya, but I think all Carpathians would sleep better knowing our prince had the care of the book rather than knowing it was floating around somewhere the vampires could find it."

"What if the book corrupts those who touch it? Power corrupts."

"That is something we do not have to think about yet, Natalya. The truth is, you want to exchange blood with me not because you are committed to *me,* to our relationship, but because you believe something is wrong with you."

The gentleness in his voice made her want to weep and she turned her face away from his so he wouldn't see tears glittering in her eyes. "It isn't what you think."

"It is, *ainaak enyém,* you think your blood is tainted and you wish to escape from it. Not all of the mages were evil. Most were kind and intelligent and so generous. Our people were friends. Even Xavier, at one time, was well respected and a tremendous help to all who sought his advice. You said yourself power can corrupt. I do not know how it happened, but it was not the blood running through his veins."

She pulled out of his arms and made her way to the small waterfall, catching the water in her hand to rinse her mouth. She was still so cold. She couldn't seem to find warmth in spite of the natural heat in the cave.

Vikirnoff could feel her anguish and cursed his own inadequacy at taking her pain from her. There was no way to ease betrayal, no way to kiss and make her better. His throat was raw with the need to help her, but he couldn't undo this terrible tragedy.

"Maybe it wasn't his blood, Vikirnoff, but I'm tied to them. They invaded my mind. *My mind.* They removed memories and planted stories. They traded on my love for my brother and corrupted my good memories of him." She ran her hand over her ankle again. "And they put parasites in my body. I don't want them to know me. I don't want them to *ever* crawl inside my mind again."

He stood up and followed her across the chamber. "The conversion will change your entire life."

She stepped into the heat of the pool. The water felt hot on her icy skin. Even her insides felt ice cold. She hoped the heat of the springs would stop her shivering. "My entire life has already changed." She held out her hand to him. "For the better." A faint smile rose up unexpectedly. "I've decided you're trainable."

His eyebrow shot up as he stepped into the pool beside her. "Trainable?"

She nodded. "You can't possibly think you're going to get away with bossing me, right? So once you're past the fact that I'm always right, we'll get along just fine."

He shook his head. "You are impossibly optimistic for your chances." He pulled her down into the water with him so that she was tucked in close beneath his shoulder.

"Chances of what?" Her head felt too heavy and she leaned it against his chest.

"Of being right. I am one of those obnoxious people who know everything. You think I am bossy, but in fact, I am merely directing you when you start to go off track."

"And you expect me to thank you, I suppose, for your brilliant direction."

"I have many ways in mind for you to show your appreciation."

"I'll just bet you do." She rubbed her ankle beneath the water. "This is never going to come off, is it? It's part of my skin now."

"I do not know. I am not really a healer, although I can perform basic healing skills. When Gregori returns we can have him take a look at it. If he cannot remove the mark, we can seek out Francesca. She is in Paris and is said to be amazing."

"Is it possible the conversion would remove it?"

His hand slipped beneath the water to circle her ankle. "I wish I knew. I doubt it, Natalya. You are very different from any other I have known. I do not know what the conversion would do to you. I do not believe it will take away your skills as a mage. Rhiannon possessed more talent than most wizards. You must have received that from her as well as from the mage blood to make you so powerful. It is no wonder Xavier wanted your blood."

Natalya's eyes met his. "Razvan wouldn't allow it."

Vikirnoff's strong fingers moved over her ankle in a soothing massage.

Natalya began to relax again, the hard knot in her stomach easing. When had Vikirnoff become someone she could feel peace with? She slid her hand over his belly, without sexual intent, but needing to feel his body beneath her fingertips. "Do you think I could have held out against Xavier? If I had been the one to visit him instead of Razvan? If Xavier took my blood?" She would not call him grandfather. "Do you think Razvan could have been saved?"

"There is no way of knowing."

She looked so distraught, so different from her confident, sassy self that his heart shifted with pain. Vikirnoff touched her mind to read her, needing to know how to help her. Natalya possessed a will of iron. Her brother was her twin. They thought alike. They protected one another. They had lived through harrowing times even as young teens and found a way to survive without adult guidance.

Vikirnoff looked into her heart and found her shaken all the way to her soul.

Razvan had honorably chosen to give his blood to Xavier. He had successfully deceived his grandfather into believing he was the one with the superior skills in magick, when it was really Natalya. They had carried out an elaborate deception and Razvan was often punished when Natalya couldn't complete experiments and pass the information on fast enough to her brother. She had hidden in safety while her brother had taken all the risks and now, after all of his sacrifices, she couldn't bear to think she hadn't been there to save him as he had saved her. She hadn't been there for him and he'd turned to evil. Her guilt was soul-consuming, a terrible burden he felt penetrating his own soul.

She looked up, her gaze locking with his. "Is there a way to get him back? Can we undo the damage done to him?"

"Natalya . . ." There was a warning note in his voice. "He has Carpathian blood running in his veins. There is every possibility that he is now part vampire. I never thought vampires would ever join forces, but they have. And your brother is in league with them. Maxim and his brothers are arrogant and believe they should be ruling the world. I think that both Xavier and Razvan feel they should be the rulers and they have united with the vampires in the hopes of gaining control of everything. The vampires are using your experiment to recognize one another, those participating in this conspiracy. I found the parasites first in my brother's lifemate's blood. She had been taken as a child and converted by a vampire. She was able to defeat him, but her blood called to the others. That's how they identify the members of the conspiracy, those with the parasites in their blood. It has to be that." He gentled his tone. "You know Razvan is lost to you."

"How do I know? The healers do incredible things. Maybe he could be saved. He isn't wholly Carpathian. So if he did turn, he isn't wholly vampire." She wiped her hand over her face as if that could erase the knowledge of the extent of her twin's betrayal. "He was a good man. For centuries, he was honorable and he suffered so much."

Vikirnoff sighed with regret. "You wanted to know why he wanted children. I have seen that question in your mind many times."

She swallowed the sudden lump in her throat and refused to meet his gaze, shaking her head slightly.

"He is looking for blood just as Xavier wanted the

blood of his children to sustain his life. That is how he remained alive all these years. Not all children will carry what he needs, so he wanted several from different mothers." *And Razvan now wanted Natalya's blood just as Xavier sought it all those years ago.* Razvan would not take her from Vikirnoff. He could not be allowed to destroy the fragile threads that bound their hearts even as their souls were welded so tightly together.

"You don't know that." But it made sense. It was exactly what Xavier had done. She had witnessed it when she'd grasped the handle of the ceremonial knife.

"No, I do not. And I do not know if there is any hope for him. What I do know is there are vampires conspiring to kill the prince and kidnap you. They are hunting for a book your father gave his life to protect. He was so desperate to protect that book he put a compulsion on you to find it should someone start nosing around the cave."

"Someone went into the ice cave before us and that triggered the compulsion." She'd already figured that out for herself.

"If your father was willing to give his life to keep that book from Xavier, I am willing to bet we do not want it in his hands."

"I still think there's a chance."

"Natalya, I cannot tell you how many friends—even family I have had to hunt and kill. When we face a loved one who has become a vampire, even hunters hesitate. And when facing a hunter as skilled as your brother, hesitation is a death sentence. You cannot afford pity. You cannot afford to think he can be saved. He cannot."

"How do you know, though? Have any of you ever tried to heal a vampire? Has it ever once been tried?" She knew it was desperation, but she couldn't help pushing it. There had to be a way to save her brother. If his sacrifice for her had led to his downfall then she bore the responsibility. He had been there for her when she needed him so desperately; she had to find a way to be there for him.

Vampires were completely evil. She had seen their depravity, their joy in the killing of others. She couldn't bear that Razvan had *chosen* such a thing. That he had deliberately embraced everything they had fought against all of their lives. Vikirnoff could see her struggle to fight off the weight of guilt and fear and even repugnance. She didn't want to fear her brother. She didn't want to loathe and despise him. She didn't want to feel revulsion for what he had become.

Reluctantly, Virkirnoff released Natalya when she pushed away from him. His heart ached as he watched her swim restlessly back and forth across the small pool. He couldn't lie or soften the truth. He respected her too much for that. When they hunted for the book, they would be pursued. And they had to hunt for the book. He knew it, and somewhere, deep inside, so did Natalya. The book would surface sooner or later, maybe even in another century when memories had dulled. It was far too dangerous to leave to chance.

Vikirnoff rubbed his hand over his face, his stomach

lurching at the idea of what was to come. Natalya was an exceptional woman, but one he had never expected, one he'd thought he would never want. Yet why had he envisioned a docile, amenable woman as his lifemate? Natalya was a woman to walk beside him. He could not imagine his life without the sharp edge of her tongue, or her peculiar sense of humor.

His brows drew together as he watched her swim back and forth. The beads of moisture on her face were not from the spring water and that was painful. *Does that television set in your room at the inn actually work?* He used their more intimate path of communication deliberately, wanting her to feel him inside of her.

She halted abruptly, throwing back her hair so that water went in every direction. Blinking rapidly to clear her vision, she nodded. "Why?"

"Half of what you say makes no sense to me. If we are to communicate adequately, I have to watch your late night movies."

She sent up a spout of water straight at his face. "Don't sound like you're going to a funeral. Late night movies are fun. *Fun.* Do you even understand the concept of having fun?"

There it was again. That heartbreaking note of desperation, of strain, in her voice. She was gamely smiling at him, but her eyes were dark with sorrow. Vikirnoff waded over to her, his gaze locked with hers. All the teasing in the world wouldn't fix it. All the love in the world wouldn't take it away. All he could do was pull her into the shelter of his body, as close to his heart as possible. And tell her the real truth. She would see him for what he was. It was a risk he hesitated to take. Their relationship was so very fragile and he always seemed to make the wrong decision.

He was aware of his blood moving through his body, carrying his shame. "I do not know that Razvan willingly chose to embrace evil, Natalya."

"I don't understand what you mean. He has to be vampire. Or at least in league with the vampires. How could that not be choosing to embrace evil?"

He heard his heart thundering in his ears, trying to drown out the sound of his voice confessing. Voicing aloud what he didn't want known. What he didn't admit to himself. He rubbed his face against hers, his fingers tangling in her wet hair.

Natalya held her breath, sensing how vulnerable Vikirnoff was at that moment, sensing the cost to his pride. "Tell me."

"Before I met you. Long before I met you, I hunted the vampire everywhere I went. I was good at it, Natalya, because life no longer mattered to me. Not my life and not that of any other. I realized I was becoming the very thing I hunted so I sought my brother, hoping his close proximity would alleviate the growing darkness."

Natalya pressed closer, circling his neck with her arms, wanting to give him strength as he'd done for her. "Go on, Vikirnoff." She felt his reluctance and knew he was giving her something of himself, something that cost him dearly.

Vikirnoff drew in a tortured breath. "It helped for a few years and then the emptiness was a weight pressing heavier than ever. I backed off making the kills, allowing Nicolae to destroy the vampires after we found them. I even spent most of my time in another form."

"All good things to keep yourself going." She caught glimpses of a stark, bleak existence in his mind, but it was nearly impossible to understand without merging with him and he was holding himself away from her.

Vikirnoff closed his eyes. "You are not understanding what I am saying to you, Natalya. I am an ancient Carpathian. I am well-schooled in what happens to our males should they continue to live and hunt and destroy. There is a point of no return. A place in one's mind where a choice must be made."

Natalya frowned and pulled back to look at the lines etched into his face. "What choice?"

"Every moment of our existence, we are acutely aware of the gathering darkness. We know if we do not find our lifemate there is a time we must make a decision to protect our people and the populations of the world. Once that time is upon us, we cannot allow it to pass us by. If we do not choose to meet the dawn with honor, then we endanger our souls by becoming vampire."

Natalya reached up to frame his face. "But who can ever make such a choice?"

"It is our legacy, Natalya. We are given the ritual binding words to preserve our species, our lives. It is our only true safeguard. Without the light to our darkness we succumb inevitably to evil if we do not seek the dawn." His gaze shifted from her face, jumped back to meet her green eyes. "I was far, far past the point of no return. I knew the exact day of my choosing. I remember it vividly, but I did not do what was necessary to ensure the survival of the rest of my race. I chose life. I clung to life when I should have chosen the dawn."

She shook her head, her fingers stroking the strong bones of his face. "That's not true. You said we are lifemates. Doesn't that mean you were meant to survive?"

He shook his head. "I was too close. You sensed it in the forest long before you ever saw me. You could not tell if I was hunter or vampire. I could not tell either." He refused to flinch away from the raw truth. "I do not know if a second moment of choice ever comes after that first. I cannot tell you if Razvan even knew there was a time of choice. It had been so long since I had actually experienced emotions, experienced anything, my mind began to wander into places I know it should not have gone, but I was unable to stop it."

Natalya took a deep breath, her fingers tangling in his hair. There were so many emotions in him, running deep, carving out deep wounds of humiliation. It cost him his pride as a Carpathian hunter, as a male of his species to tell her his darkest secret, to admit the shame of his choice knowing what would inevitably happen, and the worse shame of not being able to stop himself moving inexorably toward ultimate evil.

"Razvan did not have my training. He did not have the knowledge of what could happen drilled into him for centuries. Does this make him weak? Is it a betrayal of all we love, or is the choice taken from us, lost in the haze created in our minds when everything runs together and there are no longer clear lines of definition, just awful, meaningless existence?"

She felt dazed, humbled even, looking into his dark eyes. There was pain there, the pain of centuries of emptiness. There was fear that she would reject him.

"How could you think that I could reject you? Why would I? Not for baring your soul and confessing to me because you wanted me to know Razvan didn't deliberately betray me." She pressed kisses along his jaw, trailed several to the corner of his mouth. Her tongue flicked enticingly along the seam of his lips.

"Razvan might not have meant to betray you, it may have just happened. But, Natalya, mine was a true betrayal. As your lifemate, I should have put your protection above all else and I should have chosen the dawn when that moment came to make my choice."

She kissed his mouth, soft pressing kisses over and over until he opened his mouth to her. She drowned in his taste. In his stark honesty. In the sacrifice of his pride for her. She wanted to cry for both of them. "There was no betrayal, Vikirnoff," she said softly, "only life. Just life. And it can be hard and cruel and terrifying. But it can also be exhilarating and beautiful and filled with passion for all things if you want it. We want it. Both of us. We are not willing to let it pass by. I would have clung to life as you did. As Razvan did. I don't know if he can be saved or not, but at least I feel as if he didn't choose to betray me. Thank you for that."

Vikirnoff crushed her to him, his breath exploding out of his lungs in relief. He pushed the tawny hair from her eyes, framed her face so he could drink her in, devour her. Heady relief mixed with sharp joy. Natalya's beauty ran far more than skin deep. He kissed her, a slow sizzling kiss of happiness that her heart was so open to him.

She melted into him, one leg sliding around his thigh so she pressed closer, rubbing her wet, slick body against his in invitation.

Vikirnoff lifted her easily, urging her to wrap both legs around his waist, leaving her open to him, allowing him to position her over the head of his erection. The welcoming folds of her channel were hot velvet and exquisitely tight, holding him like a fist as he buried his body deep into hers. It was a miracle to him, the way her body accepted his, stroked and gripped and milked his. Her skin was hot and soft and rubbed against his with every movement.

Her face was beautiful in the shadows from the flickering candlelight, which played over her soft curves. She leaned back, her hands clasped around his neck and began a long, slow ride of ecstasy, the pleasure on her face heightening her beauty. He let her take the lead, bringing him to the point of climax several times only to stop and tease his pulse with her tongue and teeth. Waiting. Building. He felt the powerful orgasm gathering and gathering, a force that finally took control from both of them. It rushed over him, over her, taking them with it as it thundered through their bodies and souls.

He heard his own hoarse shout, her soft cry, felt the convulsion of her strong muscles surrounding him and the blood-red tears on his face.

16

Natalya sank back onto her heels as she knelt staring at the jewel-embedded ceremonial knife. It lay on a small piece of cloth between them. The blade was slightly curved and the handle ornate. Instead of looking deadly, the knife seemed an object of priceless art.

"The knife looks so harmless, doesn't it?" Natalya asked. "And yet looks can be deceptive. It's been used countless times to murder." Her hand hovered over the blade and trembled. Natalya pulled back.

The sun had set and both she and Vikirnoff had bathed in the hot spring water after making love. It had been difficult for her to avoid taking his blood. She craved it more than ever, as if he were a drug she was ad-dicted to and now, with the knowledge that Razvan was still alive, the idea of becoming a Carpathian held both comfort and promise. They were both dressed in the clothes Vikirnoff had fashioned for them. Now, there was only one last task that stood in her way; touching this knife, accessing the violent memories that clung to the ceremonial weapon.

"I have fed and I am here as your anchor to hold you to this world and this time." He stroked a long caress over her hair. "The safeguards are in place and my duty to Gabrielle has been done. Falcon has given her the second blood exchange and we have all answered the call to heal her. This is our time, Natalya. Find out what memories the knife holds and hopefully we will have a clue to where the book is hidden. Once we retrieve it we can take the book to a safe place where it can be destroyed or guarded adequately."

Natalya took a deep breath and let it out. "Reading the knife will not be easy, Vikirnoff. We will live the memories of those that died on its blade."

His hand slid up her arm to her shoulder, fingers massaging gently. "I know this is difficult for you. If I could, I would do it for you."

She sat there with the candles flickering all around her and the knife in front of her. The sound of the water lapping at the edges of the pool soothed her and Vikirnoff's presence made her feel protected. She had "read" objects hundreds of times, yet she was reluctant to relive the death of her grandmother and worse, the murder of her father, even with Vikirnoff there to aid her. "You believe I can do this."

"I know that you can."

"Before I do, I want you to know I'm not mad at you anymore."

His eyebrow shot up. "Were you angry with me?"

She scowled at him. "Yes, I was angry with you. Sheesh! You didn't even notice?"

"We made love a dozen times, more even. You bit me a few times and there are scratches on my back, but I enjoyed you putting the marks there."

"That's because you're a pervert. And I'm not talking about that. I'm talking about your ridiculous and totally arbitrary decision to bind us together."

"Natalya?"

"What?"

"You sound angry."

"Well, of course I'm angry. You didn't even notice that I was angry in the first place. Do you realize how upsetting that is? All this time I thought you were suffering because I was mad at you, but you didn't even notice."

"I am sorry. I should have been more observant."

"You don't sound sorry." She ran her fingertips around the knife and held her palm above the blade testing the strength of the vibrations of violence. "In all honesty, Vikirnoff, I really don't want to do this."

"I know. And I understand. No one wants to relive the torture and murder of their parents or grandmother."

Vikirnoff knelt behind her, knowing she was working up her courage, chattering to cover her hesitation. "I will take the journey with you. When memories become too much to bear, I will do what I can to lessen the pain."

"What if you're trapped there with me and we can't pull out until every kill has been reenacted? It was your strength that allowed me to get away from the past."

His arms enfolded her, his hands sliding down her arms to envelop her hands in his. "You feel the violence of the knife's past without touching."

Natalya leaned against his chest, allowing her head to rest on his shoulder. "Yes, but I'm not reading the memories."

"I want to hold the knife in my hand with your hands around mine, so that your fingers brush the knife, but limiting your physical contact with it. Perhaps that will minimize the risk to you."

Natalya took a breath and let it out, trying to still her chaotic mind. She'd rather battle ten vampires than read what the knife offered, but all the wishing in the world wasn't going to change what had to be done. "Let's try it, then, Vikirnoff, but if you feel that you can't get us out, drop the knife."

"I will."

His breath was warm and comforting on the back of her head as she bent forward again, allowing her to feel his presence without distracting her. She laid her hand over his and nodded to let him know she was ready.

Vikirnoff reached for the knife. She felt her own heart
beating, strong and steady, beginning to accelerate. Her
muscles began to knot painfully.

I am with you.

She felt him, strong and solid behind her, his arms
around her, there for her. *With her*—and that meant
everything. She drew courage from his presence and her
fingers brushed the handle of the knife. Instantly she felt
the curving of time, the wrenching pull that dragged her
into the past and deeper into the violent memories the
knife contained.

The concentrated fear of so many victims rushed toward her, surrounded her and invaded her mind and soul.
Immediately she focused on the feel of Vikirnoff's hand,
the shape and size of it, the warmth of his skin. The
mounting terror lessened enough for her to slide past,
reaching for the reenactment she needed. There seemed
to be so many souls wailing with grief and crying for jus-
tice. She knew whatever the knife needed to show her had
to have occurred farther in the past before her father's
death. He had to have hidden the book and spilled blood
on the knife.

*My father wouldn't have sacrificed someone to leave behind
the information. The reenactment would be much fainter
than the ones with more violence. That would explain how I
missed it the first time.*

*Slow down. You are moving so fast I cannot catch even
glimpses of what has occurred.*

I feel the level of violence and know it is not what I want and I don't want to know what else Xavier has done or whom he killed . . . Her voice trailed off and she halted abruptly to find herself in the crystal cave. She looked around her carefully.

What is it?

Razvan. I feel him. His presence is strong in this time period.

Vikirnoff inhaled sharply, wanting to tighten his arms protectively around Natalya and order her out of there. *How long ago was this?*

I can't tell. Recently, I think. I haven't felt the presence of my father yet.

Vikirnoff's instincts shrieked at him. *This is unnecessary. You do not need to witness any violence Razvan commits. Keep moving, Natalya.*

She wanted to see her brother. She wanted to witness with her own eyes his betrayal. It seemed the only way to make herself believe that he had gone over to the side of the vampires, to Xavier, was to see the extent of his betrayal. Stubbornly she watched as her brother sauntered into the ice chamber. He carried the ceremonial knife in his hand and his eyes were glittering with some fierce emotion.

You cannot. Vikirnoff inserted a mild push into his voice, not wanting to take command of her, but the taste in his mouth was bitter with warning. Razvan looked far too much like Xavier in his youth; a madman bent on accumulating power over others. Xavier had grown in power and stature very quickly with his natural talent and he became convinced that he was destined to rule the world. The corruption of a once-great sorcerer was complete when he discovered the rush of power the taking of life gave him. Furious that the Carpathian race seemed to be immortal, something he was not, he grew to despise them with a fanatical hatred that fed his own ego and determination to stamp them out once he had gained the secrets of their blood. Razvan wore that same, smug, contempt-filled expression.

The ice chamber was the same, yet not the same. Fewer orbs lit the cavern and the ice formations were less abundant. On the far wall, the dragons were frozen in time, encased behind layers of ice.

They weren't there before. Natalya read his mind. *They are now in the hall leading to the main chamber, remember? Something terrible will happen here.*

Vikirnoff felt Natalya's heart pounding through her body, in her veins, threatening to burst, as Razvan turned and beckoned someone toward him. A young girl emerged from the shadows, a child really, forced forward by compulsion. The girl had bright green eyes and a wealth of copper curls. She shook her head as Razvan caught her arm, jerking her closer to him.

Don't! Natalya tried to pry her fingers from the knife, but something much stronger than her will held her there, mesmerized. *He wants her blood. He's taking her blood.* She winced as the ceremonial knife slashed across the little wrist and Razvan pressed the open vein to his mouth. *He's seeking immortality just the way Xavier did. That poor child.*

Vikirnoff felt sick, wanting to close his eyes against the abomination that Razvan had become. The child looked very much like Natalya must have looked as a child, yet Razvan had no feeling for her. Her use to him was that of a blood bank. He wanted to stay young. He had children for the sole purpose of finding the ones with the necessary gene to carry the bloodline he needed.

How old would she be now if she had managed to stay alive? Natalya whispered it in her mind, desperately needing the connection with Vikirnoff.

This time period cannot be long ago. Maybe fifteen years, twenty at the most. She cannot be more than twenty-five or thirty now.

He has a daughter named Colby. I met her a couple of months ago. She didn't have any memories like this. Natalya drew in a shuddering breath. *She must not have had the right blood for him to want to use her this way.*

I met her, too. She was very lucky, Vikirnoff said.

But don't you see? He is still impregnating women. If he has turned into a vampire, how could he do that? Colby was younger than this child would be now. How can this be? Have you ever heard of a vampire having a child? Yet look at her. Her eyes have changed color, her hair as well; she is of our family blood.

I have never heard of a vampire who did not kill his victims, women or children. I certainly have never heard of any capable of having a child. And what of the blood? Razvan's blood cannot be infected with the microorganisms or his children would be infected. Did Colby have parasites in her blood?

Colby had no such parasites in her blood. Vikirnoff frowned as he watched Razvan's careless disregard for the child. He didn't seem to be aware of her as a human being, a person in her own right. He didn't take her blood with care or respect, but treated her as human cattle. It sickened Vikirnoff to watch the child struggle to get free. There was determination on her face. She reminded him of Natalya, that same fierce iron will. *I am willing to bet she is still alive. Even at her age, she is thinking of how to escape. See how she grows quiet, her gaze moving through the room? I believe she has your natural talent with spells.*

Natalya stiffened. *That is Xavier.* She whispered the revelation telepathically, even though she was in his mind and no one could hear.

An older man came out of a chamber, his robes rustling as he moved. His features were indistinct, blurring as he shuffled across the ice floor, but Vikirnoff had the impression of great age and snow-white hair and beard. A wrinkled hand stretched toward the child. She shrank away from the older man and Razvan jerked her out of the dark mage's reach.

"You will not touch her." Razvan snarled. "You have your own supply."

"I can no longer use them as you well know. They have become far too powerful to control. I need the

book. We must find the book." Xavier stumbled closer to
the child, his clawlike fingers extended toward her. "Once
I have the book, they will not be able to defy me."

Razvan held the girl just out of reach, an evil smile on
his face. "This one is mine and you will not touch her."

"Do not presume to give me orders. I grow old, but I
still have my abilities and you do not." Xavier drew himself up to his full height, and immediately Razvan seemed
to shrink before him, but he still kept the child shielded
behind him.

Look at her, what she is doing. Vikirnoff nudged Natalya
with his chin.

Natalya tore her horrified gaze from her brother to
glance at the young girl. She bent her head and licked at
the wound on her wrist. Immediately the drops of blood
ceased. *She has a healing agent in her saliva. She carries a
strong Carpathian gene.*

*That is why they both want her blood. They are using her to
keep them young. Razvan does not want to share her.*

Memories rushed over Natalya. Razvan rocking back
and forth, struggling to hold back tears, his wrist
raggedly torn. How had she forgotten? She had been the
one to heal the wound, using her own saliva. It had taken
Xavier a long time before he realized Razvan's blood did
him no good other than to feed. The dark mage had begun to age and that had sent him into wild rages.

She felt tears on her face and for an instant was aware
of her own body, far from the time where her spirit

watched unclean events unfolding. Razvan knew what it was like to be subjected to such a horrific life, yet he held the young girl prisoner to feed off of her.

Revolted, Natalya turned her attention back to the child. Razvan and Xavier began arguing. Razvan no longer paid attention, releasing his hold on the girl when she ceased struggling. She inched closer to the wall where the dragons were encased in ice. *Vikirnoff? Are they alive? Are the dragons talking to her? Can you tell?*

The child's head was tilted toward the dragons as if listening. Vikirnoff found he was holding his breath. The wall around the dragons began to bulge, the ice fragmenting in great chunks.

"Stop them!" Xavier leapt back away from the splintering ice as he yelled the warning.

A bright red dragon burst through the ice, great claws stretched toward Razvan as a second blue-colored dragon bent its wing to the young girl. The child didn't hesitate, but jumped agilely onto the wing and climbed to its back as the dragon took to the air, rising sharply toward the surface while the first dragon held Xavier and Razvan at bay. It was easy to see both dragons were weak and pale, very sick; their movements, after the initial attack, lacked power.

Razvan lifted the knife and sliding quickly between the claws, plunged the blade deep into the chest of the red dragon. It screamed in pain, as did the one carrying the child. Valiantly, the flying blue dragon deposited the little girl far above the chamber where she had a chance to escape, before turning back to join her wounded comrade.

Xavier stepped forward and held up one hand, his voice commanding. The red dragon ceased thrashing to lie still, panting loudly, precious blood draining onto the ice. The blue dragon settled beside it, nuzzling the injured dragon with its long neck and tongue in an effort to save it.

We must go. There was urgency in Vikirnoff's voice. *We have little time.* Part of him was still scanning in real time, and he felt the tear in the night sky even from deep within the cave as evil passed directly over their shelter.

The events unfolding before Natalya had happened years ago. The bodies of the dragons were now encased in the great hall behind several feet of thick ice. Natalya already knew the price they paid for saving the little girl. As for the child, she could only hope the girl had successfully made her escape and was hidden somewhere in the world, safe from Razvan and Xavier. Unfortunately, there was no way to change history. She could only watch it unfolding before her and hope the dragons had bought the child enough time to escape. Natalya had no choice but to move backward to find the time when her father had hidden the book.

She allowed the vision to end and actively began to search for a sign of her father. There was so much blood, so many deaths she began to feel nauseated.

The small vignette Vikirnoff had witnessed between

Razvan and Xavier led him to believe that the two men, although in league with one another, were in a power struggle. Razvan couldn't hope to defeat Xavier with mage skills—unless he had Natalya. It was suddenly very clear to Vikirnoff. Natalya had the natural talent and she was highly intelligent. Instead of developing his own talents, Razvan had relied on Natalya throughout their childhood and early adulthood. Xavier had bought into the deception, thinking he had the twin with the natural skills.

Where does Razvan's skill lie? Natalya's twin may have been lazy in some regard, but he had to possess the same keen intelligence as his sister.

There was a small silence. Vikirnoff felt her hesitation. *In the planning of battles.*

Something inside Vikirnoff shifted. Of course it had to be Razvan. Xavier and his grandson had joined forces with the vampires, had actually managed to unite an apparently large group of them in spite of their perpetual self-interest. The Malinov brothers were a huge boon to them. The brothers had already conspired to destroy the prince and finding Xavier with his talents and hatred of the Carpathians to match their own, must have seemed providence to them. Xavier would have kept Razvan around only if he was useful. And he had to be extremely useful.

If Razvan held talents as a planner of battles, as extraordinary as his twin was in other areas, then the Carpathian people could very well be in trouble. The vampires had been harassing the prince and his hunters, continually weakening them with small battles, while sacrificing only pawns.

I feel the pull of my father. There is much more violence associated with this than I expected.

Vikirnoff heard the wariness in her voice and his heart went out to her. *I am with you, Natalya. You are no longer alone. What was done happened years ago and there is no changing the past. Try to view whatever happens from a distance if at all possible.* How could she view the torture and murder of her parents from a distance? He desperately wanted to spare her what was to come and he felt helpless to prevent her pain.

Natalya allowed his nearness to help comfort her as she reached for the events of the past. Her father came into view, striding through carnivorous plants, shrubs and trees while the ground trembled beneath his feet. The surrounding water, the color of dried blood, marked the area as a bog. She frowned, trying to recognize landmarks. He carried a package wrapped in oilskins and was obviously wary, continuously looking over his shoulder and scanning the area around him.

He isn't carrying the ceremonial knife. For some reason that alarmed her more than the darkened skies and flicker of lightning at the edges of the overhead clouds. She found herself straining to see through the foliage around her father. It was so dark, the heavy clouds blocked any moonlight.

Yes, he has it in his belt, Natalya. He also carried a small bag that looked as if some live creature wiggled inside of it. Distaste was strong in Vikirnoff's mouth.

Natalya let her breath out slowly. Her father moved with such confidence she almost missed the fact that there was a pattern to his steps. The bogs held sink holes, the surface treacherous to those who didn't know their way through.

I have to start again.

Vikirnoff remained silent, as careful as Natalya to mark the way through the bog. If they were to recover the book, they would need to know their way through the spongelike marsh. His own heart tried to regulate the pounding of his lifemate's. Together they etched out the pattern of steps used to gain the middle of the most wild and overgrown part of the bog. Her father knelt carefully and pushed the book deep into the stained waters, watching it sink slowly beneath the surface. All the while his lips moved as he murmured something softly and his hands wove a graceful pattern in the air.

Could you see his safeguards, Natalya? Vikirnoff had caught some of the spell, but it was unfamiliar to him.

Yes. The weave is complicated, but given time, I can unravel the spell. His unspoken safeguard adds to the strength and complexity. I should be able to reverse the pattern and bring the book to the surface. I just don't know if anyone wants such a heavy responsibility. I doubt the book can be destroyed easily.

If you found it, others will be able to find it as well.

We can destroy the knife. Natalya watched as her father

got to his feet and began the arduous journey through the large peat bog back to solid ground. He walked as if a great weight had been lifted from his shoulders. As he neared the very edges where the sphagnum moss grew the thickest, she saw movement in the surrounding bushes. The leaves swayed and dark shadows glided from one shrub to another. Her father continued his journey, moving into the meadows, turning toward the nearest village.

He came to a halt and pulled a squirming rabbit from the bag. She knew he had brought the animal as a sacrifice and she couldn't look at Vikirnoff. She felt his disgust. She could see the dark shapes in the bushes directly behind her father. The urge to call out, to warn him was overwhelming.

The dark shape leapt on him, wrestling the ceremonial knife from his hand and slashing it across her father's calves. It wasn't Xavier, but several of his minions, sent to bring her father back to the ice caves. He went down hard, the tendons cut so it was impossible to walk. Without preamble, the largest one lifted him and, ignoring his cries of pain, began to carry him back toward the mountain.

Drop it now. Vikirnoff ordered, giving a hard "push" as he did so. His hands were already loosening around the handle. She did not need to see what her father had been subjected to as Xavier tried to get the whereabouts of the book from him. It was only good fortune that the dark mage's henchmen had not seen Natalya's father coming from the bog itself, but rather circling the outskirts of it.

Natalya found her fingers obeying even when her

mind tried to cling to the sight of her father. The knife slipped from her hand and Vikirnoff allowed the weapon to drop to the floor. "Destroy it," she said. "I don't care how you do it, just please get rid of it."

He wrapped her up in his arms, rocking her gently back and forth. "I will be happy to rid the world of it, Natalya, but we cannot take chances with the book. Xavier must have questioned his servants closely and he knows the area where they found your father. He must suspect the book is hidden somewhere in that region."

"Not necessarily. He may not know when my father actually hid the book. It may have been weeks earlier. He may have thought my father gave the book to your prince." She laid her head back against his shoulder, grateful for the solid feel of him. Vikirnoff had somehow gone from enemy to her solid foundation. It had happened without her even being aware of it. Was it the binding words she railed so hard against? Or was it always sharing his mind and knowing his thoughts so intimately? Her hand slipped into his. "Without you, I would feel so alone."

His heart gave that funny little lurch that bothered him so much. Natalya was a fighter, a woman of tremendous courage and Razvan's betrayal was breaking not only her heart, but her spirit. Vikirnoff found it was the last thing he wanted. He had grown fond of his tigress and her astonishing smart mouth. He didn't want her broken and bruised or so vulnerable even when she was turning to him for comfort.

He caught her chin and drew her head around so he could find her mouth with his, kissing her long and making a thorough job of it. When her eyes had gone opaque with desire and she was matching his hunger, he pulled away abruptly. "I'm so pleased you finally see that I was right all along."

She blinked, drawing a little away from him, wariness creeping into her expression. "Right? About what?"

"The ritual binding words of course. It was a good thing I said them and tied us together. With your stubbornness we probably would still be dancing around one another."

"*My* stubbornness?" Her green eyes glittered at him. "I think you invented the word." She pushed a hand through her tawny hair, sweeping it off her face to glare at him. "In fact, if you look up the word 'stubborn' in the dictionary, your picture is right there as the definition."

Vikirnoff thought she was the most beautiful woman he'd ever seen. He wrapped the ceremonial knife in a white cloth and tucked it inside his shirt, out of her sight. "You still have not wanted to admit it was the best thing I could have done for both of us."

She scrambled to her feet, sliding weapons into the loops on her pants. "And it will be a cold day in hell before I ever do. I don't think bringing that up is in your best interest, but thank you for trying to distract me." She blew him a kiss. "I don't really rise that easily to bait."

"Sure you do. You cheated. You were lurking in my mind."

"I wanted to see what you really thought about just leaving the book where it is. I have reservations about turning it over to your prince." She thrust the pair of Arnis sticks into the loops on her belt. "I'm not certain it would be entirely safe with him."

"Because Razvan is plotting to kill him."

She winced but nodded as she strapped on her twin holsters. "Razvan's very good at what he does, and quite frankly, with the vampires, Xavier and Razvan against him, I don't think your prince is up to it."

Vikirnoff watched as she slid extra clips into several compartments of her pants. He was very aware she was pleased with his creation, nearly matching her original design, but improving slightly so she could move easier and reach whatever she needed quickly. "Mikhail will not be defeated by any of them."

"How do you know that? You don't even know him. I searched your mind for memories of him, but he was not fully grown when you left these lands. How do you know his strength? Why do you even trust him? That book is more dangerous than you can know and no Carpathian prince will easily destroy it, nor can he hope to wield its power. Once the book is in his hands, they will send everything and everyone they have after him. You'll be condemning him to death."

"Mikhail Dubrinsky will not be defeated by those who seek his death. He is extremely powerful, Natalya. It is in his blood, bred into his very genes, his bone and spirit and veins. He can be wounded, yes, but when push comes to shove, he can unleash a power greater than Xavier imagines. Mikhail will find a way to destroy the book and in the meantime, he will protect it."

She turned to face him, staying partly in the shadows to hide her expression. "What if I don't want to turn the book over to him, Vikirnoff? You never asked me how I felt about it. You assumed I'd be willing, but I am not someone to follow so easily."

Vikirnoff studied every nuance of her tone, for the first time uncertain if she was challenging him to make a point, or if she really meant it. Her mind was closed to him, and, although he could breach the barrier she had erected, it seemed an insult when she clearly wanted her privacy.

Of course they had to turn the book over to the prince. What else would they do with it? He paced away from her, knowing she would read his agitation, but he didn't care. "What would you want to do with the book?" He made every effort to keep his tone flat, without any inflection whatsoever.

Natalya shrugged. "I haven't decided yet, but I'm not about to be railroaded into something I'm not certain is the right thing to do. The book is enormously powerful. It contains thousands of spells, magick so complicated and so dangerous that I don't think any but a mage should ever possess it."

Vikirnoff stiffened. "You would use this book?" His gut churned with protest and his lungs began to burn for air.

Her eyes took on a faint amber glow. Bands of light

streaked across her face and hair as she shifted closer to the candlelight, reaching for the long sword in its scabbard against the wall of the cavern. At once she was far more difficult to see, blending into the shadows.

"If I chose to use the book it would be my business, Vikirnoff. You cannot dictate to me that I must retrieve this book and then turn it over to someone I don't know, I don't trust and I don't respect."

Vikirnoff remained silent, forcing back his first response. She knew very little about his people and it was true, he had arbitrarily decided for her what she should do with the book once she had recovered it. And he was pushing her to recover it. Natalya was not a woman to be forced into anything. Right now she felt cornered and she was fighting back. "Have I earned your respect?"

Her amber eyes glittered, taking on the eerie glow of the night creature. "Yes, of course. One has nothing to do with the other. You aren't Mikhail Dubrinsky. You aren't asking me to give you the book for safeguarding, you're *telling* me to give it to him."

"Would you give me the book?"

"Yes." She didn't hesitate. "But not to give away. Only to safeguard."

Vikirnoff let his breath out. She disarmed him so easily. The tension began to ease from his body. "Do you want to keep this thing? I think of it as evil. Am I wrong to feel that way about it?"

"The blood of my grandmother and two others sealed this book. Of course I think of it as evil and more than ever, that means it can't fall into the wrong hands. I don't know your prince and I don't find memories of him in you. How do you know his heart or his soul, Vikirnoff? You want to hand him a weapon that could be the ruin of us all and yet you do so on blind faith." She shook her head. "I can't do it."

"Are you concerned that Mikhail will be in more danger?"

"Partly."

"No one has to know he has the book. He will not try to wield the power, only to study Xavier's plan to rid the earth of our species. Xavier must have spent centuries developing a spell to use against my people."

"I'm certain he did. The point is this. You asked me to locate the book and I did. Now you want me to recover the book and hand it over to someone I don't know. Does that make sense to you?"

"If you trust me, then there is no problem. We do not want to keep this thing."

"Isn't it better to leave it where it is for the time being and if it becomes apparent Xavier is getting close to discovering its whereabouts, then retrieve it?" Natalya stepped out of the shadows. "Don't ask me to do this, Vikirnoff. I can't go against what I feel is right, not even for you."

"You believe it is better to leave the book there? Why do you think vampires are looking for psychic women who have the ability to touch objects and read the past? Why do you think so many have gathered here? A war between vampires and Carpathians? I believe they are searching for the book. Xavier knows your father was found near the peat bogs. He has to be searching there."

"The safeguards will hold."

"Will they? Who taught your father the safeguards? Who taught you? Even Razvan knows the safeguards you use. They will not hold and I think you know that."

"Then I'll guard the book. I'll hide it somewhere else, halfway around the world, somewhere he'll never think to look."

"Natalya."

She threw her head back, exposing her throat, but her fists were knotted at her sides. Her name. Just that, nothing else, a wealth of expression in his voice. "I'll find the damn book, Vik, but I'm not handing it over to the prince until *I'm* certain it will be safe."

"That is good enough for me, *ainaak enyém,* I cannot ask for more." He held out his hand. "Let us go find it."

17

The peat bogs were unexpectedly as beautiful as they were eerie. Natalya paced carefully around the nearest edges just along the pine forest, where the water drained from above and seeped up from below to form the enormous marsh. Sphagnum moss grew in abundance, the feathery stems and leaves stretched out invitingly over the surface beckoning her to come closer. Orchids and a dozen other plants flowered in or around the dark water. The ground, even close to the edges was spongy and each step she took shook the nearby trees. "Some of these plants are huge."

"They are carnivorous. They eat insects," Vikirnoff said.

"Still . . ." Natalya glanced up at the mountain rising

sharply above them. Parts of it were totally obscured by the thick mist. Pine trees grew in abundance and some low branches partially dipped into the wide bog, so that needles floated on the surface along with the thick vegetation. She pressed her palm over the birthmark that warned her when vampires were near. "I don't think we're being watched. Do you feel any danger?"

"Not from vampires, but lately I haven't been able to feel them close by. I think it has something to do with the parasites in their blood. I have no idea how they mask their presence, but it seems to be effective." He was still uneasy. The forest pressed too close and the smell of the peat bog was overwhelming. "Can you unravel the safeguards from here, Natalya?" There was more fighting room. He preferred the solid ground to the spongy, waterlogged terrain.

"No. I'll have to be in the exact spot my father was. He'll have set it up that way as part of the protection. If they come, you'll have to keep them off of me while I retrieve the book. Once they know we're looking here, they'll drain the bog before giving up." The marsh was huge with sinkholes everywhere. In the moonlight, the stagnant water appeared deep and treacherous, despite the many plants blooming on the surface.

"You be very careful, Natalya." It was an unnecessary thing to say, but her hesitation, coupled with the heavy oppressive weight settling between his shoulder blades, increased his feelings of unease.

Natalya tossed him a quick, saucy grin. "Careful is my middle name."

Vikirnoff scowled at her. "This is a *serious* situation, Natalya."

Her eyebrow shot up. "Really? I would never have guessed. I thought maybe it would be cool, campy fun like in *The Creature from the Black Lagoon.* It didn't actually occur to me that it could be *serious.*"

"There is such a thing as overconfidence." There was a small pause. "What is *The Creature from the Black Lagoon?*"

Natalya shook her head in disgust. "Just what have you been doing all these years? Don't you ever watch television? *The Creature from the Black Lagoon* is a classic. A must-see movie right up there with *King Kong* and *Godzilla.* You had to have watched them." When he looked blank, she sighed. "A scientist becomes this mutant creature and lives in the lagoon . . ." She trailed off. "Never mind, but we have to work on educating you about movies. You're missing some great stuff. It's *education.* How do you think I learned about vampires?"

Vikirnoff shook his head. "I do not even want to know."

"*Movies,* of course. I've decided I'm going into the film business. I can make great vampire films." She took her first step onto the thin layer of earth that stretched over the waters of the bog. "These mountains make a perfect setting, with the way the wind can't reach certain areas and blasts others, and how the fog lies in so thick, not to mention all the bogs and ice caves."

"I think it's been done," he answered. His voice was husky and she glanced at him sharply.

Vikirnoff's heart beat in his throat as he watched her following in her father's precise footsteps, a pattern they had both memorized. It didn't matter that she was so careful and light on her feet, almost gliding as she placed her feet on the tufts of grass, he was afraid for her. Fear took on an entirely new meaning when it was for a loved one.

Love. He tasted the word—tried it out tentatively. How did one equate the terrible, overwhelming emotion that had somehow crept up on him with that small word? Did he feel this way because she was his lifemate? Or because of who she was? What she was? He couldn't image wanting a woman without her penchant for late night movies. And as exasperating as it could be, when she didn't have a sassy, smart comment to make, it worried him. Was it love to wake up thinking of her before anything else? For centuries hunger had been his every waking thought and yet now, even that had taken a back seat.

Natalya paused staring down at the two small blocks of grass, side by side, both looking as if they were solid. "Look at this, Vik, does this look the same? I don't remember two patches so close to one another."

He swore under his breath as he took to the air and hovered just above her. There had not been two patches so close together. Over time, the bog had changed, plants growing, multiplying, and dying off naturally. Natalya was risking stepping into a sinkhole by following the pattern her father had provided. "We could try finding the last step and I could carry you to that spot."

Natalya shook her head, glancing at him sharply. "The pattern is part of the safeguard."

Vikirnoff was ashamed of himself. He had known the steps were important, just as she did, but as she got deeper into the bog, his uneasiness grew stronger. He was well aware of the weather patterns in the Carpathian Mountains, of the places where there was a lack of wind and the fog hung for weeks on end. He knew there was fire and ice beneath the mountains and that many oddities were really natural and not made by either Carpathian or vampire, yet the stillness in the valley was oppressive to him and the stagnant water, so naturally the color of old blood had become sinister.

"I do not feel easy about this, Natalya."

Her eyebrow shot up. "You aren't helping. I'm trying to remember if he stepped forward with his left foot or with his right."

"His left." The answer came out of his memory, minute details recorded automatically without thought. "He switched leads."

She flashed a grin at him as she wiped beads of sweat from her face. "You might be useful after all." She pointed toward the edge of the bog. "Wait over there. I don't want you hovering over me, making me nervous." She waited until he complied before leading with her left foot.

Vikirnoff folded his arms across his chest, assuming his expressionless mask. "It is good to know you are finally coming to the conclusion that I am useful." His fists clenched so tight his knuckles turned white and his muscles began to ache from the terrible tension that continued to rise in his gut.

In the forest behind them the trees started to sway gently, almost imperceptible at first, but Vikirnoff's acute hearing picked up the rustle of the pine needles and he swung around alertly. There was a little moonlight shining through the woods and the branches were illuminated in a ghostly silver. The needles appeared more like skinny fingers with sharp nails reaching out toward the bog. The ripple of unease grew stronger. Vikirnoff turned so he could watch both the forest and Natalya as she proceeded through the swamp.

She stepped forward a second time with her left foot, swayed precariously so that his heart jumped into his throat. Natalya regained her balance and took several more steps, each with more confidence, so he was surprised when she halted again abruptly.

"What is it?"

"I don't know." Her hand slid to her sword, touching the sheath for the comfort of knowing it was close. "Did you hear something?"

"The wind?" But it wasn't the wind. There was barely a wind. Voices sounded in the distance, wailing and crying, the rise and fall faint, but discernable.

"You wish it was the wind. It's going to be something

nasty," Natalya predicted. "The sound has increased with every step I've taken. And look at the surface of the water."

Vikirnoff stepped closer to the edge of the bog. The ground shook and several plants vibrated with the motion. He halted instantly, his gaze riveted to the surface rather than the plants. The water was stagnant and should have been still, but it moved in peculiar patterns, not fast or abruptly, but rather so slowly that it was almost imperceptible, yet when he peered closer, faces seemed to stare back at him.

"Are there bodies in the bog?"

"Ugg!" Natalya drew back, staring down at the surface, her fingers grasping her sword hilt. "That's gross. I didn't even think of that. I don't think there are bodies in the swamp, but now I'm worried something dead is going to reach up and grab my ankle and yank me in." The moment she uttered the words there was a small silence. She reached down to rub at the finger marks on her ankle. "Do you think he's here?"

Vikirnoff knew she meant Razvan. "Let's get out of here, Natalya. You do not have to do this." He took another step toward her and sank to his ankles.

"Don't!" she said it sharply, shaking her head adamantly. "I have to do this. We both agreed. If I don't now, I'll never come back. I need you to give me confidence."

He swore under his breath, resisting the urge to take to the air and snatch her back from the center of the bog. "You do not ask very much of me, do you?"

"You know, when you started in about the entire life-mate thing, I didn't protest too much, because you were kind of cute." Natalya pulled her gaze away from a shimmering face with its mouth open in a scream. She took several more careful steps, sure of the pattern, and stopped only feet away from where her father had hidden the book. "At the time, I didn't realize how incredibly bossy you are or how grumpy you can be."

"Kind of cute? You didn't protest too much?" Vikirnoff echoed. "In all your late night movies did you ever come across a character named Pinocchio?"

Natalya burst out laughing. "Of all the movies, you had to have seen that one. That's so you."

He grinned at her. "Actually, I did not see it. I read the book, but I knew it was made into a movie and the character was someone you could relate to."

"It's a good thing you're over there and I'm over here. I'd push you into one of the sinkholes and just leave you to contemplate your sins." Natalya gave a little sniff. "I may have stretched the truth *slightly,* at least the kind of cute part, but I didn't lie."

She took the last few steps through the bog, until she was standing in the exact spot her father had stood in years earlier. "This is it. I feel my father here. Now it gets complicated."

All around the small island of grass where she stood, the faces forming in the surface of the water gathered, mouths gaping open, sightless eyes wide. Some of the faces were larger than others, rising up like small waves and trembling as if made of gelatin. "See, this is the kind of thing to put in movies," Natalya said. "Only no one would believe it. It's plain freaky."

"What do they want?"

"They are the guardians of the book. I imagine, if I make a wrong move, they're going to let me know very fast." She took a breath and let it out, slowing her pounding heart and stilling the strange roaring in her ears. "If they grab me, I have high expectations that you'll dive into the water and do something to get me back."

He shrugged, feigning nonchalance. "It has taken me a while to train you in the ways of submissive lifemates. I would not want that time to be wasted."

She flicked a quick glance at him. Just his presence, calm and confident, his wide shoulders and strong, beloved masculine face calmed her churning stomach. "So let's get it done and when it's over, you are going to strike the word 'submissive' from your vocabulary right along with your 'little slip of a girl.'"

"At this rate I will not be allowed to speak."

"And your point would be?"

"I am not making any promises."

She smiled. It was barely there, a brief curve of her mouth and then gone again, but his heart contracted. "Somehow I knew you'd say that." The warmth faded from her eyes to be replaced by fear. "Seriously, Vikirnoff, if anything happens to me, remember that whatever is in this book, is worth dying for. Xavier killed to seal the book and he's killed again and again to get it

back. You have to find a way to destroy it. Don't let anyone try to use it."

"I will be damned angry if anything happens to you
and you have never seen me truly angry before. Get it
done and let us leave this place."

She rolled her eyes. "I love it when you get all bossy on
me. It's silly and never works, but it's kind of cute."

Natalya turned away from him, grateful she'd had the
last word. She was already feeling the pull of the book. It
called to her, a treasure lost, a book filled with centuries
of work, recipes for good, for healing, for working mira-
cles. Xavier, a brilliant man lost to the corruption of
power and greed, had distorted the work of so many.
When had Xavier been derailed? Had it been a gradual
decline? It must have been. The Carpathians had once
been friends with him, trusted him. Rhiannon had studied under him. Had that been the start of the tragedy?
Had he craved her immortality? Her beauty? Had he
grown old while she stayed young?

Natalya shook her head to rid herself of all thoughts.
She needed to concentrate, to think only of the complicated pattern her father had woven into the air when he
set the safeguards. She had to reverse his spell, using his
words, but backwards, paying particular attention to
every syllable he had enunciated. She felt Vikirnoff with
her, merging firmly, his mind and memory open to her
and that added to her confidence. She was a natural talent
and she had worked hard to hone her skills. Although she
feared Xavier, she was very aware that she had outmaneu-

vered him several times and that her talent as a mage was nearly on par with his in spite of her comparative youth.

Do not think you can go up against him. Vikirnoff snapped the order, uncaring that she might get angry. *If I thought for one moment that you would do something so stupid, I would not only forbid such a thing, but I would prevent you from such a folly. Rhiannon believed she could match him with her talent and you know what happened to her.*

I am not nearly as egotistical as you seem to think I am. I'm busy here, Vik, don't be bothering me. It occurred to her even as she turned away from him that Vikirnoff was as reluctant for her to put her hands on the book as she was to touch it. She brushed his mind with warmth, with reassurance.

Vikirnoff held his breath as she began to weave a graceful pattern in the air. She turned slightly to mimic the exact angle her father had taken. Her voice, soft and melodious, but commanding, called on the elements to aid her. The air around the bog grew heavy, pressing on them, nearly suffocating them, as she murmured the reverse of the safeguards, choosing each word carefully and using her father's peculiar rhythm.

The moaning of the wind increased. The branches in the pine forest clacked together and needles flew like sharpened darts through the air. Vikirnoff shifted slightly as the water began to rise and seep around his feet. Tuffs of grass disappeared. Anxiously, he looked at the spot where Natalya stood. Water lapped at the toes of her boots. The faces on the surface surrounded her tiny square of grass, empty eye sockets watching her every move. Waiting for one mistake. One misstep.

Admiration grew for Natalya as he watched the way her hands swayed in the air, never faltering, never trembling. Merged as deeply as he was with her, he knew her fears, yet she stood in the center of the bog encircled by danger without flinching, looking magnificent. *He* was the one with the beads of sweat trickling down his body. He was the one with his heart in his throat. He was on the balls of his feet, ready for action, ready to take to the air and reach her should something go wrong. All the while he watched her, his heart swelled with pride. It was nearly impossible to believe she was really his lifemate. She seemed an extraordinary miracle of which he would never be worthy.

The air shimmered as her hands dropped to her sides. The faces in the water moaned softly, emitting cries of protest as the book ascended from the murky depths. Red water poured off the oilskins, looking like trails of blood as the thick tome emerged. Small waves crested around the small square of grass, covering Natalya's feet.

Vikirnoff leapt into the air and was on her in seconds, grasping her around the waist and jerking her out of the bog as the book floated into her outstretched hands. A loud hum was his only warning and he wrapped his arms around her firmly, protecting her with his body as he threw shields up around them. Insects crashed into the barrier, the sound breaking the stillness of the night.

Natalya hooked one arm around his neck and wedged the book between them. "It's heavy."

It also smelled foul and dripped water down the front of them. Vikirnoff immediately cleaned and dried the package even as he streaked away from the bog back toward the mountains and the caverns he loved.

You were incredible.

I know. Shocking talent, aren't I? Natalya did her best to see in every direction as they streaked across the sky. *I'm getting used to traveling this way. I kind of like it.*

It is very convenient.

Natalya felt him nuzzle her hair. Unexpected desire shot through her. It was such a casual gesture, but at the same time, it felt intimate. *My birthmark is beginning to burn just a bit. A vampire is coming close to us.*

I do not want to take any chances as long as we have the book. We should go back to the caverns and decide what to do from there. Do you think Xavier is tied to the book in some way? Will he know it is out of the hiding place?

Natalya shook her head. *I doubt it. If he could have traced the book, he would have known it was in the bog and he would have sent someone to search the place until they found it. He wouldn't have dared to go himself. The bog is located too deep in Carpathian territory, and he feared Carpathians more than anything else.* It was strange to remember small details denied to her for so long. Vikirnoff's safeguards obviously prevented Razvan from being able to suppress her memories. The longer her brother was out of her mind, the stronger her memories became.

I doubt he would have trusted anyone else.

Razvan. He would have sent my brother. Razvan has little natural skill as a mage. He wouldn't have noticed the safeguards for what they were. He would have done a cursory inspection of the area and gone back to Xavier and told him the book wasn't there.

Vikirnoff took them through the small opening in the chimney and dropped through the mountain until it widened out into the larger chamber. He waved his hand and flames leapt to life on the candles as he placed her feet carefully on the floor.

"Where are we going to put the book?"

Vikirnoff took it from her and slipped it into her backpack. He didn't even glance at the book for which they'd risked so much. "This will do for now. We'll discuss a safer place to hide it later."

"Sounds good to me."

"I realized, there in that foul smelling bog, that revelations occur in the most unlikely places."

Natalya's eyebrow shot up. "Really? What world-shattering revelation was imparted to you there in that foul-smelling bog?"

"Just that I never wanted Donna Reed or June Cleaver. It has always been Xena, warrior woman who had my heart." His tone was casual, matter-of-fact, not at all as if he were handing over his heart to her.

"The revelation just came to you right there in the

middle of the bog, did it?" Natalya slipped out of her double harness and removed several clips. "Somewhere between the water making nasty faces at me and the rather pathetic audio effects?"

He nodded. "Yes. It became very clear to me."

"You're just a tiny bit slow on the uptake, there, Gomer." She set her sword up against the cavern wall and laid several knives in a semicircle around it. "You should have figured it out in the forest when I saved your butt the first time we met."

"Gomer?"

"Pyle. I'll explain later. Right now, I want to hear more about your revelation." She placed her backpack in the center of the semicircle directly in front of the sword.

"The last time I tried to bring up Xena, you terminated the discussion," he pointed out, folding his arms across his chest.

"Well, now you've had a revelation, haven't you? That changes things."

"Would you like me to set the safeguards for that?" He indicated the backpack with his chin.

"You may as well. If I do it, my brother will be able to track us immediately." She tilted her head, studying him as he glided over to the cavern wall. She loved watching him move. "You could take your shirt off while you're working. I wouldn't want you to get hot or anything."

His eyes went dark with heat as he shrugged out of the shirt and tossed it aside. She watched the play of muscles across his back as he raised his arms to weave the safeguards.

"You're breathtaking, you know that? I guess I can forgive you for being an absolute dope sometimes."

Vikirnoff laughed, the sound startling both of them. He rarely laughed and when he did it warmed his eyes and took the hard-edged expression from his face. Natalya found an answering grin on her own face.

"Your adoring compliments take my breath away."

"Well, don't let them go to your head. I'm only feeling this way temporarily. You said something nice for a change." Natalya held her breath as he sauntered toward her. He could look so powerful just walking. Just breathing. The effect he had on her was absolutely idiotic.

"I am reading your thoughts."

"Really? Are you getting the part about what an incredible lover you are and how I might be able to put up with your bossy nonsense if you keep me happy in other ways?" She shrugged. "Just asking, in case, you know, you wanted to start keeping me happy."

Vikirnoff was suddenly crowding her so that she took several steps backward. "Where do you think you are going?" His hand snaked out to wrap around the nape of her neck, abruptly stopping her.

"Nowhere. You just move so fast sometimes."

"Are you saying I intimidate you?" There was a wealth of amusement in his voice.

"As if." She moved into the shelter of his body, loving the way his skin heated her as if he absorbed her, or she just melted into him. "I am not easily intimidated." She ran her fingertips over his chest, trying to press closer, inhaling him to take him into her lungs. Vikirnoff was like a rock, solid and steady. "Especially by you."

"That is a good thing." He bent his head to hers.

Natalya loved how slowly his mouth descended to capture hers. His breath was warm. His eyes changed right before his lips claimed hers, going dark with desire. There was the feel of his hand tightening on her neck, the pad of his thumb sliding over her skin. So many sensations, all before his mouth took possession of hers. He created intimacy between them with so many small details, each one making her feel like she belonged to him. Like he belonged to her.

She closed her eyes and gave herself up to the wonder of his mouth. She allowed the heat to claim her, to sweep through her body so that she caught fire from him. She wanted to kiss him forever, to drown in the taste and scent of him. His arms closed around her, strong, reassuring, possessive even, dragging her closer, setting off a multitude of butterflies winging their way around her stomach.

Vikirnoff wanted to kiss her forever. He called her *ainaak enyém,* forever mine, and he had all along. His mind had known and his body had known, even his soul had known, but it had taken spending time with her before his heart had caught up. She was so much more than *ainaak enyém*, she was *ainaak sívamet jutta,* his 'forever to my heart connected', and she would be for all time. The crazy thing was, he didn't even know how it happened.

"I love what you're thinking." Natalya framed his face with both hands. "I really do." She punctuated it with small kisses and teasing nibbles on his lips. "But I want all of your attention on making love to me. The *actual* making love to me, not thinking about how much you love me." She gave him a small sexy smile. "You can do the thinking about loving me so much *afterward*."

Amusement crept into his eyes, stealing her breath. "You want the *actual* thing?"

She nodded.

"My *entire* attention?"

"Absolutely."

"You are a demanding little thing."

"High-maintenance. I told you." She went up on her toes to kiss him. She loved kissing him, loved the silken heat of his mouth. She could stay there for eternity.

Vikirnoff drifted on a rising tide of lust and love. He let the feel of her skin, the brush of her hair and the fire of her mouth take him over. Electricity arced from Natalya to him. Flames raced over his body and poured like molten lava into his veins. His every nerve ending leapt to life, craving her. His fingers tangled in her hair, his mouth devouring hers, wanting more. Needing more.

"Vikirnoff." She murmured his name, breathed it into the heat of his mouth. Her voice was soft and sensual, her lips swollen with his kisses and her vivid eyes dark with desire.

His body was as hard as a rock, painfully full. She could do that to him so easily. All of his centuries-old control seemed to vaporize when his mouth was on hers. He dispensed with her clothing in caveman style, jerking the material off her in strips, exposing the rise and fall of her breasts, the tight beckoning nipples, the globes of her buttocks and the invitation glistening at the junction of her legs.

He blazed a path from her lips to her breast, his mouth clamping greedily, teeth scraping and teasing while his tongue laved and soothed. She cried out, stunned pleasure on her face. His hand caressed her belly, touched her small golden hoop, and moved lower. The moment his fingers brushed her wet mound, her entire body shuddered, a low moan escaping.

"You are so hot, Natalya." His fingers plunged deep, felt the contraction of her tight muscles, hot and moist and so velvet soft. His erection, heavy and thick, pulsed with the need to be buried deep inside her, surrounded by her feminine sheath.

She bucked against him, a helpless thrusting of her hips, riding his hand with a small sob of pleasure. Vikirnoff couldn't stand it anymore and lowered her to the floor, hanging onto enough of his intellect to remember at the last moment to cushion her with something soft between her body and the cave floor. His mouth found hers again, feeding on her taste, the sweetness he could never quite get enough of.

She groaned into his mouth, and fire raced over him, hot and pure, his body hardening past the point of pain. He kissed her throat, her breasts, spent time on her small golden ring, teeth tugging and teasing and returning to her hard nipples. She gasped when his hands parted her thighs, his fingers stroking so close to her heated center that her body shuddered and her muscles clenched with a need so agonizing tears shimmered in her eyes.

"Please, Vikirnoff. I need this. I need you."

That soft little plea was more than he could stand. He bent his head and lapped at the welcoming liquid. Her body jerked beneath his hands and his tongue speared deep. She screamed, her hips bucking but he pinned her with hard fingers, holding her to him to drive his tongue hard and deep.

Stars seemed to explode around her, lights dazzled her. Natalya couldn't catch her breath, couldn't think. Her body fragmented, shattered her so that she thought she might die from sheer pleasure. He didn't stop, teasing her with lightning-quick flicks of his tongue, stroking the hot knots of nerve endings into another hard release that left her lungs burning and her head spinning.

He heard her cries, felt her fists tugging at his hair, her body thrashed beneath him but he couldn't stop, craving the honey from her body, her screams of pleasure that only fed the building inferno in his body. He suckled her, tongue thrusting and probing, forcing her body into another tier of sensation where she could only mindlessly plead with him and her body was slick and hot with the shocks of multiple orgasms.

Vikirnoff rose over her, his eyes black with hunger, a snarl of possession on his lips. His hands kept her thighs apart as he pressed against her pulsing entrance. Natalya could feel the thick head entering her with excruciating slowness. He seemed far too big for her, even as slick as she was and with her nerve endings so sensitized she could only wail at the intensity of the pleasure engulfing her.

"Hurry. Please. Hurry, hurry." It was a mindless chant, her head thrashing back and forth, her body in a frenzied grip of need. The loss of control was so shocking, frightening even. She could only hang onto him for an anchor in reality as he took her over the edge of reason.

He gave one powerful thrust, surging forward, burying himself deep, stretching her tight muscles impossibly, driving into her hot core. She screamed again, her body convulsing instantly around his, inner muscles squeezing so powerfully, he nearly lost control. Her nails bit deep into his shoulders and her hips jerked beneath him.

Vikirnoff clamped his fingers around her wrists and slammed them to the cavern floor, holding her helpless beneath his assault, his body relentless, using a hard, merciless tempo, pounding into her over and over.

His face was edged with lust, his eyes dark with hunger and need as his mouth found her throat. Natalya couldn't think past the pleasure/pain of his body taking hers with such wild abandon. She felt the sharp sting of his teeth at her throat and it only increased her pleasure until she thought she might die with it. His teeth scraped back and forth at the swell of her breast, just above her heart, and then sank deep.

Her body imploded, splintered and shook with the

force of her orgasm. His fingers tightened in hers, holding her beneath him, his body building and building with the force of his need. She felt him in her mind, sharing the taste of her, the pleasure rocking him, and then his tongue swept across her breast.

"Taste me, Natalya." His voice was harsh, sexy with his lust. "Come to me now. Come into my world." It wasn't a plea, it was a command. His hands tightened around her wrists. He didn't help her, his chest above her mouth, his body so tight it stretched hers to the limit. "Damn it, woman. Do it now."

She was desperate for relief. If he kept pounding into her she wasn't going to live through the night. Could a woman die of pleasure? In any case, her incisors had already lengthened and her body gushed with anticipation, making her sheath so hot and slick it only allowed him deeper until she thought he would climb into her womb. She licked across the heavy muscles of his chest and sank her teeth deep. At once his ancient blood poured into her like flowing nectar. His body thickened, hardened, pistoned into hers without mercy. His erotic images and his overwhelming pleasure burst through her mind even as her own muscles tightened around him, gripping him desperately.

She drank, choked, swept her tongue across him to close the pinpricks. Nothing could stop the forceful driving of his body into hers. Her orgasm ripped through her, somewhere between pain and pleasure, rocking her body, the shudders refusing to stop, gripping her with the same intensity as her muscles milked him. She felt him exploding, jetting into her with his seed, hot spasms that had a guttural sound tearing from his throat.

Vikirnoff buried his face in Natalya's throat, desperately trying to regain a steady heartbeat, to pull air into his lungs. She had been so tight and hot, her vaginal grip on his sensitive erection torturing him with pleasure as she clasped him to her, draining him completely. She was going to kill him if their lovemaking got any better, but it was a great way to go. He lifted his head enough to nuzzle her breast. Her nipples were tight hard beads, tempting him. His tongue flicked and teased.

Her body jerked around his, tightened on his flesh so that he groaned as fire raced through him, spreading through every nerve ending. "I love you, Natalya."

"I don't think I can ever do that again. It scared the hell out of me. Worse than any vampire." Her fingers tangled in his hair. "I couldn't stop. It just went on and on and I didn't have any control at all."

He smiled against her breast. "It will only get better."

"We're both going to die, you know that don't you?"

"It occurred to me," he admitted. He kissed her again, gently this time. "You know you will be going through the conversion soon. I have heard it can be painful." He lifted his head to look into her eyes. "I will do my best to spare you and the moment it is safe, I will put us both in ground."

Fear etched tiny white lines around her mouth. Her eyes were enormous but she nodded at him. "Don't forget the book and the safeguards."

He rolled off of her and drew her into his arms, holding her close. "I will not forget anything. Thank you for giving yourself to me."

Natalya laughed. "Is that what I did? I thought you took me for yourself and there was no going back."

"There is no going back now." He murmured as the first ripple of pain took her, driving the air from her lungs.

18

"Hold on to me, *ainaak sívamet jutta,* I fear this will hurt like hell." Vikirnoff's eyes held panic, something Natalya had never seen in him, just as she'd never heard that particular tone in his voice.

She reached for his hand, tangled her fingers with his. "I'm not the first woman to do this, you know. We'll get through it." As the pain radiated through her with all the intensity of a blowtorch, she wasn't altogether certain she was telling the truth. It took her breath, leaving her gasping.

Vikirnoff turned pale. "Damn it, I should never have let this happen."

He startled her with his swearing. He often said things in his ancient tongue, but rarely did he curse. His blatant lack of control shocked her into focusing on him rather than the pain tearing through her body. Vikirnoff was already sweating, his eyes alive with fear for her.

When the first wave eased enough to allow her to breathe again she pushed her hand through his hair, her touch tender. "You're such a baby. It never occurred to me you'd be a baby."

A baby? He wanted to kill someone with his bare hands. He didn't feel like a baby. He felt like a berserker, a wild, out-of-control demon, ready to rend and tear anything in his path. He couldn't believe the conversion would be like this, the pain ripping through her body with the force of a tidal wave. Against such agony, his tremendous power was utterly useless. "This is . . ." He spat out a series of words in his ancient language, his voice low and mean.

"I so don't want to know what any of that means," Natalya said, trying to smile. The smile died swiftly as the pain began swelling again, gripping her so hard her body convulsed. Fire, hot and ferocious, tore through her body. She bit back a scream, desperate to hide the extent of the pain from him.

Small beads of blood formed on Natalya's brow. Vikirnoff swept back the tangled mess of her damp, tawny hair. Small stripes banded over her body, shades of orange, white and black, faint streaks tinged with blood. Raw fury burned through him and he cursed who and what he was. The way she tried to be so damned protective of him shredded his heart. He came up on his knees, soaked his shirt in the coolest pool in the cavern and wiped the sweat from her face as gently as he could.

Natalya suddenly pushed at him, tried to pull out of his mind, turning her face away from him, but he stayed firmly merged, his blood pounding through his veins. This was emotion at its worst. He rode the wave out with her, striving to find a way to help her, searching for calm. For centuries, his world had been unemotional, and now, when he needed it most, he couldn't find the balance that was so necessary to aid her.

She went white, so pale her skin was nearly gray. The bluish tinge to her lips had his heart pounding in alarm, but his hands were gentle as he wiped her face and throat.

She caught his arm. "Stay with me."

"I am not going anywhere."

"You can't possibly become vampire, can you, Vikirnoff?"

He knew her fears were because of her twin brother. She had lost him. The last person in her life to really love her. Now, she feared losing Vikirnoff. He brought her hand to his mouth, kissed her knuckles, opened her clenched fist and pressed a second kiss to the center of her palm. "Thanks to you, no. Not ever."

She attempted a smile, trying to tease him, wanting to reassure him. "Then you owe me big time. *Big* time. And I intend to collect." It was starting again, the torch in her stomach, burning through her lungs and heart and every organ. She tried to breathe through the pain, was desperate for air, for a way to stop the agony just for a moment so she could regroup. Tears burned in her eyes and streaks of blood ran down her face. "I'm sorry," she whispered, her fingers tightening around his. "I'm going to be sick."

"That is good." He swallowed the bile in his own throat, feeling desperate. He wanted to wrap his body around hers, find a way to protect her, to take away every second of the pain. "That is a good thing. It will help you rid your body of toxins."

She tried to crawl away, wanting to get into the shadows, but she was too sick, her body shuddering with pain, collapsing before she could reach the darker edges of the cavern. Vikirnoff tried to touch her, to help her, but she shook her head, pushing his hands away, unable to bear being touched with her skin so sensitive. He waved his hands at the candles flickering closest to her and the lights went out, leaving her with a semblance of privacy as she was sick over and over.

"This sucks," she announced, rolling over to lie still, conserving her strength for the next round. "I know you can make that go away"—she pointed to the mess she'd made—"and I really detest throwing up, so remove it please." She took the water bottle he handed her and rinsed her mouth, grateful he was thoughtful.

Vikirnoff complied, making certain all evidence that she had been ill was removed. "I want to try to do this together, Natalya. Do not hold yourself away from me or try to protect me. You are my life and I need to do whatever I can to help you through this. Let my heartbeat lead yours. Let my breath be yours." He couldn't be a bystander while she suffered so much. He had to find a way to help her.

Natalya reached out her hand for his. It was almost comical to see him so shaken. Her big bad Carpathian. He was actually trembling. Worse, he looked ready to kill something, or someone. Who knew he would react like that? "What are you going to do if I ever have a baby?"

His face paled visibly and his eyes darkened even more. "I cannot think about it now. Not for a long time. Centuries maybe. Perhaps never, if it is anything like this."

The next wave began building and she shifted her gaze to his face, her expression desperate. He brushed back her hair, noting the stripes once again stood out against her skin and hair in bands of orange and black and white. She alternated between the stripes and her pale, almost gray complexion. "Hang on, love, breathe with me. A long slow breath and ride above the pain."

Her gaze clung to his, her grip on him so tight he thought she might crush his bones, but she followed his breathing, long slow breaths, moving air in and out of their lungs, staying above the worst of the pain. Her body shook and the pinpoints of blood seeping through pores alarmed them both, but she was able to get through the wave without convulsing.

"I don't want to lose my tigress." She lifted her head when he put his arm around her neck to hold her up so she could rinse her mouth again. "It wants my tigress and she is fighting it. I don't want to give her up. She's a part of me, just like breathing." There was anxiety in her voice, a plea in her eyes.

"The conversion is reshaping organs and tissues; essentially you are reborn as a Carpathian. I can still see the stripes. It is your *nature* to be a tigress, not part of your *species*. I do not believe you will lose who you are." He brushed the damp strands of tawny hair from her face. "You will always be Natalya and the tigress is part of your soul. I feel her locked with me. You will not lose her." He repeated the reassurance a second time as the next pain welled up sharp and fast, lifting her from the cavern floor and slamming her back down so hard her bones seemed in danger of breaking.

Natalya kept her gaze fixed on Vikirnoff. He was her lifeline. As long as she looked at him, saw desperate love and worry etched into his face, in the black eyes, she knew she could be strong. She'd never had a man look at her like that, as if his world was shattering because she was suffering. She could feel him trying to take the pain from her and it only made her love him more. He was such a powerful, steadfast man, yet all his personal stoicism dissolved in the face of her suffering.

She stroked his face, her fingertips smoothing the deep lines as the pain subsided. "I'm not afraid of this, Vikirnoff. I'm really not."

He swore again. She hadn't heard him say so many swear words in all the time they'd been together. "I am. I knew it was bad, but not like this." He pressed his forehead against hers, smearing blood across both of their brows. "It has to be over soon."

"It will be." She was calm now, resigned to the waves of pain, able to hang on because she could get through anything for a short period of time and he was there with her, looking ravaged and drained, so distraught she wanted to soothe him.

Vikirnoff thought he might lose his mind. Time dragged, each second agonizingly slow, an excruciating endless anguish that had him praying when he hadn't prayed in centuries. He had never felt so helpless—or use-less in his life. His Natalya, so courageous, undergoing such torment for him. For his way of life. When finally he thought it would be safe to send to her sleep, she smiled at him. *Smiled.*

Vikirnoff wanted to weep. The way she looked at him, with such love in her eyes, humbled him. He couldn't be-lieve she could see him that way, not after such an ordeal. There was love in her eyes, a warmth that seeped into the coldness of his bones and brought him back to life.

You really are a baby, you know. There was utter weari-ness in her voice. She was so tired, yet she couldn't help wiping at the blood-red tears streaking his face.

Only where you are concerned. I am going to lock you in a tower and keep you safe for well over a hundred years. It will take at least that long to get over this night.

I really hate to have to admit this because I've almost worked out the counter spell to undo the binding ritual, but I have fallen madly in love with you. There was a small deliberate sigh in her voice, as if she were annoyed that she could possibly have fallen in love with him.

His burning lungs found air. That small sigh was enough to tell him she was still Natalya, his warrior woman and she wasn't going to cave in because she was flat on her back. *I hate to disagree with you when you are obviously unable to defend your position, but the ritual binding words are not a spell. You cannot undo our marriage.*

She closed her eyes but a faint smile curved her lips. *Then I shall endure.*

He burst out laughing, a mixture of relief and amusement, tears still leaking from his eyes, gathering her up in his arms as he opened the ground, exposing the rejuvenating soil rich in minerals. "I am putting you to bed where you will not be able to torment me. I need recovery time from this ordeal."

Her eyebrow shot up. *You need the recovery time?*

I nearly had a heart attack.

The pain was welling up again, seizing her organs, squeezing like a vice so it felt as if she might really be having a heart attack. *Stop talking and more action.*

Vikirnoff sent her to sleep instantly, a strong command that was probably unnecessary, but he wasn't taking any chances. He sat for a long time cradling her in his lap, rocking gently back and forth, more to soothe himself than her. He stared down into her beautiful face. When had he become so consumed by her? He couldn't imagine his life without Natalya. Her lashes were thick and black, feathery crescents under her eyes. He noted the dark circles that hadn't been there before.

He had never considered himself a man of violence. He lived in a world of violence and did what he had to do. Hunting was a way of life. Battles and wounds and destroying evil were simply how he lived. It was never personal, never emotional. Yet now, with Natalya, all that had changed. He couldn't bear her to be in pain. Not physically and certainly not emotionally.

He buried his face against her throat. He had a demon in him and it wasn't the monster who had lived and roared for blood. This unexpected demon had risen up, demanding retribution, wanting to smash and destroy simply because Natalya was in pain. He couldn't stand to see her that way, so pale, in agony, trying valiantly to protect him. Vikirnoff didn't like discovering he was a violent man, but it was there, deep inside and he wouldn't hide from it. Natalya had seen him, demons and all, and she hadn't turned away from him. For that alone, he loved her.

He carefully unraveled the safeguards surrounding Natalya's weapons and her backpack. The book would have to be with them at all times until he could convince Natalya to turn it over to the prince. He could understand why she wanted to safeguard the tome herself. She knew next to nothing about the Carpathians, a dying species, with too few women and even fewer children. And that meant she didn't know the prince or his capabilities. Mikhail was one of the most powerful Carpathians alive and if anyone could keep the book safe—or find a way to destroy it, it would be Mikhail.

The backpack floated into his hand and he settled down into the rich soil. He would need to rise first and feed enough for both of them before taking her to the great healing caverns where Mikhail and Falcon would give Gabrielle the third blood exchange to convert her. In spite of the tremendous odds against it, Gabrielle was still alive, and Vikirnoff was still guarding her spirit. He needed to be there when she underwent the conversion. The idea was unsettling, especially after he had just gone through it with Natalya.

Vikirnoff stretched out in the welcoming soil, feeling it cushion and embrace him. He settled Natalya's limp body beside him, while he curled up around her, the backpack under both of their palms where it would be safe and she would see upon awakening that he had kept his word. The safeguards were some of the strongest he'd ever woven, wanting to ensure Natalya's safety. He swept his hand across her bare skin. "Sleep well, sleep deep." He brushed a kiss over her lips and lay still beside her, calling to the soil to cover them.

Vikirnoff woke hours later at the precise moment the sun set. All Carpathians were aware of the rising and setting of the sun, yet it was so ingrained in them they gave it very little thought. He scanned the caverns above and below them and then finally the open areas surrounding the caves before opening the earth. As he gathered Natalya in his arms, he thought for the first time in centuries about the sun and how important a part it had played in the life of his lifemate.

He carried her body to the pool where he could wash all evidence of the conversion from her body along with remnants of the rich soil. He didn't want her to wake afraid—or worse, sorry that she had chosen the Carpathian way of life. He loved the night, embraced it as his world, but someone who had walked in the sun might have trouble adjusting.

He nuzzled Natalya's throat, whispering to her to awaken. He caught her first breath in his mouth, took it into his lungs and held it there, feeling her heart flutter against his hand. She sighed, a soft sound of love that made his heart leap. The pads of her fingers trailed over his chest, a wisp of movement so light it felt like the flutter of wings, yet it seemed she burned her brand forever into his skin. Her fresh scent rose up to torment him, to tease his senses and harden his body.

Natalya's long lashes lifted and her brilliant green gaze stared into his, darkening with hunger, with desire. "Hello." Her voice was soft, incredibly sexy and every muscle in his body tightened and hardened.

"Hello." She couldn't fail to notice the evidence of his desire, thick and pulsing with energy and heat.

"I'm alive." Her fingertips smoothed over his face. A slow smile curved her mouth. "Hang on one minute and let me make certain everything is working properly."

Vikirnoff frowned as she rolled over and jumped to her feet, stretching lazily. He propped himself up on one elbow, a faint smile on his face as she shifted shape. The tigress bounded around the cavern, joy in the playful leaps, before she rubbed her fur along his body. He sank his fingers into the thick pelt and caressed her face as she lay beside him.

Natalya shifted back again, laughing up at him. "She's still there."

"I knew she would be."

Natalya sat up, a fluid movement of grace and elegance, shifting to straddle his lap. Her body was already hot. He could feel her wet and slick pressed into his thigh. His hands caught her hips, trying to position her where he could join them, but she resisted, shaking her head. "I want luxury this evening. I think I deserve it."

He swallowed hard. Luxury might be the death of him. "You deserve anything you want."

"I want to touch you." She lowered her head so her lips could skim his chest, featherlight, just enough to drive him mad. "Like this. I love touching you." She wanted to make love to him. A long slow passionate time where every touch showed him her love. Where her new senses could heighten what she already felt when he touched her. She needed this time with him to feel loved in every way.

His hands cupped her buttocks, lifted, massaged and rubbed, pressing her closer to him, his body so eager for hers his heart was nearly exploding out of his chest. She lifted her head, her gaze slumberous and sensual, her mouth finding his, teeth tugging gently at his lower lip, her tongue teasing his with tiny stroking caresses. He felt each one vibrate through his body, coming together in his groin. The ache grew into a distinct pain, his erection heavy and stiff and throbbing for relief.

Her mouth left his and she alternated tiny kisses and bites across his throat and down his chest. Her hands pushed at the wall of his chest until he leaned back, resting against the side of the pool. Water lapped at his thighs and legs, splashed droplets over him. Natalya didn't seem to notice, intent on tracing every muscle with her tongue and teeth. She was tortuously slow as she moved down his chest to his belly with slow licks and tiny kisses. The fire racing through his veins found its way to the building volcano in his groin. "I am not going to live through this."

"Well, you'll just have to, because I want to *feel* the way I love you and the way you love me back."

She moved her hips, sliding the moist heat of her mound back and forth over him until he groaned, his fingers digging into her hips to set her on him. Smiling, she slid lower, pressing kisses against his flat belly, her legs sliding into the water, giving him a delicious view of her curved bottom. He couldn't stop his hands from massaging her, fingers dipping low to invade her body. His breath was coming in ragged gasps.

Her breath moved over the head of his erection, warming the glistening drops there, and stilling his heart. "This is what you did to me. I couldn't think or breathe. I could only feel, Vikirnoff. I want you to feel how much I love you."

Before he could answer, her mouth closed around him, tight and hot, her tongue doing some incredible dance while her fist grasped him with sure fingers. Lightning raced up his body, sizzled in his veins. The sound of his breathing was harsh, even to his own ears. He watched her through half-closed eyes, his body going up in flames. When he thought he would die, when he couldn't feel anymore without exploding into a million fragments, she took him deeper so that his hips thrust helplessly. The small suckling noises coupled with her tight mouth and licking tongue nearly drove him out of his mind.

Her fingernails raked his scrotum, her fingers tightening and squeezing gently, her mouth so hot it was a cauldron of fire wrapped around him. His fists bunched in her hair and he thrust deeper. Her breasts moved against his thighs, her nipples hard pinpoints of heat. He couldn't resist the invitation of her curved bottom, thrust upward in the air as she suckled. His hand came down open-palmed, stroked and caressed, massaging, his blood pumping so hard through his veins he was afraid he might spontaneously combust.

Vikirnoff groaned her name, dragged her head back,

needing her body, needing the feel of her wrapped tightly around him, gripping with such force he knew she needed him every bit as much. He could devour her later, her sweetness pouring into him, her cries bringing him intense pleasure, but not now. Now he was too frenzied with lust, too high on love. The two emotions were so mixed together he couldn't separate them.

He rolled her over, coming up on top of her. Her breasts were beautiful, the full mounds tipped with darker pink nipples, rising and falling with each breath she dragged into her lungs. Water splashed around them, her hair floating in strands on the surface. The ledge held her in position, her bottom firmly lodged in the cradle of rock. He stroked her soft skin from her neck to her hip, stretching her beneath him like a sacrifice. "I love the feel of you. Do you have any idea what it is like for me to touch you like this?" He stroked her again, this time his palm taking a path over the swell of her breast to the V at the junction of her legs. Deliberately he merged his mind with hers so she could feel the fiery sensations in his own body, the driving need of the male of his species to dominate and control.

Her eyes darkened with hunger, with excitement. The tigress in her would never accept a mate less than Vikirnoff. His touch on her breast roughened as he rolled her nipple between his thumb and finger, but he leaned forward and brushed a gentle kiss across her lips, his tongue sweeping into her mouth with stroking caresses.

The contrast between the tenderness of his mouth and the roughness of his hands sent heat sweeping through her body and left her womb clenching in desperation.

His teeth nibbled on her chin, his hair sliding like silk over her so that every nerve ending jumped to life. He licked her nipple. Paused. Lowered his head to taste again. His tongue flicked her several times making her so aware of the sensual erotic spot. Teeth scraped, lips kissed. Her head thrashed back and forth and when his mouth closed, hot and tight over her breast, suckling strongly, she cried out his name, fingers tugging at his hair, nails digging into his back.

"Hurry up." She panted the command.

He lifted his head, his smile wicked. "You wanted slow and lazy. I am giving you what you wanted." Deliberately he kissed his way across her belly, tonguing the ring, teeth tugging at it, before dipping lower.

"No. I *need* you in me. Right. Now." She could barely get the words out.

"One taste." He sank his finger into her, watching the shattering pleasure on her face. "That is what I need. To see you like that, Natalya, to see you come apart for me." He pushed a second finger in, deeper this time, finding her most sensitive spot and rubbing with hard, strong strokes. "The tigress is close when you make love. Do you realize that? Your eyes go midnight blue and then opaque when you are very aroused." It was the biggest turn-on, watching her eyes change color, watching her face and body flush for him, her nipples taut and elongated, her breath coming in ragged, harsh gasps.

His eyes, dark with sensuality held her gaze captive as he began a slow assault of her body. His tongue and fingers stroked and thrust into her; his licks and the tiny bites of his teeth drove her to the very edge of sanity. She couldn't think straight, couldn't find the breath to gasp out a protest as he took over her body, playing it like a finely tuned instrument. He was everywhere, claiming every inch of her as his own, building her need and hunger into a frenzied lust. She screamed through two orgasms, her body inflamed, burning out of control.

He rose above her, gripping her thighs, desperate hunger running through his body. Every muscle was strung so tight he felt coiled and ready, an explosion waiting to happen. Looking at her face, so beautiful, so filled with hunger and need for him—*for him*. There it was, the miracle he had been gifted with. She had been made for him. Her body, this body, fit so perfectly with his; it was designed for pleasure, and he meant to take every drop and give her back tenfold.

He sank his shaft deep, a hard, driving stroke to take him as far into the hot inferno of her channel as he could get. She was so tight and wet, gripping him with her inner muscles, that he let loose a guttural growl of sheer bliss. Catching her legs, he wrapped them tightly around his waist, forcing her closer to him, so that he could pound deeper and harder with long, sure strokes. He felt her body tighten and shudder around him, but he kept thrusting, in and out, over and over, never wanting it to end. Her second climax began before the first had faded away, throwing her into another much more violent one.

Her hands clamped onto his shoulders, an anchor for her when he kept going, taking her even higher, forcing her into an explosive third orgasm. It shuddered through her body with the force of a freight train, rocking her, setting off the same explosion in him. He felt the drawing, the tightening until his very bones ached with the contraction. Her sheath, so hot and tight, gripped him, squeezing him to the point of pain, convulsing around him, a fist of hot velvet, until he was helpless to stop the volcanic eruption, spurting into her over and over.

Natalya stared up at him, dazed and slightly shocked. Her body refused to relax, refused to release him, every aftershock sending shudders of pleasure through her. She couldn't talk, couldn't find a way to drag air into her lungs. She could only lie there with the water lapping at her body, staring into his face.

"You are more beautiful than any woman I have ever seen." And more sensual. She looked a siren there, spread out before him like a feast. "Again, Natalya. I want you again. And I want your blood and I want to give you mine. I want everything this time."

She shook her head, a faint smile curving her mouth. "You already took everything. I can't move."

"I do not want you to move. I want you to feel."

Natalya couldn't move. Exhausted, her body still crying for more, she looked into his eyes, so dark, so intense with desire. His hands were everywhere, his teeth and mouth and his tongue. She pressed her mouth to his chest, drinking when he demanded, fire pulsing through her, multiple orgasms rocking her when his teeth pierced deep and his body thrust again and again into hers. She couldn't believe she could want more, but desire consumed her, Vikirnoff's needs feeding her own. She couldn't seem to get enough of his body and there didn't seem to be enough ways for him to sate himself with hers. "We're going to die if we keep this up," she warned, when she could talk again.

"I have centuries to make up for." His hands stroked her breasts. "I will never get enough of touching you like this."

Natalya rolled over into the heat of the pool. "I'm going to be so sore I won't be able to walk. You look pale. I think you need to feed." Even as she said it, a flare of jealousy spurted through her. What if he bent his head toward another woman, knuckles brushing her breast? What if the woman looked at him with desire, her body growing wet and hot as he approached her? A low snarl escaped and Natalya swam toward the center of the pool. If she *ever* smelled another woman's scent on him, he would find out what it was like to rouse the tigress.

Something was wrong, but Natalya couldn't figure out what it was. They'd made love, she had been so happy, but with her mixture of heightened tigress and

Carpathian senses, she suddenly felt the presence of another woman. She did. He might deny it all he wanted, but there was another woman in his life.

Vikirnoff watched her with speculative eyes. Very soft stripes banded her hair and flesh as she moved through the water. He touched her thoughts and smiled. How she could think he might want another woman was a puzzle to him. He followed her, pacing right beside her.

Natalya flashed him an irritated glance. "I need space." She sent up a column of water with a single bat of her hand. Or paw. In the flickering candlelight, even with his amazing night vision, he couldn't tell whether she had partially shifted. Her blue cat's eyes had gone stormy, opaque, shimmering with translucent colors and a warning.

His body tightened all over again. Natalya's warrior woman brought out the dominating male in him. He couldn't help it or the intense desire sweeping through him. "You need me."

Her eyes glowed with heat. "Back off, Vik, before you get into trouble. I feel her so close to you."

He reached out and caught her to him, standing up so the water pooled around his hips. "There is no other woman and there will never be another woman." The words hissed between clenched teeth.

"I *feel* her." Tears shimmered in her eyes and she tried to push him away with the flat of her hands.

He caught her wrists, seeing her very real distress.

"This makes no sense. . . ." His voice trailed off. "Gabrielle." He whispered the name. "You feel Gabrielle, *ainaak sívamet jutta*. You feel Gabrielle calling to me." His thumb slid over her bare arm in a caress. "You cannot hold Gabrielle against me when you asked me to save her. You knew what it entailed."

She shook her head. "I didn't. I asked before I thought. I didn't know how it would make me feel to know she is there with you."

"Her spirit is light. She is uncertain whether she wishes to remain when her life will be changed for all time. I am the holder of her spirit and I can give her freedom. Release her into the other realm. Is that what you wish?"

The tigress fought for supremacy, struggled to rule when jealousy ate at her.

"You are my heart and my soul. You are my woman. It is your body I wish to possess. Your body I fantasize about and your blood I wish to taste. I do not want you to feel afraid that I will betray you, especially after all you have given for me."

Natalya covered her face with her hands. "Stop! Don't tempt me. What a horrible person I am to even consider such a thing. Don't you dare allow her to slip away. I have every confidence in myself as a woman." That might be more bravado than she wanted to admit. Vikirnoff's appetites had not only surprised, but slightly shocked her. He had a way of making her so out of control, so filled with desire she would do anything for him and that not only was terrifying, but fascinating to her. "If you did betray me with another woman, I doubt I could hold the tigress in check."

"Lifemates cannot lie to one another. We are too often in each other's mind for a deception to be effective. I neither want nor need another woman." He drew her closer, pressing his body against hers. "They call us to the healing cave. Mikhail will convert Gabrielle and bring her into our world. Once it is safe, she will be put into the ground for several days to give the soil a chance to heal her. Joie and Traian, Gabrielle's kin, will have a chance to complete their journey to be here when she rises. I will no longer be needed." His arms went around her and he rested his cheek on the top of her head.

"I'll need you." She rubbed her hands down his back. "I'm sorry I'm not those perfect women."

"Perfect women?" He lifted his head to look down at her, confused as usual. He could never follow her train of thought and he even had the advantage of getting into her head. "I have no idea who you are talking about."

"June Cleaver and Donna Reed. Your pinup fantasy women." There was a bite in her voice, even when she tried to tease.

He groaned. "Are you ever going to let me off the hook? I do not want those women. Or any woman like them. I want you." His teeth bit into her shoulder in a small reprimand. "*Only* you."

"I can hear the Carpathians calling us now. How many of them will be there?"

Vikirnoff heard the apprehension in her voice. Fighting vampires, coming into his world, being his woman, even making love to him for hours on end was undaunting to her, but meeting other Carpathians was frightening. She tried to hide it, but her body was pressed tightly against his and he could feel her trembling.

He carried her out of the water. They dried their bodies and dressed in the clothes Vikirnoff wove for them. He provided her with her battle outfit, the one she was most comfortable wearing. She loaded up with weapons in silence and accepted the backpack from him, slipping it onto her shoulders before sliding her Arnis sticks into the loops of the pack.

"Mikhail and his lifemate, Raven, will need to be present. I am certain Falcon and Sara will be there as well." He sent a question winging to the prince, waited for the answer and relayed it. "Mikhail said that Jubal is with Slavica watching over the seven children Falcon and Sara care for."

Natalya slipped her arm around his neck, as he shifted shape. "Not too many people. I can handle it." As they took to the night sky, with her clinging to his giant bird back, she hoped it was true. Colors dazzled her eyes. Everything, including her emotions seemed so much more acute. She was far more aware than she'd ever been, to the point where she actually had to experiment with turning down the volume in her ears to avoid hearing snippets of conversations as they flew over the village.

The healing cave was beautiful, made of crystals and

flowing water. Heat and humidity blended together so at first Natalya found it heard to breathe. Ice-cold water flowed from one wall, dropping several feet into a hot mineral spring so that the steam was thick and white, floating above the shimmering water like clouds.

Gabrielle lay in the center, the earth already open to welcome her, the soil nearly black with richness. She looked pale, so still and white, Natalya's heart went out to her and she was ashamed of her earlier jealousy. She touched the other woman gently, determined to help Vikirnoff do whatever it took to save her.

Sara and Raven greeted Natalya with a hug and very welcoming smiles. The men greeted Vikirnoff by gripping his forearms in the way of the ancient warriors. Both Mikhail and Falcon bowed from the waist at Natalya with old-world courtesy. A third man stepped from the shadows, startling her so that she drew her sword before she realized he, too, was Carpathian.

"I did not mean to frighten you." If there was amusement on his face, it didn't show. The centuries spent in Brazil had given him a slightly different look. Aloof, aristocratic. Very handsome like his kin, but dressed in a completely different style, looking more like a wealthy rancher. "I am Manolito De La Cruz, at your service."

Natalya lifted her chin. "You didn't frighten me." She met the black eyes without flinching.

Mikhail turned away with a faint smile. "Manolito brought us news of a small group of Jaguar men committing atrocities against their women. His family believes they may be in league with the vampires. He also carried back the news of another Morrison laboratory and a very lethal poison they've developed to use against us."

Natalya turned to Vikirnoff, her eyes wide with apprehension. He moved closer to her, but didn't touch her, recognizing her need to feel strong. "Did you bring back a sample of the poison?"

Manolito shook his head. "I have the images sent from my brother. I have given them to the prince. Riordan broke down the compound and sent it to me to deliver to the Mikhail."

Mikhail knelt beside Gabrielle's still body and gestured for everyone else to take their places in a loose circle. "We must complete this before we lose her. Vikirnoff has guarded her spirit carefully for days, but he tells me she fades more with each rising."

Vikirnoff positioned himself at Gabrielle's head, his hands resting on either side of her. Natalya knelt beside him and merged her mind firmly with his. At once she touched Gabrielle's spirit. It was light and fragile, staying only because Vikirnoff kept her with them, refusing to allow her passing. He murmured to her softly, encouraging her as the others began the ancient healing chant and Mikhail bent to take her blood for the third exchange.

Merged so deep, Natalya felt Gabrielle wincing away, trying to be brave, but doubts and fears rose up in spite of Vikirnoff's comforting voice. Tears welled up in Natalya's eyes as she realized Vikirnoff had been soothing and comforting Gabrielle each time she was awake. *I should have been helping you. I should have been there for you.*

She was his partner and this keeping of Gabrielle's spirit hadn't been easy for him. He didn't have the connection to Gabrielle the others had, yet he had guarded her soul and refused to let her die. Natalya was determined to rectify her mistakes. She bent close to Gabrielle, brushing her own spirit against the other woman's.

You must cling to life. Natalya told Gabrielle. *There are so many who fight for you. So many who love you. Do you have any idea how very precious that is? These people give of themselves freely to you. They offer life with them. Do you want to leave only out of fear? Fear can be overcome.*

The answer was a small fluttering in Natalya's mind. In her heart and soul. *Gary.* A single name. A single cry of anguish.

He would want you to choose life. With life there is always a way. Take my hand. Take the blood your prince offers you and choose life.

I have heard the conversion is painful and I cannot bear more pain. It seems to have become my life. I don't have Gary or my sister here with me. I'm so afraid.

I will be with you. Vikirnoff will be with you, Natalya said.

As will I, Raven murmured it softly, connecting through the prince.

I am here, Sara added, connecting through Falcon.

We have all suffered the conversion and come through to the other side. We will be with you every moment.

Gabrielle opened her mouth and accepted the life-giving offering of the prince.

19

*T*he *Dubrinsky home* was beautiful, with high ceilings, a stone fireplace and wood floors. Most of the rooms had floor-to-ceiling bookshelves. Natalya was surprised the house had a huge, well-stocked kitchen.

Raven grinned at her. "We always maintain the illusion of being human."

Vikirnoff was close, so close Natalya could feel his breath on the nape of her neck. They had fed together, finding a farmer and his grown son before joining the others at the Dubrinsky home. Vikirnoff had snarled over her luring the son to her and ever since he'd been hovering. Natalya threw a quick, repressing glance over her shoulder at him, but he didn't seem to notice the hint.

Raven laughed. "They're all like that. I think it comes

of being ancient. They were born so long ago they can't quite make it out of the caves."

"What do you know of this poison Manolito has told us about," Mikhail asked Natalya. "Have you seen it before?"

There was instant silence. The men had been talking together in the corner, but suddenly they were all focused on her. She stood her ground, her fingers running back and forth over the hilt of her knife.

Mikhail wrapped his arm around Raven and pulled her back into the shelter of his body, nuzzling her hair as he did so. It was a brief, affectionate gesture, one Natalya found somewhat endearing. A man couldn't be all bad if he loved his lifemate. She glanced at Vikirnoff. He trusted the prince far more than she did. "I would need to see the compound."

Mikhail easily put the images and information into Natalya's mind. He did it fast, with no preliminaries, no gentle asking. He obviously had a path to her mind despite the barriers and that made her feel very vulnerable and extremely uneasy.

He is able to do so through me. Vikirnoff reassured her.

Natalya took her time examining the structure of the poison, ignoring the conversations flowing around her.

Ordinarily, Natalya wasn't nervous in social situations. She never had anything to lose, but she knew how tied to these people Vikirnoff really was. He hadn't spent time with them in centuries, but he thought of them, fought for them, identified with them whether he realized it or not. She didn't want to embarrass him by saying or doing the wrong thing. She knew she had a smart mouth and curbing it in the face of so much testosterone was going to be difficult.

At once Vikirnoff flooded her mind with warmth and silent laughter. *I will enjoy watching the show.*

Ha. Ha. Ha. I'm so glad you like fireworks. She flashed a small grin at him.

I'm extremely fond of fireworks.

"I recognize parts of this poison, but it isn't all mine. They've mixed some of my earlier experiments."

Mikhail nodded. "Gary Jansen developed a poison against us some time ago and parts of his poison are mixed with the newer chemicals."

"The vampires are definitely in league against us," Falcon said. "They have been planning for some time."

"Xavier is involved," Vikirnoff announced, reaching for Natalya's hand. "He is alive and conspiring with the Malinov brothers."

As Vikirnoff was speaking, another man entered the house. He was tall with broad shoulders, thick black hair and startling green eyes. "That Xavier lives, does not surprise me in the least." His gaze swept past Vikirnoff and found Natalya. He went utterly still. For a moment it seemed as if he had ceased to breathe. "You are the exact image of Rhiannon."

His penetrating gaze seemed to see straight through

her to every dark deed she'd ever committed. "Rhiannon was my grandmother," Natalya said.

"*Was?*"

Ordinarily the demand in his voice would have irritated her, and Vikirnoff was already moving to put himself between her and the stranger, though for her protection or the stranger's she wasn't certain. Something in the man's face saddened her. The man, whoever he was, bore an uncanny resemblance to her father. "Xavier killed Rhiannon long ago," she explained.

"She is dead?" Though no expression crossed the man's face, she was certain the news struck him hard. "You are certain?"

"I'm capable of accessing the memories in objects, particularly if violence is associated with the object. Xavier used his favorite ceremonial knife to kill her. I saw it happen through the knife and Vikirnoff witnessed it as well." The man closed his eyes as if in pain. "I'm sorry," she added. "Did you know her?"

"Forgive me, little sister. I should have introduced myself. I am Rhiannon's brother, Dominic. I have long sought my beloved sister in the hopes of finding her alive. It is good she lives through you." Dominic clasped Vikirnoff's arms. "*Ekä, kont.* I had hoped one day to see you again."

"You are wounded."

Dominic shrugged. "I had a run-in with Maxim Malinov and we had ourselves quite a little battle."

He was the dragon in the sky the other day, wasn't he? Natalya asked Vikirnoff, excited. *What did he call you?*

Yes. He has always been a superb warrior. He called me brother and warrior. Coming from Dominic, it is a great honor.

"It is why I was late this rising. I meant to attend the healing, but fear my wounds needed a few extra hours in the soil to ensure I was fit to aid our people should the need arise." All the while he spoke, his gaze continued to flicker over Natalya. "I would see the memories of the murder of my sister with my own eyes, Vikirnoff."

Vikirnoff readily complied and Natalya looked away, out the window, refusing to brush their minds while they exchanged information. She could not bear to relive the past again.

"I have long used the disappearance of my sister as my reason for remaining on this earth. I thought once I knew what happened to her I would seek the dawn, but I must know about her children."

"My father is dead," Natalya spoke up. "Xavier murdered him. I don't know what happened to my aunts. They were triplets, two girls and a boy. My father thought his sisters had to be dead. He rarely spoke of them." Natalya pressed a hand over the suddenly burning birthmark and looked anxiously at her lifemate. "Vikirnoff? They are coming."

"Who is coming?" Falcon asked, rising from where he'd been sitting with Sara.

"Vampires," Dominic answered, his palm covering his

side over the same birthmark. "The dragon is burning. They are already here."

Mikhail thrust Raven behind him, looking out his window. "I do not feel their presence."

"Nor do I," Falcon agreed. He was at the opposite window.

"I feel them only through Natalya," Vikirnoff said. "This is what has been happening everywhere and must have something to do with whatever they are putting in their blood."

The first explosion rocked the house, sending a shower of wood and debris down on them. An orange-red ball drove through the roof, the top story, past them and down to the basement below, spreading flames everywhere it touched. Instantly several more fireballs hit the house from every direction. Explosion after explosion shook not only the house, but the ground. Flames shot up the walls and danced across the ceiling. Faces appeared in the rolling waves of fire, laughing and taunting. The ceiling collapsed in large, burning chunks.

Vikirnoff drove Natalya to the floor, covering her body with his own as he threw up a hasty shield, trapping oxygen inside. Mikhail and Raven and Falcon and Sara huddled together, while Manolito and Dominic raised similar barriers. The breath slammed out of Natalya's lungs, leaving her gasping and fighting the weight of Vikirnoff's larger frame. She pushed at him, trying desperately to get at her weapons.

"Mikhail is creating a vacuum, sucking all the air from

around us to put out the fire. Be still." Vikirnoff gripped her shoulders, holding her down with the casual strength of his species.

"Freakin' idiot, next time warn me. I might have slit your throat thinking you were the enemy," Natalya snapped. Her heart was pounding. The world was in flames around her. The fire roared so loud it hurt her ears and the faces writhing in the conflagration stretched their lips wide with wild shrieks of laughter. The tigress didn't want to be held down. Every survival instinct was roused, desperate to fight for freedom; Natalya focused on lying still beneath Vikirnoff to keep from running.

There was a *whoosh*ing sound that rocked the house as Mikhail removed the oxygen and immediately the flames vanished, leaving a blackened shell with most of the roof gone. The eerie silence clawed at Natalya's nerves. Before they could move, the orange-red fireballs began pounding what was left of the structure again and the flames leapt to life. Several bombs rained down on them from directly overhead, tearing gaps in the floor, exposing the chambers beneath in the basement.

We have to get out of the house. Get to the underground chamber and go through the ground to safety.

Natalya recognized Mikhail's voice. He was calm, but there was an underlying urgency. At once their shelter disappeared and Vikirnoff's weight lifted from her body. She sprang to her feet and raced toward the nearest hole in the floor. Walls of flames raged around them, the heat so intense she could barely breathe.

No! We cannot go that way. Vikirnoff gripped Natalya's arm before she could jump, dragging her back against him, pressing her face into his chest to help alleviate her burning lungs. *That way is closed to us, Mikhail. They await us with traps in the ground.*

You are certain? Mikhail asked.

Vikirnoff nodded. *Trust me.*

Natalya touched Vikirnoff's mind and realized he was using her connection to Razvan. He had turned the tables on her brother, reaching out on her telepathic path to her twin, unraveling the familiar safeguards and searching his mind for information.

I should have thought of that. And maybe she had. Maybe she just couldn't accept what Razvan had become. *I'm sorry.*

Vikirnoff hissed something at her between clenched teeth, the images he was receiving from Razvan evidently infuriating him. *We'll have to shift. I will hold the image of mist uppermost in your mind and we will shift together as soon as it is safe to move.*

Natalya nodded. She was furious at being trapped like a rat in a cage. It took two heartbeats to realize it was Vikirnoff's fury she was feeling more than her own.

Get down. When I extinguish the flames after all of you escape quickly, and remember, they will know we are coming. Mikhail accepted that they had no choice but to use the common path of communication in the midst of the roaring flames and black smoke.

Natalya went to the floor, not waiting for Vikirnoff to

drag her down. This time smoke mixed with oxygen within the hastily erected shield, but the air was still breathable. Vikirnoff settled on top of her and the tigress growled in protest, but remained still.

She was more prepared this time for the ground trembling and the force of the air being removed from the building. Again there was the same eerie silence. The Carpathians threw off the shields and began to shimmer into mist. Vikirnoff's fingers curled tightly around hers as he pushed the image of vapor into her mind.

Stop! The order came from Vikirnoff again as he delved even deeper into Razvan's brain, reading the battle plan. *They have devised a method to keep us from restructuring. Xavier and Razvan have constructed a net to entrap us. If we shift, we will be caught in that form, unable to change. It is what they expect of us.*

Are there any flaws in it? Mikhail didn't waste time with argument or bother to hide the conversations from the vampires. They wouldn't know yet where the Carpathians were getting their information. *Let us all see what they have done.*

It is much more than that, Natalya confirmed. *If we try to use much of our magick it will backfire on us. I think we have only the weather left to us. He could not prevent that.*

Dominic backed her up. *She is right. Do not try to shift or use magick of any kind other than the lightning or the wind and rain. They think to force us to use the old ways to fight. And they hear us. Feel their triumph?*

Natalya reached for Vikirnoff on their private telepathic path. *Razvan and Xavier cannot spread the shield too thin. If we get to the forest we will be able to shift. Find a way to get that message to them all.*

Will do.

Natalya's heart nearly exploded in her chest it was pounding so hard. The urge to run was nearly overwhelming. She glanced at the other two women and saw the same desperation on their faces. Sara's hands covered her stomach protectively and Natalya's heart lurched. She met the other woman's gaze and Sara nodded slightly at the question in Natalya's eyes. *Vikirnoff! We have to get out of here right now.*

Already the fireballs were slamming into the house, this time coming through the sides of the structure. *We have to fight our way out.* Mikhail sounded calm. *Keep the women in the center.*

Natalya drew her guns. *Not this woman.*

Vikirnoff bent low, his fingers biting deep into Natalya's wrist as the smoke swirled heavy around them. *Stay close to me. Right beside me.*

Sara is expecting a baby. Keep an eye on her. Natalya refused to allow him to treat her as less than the warrior she was. If he couldn't handle who she was, he needed to know it now—and so did she.

We need to get out now. The entire house creaked and strained as it crumbled. The men burst through the doors and windows in a synchronized escape, the women right behind them. Natalya fell back to cover Sara as the vampires leapt on the hunters, ripping and shredding, masked with animal forms and teeth and claws.

They were everywhere. So many of them Natalya's heart froze at the sight, an army of what had to be clones, tearing at the hunters aggressively. She saw Falcon shove Sara back as a huge monster of a bear dropped from the branches of a tree directly onto his shoulders. Sara rushed the creature, intending to use her bare hands if necessary. Natalya shot the thing, emptied a full clip into the throat and heart as she ran toward it, pushing past Sara to protect her. She kept running, snapping a fresh clip into her gun and firing again almost at point-blank range. The bear fell back under the assault, shifting to its natural vampire form.

Falcon punched his fist through the chest cavity and tore out the heart. Lightning streaked from the sky to destroy the heart and incinerate the body.

Natalya caught sight of Vikirnoff, battling three of the creatures. Already his clothes hung in strips and blood gleamed on his back from several blows the vampires had landed. One already lay on the ground and she could see a fifth one creeping up behind him. Her heart in her throat, she leapt between the vampire and Vikirnoff.

She shot the huge creature again and again but it kept advancing until it was on top of her. She felt hot, foul breath on her face, saw the hatred in the red-rimmed eyes. Shoving the gun against the chest she fired in rapid succession straight into the heart. The vampire jerked with each explosion, but the claws only dug into her arms deeper. Natalya dropped the gun and palmed a knife, slamming it with all of her force into the monster's throat. "Get off of me!" She pushed him away from her, kicking out with repugnance, scoring a hit to the chest, knocking it farther back.

Vikirnoff thrust Natalya out of his way, his eyes wild with fury. Lightning arced in the sky, zigzagged overhead and punched into the earth, sizzling through the vampire's body, taking the heart as it did so. "Do not dare put yourself in danger like that again for me." He was shaking with rage and his fury spilled over into his voice. He would not lose her, not like this. The other women were accepting the meager protection of their lifemates, but not his Natalya. She had to be front and center in the battle.

Protect Sara if you must, but do not try to protect me. Damn you, Natalya. You cannot ask me to allow you to put your life in danger to save mine. I will not have it.

Damn you right back. I'm not going to let some wannabe badass kill you because your ego is too big for words. I won't have that.

Vikirnoff snarled, baring white teeth at her, but he had no chance to say anything else, meeting the rush of another small army of vampires.

Natalya glanced to her right and noted Dominic and Manolito were fighting with lightning swords, long flashing lights that sizzled with heat as they sliced through several clones. She drew her sword and grinned at Sara. "I want one of those." She indicated the light sabers with her own sword.

"You said we could use weather?" Sara asked.

Natalya nodded. "They couldn't prevent that. Razvan and Xavier were upset about it because they wanted to prevent the Carpathians from calling down lightning."

"I'll just bet they did." To Natalya's astonishment Sara jerked a knife from Natalya's belt and held her hand to the sky. What appeared to be lightning leapt from the sky and melted onto the shaft. She held it out to Natalya.

Natalya took two experimental cuts with the sword, feeling the balance, hoping she could control the dazzling light. It felt alive, a source of power, but when she gave two practice cuts it handled like a dream. She felt something behind her, and spun around, slicing with the lightning sword as she did so. A furry arm ending in long claws dropped to the ground and the creature howled in pain.

"Whoops. Sorry. Back off furball or I'm going for something much more precious to you." She held the sword at the ready, coming up on the balls of her feet and without another word, thrust straight into the furry chest. The heart incinerated immediately and Natalya grinned. "This is way cool. Much better than hairspray."

There are too many of them. We have to break through their line.

That was Dominic. Natalya could see him battling several vampires, back to back with Manolito, trying to keep them from the prince. The vampires concentrated most of their clones on the hunters, but there was no doubt they were after Mikhail and his lifemate, Raven. While the clones occupied the hunters, the more skilled of the undead attacked the prince. Raven had a sword and fought beside her lifemate, but there were just too many.

"Look to the north, toward the forest. There is an opening." Falcon caught Sara's arm and thrust her toward that direction. "Fight toward the north and perhaps we can break free."

Blood smeared all of the hunters, deep wounds they didn't have time to heal. Natalya couldn't look at Vikirnoff. He stayed close to her, battling too many opponents to handle and the slices covering his body had to be weakening him. She knew they were running out of time. She had killed several clones, but they kept coming, more and more until it seemed impossible to defeat them.

"Maxim is here and is subtly influencing us to believe we will be overwhelmed." Vikirnoff kept striding forward, slicing through the clones and burning as many as he could. It seemed an impossible task. "The forest, Natalya. Keep moving that way."

"I'm trying." The one facing her was in human form and he was no clone. He answered her lightning sword with one of his own and he looked both proficient and confidant. When his sword met hers, the shock waves went right up her arm. She staggered under the blow and just managed to parry his second blow, which came straight at her heart. She glided to one side, deflecting a third blow, allowing the force of the contact to take her sword in a small circle and right back into her opponent.

He screamed with rage, driving at her hard, forcing her to retreat *away* from the north and safety. Natalya parried blow after blow, all the while trying to move away from the direction he was taking her. There was something in his eyes, a glow of triumph that frightened her. Determined to stop backpedaling, one of the worst mistakes any fighter could make, she stepped to the left. Roots erupted around her foot, circling her ankle and holding her captive. Natalya swung her sword at the vampire and let the blade continue on its natural path, slicing through the vines. Blood erupted and the plants withered and fell lifeless to the ground.

Vikirnoff rose up behind the vampire, swinging his own lightning sword. The head went flying and Natalya thrust through the heart. They turned together to fight off the small trio of clones coming at them.

The noise around them seemed deafening. Vikirnoff dropped back in an attempt to get Natalya out in front of him where he could better defend her. All the while his sword was thrusting and parrying, a part of him watched her. It occurred to him they would probably die here. The rage in him calmed. She was fighting beside him. His warrior woman, his miracle, the ultimate lifemate created to be his match in every way.

If they had to go down, they would go together—as

they were meant. Tears stung his eyes at the realization of what she was, the skills she possessed and the way she loved him. Enough to place her body between his and death. *I love you.* He had to tell her. Had to let her know he understood what he had in her, even there in the midst of the battle—especially there.

She sent him a small smile as she thrust her lightning sword straight through a clone's heart. *Of course you do. How could you not?*

Go! Vikirnoff's voice was urgent.

Natalya turned and ran, trying to make for the forest and the tight knot of Carpathians fighting their way towards the one small hole in the enemy lines. Sudden awareness wrenched at her mind and pulled her back around. She was yards from Vikirnoff, but she could see him clearly and he was surrounded. Worse, far worse, the ground around him had erupted into several heaps much like termite mounds. Insects boiled out of the mounds, and right behind them, Razvan stepped into the open.

Everything in her stilled. The battle seemed far away. There was her brother. Her twin. She hadn't seen him in a century, but the moment she laid eyes on him, the years dropped away to leave her that young child again. He turned, green eyes glittering, going midnight blue, and met her gaze over the heads of two vampires. Tears filled her eyes. She didn't know if she was weeping in sorrow or happiness.

Vikirnoff's blade sank into one of the undead, but another directly behind him struck hard, driving him to his knees. The sight of him on the ground galvanized Natalya into action. She raced forward and sprang into the air, kicking at the head of the nearest clone as she went over him and swinging her sword at another, cutting him nearly in two. She landed on the run, still a great distance from her goal.

Vikirnoff somersaulted, coming up to his feet, his sword flashing as he parried several attacks, scored a direct hit on a heart, incinerating it and slicing the last vampire across the throat. He stood facing Razvan. His lungs burned for air. He became aware of every wound, every cut, the precious blood seeping from his body. He had no idea how many clones he had destroyed, but as fast as they went through them, Maxim created others to take their places. These were all pawns to be sacrificed while Maxim remained safe, waiting for the hunter's strength to be worn down. Natalya's brother waited, too.

Vikirnoff knew who he was immediately. Razvan was not Natalya's identical twin, but the eyes were the same and looking into those dark, midnight-blue eyes, sorrow welled up in Vikirnoff. He had no choice but to take this man's life and the deed would haunt him for all time.

"So you are the man who captured the heart of my sister." Razvan sighed softly. "I had hoped I could keep her from your kind. I kept her from Xavier and yet I could not prevent you from finding her."

Vikirnoff remained silent. Razvan's voice was a soft

beguilement. It was unlike that of the vampire, which was a mere illusion. Razvan's voice was real, filled with purity and truth. How could that be if he had turned vampire? Why wasn't he attacking?

"I cannot allow anyone to harm her. What trick you have used to make her believe you love her, I do not know, but I will find a way to clear her mind."

Vikirnoff frowned. Had Razvan actually committed the hideous crimes he was accused of? Had Xavier managed to corrupt the scenes of the past? He shook his head, trying to think clearly. The things Razvan said made no sense.

Natalya knew she would never get there in time. She could see Razvan inching closer to Vikirnoff. His movements were so slow he didn't appear to move, but he was. She touched Vikirnoff's mind and read his confusion. Razvan was a master of using his voice. She had forgotten that, forgotten to warn Vikirnoff. Worst of all, *she* had put the reason for hesitation in Vikirnoff's mind and Razvan was capitalizing on it.

Razvan inched closer to Vikirnoff, drawing a curved dagger from his sheath and palming it, the blade against his wrist where Vikirnoff couldn't see it—but she could. Despair overtook her. Terror for Vikirnoff choked her. *Kill him Vikirnoff!* She issued the order even as she threw her sword. Natalya knew she was too far away, but she had to try. She used every bit of strength she had, forgetting she was now completely Carpathian. The sword whistled through the night, the light spinning, a dazzling display that hurt her eyes. Razvan lunged at Vikirnoff just as the sword penetrated his back and slammed through his body to the hilt.

There was no sound. No scream. Razvan turned his head to look at her as he went down on his knees, both hands coming up toward the sword. The ground around him caved inward and he disappeared. His blue gaze went green and locked with hers as he slipped beneath the soil. The last thing she saw was the shock and horror in his expression.

Natalya screamed as she covered the distance to her brother, reaching toward him. She hadn't had time to think. She could only choose, not weigh whether or not Razvan could be saved and now it was too late. What had she done? Why had she been so accurate when she'd thrown the sword? The earth was already filling in over him. She dropped to her knees and began to dig with her bare hands, great sobs choking her. "What have I done? What have I done?"

Natalya's shattered cry nearly tore Vikirnoff apart. He ran toward her, catching her up, his arm a band around her waist, jerking her off the ground. "Natalya, stop it! Leave him! We have to go! Do you hear me? We have to go now!"

The clones surged toward them and Vikirnoff shook her. His gut twisted with pain. "Natalya!" He refused to let her go, even when she looked at him without recognition, when she looked so bruised and tormented and fought him like a madwoman. "Look at me, damn it." He shook her again. "Look at *me*."

She swallowed hard, her gaze focusing on him. Quickly she looked over to the clones converging on them. "I'm all right now. Really." She swiped at her eyes and drew her other gun, firing several rounds into the clones, temporarily driving them back.

Vikirnoff shoved her in front of him, pushing her toward the Carpathians fighting their way to punch through enemy lines. Manolito had turned back to aid them, running in front of Natalya and for once she didn't object to the protection.

Vikirnoff knew they were in trouble. They had to get out of the trap Maxim had set for them or they would all die here. There were far too many clones and all of the hunters had suffered injuries. Worse, Maxim hadn't even shown himself.

"Mikhail says help is coming," Manolito reported. "We have to make it to the forest and hold out a few more minutes. Gregori and Jacques have returned and are coming as quickly as possible."

Vikirnoff glanced toward the prince fighting his way toward the other Carpathians. He was still a distance away to their left and in spite of the desperate situation, looked calm. Mikhail fought back two of the lesser vampires to give Raven time to follow Dominic through the narrow gap in the enemy line. At once the prince found himself surrounded and cut off from the other hunters. The vampires and their clones began to converge upon him like a wild pack of frenzied wolves. The others were too far away to help. Vikirnoff shifted directions and went to aid Mikhail.

Natalya ran in a fog of misery, feeling crushed under the weight of losing her brother all over again. She knew she had no choice, but she wished she'd had more time. She glanced over her shoulder to assure herself that Vikirnoff was alive and well. She couldn't bear to lose him, too. Skidding to a halt, she spun around. He was off to her left already battling his way toward the prince.

What are you doing? Go with the others! Vikirnoff joined the battle, whirling like a mad demon, his sword slicing bodies and driving through the clones to get to the vampires pressing Mikhail. He cut a wide swath, shouting for the prince to work back toward him.

Natalya snarled, the stripes in her hair and on her skin more pronounced than ever as the tigress rose close to the surface. She shot at the vampire nearest Mikhail, targeting first his heart, then his throat. If she could get him down, even for a few minutes, with Vikirnoff taking out the others, Mikhail could fight his way free to join the other Carpathians. Once out into the forest, they could shift and use other skills. Then the tide just might turn in their favor.

The vampire shuddered and turned toward her, his mouth gaping wide with curses, his teeth bloody and jagged. The glowing eyes settled on her with hatred and fury and he took to the air, flying straight at her. Out of the corner of her eye she saw Mikhail cut down the other vampire, ripping the heart from the chest. Lightning arced and to her astonishment, it struck the vampire flying at her, knocking him right out of the sky. Vikirnoff glared at her and she knew he had been the one to aid her.

Show-off. She fell in beside him as he flanked the prince, sprinting toward the north and safety.

Dominic raced ahead of all of them, leading the way toward the forest, cutting through the few enemies in their path. Sara and Raven ran directly behind him and Falcon and Manolito brought up the rear. They were close to the timberline and Natalya felt a sense of relief sweeping through her even though the clones were rushing to fill the break in the line.

To her horror, Dominic hit something invisible. Sparks flew, rained from the sky and electricity sizzled and arced, a hot orange-red streak, burning down the left side of the Dragonseeker and welding him to the hidden barrier. He was held there, his arm burning, unable to get free.

Pain radiated over his face, but he remained steadfast, turning as far as he could, transferring the lightning sword to his one good arm. The Carpathians came to an abrupt halt, formed a loose semicircle facing outward and waited for the master vampire to appear.

Natalya stepped up close to Dominic where his arm continued to burn, caught in the hidden shield. The edges of the weave were more evident close to his arm. She studied it carefully, the various strands broken from catching the Dragonseeker in its mesh. "I think I can bring this down." Natalya made the announcement in a low voice. "If you buy me some time, I can bring it down."

Mikhail glanced sharply at Vikirnoff, who nodded at the unspoken question. "She's good. Better, maybe, even than Rhiannon."

"Take it down then," Mikhail said.

She shoved a full clip into her gun and handed it to Sara with extra ammunition. "If you and Raven help me, we can get this done fast."

Sara nodded. "I'm with you. Tell me what to do."

Raven stepped up beside them and the three women moved close to the barrier, inside the loose circle the men had made.

Natalya blocked out the rising fear and the sound of battle to concentrate on the feel of the shield. It was little different than a safeguard, the spell had been twisted for evil purposes, but it was still just magick. And she knew magick.

She held her palms up to feel the strength of the weave. Maxim. She had felt him in her mind and knew his touch. This was his work. It had been a terrifying experience to be touched by evil, but she had also been in his mind. She knew how he worked—and Razvan had aided him in weaving such strong magick. Razvan had used *her* safeguards and spells. It was only a matter of time before she could figure it out. "Oh, yeah," she said softly, "I can bring this baby down."

Vikirnoff kept his eye on Natalya as he fought off the next wave of clones. He knew the other hunters were growing tired. All of them had been relatively lucky. They all had sustained grave injuries, mostly deep cuts, but no one was out of the battle other than perhaps Dominic. The Dragonseeker still fought valiantly, pinned to the barrier as he was, but in the end, if Natalya didn't bring it down, they were all going to die.

There was a sudden silence. The air stilled and the clones backed away from the loose knot of Carpathians. Maxim had arrived. The vampires parted and he stood there. Powerful. Ancient. His sneering face revealing his depravity and his contempt of them. His gaze fell on Dominic. "We meet again. You do not look well, my old friend."

"I was never your friend, traitor," Dominic answered. He made no move to try to free his arm from the barrier, even as blisters continued to rise and the smell of burnt flesh drifted on the breeze.

Vikirnoff glanced again at Natalya. Raven and Sara stood side by side in front of her, shielding her from the vampire in an effort to keep him from seeing what she did. Occasionally a graceful hand moved from behind the two women as Natalya sketched patterns in the air. Before Maxim had a chance to notice, Mikhail stepped forward to face him.

The movement of the prince triggered a restless murmuring of the clones and they pressed forward until Maxim held up his hand. "They are eager to kill you, Dubrinsky. I wonder why so many despise your very existence."

"You will not win." Mikhail's voice was low but carried power and authority.

Maxim smiled. "Oh, but you are wrong. We have already won. You think that your second-in-command comes rushing to your aid, but he cannot help you. He will die just as your brother and your daughter and every member of your family will die. There will be no Dubrinsky left on this earth and we will have stamped out the hunters for all time."

How close are you, ainaak enyém?

Natalya's derisive snort was loud in his mind. *So now I'm conveniently forever yours again, now that you need my skills. Wasn't if five minutes ago you were telling me to get the hell away from you?*

Vikirnoff sighed. *I never said that.*

Not only did you say it, Lone Ranger, but you thought it. And punishment? If I didn't obey you were going to punish me? I saw that, too, by the way, floating around in your silly brain. I do not obey anyone.

How well I know that. How much longer?

If you'd leave me alone, I might get it done. He's used a very complicated spell. Dominic is aiding me. Attached as he is to the barrier, he can feel some of the strands that I cannot. Between us, we are unraveling it. A few more minutes. Gregori is close; has he been warned not to approach the barrier?

Mikhail has kept him informed.

Vikirnoff inched forward, keeping the movements imperceptible, not wanting to draw attention to himself. The hatred Maxim felt for the prince was so strong it was almost alive. The vampire was on the edge of violence, a driving need to kill overriding his need to gloat. Every bit of emotion he had managed to find as a vampire, in his highest moments when he killed his victims and feasted on the adrenaline-rich blood, he had dreamt of this moment, when he could take his revenge on the Carpathian hunters by killing their prince.

The air grew still. No one moved. There was no shuffling of feet or rattle of weapons. Vikirnoff gripped the hilt of his sword, silently swearing. The Carpathians were severely handicapped without the use of their magick. Maxim had the full use of his powers and an army he could replenish at will.

The sky erupted right in front of them with an army of vampires and clones, so many they hindered one another as they flew at the small band of hunters. Mikhail stepped forward to meet the attack, but Vikirnoff, Falcon and Manolito stepped in front of him. Lightning swords streaked through the air, cutting everything in the path. As fast as body parts fell to the ground, animals sprang up, rats with sharp teeth rushing at their legs to cut them down.

Sara stepped forward and began to fire steadily, one bullet at a time, a calm display of marksmanship in the midst of the chaos. Raven caught up the sword Dominic threw to her while he forged a new one. She went back to back with her lifemate, fighting off the airborne attacks.

Suddenly Maxim appeared behind Manolito, ripping the sword from his hand and slicing a razor-sharp talon across his throat. He moved with such speed he was a blur. Vikirnoff whirled around, slicing through the vampire's leg with his sword, but Maxim was only a shadow, insubstantial, already gone, melting away behind his frenzied army. Manolito went down and several rats rushed him. Vikirnoff kicked two of them away and was forced to fight off several clones flying straight at him.

Natalya! Get the damned thing open, they are all over us.

I've got a small opening. Dominic is covering it. Can you get the information to Gregori? I'll keep working to bring it down. It is very complicated

Hurry, Natalya. We cannot hold them off much longer.

Keep your panty hose on.

Vikirnoff wasn't about to ask what that meant or where she got the phrase. Most likely a movie. He had tried to convey the urgency of the moment, but he knew unraveling a spell of such magnitude wasn't easy and in some cases, impossible.

His sword cut through two others. Sara and Raven rushed to his side and dragged Manolito back behind the fighting hunters to Dominic. Raven knelt beside him, her hands pressed to his throat, the healing chant filling their minds as they fought. Mikhail took Manolito's place, and the sight of him whipped the vampires into a killing frenzy.

Falcon staggered back, several deep cuts on his chest and face. Vikirnoff leapt the distance between them to cover him, taking great sweeping cuts with his sword. When he glanced back at Mikhail, he couldn't even see the prince with the army swarming around him. Darker shadows swept across the knot of fighters and Vikirnoff's heart sank as Maxim appeared. He had no choice but to abandon Falcon to aid the prince. Should they lose Falcon, they would lose Sara and her unborn child.

Vikirnoff took two steps toward the prince and was driven back by several clones. He heard a groan and turned his head just in time to see Gregori burst out from behind Dominic who was shuddering with pain. Small dots of blood beaded the Dragonseeker's brow. The burns had spread across his shoulder, down his arm, up his neck to his face. He clenched his teeth together as Jacques pushed past him, rushing to join the battle. Only then did Dominic free himself from the barrier and slump to the ground.

Gregori went straight for the knot of vampires, wading through them with his incredible strength, his silver eyes blazing. Jacques dragged Falcon back and together with Vikirnoff tried to hold back the growing army. It didn't matter how many they cut down, Maxim simply replaced them, replicating them at an astonishing speed. The barrier had to come down soon or they would all die.

Gregori kicked aside a rat, tossed a clone into the barrier where it sizzled and howled, and snapped a second clone's neck to make his way to the prince's side. As Maxim reached for Mikhail, Gregori slammed his weight into him. He went through the vampire, staggered and caught himself, whirling around to find the master vampire close, a small, smug smile very much in evidence.

"I had hoped you would join us." Maxim greeted him.

"I always oblige." Gregori circled to the right.

Everything is connected! Natalya's voice was filled with excitement. *Tell the prince. It is all connected. When the barrier falls, so will all of his other shields. All of you will be able to shift and use whatever works to win this battle.*

Bring it down now, ainaak enyém, *or none of us will survive the next ten minutes.*

Maxim stepped even closer, matching Gregori's steps as if dancing with him. All the while that small ugly smile of contempt played over his thin lips. As Gregori slammed his fist deep, Maxim twisted slightly, taking the punch, trapping the hunter's hand in his body, his ribs squeezing sharply, acting like a guillotine. Gregori's face blanched and he dragged his arm back without his hand. A fountain of blood poured out. All of the Carpathians could hear Gregori's lifemate's scream of agony reverberating through their minds.

Maxim plunged his own fist into the hunter's chest cavity, driving through bone and muscle to reach the beating heart of the prince's second-in-command.

"It's down! It's down!" Natalya cried and whirled to join the battle.

"Stop." The single word was issued with such authority and power everyone stilled. Mikhail stepped close to Gregori. "Release him, Maxim."

"I am going to tear out his heart." The fingers dug deeper, ripping at arteries. "You have far too high an opinion of the Daratrazanoff family as your second-in-command, Mikhail. You would have been better to look to the Malinov family."

Gregori, instead of making a second attempt to get at the master vampire's heart, reached back toward Mikhail. His torn body shuddered. The only thing keeping him standing was the fist burrowing around his heart. He made no sound, but he reached for his prince with his bloody stump of an arm.

Mikhail stepped forward and gripped Gregori's wrist, cauterizing the wound as he leaned close and sank his teeth deep into his jugular.

There was a stunned silence, broken only by Maxim's scream of rage as he dug frantically, trying to remove the hunter's heart. Mikhail's other hand caught Maxim's forearm and pulled as he swept his tongue across Gregori's neck to close the pinpricks. When Mikhail lifted his head, he looked different. His skin glowed a warm golden color. He forced Maxim's arm out of Gregori's chest and the hunter fell to the ground, clutching his mangled body.

Mikhail stepped away from the other Carpathians, his arms outstretched, his eyes closed, his mind reaching, drawing, expanding. Streaks of light flashed from Mikhail to Gregori, to Falcon, Dominic and Jacques. The bands of light connected Raven, Sara and Natalya, leapt to Vikirnoff and Manolito. The power swelled until the earth vibrated with it.

Natalya felt the connection of *all* Carpathians, near and far, ancient and new, vampire or hunter. Every skill, every talent, every bit of knowledge poured from their minds into a single person. She blinked rapidly in astonishment as Mikhail's feet left the ground. Blinding light shot from his fingertips, from his mouth and eyes, streaking across the army of clones, shattering them, so that they fell empty and lifeless all around the master vampire.

The lesser vampires began to burn, skin smoking and melting, faces distorting. They ran in circles howling in fear.

Maxim tried to shift, sliding back to his shadow spirit, a form he often used to move quickly and without being seen, but Mikhail's light was too strong. There in the dark of night, there were no longer any shadows to slip into. The light struck his face, his skin and small holes began to form, little pinholes enlarging slowly all over his body. He roared his hated. He thrashed, spewing insects and acid, fighting to get away from the light.

Mikhail only rose higher, shedding more light, until even the eyes of the hunters burned and they had to shield their eyes. Maxim's skin began to split and peel. Long strips fell to the ground and sizzled under the heat of the unbearable light. His long pointed nails curled and turned black. Noxious smoke poured from his body and rose upward, absorbed by the light and Maxim shrieked louder, raising his arms in an effort to take back his fading spirit.

The vampire's chest split apart and worms poured out of his body, the blackened, wizened heart spilling into the radiant light. Maxim stretched his arm toward the organ. The heart tumbled back toward the vampire, but it was already beginning to smolder. The organ burst into flame and the vampire could only watch in horror. His hair, skin, even his teeth began to smoke.

Gregori stirred and with an effort, dragged himself over to Mikhail. The hunter staggered to his feet and reached his one good hand toward his prince. Mikhail caught it. The light arced between, surrounded them and for one long moment shone through them. When Gregori pulled Mikhail back to the ground, Gregori's hand had already regenerated.

Mikhail walked over to Maxim and stared into the red eyes. "My opinion of the Daratrazanoff family will always remain the same."

Maxim slid to the ground in a puddle of melted flesh, the eyes staring up at Mikhail and Gregori. Black smoke drifted up from the pupils. Tiny flames burst through the smoke to incinerate the last of the vampire. There was a long silence. A wind rose and cleared away the stench of blood and battle.

Natalya let out her breath slowly and reached for Vikirnoff's hand. "Okay," she said. "He can have the book."

20

Vikirnoff stood shaking his head, his narrowed gaze on Natalya as she leapt over a boulder, danced through a small creek, all the while wielding her lightning sword in and out of the trees fighting imaginary opponents. "Nothing is safe anymore. You have lost your mind."

Her laughter floated back to him, touching him, warming him. "I'm practicing to be one of the three Musketeers. Or better yet, Luke Skywalker. I could see myself being Luke Skywalker. Totally."

"Why not Princess Leia?"

Natalya stopped and spun around, mouth open in astonishment, her sword pulsing with light. "You've seen *Star Wars*."

He folded his arms across his chest and grinned at her. "I believe everyone has seen *Star Wars*."

Natalya held the lightning sword in the air and grinned. "No wonder you all thought of making these swords. They negate the need for hairspray and flamethrowers."

"I have never needed either." He indicated the pulsing blade of the sword with his chin. "We use lightning. It is much more lethal to reshape it."

"I didn't have that advantage." She stared hard at the sword and it wavered, but didn't disappear. "Bloody thing annoys me when it doesn't mind."

He shook his head, laughter warming his eyes. "You are trying too hard. Picture it gone. It is not quite the same thing as using a spell. You always think first of spells."

It was true, Natalya knew, but it was still aggravating. Vikirnoff had awakened her with kisses, made love to her several times and even provided blood for her. She found it amusing that he had gone hunting without her, not wanting her to feed from another man. Perhaps she felt the same way about his taking blood from a woman, but she wasn't going to admit that to herself — or him.

She concentrated on the sword and thankfully it disappeared. She had a tendency to get violent with weapons if she happened to have a bad practice session. "You know, Mr. Smug, it might be good for you to practice a bit every now and then. I thought your skills with a sword were a little rusty. You rely too much on other things and when the melting vamp, which was disgusting by the way, took your toys away, all of you bad boys had a bit of difficult time. It was a good thing I was there to save you."

"Yes, it was."

Vikirnoff was standing just below the fallen tree trunk she was balancing on. Natalya leapt off and he caught her, just as she'd known he would. Happiness burst through her. Of course he would catch her, he was always there in her mind, loving her, wanting her, feeling it was such a miracle to have her. She wrapped her arms around his neck and her legs around his waist. "Yes, it was, and you remember that next time you get all He-Man on me."

Natalya bent her head to his, her hair falling like silky rain on his skin. It was the most sensual thing in the world and she'd barely touched him. He felt a series of small butterfly licks over his pulse and immediately his blood began to pound in response.

"You always smell so good. Even in the heat of battle, you smell good," she murmured, her body rubbing much like a cat's along his. Her tongue did another flickering dance over his pulse and down his throat. Once her teeth scraped, featherlight, but her touch seemed to burn right through his shirt to brand his skin.

"Sometimes, Natalya, I do not think I can survive

without touching you." His hands cupped her rounded bottom, giving her support. At the same time he applied enough pressure to press the heat of her core tightly against his suddenly hard erection.

"I never imagined being this happy," she confided, resting her head on his shoulder, her teeth tugging at his ear. "Even when I thought we might not make it through that battle, I looked at you fighting and you were breathtaking. I was proud that you were mine."

Her tongue did a little foray over his pulse again and his erection thickened, jumped in response, his blood catching fire. "I do love you for yourself, Natalya, never doubt that. I may have a difficult time accepting you in a dangerous situation, but who you are is exactly what I want."

Her soft laughter teased his senses, gave him another heady rush. A strange roaring started in his ears. Vikirnoff sank down onto the fallen log urging her to straddle him. She cuddled close, fitting snugly in his lap, just the way he loved. "I'm what you *need*. If it wasn't for me, Vik, you'd be a bossy, snarling grump." Her teeth tugged at his bottom lip. "Don't get me wrong, it's a little thrilling to have you get all masterful and try to be the dictator." Her tongue fluttered along the seam of his lips, sent a flame burning through his body.

Her touch was so light, barely felt, yet it shook him, tightening every muscle until the blood rushed to his groin to center there, but more than that, he felt the shift in his heart that left his eyes burning with unshed tears. She tasted his skin, her tongue a delicate velvet rasp traversing along his collarbone. He had never thought that might be an erotic spot, but his entire body was strung as tight as bow.

"You have too many clothes on, Natalya." His husky declaration was somewhere between a plea and a command. He discarded his own clothes when the material of his trousers became too painful to bear over his bulging erection. If he got any larger he was afraid he might split his skin open.

"Do I?" She nibbled her way down his chest, sounding slightly distracted. "If I take off my clothes, I won't get to play anymore. You'll get all serious on me."

His fingers bit into her waist. "I am getting *very* serious here. Feel how serious I am." He grounded his body against hers, feeling the answering heat of her right through her clothes. The friction made him groan with need.

"I love it when you're wild and crazy and can't take me fast enough," Natalya admitted, her fingernails scraping along his chest with a small bite. "But this is so perfect. Lazy and slow. Eating you up. I love this muscle right here." Her tongue teased and flicked as she kissed her way over his chest.

"I would not mind eating you up," he said. The sight of her, eyes going dark with hunger, the sensual look on her face, the slow torture of her hands and mouth were all going to kill him. He'd just had her two hours earlier and yet he was burning from the inside out, so hot, he feared he might go up in flames. She was so soft, so delicate, yet steel ran through her and that excited him nearly as much as her wandering mouth.

"The idea has possibilities." She sat up, deliberately moved her hips restlessly, her mound in direct contact with his groin. Her fingers slipped the first button free and his breath caught in his throat.

Her blouse gaped open slowly, the unwrapping of a present. He moistened his lips with his tongue. She was driving him out of his skull. His body was pulsing, throbbing, his heart pounding blood through his body, gathering every sensation into one point in his body.

The blouse fell away to reveal her breasts rising and falling with each breath she drew into her lungs. "I ache for you." She tunneled her fingers through his hair and drew his head to her breast, arching back when he latched on with a growl of pleasure, suckling strongly, his tongue and teeth tormenting her.

He opened his eyes to look into hers. The dark hunger in his gaze robbed her of breath and spread heat through her body. "Get rid of the pants the Carpathian way," he commanded.

There was such a husky need in his voice everything feminine rose up to respond. She closed her eyes and wished herself out of the confines of her jeans. She wanted nothing but bare skin between them. His mouth was so hot she thought she might not survive the pleasure. "I'm not very good at this," she said with a sigh when nothing happened. "How long did it take the others to get this?"

"You are great at this. Perfect. I distracted you." He sounded unreasonably pleased.

"That must be it. I'm usually a very fast learner."

Vikirnoff threw his head back and laughed. She sounded so peeved right in the middle of their lovemaking that he couldn't help it. "You are so competitive."

"I am not. I just ought to be able to do this, that's all." Her eyes glittered green-blue, at him. "It can't be that hard. I picture it, right? That's all I need to do."

"Visualizing is not the same as thinking it. If you are thinking, 'Make it go away' it will not happen. You have to visualize the pants gone." He massaged her bottom. "I can remove them for you."

Her gaze narrowed and temper flitted across her face. "Don't you dare. I'll do it. I just gained a little weight and the stupid things are extra tight."

His eyebrow shot up. "That's the problem? Weight gain?" His hand shaped the soft curves. "Could be. Maybe a few pounds."

She shoved at his chest. "You're really asking for trouble now."

His palm slid around to her belly. "I love this little hoop, but when you have our child growing in you, and you *really* gain weight, are you going to leave this in for me to play with?"

Natalya sobered completely at the thought of children. She swallowed hard, her gaze suddenly avoiding his. "You know that Xavier is always going to be a shadow in our lives. As long as he is alive, he will always be a threat to us and to any children we have."

"I have no doubt that is true." His hand slid a caress through her hair, more comfort than sexual.

"You don't seem very disturbed by it."

"Xavier is his own worst enemy. He has been trying to stamp out our species for centuries, yet he lives in isolation, in fear. I do not see the point of living such a life. We are free to live out lives the way we are intended. We have the ability to be happy and he does not. I do not fear Xavier. He fears us."

Her teeth bit at her lower lip. Vikirnoff frowned. "What is it, *ainaak sívamet jutta*? Tell me. I will not take it from your mind if you do not wish to share it with me."

The tenderness in his voice was nearly her undoing. She swallowed the lump threatening to choke her and rubbed at her burning eyes. "Razvan. Do you think he's really dead? I've always been so accurate, and I thought I'd killed him, but when I replay the battle over in my head, I'm not so certain. You saw Maxim, and even Gregori regenerated his hand, or Mikhail did it for him, but the point is, there were so many unbelievable things. What if I didn't kill Razvan? What if he's still alive? The threat to us would be so much more. He'll never forgive what I did."

Vikirnoff drew her closer to him, stroking caresses down her hair, his heart beating in time with hers. "If Razvan is dead, Natalya, he will not only forgive you, but he will thank you. If he still lives, it is not really Razvan. His soul is long gone and only the shell of his body remains."

"I've gone over it a million times in my mind." Anxiety mixed with sorrow filled her eyes. "I swear my every intention was to kill him. I knew what he was doing the moment I looked at your face and I wasn't going to allow him to hurt you."

"I am sorry you had to be the one."

"No, it had to be me. I wouldn't have wanted anyone else to take his life. I love him. I'll always love him and I'll mourn the brother I lost forever. It was my job. Had I been the one to turn on the people I love, to become that evil a creature, I would hope my brother would love me enough to destroy me."

Vikirnoff framed her face between his hands and kissed her gently, tenderly. "That is the way a true Dragonseeker would think. Rhiannon would be so proud of you. I know Dominic must be."

"Have you heard how Dominic and Manolito are?"

"Both are in the ground healing. It will take some time for Dominic. Manolito's wounds were very serious, but Dominic remained on the barrier burning while he aided you in unraveling the safeguards. The burns were very severe. Gregori feared there would be scars and Carpathians rarely scar."

"How awful. I could feel his pain occasionally, but he shielded me for the most part. I couldn't help him at all, even though I knew he was suffering."

"Carpathian males protect our women, Natalya. It is who we are."

She rubbed his arm lightly, back and forth. "I know I'm difficult."

"We will work out the kinks. All relationships have them."

She pulled back enough to look into his eyes. "We won't be working anything out if you mean I'll be tucked away in a corner when trouble comes."

"I can only wish." He kissed her nose. "I was proud of you during Gabrielle's conversion. You really helped her get through it. Hopefully, when her sister arrives and she awakens, she will be happy."

"I think she will. Her main concern seemed to be for Gary and what the Carpathian males will expect of her now. If she loves Gary, I can't imagine anyone objecting to her being with him."

Vikirnoff remained silent, his hands sliding up and down her bare skin just to feel how soft she was.

Natalya shivered under his touch, leaning closer so that the tips of her breasts pushed against his chest. "I don't suppose your Mikhail can find a way to destroy the book?"

"Even if he cannot, it will be safe in his care. He has no wish to open it, let alone use it, so I believe, until he figures out a way to get rid of it, we will not have to worry."

"I'm glad I don't have the responsibility of it. He was amazing. Have you ever seen that before?"

Vikirnoff shook his head. "There were rumors, legends of the Dubrinsky and Daratrazanoff alliance, that there was some weapon that could be unleashed, but I am uncertain just what happened. I am just grateful that it did happen."

"Me, too. And did I say thank you for getting rid of that knife? I couldn't stand to know it was still in the world and might find its way back to Xavier."

He caught her hips and lifted her off of him, setting her to one side. Natalya gave a small cry of joy. "Hey! I'm getting the jeans off."

"Yes, you are." He flicked his hand toward her and the offending material vanished. "We will practice removing your clothes hour after hour, but for now, I cannot wait any longer." He moved up behind her, bending her forward, bracing her palms on the log. His hand slid between her legs, stroking and caressing, fingers dipping deep.

Her entire body shuddered and she pushed back against him. "So impatient," she teased. "But then, so am I."

He thrust into her, a long deep stroke, welding them together, hearing her soft cry of pleasure and feeling fire streak through his body. It would take several lifetimes to ever sate him. It would take even more before he could fully believe the miracle he had been given. "You are *ainaak sívamet jutta*. Forever to my heart connected."

"As you are to mine."

Appendix 1

Carpathian Healing Chants

To rightly understand Carpathian healing chants, background is required in several areas:

- The Carpathian view on healing
- The "Lesser Healing Chant" of the Carpathians
- The "Great Healing Chant" of the Carpathians
- Carpathian chanting technique

1. The Carpathian view on healing

The Carpathians are a nomadic people whose geographical origins can be traced back to at least as far as the Southern Ural Mountains (near the steppes of modern day Kazakhstan), on the border between Europe and

Asia. (For this reason, modern-day linguists call their language, "proto-Uralic," without knowing that this is the language of the Carpathians.) Unlike most nomadic peoples, the wandering of the Carpathians was not due to the need to find new grazing lands as the seasons and climate shifted, or the search for better trade. Instead, the Carpathians' movements were driven by a great purpose: to find a land that would have the right earth, a soil with the kind of richness that would greatly enhance their rejuvenative powers.

Over the centuries, they migrated westward (some six thousand years ago), until they at last found their perfect homeland—their *"susu"*—in the Carpathian Mountains, whose long arc cradled the lush plains of the kingdom of Hungary. (The kingdom of Hungary flourished for over a millennium—making Hungarian the dominant language of the Carpathian Basin—until the kingdom's lands were split among several countries after World War I: Austria, Czechoslovakia, Romania, Yugoslavia, Austria, and modern Hungary.)

Other peoples from the Southern Urals (who shared the Carpathian language, but were not Carpathians) migrated in different directions. Some ended up in Finland, which accounts for why the modern Hungarian and Finnish languages are among the contemporary descendents of the ancient Carpathian language. Even though they are tied forever to their chosen Carpathian homeland, the wandering of the Carpathians continues, as they search the world for the answers that will enable them to bear and raise their offspring without difficulty.

Because of their geographical origins, the Carpathian views on healing share much with the larger Eurasian shamanistic tradition. Probably the closest modern representative of that tradition is based in Tuva (and is referred to as "Tuvinian Shamanism")—see the map above.

The Eurasian shamanistic tradition—from the Carpathians to the Siberian shamans—held that illness originated in the human soul, and only later manifested as various physical conditions. Therefore, shamanistic healing, while not neglecting the body, focused on the soul and its healing. The most profound illnesses were understood to be caused by "soul departure," where all or some part of the sick person's soul has wandered away from the body (into the nether realms), or has been captured or possessed by an evil spirit, or both.

The Carpathians belong to this greater Eurasian shamanistic tradition and shared its viewpoints. While the Carpathians themselves did not succumb to illness, Carpathian healers understood that the most profound wounds were also accompanied by a similar "soul departure."

Upon reaching the diagnosis of "soul departure," the healer-shaman is then be required to make a spiritual journey into the nether worlds, to recover the soul. The shaman may have to overcome tremendous challenges along the way, particularly: fighting the demon or vampire who has possessed his friend's soul.

"Soul departure" doesn't require a person to be unconscious (although that certainly can be the case as well). It was understood that a person could still appear to be conscious, even talk and interact with others, and yet be missing a part of their soul. The experienced healer or shaman would instantly see the problem nonetheless, in subtle signs that others might miss: the person's attention wandering every now and then, a lessening in their enthusiasm about life, chronic depression, a diminishment in the brightness of their "aura," and the like.

2. The Lesser Healing Chant of the Carpathians

Kepä Sarna Pus (The "Lesser Healing Chant") is used for wounds that are merely physical in nature. The Carpathian healer leaves his body and enters the wounded Carpathian's body to heal great mortal wounds from the inside out using pure energy. He proclaims, "I offer freely, my life for your life," as he gives his blood to the injured Carpathian. Because the Carpathians are of the earth and bound to the soil, they are healed by the soil of their homeland. Their saliva is also often used for its rejuvenative powers.

It is also very common for the Carpathian chants (both the lesser and the great one) to be accompanied by the use of healing herbs, aromas from Carpathian candles, and crystals. The crystals (when combined with the Carpathians' empathic, psychic connection to the entire universe) are used to gather positive energy from their surroundings which then is used to accelerate the healing. Caves are sometimes used as the setting for the healing.

The lesser healing chant was used by Vikirnoff Von Shrieder and Colby Jansen to heal Rafael De La Cruz whose heart had been ripped out by a vampire in the book titled *Dark Secret*.

Kepä Sarna Pus (The Lesser Healing Chant)

The same chant is used for all physical wounds. "sívadaba" ["into your heart"] would be changed to refer to whatever part of the body is wounded.

Kuńasz, nélkül sivdobbanás, nélkül fesztelen löyly.

You lie as if asleep, without beat of heart, without airy breath.

[Lie-as-if-asleep-you, without heart-beat, without airy breath.]

Ot élidamet andam szabadon élidadért.

I offer freely my life for your life.

[Life-my give-I freely life-your-for.]

O jelä sielam jŏrem ot ainamet és soŋe ot élidadet.

My spirit of light forgets my body and enters your body.

[The sunlight soul-my forgets the body-my and enters the body-your.]

O jelä sielam pukta kinn minden szelemeket belső.

My spirit of light sends all the dark spirits within fleeing
    without.

[The sunlight-soul-my puts-to-flight outside all ghost-s
    inside.]

Pajńak o susu hanyet és o nyelv nyálamet sívadaba.

I press the earth of our homeland and the spit of my
    tongue into your heart.

[Press-I the homeland earth and the tongue spit-my
    heart-your-into.]

Vii, o verim soŋe o verid andam.

At last, I give you my blood for your blood.

[At-last, the blood-my to-replace the blood-your give-I.]

To hear this chant, visit: http://www.christinefeehan.com/
members/.

3. The Great Healing Chant of the Carpathians

The most well-known—and most dramatic—of the
Carpathian healing chants was **En Sarna Pus** ("The
Great Healing Chant"). This chant was reserved for
recovering the wounded or unconscious Carpathian's
soul.

Typically a group of men would form a circle around
the sick Carpathian (to "encircle him with our care and
compassion"), and begin the chant. The shaman or
healer or leader is the prime actor in this healing cere-

mony. It is he who will actually make the spiritual journey into the nether world, aided by his clanspeople.
Their purpose is to ecstatically dance, sing, drum, and
chant, all the while visualizing (through the words of the
chant) the journey itself—every step of it, over and over
again—to the point where the shaman, in trance, leaves
his body, and makes that very journey. (Indeed, the
word "ecstasy" is from the Latin *ex statis*, which literally
means "out of the body.")

One advantage that the Carpathian healer has over
many other shamans, is his telepathic link to his lost
brother. Most shamans must wander in the dark of the
nether realms, in search of their lost brother. But the
Carpathian healer directly "hears" in his mind the voice
of his lost brother calling to him, and can thus "zero in"
on his soul like a homing beacon. For this reason,
Carpathian healing tends to have a higher success rate
than most other traditions of this sort.

Something of the geography of the "other world" is
useful for us to examine, in order to fully understand the
words of the Great Carpathian Healing Chant. A refer-
ence is made to the "Great Tree" (in Carpathian: *En
Puwe*). Many ancient traditions, including the Carpathian
tradition, understood the worlds—the heaven worlds,
our world, and the nether realms—to be "hung" upon a
great pole, or axis, or tree. Here on earth, we are positioned halfway up this tree, on one of its branches.
Hence many ancient texts often referred to the material
world as "middle earth": midway between heaven and

hell. Climbing the tree would lead one to the heaven worlds. Descending the tree to its roots would lead to the nether realms. The shaman was necessarily a master of movement up and down the Great Tree, sometimes moving unaided, and sometimes assisted by (or even mounted upon the back of) an animal spirit guide. In various traditions, this Great Tree was known variously as the *axis mundi* (the "axis of the worlds"), Ygddrasil (in Norse mythology), Mount Meru (the sacred world mountain of Tibetan tradition), etc. The Christian cosmos with its heaven, purgatory/earth, and hell, is also worth comparing. It is even given a similar topography in Dante's *Divine Comedy*: Dante is led on a journey first to hell, at the center of the earth; then upward to Mount Purgatory, which sits on the earth's surface directly opposite Jerusalem; then further upward first to Eden, the earthly paradise, at the summit of Mount Purgatory; and then upward at last to heaven.

In the shamanistic tradition, it was understood that the small always reflects the large; the personal always reflects the cosmic. A movement in the greater dimensions of the cosmos also coincides with an internal movement. For example, the *axis mundi* of the cosmos also corresponds to the spinal column of the individual. Journeys up and down the *axis mundi* often coincided with the movement of natural and spiritual energies (sometimes called *kundalini* or *shakti*) in the spinal column of the shaman or mystic.

En Sarna Pus (The Great Healing Chant)

In this chant, ekä *("brother") would be replaced by "sister," "father," "mother," depending on the person to be healed.*

Ot ekäm ainajanak hany, jama.

My brother's body is a lump of earth, close to death.

[The brother-my body-his-of lump-of-earth, is-near-death.]

Me, ot ekäm kuntajanak, pirädak ekäm, gond és irgalom türe.

We, the clan of my brother, encircle him with our care and compassion.

[We, the brother-my clan-his-of, encircle brother-my, care and compassion full.]

O pus wäkenkek, ot oma śarnank, és ot pus fünk, álnak ekäm ainajanak, pitänak ekäm ainajanak elävä.

Our healing energies, ancient words of magic, and healing herbs bless my brother's body, keep it alive.

[The healing power-our-s, the ancient words-of-magic-our, and the healing herbs-our, bless brother-my body-his-of, keep brother-my body-his-of alive.]

Ot ekäm sielanak pälä. Ot omboće päläja juta alatt o jüti, kinta, és szelemek lamtijaknak.

But my brother's soul is only half. His other half wanders in the nether world.

[The brother-my soul-his-of (is) half. The other half-his wanders through the night, mist, and ghosts lowland-their-of.]

*Ot en mekem ŋamaŋ: kulkedak otti ot ekäm omboće pälä-
    janak.*
My great deed is this: I travel to find my brother's other
    half.
[The great deed-my (is) this: travel-I to-find the brother-
    my other half-his-of.]

*Rekatüre, saradak, tappadak, odam, kaŋa o numa waram, és
    avaa owe o lewl mahoz.*
We dance, we chant, we dream ecstatically, to call my
    spirit bird, and to open the door to the other
    world.
[Ecstasy-full, dance-we, dream-we, to call the god bird-
    my, and open the door spirit land-to.]

Ntak o numa waram, és mozdulak, jomadak.
I mount my spirit bird and we begin to move, we are un-
    der way. [Mount-I the god bird-my, and begin-to-
    move-we, are-on-our-way-we.]

*Piwtädak ot En Puwe tyvinak, ećidak alatt o jüti, kinta, és
    szelemek lamtijaknak.*
Following the trunk of the Great Tree, we fall into the
    nether world.
[Follow-we the Great Tree trunk-of, fall-we through the
    night, mist, and ghosts lowland-their-of.]

Fázak, fázak nó o śaro.
It is cold, very cold.
[Feel-cold-I, feel-cold-I like the frozen snow.]

Juttadak ot ekäm o akarataban, o sívaban, és o sielaban.
My brother and I are linked in mind, heart, and soul.
[Am-bound-to-I the brother-my the mind-in, the heart-in, and the soul-in.]

Ot ekäm sielanak kaηa engem.
My brother's soul calls to me.
[The brother-my soul-his-of calls-to me.]

Kuledak és piwtädak ot ekäm.
I hear and follow his track.
[Hear-I and follow-the-trail-of-I the brother-my.]

Saγedak és tuledak ot ekäm kulyanak.
Encounter-I the demon who is devouring my brother's soul.
[Arrive-I and meet-I the brother-my demon-who-devours-soul-his-of.]

Nenäm ćoro; o kuly torodak.
In anger, I fight the demon.
[Anger-my flows; the demon-who-devours-souls fight-I.]

O kuly pél engem.
He is afraid of me.
[The demon-who-devours-souls (is) afraid-of me.]

Lejkkadak o kaηka salamaval.
I strike his throat with a lightning bolt.
[Strike-I the throat-his bolt-of-lightning-with.]

Molodak ot ainaja komakamal.
I break his body with my bare hands.
[Break-I the body-his empty-hand-s-my-with.]

Toja és molanâ.
He is bent over, and falls apart.
[(He)bends and (he)crumbles.]

Hän ćaδa.
He runs away.
[He flees.]

Manedak ot ekäm sielanak.
I rescue my brother's soul.
[Rescue-I the brother-my soul-his-of.]

Alɔdak ot ekäm sielanak o komamban.
I lift my brother's soul in the hollow of my hand.
[Lift-I the brother-my soul-his-of the hollow-of-hand-
    my-in.]

Alɔdam ot ekäm numa waramra.
I lift him onto my spirit bird.
[Lift-I the brother-my god bird-my-onto.]

Piwtädak ot En Puwe tyvijanak és saɣedak jälleen ot elävä
    ainak majaknak.
Following up the Great Tree, we return to the land of the
    living.
[Follow-we the Great Tree trunk-its-of, and reach-we
    again the living bodie-s land-their-of.]

Ot ekäm elä jälleen.
My brother lives again.
[The brother-my lives again.]

Ot ekäm weńća jälleen.
He is complete again.
[The brother-my (is) complete again.]

To hear this chant, visit: http://www.christinefeehan.com/members/.

4. Carpathian chanting technique

As with their healing techniques, the actual "chanting technique" of the Carpathians has much in common with the other shamanistic traditions of the Central Asian steppes. The primary mode of chanting was throat chanting using overtones. Modern examples of this manner of singing can still be found in the Mongolian, Tuvan, and Tibetan traditions. You can find an audio example of the Gyuto Tibetan Buddhist monks engaged in throat chanting at: http://www.christinefeehan.com/carpathian_chanting/.

As with Tuva, note on the map the geographical proximity of Tibet to Kazakhstan and the Southern Urals.

The beginning part of the Tibetan chant emphasizes synchronizing all the voices around a single tone, aimed at healing a particular "chakra" of the body. This is fairly typical of the Gyuto throat chanting tradition, but it is not a significant part of the Carpathian tradition. Nonetheless, it serves as an interesting contrast.

The part of the Gyuto chanting example that is most similar to the Carpathian style of chanting is the mid-section, where the men are chanting the words together with great force. The purpose here is not to generate a "healing tone" that will affect a particular "chakra," but rather to generate as much power as possible for initiating the "out of body" travel, and for fighting the demonic forces that the healer/traveler must face and overcome.

Appendix 2
The Carpathian Language

Like all human languages, the language of the Carpathians contains the richness and nuance that can only come from a long history of use. At best we can only touch on some of the main features of the language in this brief appendix:

- The history of the Carpathian language
- Carpathian grammar and other characteristics of the language
- Examples of the Carpathian language
- A much abridged Carpathian dictionary

1. The history of the Carpathian language

The Carpathian language of today is essentially identical to the Carpathian language of thousands of years ago. A

"dead" language like the Latin of two thousand years ago
has evolved into a significantly different modern language
(Italian) because of countless generations of speakers and
great historical fluctuations. In contrast, many of the
speakers of Carpathian from thousands of years ago are
still alive. Their presence—coupled with the deliberate
isolation of the Carpathians from the other major forces
of change in the world—has acted (and continues to act)
as a stabilizing force that has preserved the integrity of
the language over the centuries. Carpathian culture has
also acted as a stabilizing force. For instance, the Ritual
Words, the various healing chants (see Appendix 1), and
other cultural artifacts have been passed down the centuries with great fidelity.

One small exception should be noted: the splintering
of the Carpathians into separate geographic regions has
led to some minor dialectization. However the telepathic
links among all Carpathians (as well as each Carpathian's
regular return to his or her homeland) has ensured that
the differences among dialects are relatively superficial
(e.g., small numbers of new words, minor differences in
pronunciation, etc.), since the deeper, internal language
of mind-forms has remained the same because of continuous use across space and time.

The Carpathian language was (and still is) the **proto-
language** for the Uralic (or Finno-Ugrian) family of
languages. Today, the Uralic languages are spoken in
northern, eastern and central Europe and in Siberia.
More than twenty-three million people in the world

speak languages that can trace their ancestry to Carpathian. Magyar or Hungarian (about fourteen million speakers), Finnish (about five million speakers), and Estonian (about one million speakers), are the three major contemporary descendents of this proto-language. The only factor that unites the more than twenty languages in the Uralic family is that their ancestry can be traced back to a common proto-language—Carpathian—which split (starting some six thousand years ago) into the various languages in the Uralic family. In the same way, European languages such as English and French, belong to the better-known Indo-European family and also evolve from a common proto-language ancestor (a different one from Carpathian).

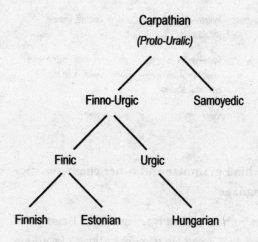

The following table provides a sense for some of the similarities in the language family.

Note: The Finnic/Carpathian "k" shows up often as Hungarian "h". Similarly, the Finnic/Carpathian "p" often corresponds to the Hungarian "f."

Carpathian (proto-Uralic)	Finnish (Suomi)	Hungarian (Magyar)
elä—live	elä—live	él—live
elid—life	elinikä—life	élet—life
pesä—nest	pesä—nest	fészek—nest
kola—die	kuole—die	hal—die
pälä—half, side	pieltä—tilt, tip to the side	fél, fele—fellow human, friend (half; one side of two) feleség—wife
and—give	anta, antaa—give	ad—give
koje—husband, man	koira—dog, the male (of animals)	here— drone, testicle
wäke—power	väki—folks, people, men; force väkevä—powerful, strong	vall-vel—with (instrumental suffix) vele—with him/her/it
wete—water	vesi—water	víz—water

2. Carpathian grammar and other characteristics of the language

Idioms. As both an ancient language, and a language of an earth people, Carpathian is more inclined toward use of idioms constructed from concrete, "earthy" terms, rather than abstractions. For instance, our modern abstraction, "to cherish," is expressed more concretely in Carpathian as "to hold in one's heart"; the "nether world" is, in Carpathian, "the land of night, fog, and ghosts"; etc.

Word order. The order of words in a sentence is determined not by syntactic roles (like subject, verb, and object) but rather by pragmatic, discourse-driven factors. Examples: *"Tied vagyok."* ("Yours am I."); *"Sívamet andam."* ("My heart I give you.")

Agglutination. The Carpathian language is **agglutinative**; that is, longer words are constructed from smaller components. An agglutinating language uses suffixes or prefixes whose meaning is generally unique, and which are concatenated one after another without overlap. In Carpathian, words typically consist of a stem that is followed by one or more suffixes. For example, *"sívambam"* derives from the stem *"sív"* ("heart") followed by *"am"* ("my," making it "my heart"), followed by *"bam"* ("in," making it "in my heart"). As you might imagine, agglutination in Carpathian can sometimes produce very long words, or words that are very difficult to pronounce. Vowels often get inserted between suffixes, to prevent too many consonants from appearing in a row (which can make the word unpronounceable).

Noun cases. Like all languages, Carpathian has many noun cases; the same noun will be "spelled" differently depending on its role in the sentence. Some of the noun cases include: nominative (when the noun is the subject of the sentence), accusative (when the noun is a direct object of the verb), dative (indirect object), genitive (or possessive), instrumental, final, supressive, inessive, elative, terminative, and delative.

We will use the possessive (or genitive) case as an example, to illustrate how all noun cases in Carpathian involve adding standard suffixes to the noun stems. Thus expressing possession in Carpathian—"my lifemate," "your lifemate," "his lifemate," "her lifemate," etc.— involves adding a particular suffix (such as "*=am*") to the noun stem ("*päläfertiil*"), to produce the possessive ("*päläfertiilam*"—"my lifemate"). Which suffix to use depends upon which person ("my," "your," "his," etc.) and whether the noun ends in a consonant or vowel. The following table shows the suffixes for singular nouns only (not plural), and also shows the similarity to the suffixes used in contemporary Hungarian. (Hungarian is actually a little more complex, in that it also requires "vowel rhyming": which suffix to use also depends on the last vowel in the noun; hence the multiple choices in the cells below, where Carpathian only has a single choice.)

	Carpathian (proto-Uralic)		contemporary Hungarian	
person	**noun ends in vowel**	**noun ends in consonant**	**noun ends in vowel**	**noun ends in consonant**
1st singular (my)	-m	-am	-m	-om, -em, -öm
2nd singular (your)	-d	-ad	-d	-od, -ed, -öd
3rd singular (his,her,its)	-ja	-a	-ja/-je	-a, -e
1st plural (our)	-nk	-ank	-nk	-unk, -ünk
2nd plural (your)	-tak	-atak	-tok, -tek, -tök	-otok,-etek, -ötök
3rd plural (their)	-jak	-ak	-juk, -jük	-uk, -ük

Note: As mentioned earlier, vowels often get inserted between the word and its suffix so as to prevent too many consonants from appearing in a row (which would produce unpronounceable words). For example, in the table above, all nouns that end in a consonant are followed by suffixes beginning with "a."

Verb conjugation. Like its modern descendents (such as Finnish and Hungarian), Carpathian has many verb tenses, far too many to describe here. We will just focus on the conjugation of the present tense. Again, we will place contemporary Hungarian side by side with the Carpathian, because of the marked similarity of the two.

As with the possessive case for nouns, the conjugation of verbs is done by adding a suffix onto the verb stem:

Person	Carpathian (proto-Uralic)	contemporary Hungarian
1st (I give)	-am (andam),-ak	-ok,-ek,-ök
2nd singular (you give)	-sz (andsz)	-sz
3rd singular (he/she/it gives)	—(and)	—
1st plural (we give)	-ak (andak)	-unk,-ünk
2nd plural (you give)	-tak (andtak)	-tok,-tek,-tök
3rd plural (they give)	-nak (andnak)	-nak,-nek

As with all languages, there are many "irregular verbs" in Carpathian that don't exactly fit this pattern. But the above table is still a useful guideline for most verbs.

3. Examples of the Carpathian language

Here are some brief examples of conversational Carpathian, used in the Dark books. We include the literal translation in square brackets. It is interestingly different from the most appropriate English translation.

Susu.
I am home.

["home/birthplace." "I am" is understood, as is often the case in Carpathian.]

Möért?
What for?

csitri
little one
["little slip of a thing", "little slip of a girl"]

ainaak enyém
forever mine

ainaak sívamet jutta
forever mine (another form)
["forever to-my-heart connected/fixed"]

sívamet
my love
["of-my-heart," "to-my-heart"]

Sarna Rituaali (The Ritual Words) is a longer example, and an example of chanted rather than conversational Carpathian. Note the recurring use of "*andam*" ("I give"), to give the chant musicality and force through repetition.

Sarna Rituaali (The Ritual Words)

Te avio päläfertiilam.
You are my lifemate.
[You wedded wife-my. "Are" is understood, as is gener-

ally the case in Carpathian when one thing is
equated with another: "You-my lifemate."]

Éntölam kuulua, avio päläfertiilam.
I claim you as my lifemate.
[To-me belong-you, wedded wife-my.]

Ted kuuluak, kacad, kojed.
I belong to you.
[To-you belong-I, lover-your, man/husband/drone-your.]

Élidamet andam.
I offer my life for you.
[Life-my give-I. "you" is understood.]

Pesämet andam.
I give you my protection.
[Nest-my give-I]

Uskolfertiilamet andam.
I give you my allegiance.
[Fidelity-my give-I.]

Sívamet andam.
I give you my heart.
[Heart-my give-I.]

Sielamet andam.
I give you my soul.
[Soul-my give-I.]

Ainamet andam.
I give you my body.
[Body-my give-I.]

Sívamet kuuluak kaik että a ted.
I take into my keeping the same that is yours.
[To-my-heart hold-I all that-is yours.]

Ainaak olenszal sívambin.
Your life will be cherished by me for all my time.
[Forever will-be-you in-my-heart.]

Te élidet ainaak pide minan.
Your life will be placed above my own for all time.
[Your life forever above mine.]

Te avio päläfertiilam.
You are my lifemate.
[You wedded wife-my.]

Ainaak sívamet jutta oleny.
You are bound to me for all eternity.
[Forever to-my-heart connected are-you.]

Ainaak terád vigyázak.
You are always in my care.
[Forever you I-take-care-of.]

See **Appendix 1** for Carpathian healing chants, including both the *Kepä Sarna Pus* ("The Lesser Healing Chant") and the *En Sarna Pus* ("The Great Healing Chant").

To hear these words pronounced (and for more about Carpathian pronunciation altogether), please visit: http://www.christinefeehan.com/members/

4. A much abridged Carpathian dictionary

This very much abridged Carpathian dictionary contains most of the Carpathian words used in these *Dark* books. Of course, a full Carpathian dictionary would be as large as the usual dictionary for an entire language.

Note: The Carpathian nouns and verbs below are word **stems**. They generally do not appear in their isolated, "stem" form, as below. Instead, they usually appear with suffixes (e.g., *"andam"*—"I give," rather than just the root, *"and"*).

aina—body
ainaak—forever
akarat—mind; will
ál—bless, attach to
alatt—through
alə—to lift; to raise
and—to give
avaa—to open
avio—wedded
avio päläfertiil—lifemate
belső—within; inside
ćaδa—to flee; to run; to escape

ćoro—to flow; to run like rain

csitri—little one (female)

ekä—brother

elä—to live

elävä—alive

elävä ainak majaknak—land of the living

elid—life

én—I

en—great, many, big

En Puwe—The Great Tree. Related to the legends of Ygddrasil, the *axis mundi*, Mount Meru, heaven and hell, etc.

engem—me

eći—to fall

ek—suffix added after a noun ending in a consonant to make it plural

és—and

että—that

fáz—to feel cold or chilly

fertiil—fertile one

fesztelen—airy

fü—herbs; grass

gond—care; worry (noun)

hän—he; she; it

hany—clod; lump of earth

irgalom—compassion; pity; mercy

jälleen—again.

jama—to be sick, wounded, or dying; to be near death (verb)

jelä—sunlight; day, sun; light

joma—to be under way; to go

jŏrem—to forget; to lose one's way; to make a mistake

juta—to go; to wander

jüti—night; evening

jutta—connected; fixed (adj.). to connect; to fix; to bind (verb)

k—suffix added after a noun ending in a vowel to make it plural

kaca—male lover

kaik—all (noun)

kaŋa—to call; to invite; to request; to beg

kaŋk—windpipe; Adam's apple; throat

Karpatii—Carpathian

käsi—hand

kepä—lesser, small, easy, few

kinn—out; outdoors; outside; without

kinta—fog, mist, smoke

koje—man; husband; drone

kola—to die

koma—empty hand; bare hand; palm of the hand; hollow of the hand.

kont—warrior

kule—hear

kuly—intestinal worm; tapeworm; demon who possesses and devours souls

kulke—to go or to travel (on land or water)

kuńa—to lie as if asleep; to close or cover the eyes in a game of hide-and-seek; to die

kunta—band, clan, tribe, family

kuulua—to belong; to hold

lamti—lowland; meadow

lamti ból jüti, kinta, ja szelem—the nether world (literally: "the meadow of night, mists, and ghosts")

lejkka—crack, fissure, split (noun). To cut ø hit; to strike forcefully (verb).

lewl—spirit

lewl ma—the other world (literally: "spirit land"). *Lewl ma* includes *lamti ból jüti, kinta, ja szelem*: the nether world, but also includes the worlds higher up *En Puwe*, the Great Tree

löyly—breath; steam. (related to *lewl*: "spirit")

ma—land; forest

mäne—rescue; save

me—we

meke—deed; work (noun). To do; to make; to work (verb)

minan—mine

minden—every, all (adj.).

möért?—what for? (exclamation)

molo—to crush; to break into bits

molanâ—to crumble; to fall apart

mozdul—to begin to move, to enter into movement

nä—for

ŋamaŋ—this; this one here

nélkül—without

nenä—anger

nó—like; in the same way as; as

numa—god; sky; top; upper part; highest (related to the English word: "numinous")

nyelv—tongue

nyál—saliva; spit (noun). (related to *nyelv*: "tongue")

odam—dream; sleep (verb)

oma—old; ancient

omboće—other; second (adj.)

o—the (used before a noun beginning with a consonant)

ot—the (used before a noun beginning with a vowel)

otti—to look; to see; to find

owe—door

pajna—to press

pälä—half; side

päläfertiil—mate or wife

pél—to be afraid; to be scared of

pesä—nest (literal); protection (figurative)

pide—above

pirä—circle; ring (noun). To surround; to enclose (verb).

pitä—keep, hold

piwtä—to follow; to follow the track of game

pukta—to drive away; to persecute; to put to flight

pusm—to be restored to health

pus—healthy; healing

puwe—tree; wood

reka—ecstasy; trance

rituaali—ritual

saɣe—to arrive; to come; to reach

salama—lightning; lightning bolt

sarna—words; speech; magic incantation (noun). To chant; to sing; to celebrate (verb)

śaro—frozen snow

siel—soul

sisar—sister

sív—heart

sívdobbanás—heartbeat

soŋe—to enter; to penetrate; to compensate; to replace

susu—home; birthplace (noun). at home (adv.)

szabadon—freely

szelem—ghost

tappa—to dance; to stamp with the feet (verb)

te—you

ted—yours

toja—to bend; to bow; to break

toro—to fight; to quarrel

tule—to meet; to come

türe—full, satiated, accomplished

tyvi—stem; base; trunk

uskol—faithful

uskolfertiil—allegiance

veri—blood

vigyáz—to care for; to take care of

vii—last; at last; finally

wäke—power

wara—bird; crow

weńća—complete; whole

wete—water

Turn the page for a look at

Dangerous Tides

by

Christine Feehan

Coming in July from Jove Books

Seventeen-year-old Pete Granger glanced toward the ocean and caught a glimpse through the drizzling rain of something—or *someone*—moving on the rising cliffs above Sea Lion Cove. His heart lurched in his chest as he slammed on the brakes to his old battered truck. Fortunately there wasn't anyone behind him, and he peered at the sheer wall of rock rising above the churning ocean, swallowing the sudden lump of fear clogging his throat.

Instinctively, he reached for his cell phone, remembering, as he put it to his ear, that there was only limited service on the coastline and he wasn't on the one bluff that allowed him to make a call. Frustrated, heart pumping, he set the truck in motion, racing through the series of hairpin turns before turning onto the dirt road leading to the cliffs. He nearly forgot to put on the brakes as he parked.

The wind hit him hard as he threw open the door and ran across the muddy ground to the top of the bluff. His cap blew off and the wind tugged at his shirt. Ignoring the small fence and the warning signs to keep away from the crumbling edge, he dropped to the ground, stretching his body out flat as he crawled to the edge and peered over.

"Drew!" The name was lost in the boom of the boiling sea. Pete cupped his hands together and tried again, putting everything he had into it. "Drew! Are you all right?" He doubted if his friend could hear the words, but then something alerted him, maybe the small trickling of dirt he'd displaced, because Drew turned his face upward toward Pete.

Drew Madison was several feet down the muddy cliff face. Nearly one hundred feet below him the waves crashed over large, jagged rocks, throwing white spray high into the air. The boom of the ocean was loud, reverberating off the sheer rock wall. The rain appeared a dank silver-gray, the steady drizzle making it much more difficult for Pete to catch glimpses of Drew's stark white face.

Drew appeared small and helpless, his face streaked with mud. He shook his head and waved Pete off, hunching against a spray of ocean water as a wave dashed against the large rock formation directly below him. Pete could see skid marks in the mud, where Drew's body had gone over, sliding down the cliff face until he hit the small outcropping where he now clung.

Pete held up his cell phone and made the motion of

throwing a rope. To his astonishment, Drew shook his head harder. The rain beat down steadily, getting in Pete's eyes so that he had to use his knuckles to wipe the water away, for a moment cutting off his view of Drew's white, desperate face. When his vision returned, Pete's heart leapt to his throat. Drew was gone.

"Drew!" Pete screamed the name until he was hoarse. He inched forward until he actually slid in the mud and had to anchor his own body by hooking his boots into the fence. Frightened, he peered below to the raging water, the white caps of foam and the spray blasting over the rocks and churning up the cliff face, searching for a body. It seemed impossible to survive the fall. Even if Drew had avoided the rocks he would have fallen into the roiling sea.

Tears blurred his vision. He stared at the top of the rock formation so long it appeared as if something were moving in slow motion. He wiped at his eyes with his knuckles and looked again. There were several outcroppings making the angle more difficult, so he slithered back and repositioned himself. At once he could see that on the rocks rising to meet the cliff Drew lay in a crumbled heap, and he was moving! Excited, Pete cupped his hands around his mouth.

"Drew!"

There was no answer, but he knew Drew was alive. He looked to be wedged between two boulders jutting up out of the sea that were part of the formation of the caves below the water line. It seemed impossible that he could still be alive, but he definitely moved.

"I'm getting help. They'll be coming for you, Drew!"

Pete scuttled backward like a crab until he crawled under the fence to safety and rushed back to his truck. He needed to get out a little farther on the other side of the cove where the cell phone service actually worked. It was tricky—he had to stay in one place when his body was flooded with adrenaline and wanted to move—but he gave the details to the sheriff's office.

He was almost back to the cliffs when he heard the wail of sirens and knew Jonas Harrington and Jackson Deveau, the sheriff and his deputy, were on the way. He sagged with relief and waited for the patrol car.

"Ty's tuning us out," Sam Chapman announced to the ring of firefighters sitting around the table playing cards. "This is his vacation, you know. He spends weeks, even months locked up in his lab at BioLab Industries. He doesn't eat or sleep and forgets everything but staring into a microscope. He doesn't talk to a soul, just stares at little wormy things dancing on a slide."

"He doesn't talk much here, either," Doug Higgens said.

"He manages to recertify for helicopter rescue every ninety days," Sam said, "but that's because he likes the rush, not us."

"I don't like you all that much either, Sam," Jim Brannigan, the helicopter pilot, announced. "You took all my money the last card game."

Tyson Derrick barely registered the continuous ribbing of the other firefighters at the Helitack station as the conversation flowed around him. It was true, he often forgot to eat and went days without sleeping, so focused on his research he forgot the world around him. Working the fire season provided him with a small respite, an opportunity for interaction with others as well as the adrenaline rush he needed outside the lab. Yet even that no longer seemed to be working for him. Something was missing. He *had* to get a life.

"Wake up, Ty." Sam Chapman slapped him on the back. "You haven't heard a word I've said."

"I heard," Tyson conceded. "It just didn't merit a response. And by the way, Sam, I keep telling you odds are always against you in cards. Right now you're looking at two-hundred-and-twenty-to-one odds. That's just not that good. Sean has a much better chance at forty-three-point-two-to-one."

"Thanks so much for that little lesson," Sam said, tossing his cards on the table. He grinned at the circle of faces surrounding them as he ribbed his cousin. "Ty told me last night he's ready to settle down with the perfect woman. He just needs to find himself a woman who doesn't mind him disappearing for weeks or months on end while he works in his lab, or goes skydiving or parasailing or mountain climbing. You know, a saint."

A roar of laughter went up at Ty's expense. He wasn't easy-going and comfortable like his cousin, Sam. Sam just fit in anywhere and he had a natural ability to make others laugh. Ty forced a faint grin. "That's what I should be thinking about," he agreed. "I can't seem to get my mind off one of the projects at BioLab."

Sam groaned. "I thought you completed all your projects and whatever you were working on . . ."

"Not exactly, it's an ongoing project to identify a series of compounds that are potent in vitro inhibitors . . ."

"Stop, Ty." Sam shoved his hand through his hair. "You're going to give us all a headache. No wonder you're thinking of settling down. No one could live full-time worrying about things like that. I probably can't pronounce half the things you work on."

Ty shrugged, a frown settling over his face. "It isn't my Hepatitis-C project. Some time ago the company began developing a new drug using the basic findings of the cellular regeneration study for external wounds I did a few years ago. They believe they have a potential internal drug to fight cancer, but I just have this hunch that something's not right with it. I've been doing a little moonlighting . . ."

"Ty," Sam shook his head. "You're supposed to be putting all that behind you when you come here. You looked like hell when you showed up for training. You might as well be in prison the way you get so wrapped up in all that."

"It's just that this drug has the very real potential to help a lot of cancer patients if they get it right. Harry Jenkins is heading up the project and he isn't as thorough as he should be. He tends to take shortcuts because he wants recognition more than he wants to get it right." He was suddenly all too aware of the silence of the others around him. That was the way it was with him. He didn't fit in, no matter how hard he tried. Most conversations seemed trivial to him when his mind was always working on unlocking some key, and it preferred to keep working no matter how hard he tried to shut it off.

"This internal drug isn't even your department?" Sam said. "I'll bet old Harry doesn't like you much, does he?"

"Well, no." Ty admitted reluctantly. Harry didn't like him at all. He doubted if many people did. He wished it mattered to him, but only Sam really counted. He didn't like letting Sam down. "But it isn't a popularity contest. This drug could save lives. And the new drug is based on my earlier work in cell regeneration. If they get it wrong, I'd feel responsible."

"Great. You're going to spend your off time in that makeshift lab in our basement, aren't you?" Sam asked. "I planned whitewater rafting and a couple of rock climbing trips as well as parasailing. You'd better not back out on me again."

Ty sat back in his chair and studied his cousin's handsome face. Sam managed to look petulant at times. He was the only man Ty knew who could pull off the look and still appeal to women. He'd seen it a million times. Sam had charm. Ty often wished he had just a little of whatever it was that Sam had. Sam got along with people. He could bullshit with the best of them and everyone liked him.

Ty knew he had embarrassed Sam more than once through the years with his abrupt, abrasive manner. How many times had he missed some trip or outing Sam had planned because time got away from him and fun with the boys wasn't nearly as exciting as the trail of an inhibitor that might work on T-cells. The bottom line was, it didn't matter that he had an enormous IQ, he felt awkward in the company of others—and he probably always would. He just didn't care enough to make time for improving his social skills.

It was always an adjustment, living with Sam for those three months out of the year. Ida Chapman had left her son, Sam, and her nephew, Tyson, her house when she'd passed away five years earlier. Ty always looked forward to visiting Sam, but that first month was difficult. Ty was used to being alone, without speaking to anyone, and Sam liked conversation. "I don't back out of our trips," Ty said. His frown deepened as Sam remained silent. "Do I?" He rubbed the bridge of his nose. He probably had, more than once. Disappointing Sam yet again.

Sam shrugged. "It doesn't matter, Ty. I'm just giving you a hard time. You're a biochemist. They're all crazy."

"And helicopter crews aren't?"

A roar of laughter went up. Sam held out his hands, palms up. "All right, you've got me there."

"I want to hear more about Ty's saint. Is she blond and built?" Rory Smith asked. He rubbed his hands together. "Let's get to the good stuff."

"That's your idea of the perfect woman, Rory," Doug

Higgens said, jabbing the firefighter in the arm. "And you definitely don't want a saint. What does she look like, Ty? You found her yet?"

Sam's mouth tightened. "He thinks he's found her."

An image flashed in his mind before Ty could suppress it. Her face. Pale. Midnight black hair. Large green eyes. A mouth to kill for. Ty shook his head. "She has to be intelligent. I can't spend more than a couple of minutes with someone who's an idiot." And that was the problem, would always be the problem. He wanted to talk about things he was enthusiastic about. He wanted to share problems at work with someone. Not even Sam had a clue what he was talking about and Sam actually tolerated him. Most women's eyes just glazed over when he started talking. And God help him if a date started talking about hair and nails and make-up.

"Geeze, Ty. What the hell is wrong with you? Who gives a damn if they have brains? You're just doing the wrong things with her," Rory said. "Stop trying to talk and get on with the action. You need help, man."

Another round of laughter went up.

Three tones blasted through the air and the men went instantly silent. The three tones chimed again and they were on their feet. The radio crackled and command central announced an injured climber on the cliffs of Sea Lion Cove just south of Fort Bragg.

Ty and the others grabbed the rescue gear, loading it into the Huey as fast and as systematically as possible.

"Ben, go to the Fort Bragg command center first, but

I'll want you to get as close as possible," Brannigan, the helicopter pilot, told the fire apparatus engineer. Ben would drive the heli-tender carrying the fuel for the helicopter as well as extra stokes, the baskets they put the victim in, and everything else needed in emergencies. He would have to take the large truck over the mountainous route to reach Fort Bragg, and it would take him at least an hour or more. The helicopter would be there in fourteen minutes.

Ben nodded and ran for his vehicle. The helicopter devoured fuel and they never went anywhere without the heli-tender.

The familiar rush of adrenaline coursed through Ty's body, making him feel alive again after living in his cave of a laboratory for so long. He needed this—the wild slam of his pulse, the adventure, even the camaraderie of the other firefighters. He took his place in the back of the helicopter with the other four firefighters, the captain and pilot up front. His helmet was fitted with a radio, and the familiar checklist settled everyone down.

"Commo check," Brannigan said into his mike.

The crew chief answered, followed by each member of the team.

"ICS isolation," Brannigan announced.

In the back, Ty, along with the others, checked their communication box and turned off all radios to isolate themselves from all unnecessary chatter. During the rescue operation it was necessary nothing distracted them.

Sean Fortune, the crew chief, answered. "Isolated."

"Pilot is isolated except for channel twenty. All loose items in cabin."

"Secured," Sean answered.

Ty felt the familiar tightness in his stomach. He loved the danger and he craved the excitement. In a few minutes they would be airborne.

"Doors."

Sean inspected the doors. "Right door open and pinned. Left door is closed and latched."

"Seatbelts."

"Fastened," Sean confirmed.

"Rescue supervisor and crew chief safety harnesses."

Sam and Sean checked the harnesses very thoroughly. "Crew chief secured. Rescue supervisor secured."

"Rescuer rigging."

Sam stepped forward to inspect the rigging, giving Sean the thumbs-up. "Secured."

"PDFs," Brannigan continued with the checklist.

Tension rose in the helicopter perceptibly. They were going over water and the pilot and crew chief were required to wear personal floatation devices, or PDFs, as the pilot was more apt to be trapped in the helicopter should it go down over water.

"Donned," came the response.

"H.E.E.D.S. and pressure. Pilot's H.E.E.D.S. is on and pressure is three thousand."

The H.E.E.D.S. was the Helicopter Emergency Evacuation Device, which was a mini scuba tank with a two-stage regulator.

"Crew chief's H.E.E.D.S. is on and pressure is good."

Sam answered as well. "Rescue supervisor's H.E.E.D.S. is turned on and pressure is good."

"Carabineers."

Ty gripped the edge of the seat. This was it. They were going up and he hadn't done a short haul over water other than in training in two years. He'd kept up the training, and was confident he wouldn't let the others down, but the rescuer was determined by rotation and today he had the short straw. He was going out on the rope.

Sean responded to the pilot. "Unlocked." Over water they always flew with the carabineers unlocked, as it would take too long to unlock them in the event the helicopter went down.

"Airborne," Brannigan announced calmly to command center as he took the Huey into the air.

The adrenaline poured into Ty's veins, a rush unlike any other. Nothing compared to it, not even the time when he unlocked the key to cellular regeneration and won a Nobel Prize in medicine. Nothing felt like this, soaring into the air inside a helicopter, surrounded by the other men as determined as he was to do whatever needed to be done.

Command responded with latitude and longitude, distance and asmith, the compass bearing. Brannigan loaded the information into the GPS and plotted a route directly to the victim.

Carpathian novels from
New York Times bestselling author
CHRISTINE FEEHAN

Dark Symphony
0-515-13521-6

Dark Secret
0-515-13885-1

"A skillful blend of supernatural thrills and
romance that is sure to entice readers."
—*Publishers Weekly*

"Will appeal to everyone regardless of
gender...great creativity."
—*Examiner* (Beaumont, TX)

Available wherever books are sold or at
penguin.com